The Curse
of the
Strawberry Moon

A Caviston Sisters Mystery

by

MARY PAT HYLAND

Also by Mary Pat Hyland

Novels
The House With the Wraparound Porch ~ 2013
The Maeve Kenny Series:
   The Cyber Miracles (Book 1) ~ 2008
   A Sudden Gift of Fate (Book 2) ~ 2009
   A Wisdom of Owls (Book 3) ~ 2011
3/17 ~ 2010
The Terminal Diner ~ 2011

Short stories
In the Shadows of the Onion Domes ~ 2014

Essays
"Dear George F." (from *Lost Love Letters*—an Indie Chicks anthology)
~ 2014

First edition ~ August 2016
Printed in the United States of America
Set in Georgia typeface. Cover design by Mary Pat Hyland

Author's websites:
http://marypathyland.com
http://www.facebook.com/marypathyland

For my rockin' nephews & nieces (& their spouses),
with fond memories of when we
broke on through to the other side.

☙❧

In 2013 the Arts Center of Yates County awarded me a writer's residency at their lakeside retreat, Sunny Point. This novel was inspired partly from my stay there. Thank you for keeping alive so beautifully the legacy of author, artist and art history professor, Dr. Annie Smith.

ACKNOWLEDGEMENTS

With deepest gratitude to my editors, Elizabeth Herrington, David Craig and Jordan Nicholson. Also to my first readers, Kate Graham, Anne Woodard, Sheila Forsyth, Sharon McKinney Hyland and Diana Schleicher.

Susanne Reilly Fitch, Matthew Rossie and Thresa Granger helped with police details; Stephanie Olsen gave me a juicy tidbit of Keuka Lake lore; Rich MacAlpine and the members of the I Love Keuka Lake Facebook group introduced me to the legend of the curse of the Strawberry Moon. A quick shout out to my focus group: Ingrid J., Tami G., Joe & Julie G., Ruth S., Diana M., Melissa C., Kate P., Kathryn R., Cheryl O., Laura B., Trish S., Toni S., Ingrid F., Chris B., Darlene S. & Karen B. Also *merci* to Edwina C. Many thanks to Melissa and Joe Carroll for showing me the heart of Keuka.

As always, thank you to my support network of family and friends for your encouragement.

Finally, a special thank you goes out to tenor lead vocalist/bass player Jason Scheff of the band Chicago for his broadcasts on Periscope that gave me insight into the tour life of a rock star.

CHAPTER ONE
Friday, June 13 ~ 9:30 p.m.

The moment the bride and groom pledged their eternal love with a kiss, fireworks whooshed skyward blooming into sparkling scarlet chrysanthemums above Hare Hollow Vineyards on the West Side of Keuka Lake. No one was more surprised than the groom who paid for the spectacular display. They'd been set off an hour early.

A full red moon (tinted by California wildfires a continent away) brooded ominously above the opposite shore, though raucous guests at the nighttime wedding acted oblivious to that portent or the unlucky date. As waiters dispersed briskly through the crowd carrying silver trays of the winery's Blanc de Noirs sparkling wine, guests lifted effervescent flutes aloft cheering on the newlyweds to kiss again. The groom winced slightly, complied with a chaste buss on his wife's cheek, then whispered he had to go check on something and would be right back. She nodded, curious at his furrowed brow, but pulled him suddenly by the lapels of his white tuxedo toward her, locking him into a deep, lingering kiss. Her fingers wove into his strawberry blonde locks to a roar of approval.

A heart-shaped firework spread across the sky above them as the groom whispered one more thing before heading off toward the reception tent.

"This wasn't the plan, Esperanza. I have to go check on something."

She sighed. Ryan often became distracted by the tiniest details gone awry. Surely someone would endure a verbal lashing over this mix-up. The thing was, she loved that it was a mistake and that the fireworks went off the exact moment they became man and wife. How more romantic could you get? Esperanza pushed the veil off her shoulders, hung her hands on her hips and took a deep breath. On cue, the six bridesmaids locked arms with her, then stepped forward to join the guests watching the show from the patio balcony, the billowy tulle of her strapless gown melting into the crowd.

Outside the reception tents, juicy haunches of beef rotated slowly on a large spit releasing savory aromas that wafted down the hillside and stirred the appetites of guests, hungry for the feast to begin. Inside the main tent, the groom loosened his bow tie nervously while he asked the band the whereabouts of the rock star he'd hired to sing during the first dance. They told him Jeremiah Redfern had not yet arrived, but he was expected soon. The plan was he would surprise the bride by walking out singing their song, one of his biggest hits, as the couple took to the dancefloor. That was when the fireworks should have gone off.

About an hour earlier in a sprawling mansion across the lake, Jeremiah Redfern's practice session for the performance had been interrupted by his wife's haranguing outburst. His cellphone pinged in the midst of her screams, and he calmly set down the guitar to read a text sent from someone claiming to be the wedding planner's assistant. Ignoring his wife's latest accusations of infidelity inflamed her further. She pointed a sharp scarlet fingernail into his chest and unleashed a fusillade of F-bombs.

The text said the staging of his entrance at the reception had been changed to make it more dramatic and coincide with the fireworks display. Jeremiah grinned and nodded in approval. Back in the '80s you couldn't stage a legitimate rock concert without pyrotechnics. He walked out of the house without the slightest conciliatory goodbye or backward glance at his wife and texted "Leaving now." When the door slammed behind him, his wife kicked Jeremiah's Stratocaster guitar off its stand and its nickel-steel strings banged onto the hardwood floor, plucking a dissonant chord.

"Cheating bastard!" she yelled, then drained her glass of bourbon and flung it at the music stand. It broke into clinking smithereens and the smoky, amber liquid splattered across the wall. Sheet music fluttered in midair briefly before settling beneath the grand piano. Even though their neighbors resided a good distance behind massive bluestone walls lining the property, they couldn't help but hear her tirade that followed.

The assistant texted directions to a cottage on West Lake Road, about half a mile below the Riesling vineyards owned by Hare Hollow. Jeremiah arrived at the address but could not see a driveway anywhere. He lowered the car windows to get a better view in the dusk and saw a cellphone light flash at him.

"Park along this shoulder," a person wearing a motorcycle helmet yelled from across the road. Jeremiah made a U-turn and pulled far off the shoulder. He emerged from his platinum Jaguar dressed in expensive casual wear: fitted black jeans over hand tooled cowboy boots, a black T-shirt and white linen jacket with the sleeves pushed up. His caramel-colored hair (much lighter than the chocolate brown of his youth) spiked into blond bangs framing his thin face. A few injections of Botox and plastic surgery nips stretched and removed any sagging skin that would have given away his true age—sixty-nine. He strolled over to the person who was now waiting for him on an all-terrain vehicle idling next to a dirt road.

"This is my lift? Seriously?"

"C'mon, get on. We don't want you to be late!"

He donned the helmet offered him and boarded onto the back seat. Jeremiah appreciated that the driver steered carefully up the bumpy, acre-long path that ran deep into the bottom half of Hare Hollow's vineyards. He didn't want his outfit covered in dust.

Well, this is an adventure. Why not just deliver me by limo?

The driver paused midway up the dirt path.

"Wait with this wireless microphone by the clearing over there for the person who will lead the rest of the way to your surprise entrance." The driver pointed toward a path between the grapevines.

Jeremiah removed the helmet and set it on his seat, fluffed his hair and took the microphone from the gloved hand of the driver as he climbed down cheerily from the vehicle, waving goodbye to his ride.

"Ohhhkay then." He checked to see if the mic switch was on. *They must have planned my entrance to be something sort of James Bond-ish. Whatever floats the groom's boat.* Once the ATV vanished down the path, Jeremiah paused to take a swig of bourbon from an engraved flask in his jacket as he squinted up the hill at the illuminated tents next to the winery. The planner said there would be about three hundred guests waiting for him. It was a relatively intimate setting, yet the audience was still large enough to make his stomach flutter. *God, I hope I don't forget any lyrics tonight.* That had been an issue lately and it had been a few years since he'd sung that song live. In this age of instant social media, Jeremiah did not want to wake up tomorrow and find a video of a bad performance gone viral.

He laughed like a delighted child when the first fireworks burst right above him and then continued along the vineyard path. *Will the bride cry when she hears my voice and sees me there in person?* That image made his chest broaden slightly. He fluffed his spiky bangs once more as he thought briefly of his angry wife back home and winced, trying to remember what she looked like on their wedding day. The dim memory dissipated like dry ice smoke from a fog machine when he heard footsteps.

Someone emerged suddenly at the end of the row of grapevines, about thirty feet ahead of him. *This must be my guide.* Jeremiah strode happily toward the figure, trying to make out the person's face in the moonlight and reflected glow of the fireworks. His initial reaction of recognition changed to surprise when he got close enough to see the person's arm raise and aim a handgun at him. The fireworks were so deafening above the wedding guests that no one heard Jeremiah's pleas and for that same reason, of course, no one heard the pop of a perfectly aimed shot fired toward the center of his chest or heard his lifeless body collapse with a thud below the vines.

CHAPTER TWO
Friday, June 13 ~ 9:45 p.m.

It was calm with a promise of storms. Across the lake reflections of the fireworks shimmered on the water like lustrous patent leather. Three sisters admired the free show as they relaxed around a table on the upper deck of their home.

"Hope you've enjoyed the entertainment I've arranged for this evening." Tara laughed as she uncorked a second bottle of wine from Hare Hollow Vineyards—her employer. She was the winery's tasting room manager, and whenever they had a free night she'd treat her sisters to a flight of samples from work as a way to hone her skills. Tara filled generously the glasses held by Maureen and Kelly. The citrusy, pineapple taste of the chilled semi-dry Riesling offered perfect refreshment on this sultry June evening.

Although they displayed a definite genetic resemblance in the height of their brows and the width of their cheekbones, the sisters' personalities veered dramatically. Maureen Caviston McCarthy—the eldest—bore a regal sagacity acquired through an abrupt transitional life experience. Until the moment her husband instinctively steered the car left when it skidded right on the icy thruway outside Rochester, she had a reputation as the determined courts reporter for the daily newspaper. Both prosecutors and defenders grimaced when she'd run toward them with her notebook. She always returned to the newsroom triumphant though, bearing all the critical information sought by her editors.

The instant the tractor-trailer crushed their straying car during that sudden snow squall, she lost both her loving husband Bob and any desire for career advancement. The injuries she sustained to her back and neck were excruciating, but they would heal with time. Narcotic meds helped her cope through the pain-filled, blurred weeks afterward. The accident's emotional toll required longer-lasting therapy however, and it altered permanently the way she pondered and valued everything.

Her looks changed the most after the accident. She'd acquired a girth of fifteen extra pounds she'd yet to shake. No longer did she dye her hair auburn and fasten the long locks loosely into a bun, held in place with a ballpoint pen. Nowadays Maureen opted for low fuss, cropped bristly silver hair that belied her age of fifty-eight. When you saw the sparkle of her green eyes that caught the light like facets on an emerald, you could sense the youthful exuberance that remained despite her challenges. At this moment in her life Maureen felt once again sturdy of body, and mind, but now in addition she possessed a disarmingly gentle manner that could soothe any inflamed situation. Lowering her stress renewed her innate creativity which came forward in everything she did, from cooking gourmet meals to designing beach glass sun catchers.

Tara Caviston Grande, the middle sister, looked and acted fifteen years younger than her true age of fifty-six. Statuesque and stylish, she was a divorcee who captivated every man within her radius with a flip of her long, silky tresses. Her flawless skin bore a year-round tawny hue. She had a broad smile with perfect teeth framed by the slightest of dimples.

Tara had the knack of engaging anyone in conversation with such rapt attention from her stunning aquamarine eyes that it felt like just the two of you existed on the planet. You'd be a fool to assume she relied on her looks. Tara's intelligence, quicksilver wit and sharp tongue cut through anything she suspected to be a ruse.

Talented like her eldest sibling, she found her niche in interior design and had been the darling of the old money set in the Finger Lakes before Gianni, her ex, begged her to give up the business. His traditional upbringing clung to outmoded perceptions of women's roles in society. In his mind home duties came first, her career second. Tara's ability and Hollywood-like glamor had one downside: she commanded attention among any group of people. That made it particularly depressing for those caught in the long shadows she cast.

That was where Kelly Caviston, their younger sister, often found herself. At fifty-three she was still single but hadn't given up hope of finding love one day. Kelly was used to feeling invisible to men whenever Tara was around. To compensate for her sense of inadequacy in that respect, she focused on her studies and graduated early from Cornell with a Master's Degree in Library Science. Soon after Kelly was given the opportunity to manage a bookshop in Hammondsport known for its collection of used and rare books. The job became her career and she eventually bought the business from her boss in 2007, renaming it The Deckled Edge.

Kelly never quite figured out how to assemble her wardrobe in a way that could have transformed her into the knockout she had the potential to be. Growing up, Tara was always too preoccupied with her boyfriend of the moment to pass along beauty tips. Despite lacking fashion sense, she was a lithe, natural beauty with lush curly chestnut hair. Instead of seeking advice from a hairstylist, she tamed her mane with tortoise shell clips and barrettes. The upside of her lazy hair maintenance was that it framed her intense peridot green eyes. Through them she noticed everything around, and when paired with an innate strong intuition, they gave her the ability to size up any situation swiftly... that is, unless it focused on her.

"What's going on at the winery tonight?" Kelly dipped an orange pepper slice into the roasted garlic hummus Maureen made. "Is it another wedding?"

Tara leaned toward the plate of brie, cut a small wedge and smeared it on a slice of crusty baguette as she nodded. "Brendan O'Hare's grandson is getting married there tonight." Here was another annoying aspect of Tara's perfection. She could eat whatever she pleased and never seemed to gain any weight. "I have the metabolism of Secretariat," she'd often brag.

"I heard the father of the bride's a record producer from LA." Maureen reached across the table for a handful of candied walnuts.

"His name is Alejandro Montez." Tara exaggerated the "ja" in his name with a phlegmy "h" sound, as if she spoke Spanish fluently. She didn't. It was just that she got a kick out of over-pronouncing vivid names. "Ryan is marrying his daughter Esperanza." She cupped the side of her mouth as if she didn't want anyone else to hear her. "From what I've heard, Alejandro is not too happy about the marriage. He thinks Ryan lacks the drive to take care of his daughter in the manner to which she is accustomed. Ryan's spoiled brat outbursts have not helped his cause, either."

"Wait, did he actually say 'take care of her'?" Maureen guffawed. "Aren't we in the twenty-first century? Women can take care of themselves, Alejandro!"

Kelly leaned back in her chair and sighed toward the stars. "I tell you, at this point in my career, I wouldn't mind someone taking care of me."

Her admission amused Tara and Maureen, who both immediately groaned.

"What's the matter with you, Kelly? Trust us, you're much happier and freer when you're untethered to a man."

Maureen nodded, but felt the slightest twinge that doing so in some way disrespected her beloved late husband. Tara acted oblivious that her offhanded comment flirted with insensitivity. She prattled on.

"You know, I could have worked the reception if I wanted to, but we have a busload of tourists coming from Quebec for a special tasting tomorrow. It would have been tough to skip partying with the crew afterwards. Maybe if I drank a few pots of coffee it would have been doable."

Kelly winced. Her sister still acted like a college coed sometimes. Surely that lack of maturity was another reason why Gianni severed their relationship two years ago.

Tara's cellphone rang and she got up from the table quickly to answer it.

"What's the matter? Why does your voice sound funny? Did something happen there?" She saw her sisters listening, and turned her back to them as she walked over to the far railing.

"Who'd be calling her at this hour?" Maureen watched her sister for a few seconds and then picked up an organic purple carrot stick and dragged it through the hummus.

"Didn't she break up with that wine distributor? If it's not him, maybe it's Christophe?"

Maureen shook her head. "Probably not. He's partying with friends in Ibiza until Sunday. She must have a new beau."

Tara's conversation ended several minutes later and she returned to the table without offering any clue who called.

"OK, who'd like to try the new Cabernet Franc?"

The other two sisters held out their wine glasses eagerly.

"Of course if we were at the tasting room, I'd rinse your glasses with water dramatically and dump it to prepare you for the switch to red wine. Sorry, not in the mood. Ha! So imagine I've just done that. These Cab Franc grapes are sourced from our vineyards on the southeast shore of Seneca Lake. Swirl the wine in your glass to get some air in there, and take a good sniff inside the glass before letting the wine roll over your tongue. This will be much drier, of course, and expect to experience a dramatic depth of flavors."

"Pretty color." Kelly held her glass up to the candle lantern on the table. "I've been drawn to anything garnet-colored lately. Maybe I need to buy a garnet ring."

"No wonder, it's a shade that looks beautiful on you."

Kelly smiled at Maureen. She was always so generous with sincere compliments.

They followed Tara's directions and savored the complex layers of the dry red wine. Though the sun had long set, heat still permeated the air, still emanated from the wooden deck beneath their bare feet. Maureen fanned her face after she was overcome by a sudden sulfites-induced hot flash. She stood abruptly and carried her glass over to the railing, hoping she could lean out and catch the subtlest stirrings of a lake breeze. The air was unmovable, pinned by humidity as heavy as a wet Aran sweater. Maureen walked back to sit down and her eyes caught the reddish full moon rising behind the cottage.

"Ooh, how pretty! Look, it's the Strawberry Moon." Tara and Kelly turned to see it.

"I learned that nickname and the mythology behind it from a client today at the spa." Maureen worked as a massage therapist for Ballylough Spa at the lake's north end in Penn Yan.

"How beautiful. Is it named that because it coincides with strawberry picking time?" Kelly asked.

"Well sort of, but that's not the interesting part. Dolly said the Seneca Indians have a folktale about a brave who crossed Keuka Lake in a birch canoe with his wife and child one June night long ago. It was during the Strawberry Festival. The Senecas revere strawberries so much they believe the fruit lines the path to heaven and you'll eat them when you die. The festival celebrates the fact they are the first fruits harvested each year. As part of the event, they mix strawberry juice with water and maple syrup. Then they drink it after expressing gratefulness for the privilege of life."

Tara snorted. "Kind of like why I drink wine."

Maureen laughed, then paused to collect her thoughts.

"According to the folktale, when the brave paddled across the lake, a sudden storm capsized the canoe. He reached over the edge to grab the wrists of his wife and child, but the pull of the fierce waves wrenched them apart. Eventually he floundered to shore and collapsed. When the brave came to, he was devastated to see the overturned empty canoe lying on the beach next to him. He cursed the lake for 'devouring' his wife and child at the time when ice had retreated and all were joyous at summer's return. He raised his fist and yelled that Keuka Lake would always be hungry for more bodies when the Strawberry Moon is full, but it would never be satiated because they'd rise to the surface from summer squalls driving them ashore."

Tara looked at Maureen and blinked, drained her wineglass and folded her arms across her lap. "Well now. *That's* a real buzzkill."

Kelly chuckled. "Imagine if you had triskaidekaphobia and paired that legend with today's date. You'd end up with the perfect storm. Ha!"

Swarms of bright gold flashes punctuated the fireworks finale, chased by a sharp bang that rumbled up the shores of the Y-branched lake so loudly they felt the concussion, miles away. A faint cheer rose across the lake and when it dissipated, the thrum of contented crickets filled the silence.

"Did you hear who moved into that ridiculous Tudor McMansion on the East Side near the bluff?" Kelly asked. "Jeremiah Redfern! Can you believe it? There's a rock star living down the road from us now." Though Kelly's interests were usually steeped in topics more intellectual, she was a sucker for pop culture gossip.

"Great, that's all we need choking narrow East Lake Road: paparazzi and groupies." Tara topped off the wine in her glass. "I remember the first time I heard his hit 'Forever Gigi.' Bobby Smyth and I were fooling around in his Mustang convertible at Makeout Point. Maybe it was the Boone's Farm we'd been drinking, but when the song came on the car radio I got the giggles bad when he paused mid-kiss and said, 'What the hell kind of name is Gigi?' Still makes me laugh."

"Jeremiah sounded better before he went solo, back when he was still with Vinegar Hill." Kelly sat forward. "They were my favorite rock group. Maybe it's because I had such a wicked crush on Glenn McCann. Remember him, the keyboard player?" She sighed slightly.

"Oh yeah. You're right," Tara nodded. "Now *that* band rocked."

"I remember seeing them back in March of 1984 at the Rochester War Memorial," Kelly continued. "My friend Melissa and I drove to the show. We waited outside by the band's bus after the concert in the freezing cold for more than an hour, hoping to get their autographs. When the band finally left the building, they walked past us so fast we couldn't get up the nerve to stop them.

"Oh, I'll never forget how gorgeous Glenn was. He had to be about six-foot-five and his thick black hair feathered back across his cheekbones. He walked past with his head raised, regal nose, cleft chin, that toothy smile of his... it simply gleamed under the streetlights. Glenn exuded sexy rock star glam. He wore this shaggy Mongolian lamb fur coat over a black turtleneck and tight leather pants." She paused to fan herself. "Phew! His presence... my God, it was as if the air turned to glitter in his wake. Time froze. There was no sound. Utterly magical."

"Or, perhaps you just inhaled too much at the concert?"

Maureen guffawed, but Kelly frowned at Tara. "C'mon, you know I never did that stuff. It was the overwhelming power of his presence. The band was at the peak of its career. Know what's a funny coincidence? I just ordered some copies of the unauthorized biography of the band that came out in the '90s, *Soured Grapes*. Can't wait to read it when it arrives at the store. The description hints it has juicy details about the rock scene in that era. Wonder if they will sell out because of Jeremiah's move here?"

Maureen squinted toward the opposite shore.

"Wait a minute... you mentioned the song's title was 'Forever Gigi'. Right?" Tara nodded. "Hmm, now *that's* a funny coincidence." Her sisters gave Maureen a confused look. "One of my clients today had small tattoos on the underside of his wrists. The left one said 'Forever,' the right, 'Gigi.' I remember thinking it was so odd. Now I realize they were written in the curlicue script Vinegar Hill used for its logo."

"No way! Do you think it was Jeremiah?" Kelly gaped, intrigued by the prospect that her sister had a close encounter of the rock star kind.

"No, it wasn't him. This guy looked way older. He had white hair pulled back into a ponytail, thick black eyebrows and a white goatee. The most recent photos I've seen of Jeremiah look nothing like that."

"Maybe we shouldn't have knocked the name Gigi." Tara twirled up her mane of highlight-streaked hair to cool her neck.

"There must be something beguiling about it. I haven't met a man yet with 'Forever Tara' tattooed on his wrists."

"Give it time, sis." Maureen tipped her neck back and gazed at the faint stars above. "I wonder what the story of that man's tattoo is. Did he fall in love with Gigi and marry her? Or did he pine for her from afar, a forbidden paramour. Then again, maybe it was his mother's name." She laughed lightly. "I did sense a sadness about him and his back was a minefield of tension bombs."

"Can you read your client's personality through the massage?" Kelly asked.

"Certainly. Of course I've always been intuitive, too. That man was a seeker. Of what, I'm not sure. He lacked inner peace."

Heat lightning flashed beyond the distant vineyards toward Italy Hill.

"Storm's a comin'." Maureen stood and peered over the railing. "Is the umbrella closed on the patio?"

"I'll take care of it." Kelly rose from her chair. "Think I'm going to spend the night on the screened porch downstairs tonight unless the storms turn severe. It's so hot and I can't sleep with the rattle from that ancient air conditioner in my bedroom."

"OK. That's my cue. Wish me luck with the tour groups tomorrow, eh?"

"May the Cab Franc be with you." Maureen raised her glass in farewell and savored the last drop. Kelly carried the dishes and glasses into the kitchen as Tara crossed the sloping lawn to her little cottage next door.

It wouldn't kill her to help clean up once in a while. Kelly frowned as she filled the dishwasher.

"Pleasant dreams." Maureen blew a kiss to her youngest sister before climbing the stairs to her bedroom.

Kelly's room was on the lower floor with big windows facing the lake. She put on a lightweight nightgown, grabbed some pillows and fluffed them on the old couch on the screened porch. Before she lay down, she checked the door to make sure it was locked, propped the pillows under her head and closed her eyes. In her mind she imagined strolling down the lake road and encountering Jeremiah Redfern. They'd strike up a casual conversation about lake life. Of course she would be cool and not fawn over him. One should always respect a celebrity's private life, right? *I've got a strong feeling we will meet someday.*

Chapter Three
Friday, June 13 ~ 11:45 p.m.

Sleep eluded Kelly. She blamed it on the heat—the promise of cooler air storming in on a cold front unfortunately never materialized. Then there was the insistent moonlight which bathed the lawn so brightly she could see blades of grass from where she lay. Her mind raced through tasks that needed to be done, she pondered who might have called Tara earlier and eventually settled into a bit of a funk about her singleness. How had her life come to this?

The sisters' year-round home and its guest cottage belonged to their parents Dr. John and Mary Kennedy Caviston. It was on the East Side of the lake, about six miles south from the Village of Penn Yan. Keuka sits in the middle of the eleven Finger Lakes, scenic spans of fresh water carved by glaciers deep in the heart of upstate New York.

The Cavistons' property had been part of a large farm broken into parcels during the Great Depression. Two buildings sat about sixty yards apart from each other on the land. The main house, a crimson clapboard clad structure built in the Dutch Colonial Revival style, had been built into the sloping property in the manner that the roadside's main floor was the lakeside's second floor. Above both was a smaller floor with two bedrooms and a full bath.

A much smaller, one-story stone cottage stood on the left side of the property, halfway between the main house and the lakeshore. Legend was the farmer who owned the property built it with stones dug from his fields. It had sharp gables, a whimsical arch made partly with old farm tools stuck in the mortar, and two interlocked horseshoes hung over the front door facing the lake. The farmer dubbed it the honeymoon cottage, but it was not known if he built it for himself or someone else. Maybe it was called that because it was quite cozy, and with more than two people inside it would feel as crammed as a subway car at rush hour.

Hedges of lilacs and Japanese quince framed the sides of the property, providing a bit of privacy from the neighbors, and tall, twisted willow trees arced over the water's edge. A stand of cottonwood trees between the two houses shed fluffy "snow" in June and provided dappled shade on hot summer days. Variegated hostas rimmed the shady sides of the homes and a mix of flowering perennials including tiger lilies, bee balm and Russian sage brightened the sunny spots.

John Caviston, a beloved obstetrician renowned in Penn Yan for his dulcet rendition of "Danny Boy," used the cottage as his home office until his retirement. Ten years after he died of a heart attack. The cottage sat untouched. It was too much for his bereft widow Mary to process. She lived in the main house until her death a few years later from breast cancer. To Kelly, as their lone unmarried daughter, the house that her father christened Keuka Breeze was the only home she knew outside of college dorms. When cancer incapacitated her mother, Kelly accepted willingly the responsibility of live-in caregiver. Upon her passing, Mary left the entire property to the three sisters to keep or sell. The two older siblings deferred their shares happily to Kelly because she'd lived there for so long. They didn't need it; their lives were set.

Or so they thought. It wasn't too long after Mary's death that Maureen and her husband Bob were driving home from a Buffalo Sabres hockey game when they got into that terrible car accident. Maureen sustained a sprained back and whiplash that required much physical therapy. Her daughter Ciara's family lived in Glendale, Arizona, and it would have been difficult to leave her job and school-aged children to come home for a few months and help her mother. Her son Martin was a reporter for an international news bureau covering Eastern Europe. What could they do? Kelly shifted swiftly back into caregiver mode with the assistance of her part-time staff at the bookstore and helped nurse her sister back to health at Keuka Breeze.

During that personal trial Maureen learned firsthand the value of massage therapy for recovery. She decided to go back to college—in her fifties—to get licensed. It was just an hour's commute from Keuka to a school two lakes over near Ithaca. The program required seven months of study, Maureen took the final exam the following January, and as luck would have it, she got the massage therapist job at Ballylough soon after. Not keen on the long commute from home, Maureen accepted her sister's invitation to come back to live at Keuka Breeze. She sold her home in Rochester and moved in with Kelly.

Soon afterward, Gianni Grande dropped his divorce request bombshell on Tara. Using the grounds of irretrievable breakdown, he stated their marriage fell apart because she never seemed to embrace the duties of being an adult or maintained the household properly—to his overly demanding standards, Tara always clarified. The law firm he worked for handled high-profile clients and he felt he could never invite any of them over because Tara was usually off traipsing through designer and furnishing stores with clients, leaving their own home neglected. He said it felt like she was a wife in absentia. Tara was too proud to allow a maid in their home. Maybe she instinctively didn't trust her husband to be alone with *any* woman. Tara tried her best, but there was no pleasing Gianni.

Once the divorce papers were signed, she returned from her home in Canandaigua—one Finger Lake to the west—to the family's homestead, with ego bruised and anger simmering. Within weeks of the divorce settlement Gianni married a woman twenty years younger, a hand model from New York City. The thing that made Tara laugh was because of her replacement's career, she could not lift a finger around the house for fear of scratching her hands or chipping a fingernail. It didn't seem to bother Gianni that she wore gloves most of the time, and he didn't mind hiring a maid to do the work Luna could not do for risk of harming her prized assets. Being from a wealthy Italian family, Luna was accustomed to such pampering. Papa owned blocks of real estate across New York City's boroughs. Tara suspected Gianni was hoping some of her wealth would trickle into his pockets.

It took a few months for the three to readapt to living together again. Tara desired a bit more privacy, and in a rare domestic mood, finally purged the clutter from her father's office in the "honeymoon cottage" and moved in.

***

The moon glow insisted on tormenting Kelly with its fairyland-like "daylight." She covered her eyes with a pillow to create a shield of darkness and that helped. There were other distractions though. Crickets chirped shrill dialogues that wove together across the lawn. Loud music drifted up the lake from the wedding reception dance floor, still throbbing with happy partiers. Mixed into the pauses between songs were moments of conversations with happy voices. Those sounds under such romantic moonlight reminded her once more of love that eluded her. Another wave of self-pity swept over Kelly, eliciting a few tears until sleep finally overcame her.

In her dreams, Kelly heard the sound of something scraping across the shale pebble beach. She looked up and saw the Seneca brave Maureen described earlier emerging from a pinkish mist off the lake. It swirled around him masking his face as he gripped an empty canoe with his left hand. He extended his right hand to her.

"The time of the Strawberry Moon is nigh. Keuka is hungry."

Kelly's own screams startled her awake; she nearly rolled off the couch. Now it was the tympani beats of her pounding heart keeping rhythm with the cricket dialogues. Her dream was so vivid, she raised her head and looked toward the beach. No brave. No canoe. At least the guests at the wedding reception seemed to be getting quieter. She laid her head back on the pillow and closed her eyes, thoughts drifting back to that magical moment when Glenn McCann breezed past her outside the concert in Rochester on a night long ago, in a life far away.

CHAPTER FOUR
Saturday, June 14 ~ 1:15 a.m.

As soon as the lights dimmed in the reception tents up the hill, a figure holding a remote-control drone emerged from the vineyard's shadows. Tiptoeing to where the pink pearl-handled pistol dropped onto the ground, the person retrieved it with a gloved hand and slipped it inside a gallon-sized plastic bag. Previous practice attempts to carry the handgun away with the claws of the drone failed. Putting the weapon inside the bag made it easier for the drone to secure a grip.

Suddenly a drunken couple stumbled down the hill, laughing loudly as they wove through the vineyard toward Jeremiah's body. *Where the hell did they come from?* The person's hands trembled while sealing the bag quickly, leaving it puffy with trapped air, and then attached it to the drone's claws. The person stepped back, removed the glove and texted geographical coordinates hurriedly into a cellphone app. Rotors on the drone purred to life and it lifted above the vineyard and drifted toward the lake.

"Shush!" The drunk man held a finger to his mouth. "What's that sound?"

"I dunno, maybe it's a bat?" asked the woman. She grabbed his shoulder, unsteady on her feet as she gawked cross-eyed at the night sky.

"Ahhh, yes, it's the call of a vampire bat coming for you. I vant to drain your blood, ha-ha!" He slipped his arm around her waist and playfully nipped her neck. She giggled as they spun around and fell onto the ground in a passionate embrace, resting at the far end of the row where Jeremiah's body lay.

When the drone reached the lake it shifted direction, flying low over the black water toward the north end of the lake. The operator backed away carefully into the woods, hoping the inebriated couple wouldn't hear any footsteps.

***

An hour after The Eggleston Inn closed across the lake, some of the staff crowded into bartender Jarod Jensen's ski boat parked outside at the dock. Jarod had had a bit to drink earlier in the evening, but now he felt in control. His girlfriend Sarah, however, wobbled on the back seat of the boat. She'd done too many Jell-O shots with the other waitresses, probably because of the vicious argument the couple had earlier that evening. Frankly, he was glad she wasn't sitting up front next to him. He needed to collect his thoughts about their strained relationship.

Something intangible shifted between them recently. He'd first felt an emotional distance from her on Memorial Day during the staff picnic at the vineyard across from the inn. When she disappeared for few hours, Jarod asked Sarah's best friend Tamara where she was. Tamara looked at her feet and mumbled something about Sarah wanting to go pick wildflowers up the hill from the vineyard. After Sarah returned (with no bouquet, Jarod noted) he asked if everything was OK and she was all smiles, acting as if there was no problem. It struck him as a fake response. Their relationship felt off ever since.

Jarod and Sarah met during sophomore year of high school in Penn Yan. He'd transferred there suddenly in mid-October from a school in Roswell, New Mexico. The man his mother was seeing, Zane, threatened to hit her with a piece of steel pipe one night after he drained a bottle of mezcal. She didn't want to linger and wait until he actually used it.

They'd lived in Roswell as a cobbled-together family for nearly a decade with Zane's Aunt Imelda. She claimed to be half extra-terrestrial. Her skin had a grayish cast and she spoke so oddly in a high-pitched whine that Jarod believed her claim. Even her dog looked alien—a Frankenstein-ish mongrel whose lone decipherable genetic heritage was Chinese crested. He hated their mobile home with its dark wood paneling and scratchy crocheted throws tossed over lumpy furniture.

There was little privacy within, and whenever he wandered outside all of their buttinsky neighbors dispensed unsought opinions about Zane's unenthusiastic upkeep of the property. To escape it all, Jarod lifted free weights in his room. He detested Zane's constant bullying toward his mother and having never met his own father, Jarod's soul drifted and resentment filled its darkened void. Sometimes he imagined what it would feel like to pin Zane under a rack of weights until he begged for mercy.

It might seem odd but Jarod felt relieved when Zane freaked out, because the next morning he and his mother booked back east on the first Greyhound available. Fortune shifted for mother and son, and they soon found a tiny hillside home in the Finger Lakes that she could afford on her disability checks. She'd suffered post-traumatic stress from a previous violent relationship. His mother figured her ex-boyfriend wouldn't find them in Dresden by Seneca Lake's shores, even though he knew her parents still lived in Branchport on Keuka Lake, to the west.

Jarod's mysterious arrival drew curiosity from classmates and raised concern from the guidance counselor. He expressed an interest in sports and the counselor introduced him to the lacrosse team coach hoping he'd try out for the team. He did, and the sport came easily to him, so much so that he lied to his teammates and told them he was half Onondaga Indian.

The afternoon of the lacrosse team's game against Fairport, Jarod first noticed Sarah Washington standing on the sidelines looking thoroughly bored. Sarah rarely went to sporting events; academics consumed most of her free time. Her tenacious prowess with schoolwork scored her a permanent spot on the honor roll. She hoped to study oenology at Cornell or the University of California, Davis toward the goal of creating hybrid grape varieties.

Her friend Tamara dragged her along to the game that day, and she observed it with little enthusiasm. Tamara had a crush on one of the other players and needed Sarah there for support.

Sarah's quiet, natural beauty intrigued Jarod though he was prone to vivacious cheerleader archetypes. Who was this mysterious girl watching him? Her un-styled wavy hair and beautiful doe eyes stirred feelings he'd never experienced before. After the game as he walked by her, he paused and proclaimed to his teammates, "I'm going to marry that girl."

Sarah blushed and covered her face with her hand as she whispered to Tamara, "What the...? Is that jock talking about me?" It was incredible to Sarah that this buff, gorgeous athlete would have noticed her existence.

Tamara pinched her arm. "If you felt that then yes, he *is* talking about you." They whispered as he walked away with the pack, still watching her with a wide grin on his face.

Jarod began a campaign to win her heart. They weren't much alike intellectually, but there was an intense chemistry between them. By the end of the next lacrosse season they were one of the school's "it" couples, and everyone assumed they'd eventually marry. The relationship hit a few snags over the summer and they broke up before the start of senior year when she found him making out with some dairy princess from Dresden at the county fair. After that, Sarah decided to apply to UC Davis to put a continent between them.

Two unexpected things happened. First, she was not accepted by UC Davis but Cornell did add her to the waiting list, and later, despite her resentment at his indiscretion, they reunited. He'd gotten a decent job at his uncle's hardware store in Penn Yan and it looked as though he could be fast-tracked to manager within a couple of years after graduation. She enrolled in the nearby community college and after she graduated two years later, accepted his offer to move into his apartment off Lake Street.

Their intellectual differences dragged on their strong physical attraction. She also began to notice a short-fused temper that erupted with increasing frequency. Within three years Sarah moved out to share an apartment with Tamara. Jarod took it hard and drank heavily. Somedays he wasn't even sober when he showed up for work. He'd mock customers' questions; he'd stock hinges on power drill shelves. His erratic behavior caused him to be fired from the hardware store. Jarod lucked out when he was offered a job bartending at The Eggleston. Fortunately, he was a good friend of the owner. The new job gave him renewed hope that he could eventually buy a house and propose to Sarah. She *would* be his wife someday.

Sarah felt awful Jarod was so devastated by her move, and because of that she did not break up formally with him. The distance her move created did seem to rekindle their passion briefly, but it dimmed once again after Memorial Day. *What changed?*

Despite having Friday off, they both showed up separately at The Eggleston that evening. Mitch and Jarod chatted with regular customers at the bar before he mustered enough courage to wander over to her table and confront her.

"Sarah, you've gotta tell me. Are you seeing someone else?"

She looked at her friends sitting around the table and responded in a flat tone: "Not sure. Maybe." When she grabbed a handful of popcorn, Jarod noted she wasn't wearing the pearl ring he'd given her.

Crash! He flipped over the table and sent Sarah's friends scattering. Airborne drinks, popcorn bowls and chicken wings laden with hot sauce hit the ankles of the people sitting close to them. The manager ushered the quarreling couple outside, where they continued screaming at each other. At one point Jarod burst into tears. She tried to soothe him with a kiss, but his cellphone pinged, he read the text message, and pushed her away. Next thing Sarah saw was his car pulling out of the parking lot. Her friends rushed to her side when she went back into the bar. They spent the better part of the evening consoling her with comforting words and booze.

Jarod returned finally hours later, pulling up in his grandfather's motorboat after last call. His good friends noticed he was a bit fidgety and trying too hard to act as if nothing had happened earlier with Sarah. He soothed his simmering anger with the last beer chilling in the boat's cooler before starting the motorboat's engine. *So what if it's three in the morning now?* Vibrant moonlight belied that fact. They were pumped to continue a fun evening ahead at Mitch's cottage up the lake. Gas fumes rose from the gurgling motor beneath them as the boat idled a few minutes. Jarod drained the beer can, crushed it in his hands and tossed it into the lake. He cranked the volume to the onboard stereo and set the bass to maximum. The sides of the boat pulsed to The Killah Rappahz as he backed it away from the dock slowly, pushed the throttle forward and rocketed past Bluff Point heading up the lake toward Penn Yan. Everyone onboard yelled to talk with one another over the pounding music and engine's roar.

***

Kelly's fight to remain asleep became an unwinnable war between the stifling heat and the sneaky moonlight. During one of her barely conscious moments, hickory-scented smoke from a bonfire across the lake drifted into her senses and roused her. Kelly slipped off the couch and wandered inside, sniffing the rooms to see if the smoke was present there as well as outside. That nightmare freaked her out earlier and she was concerned if it were an omen of some sort. Convinced her home was not on fire, she returned to the porch exhausted and drifted off once more. Not long after, a whirring sound similar to a weed trimmer brought her back to a conscious state. The noise seemed to be getting louder and as her mind acknowledged that, she awoke fully. Was the next-door neighbor trimming poison ivy in the middle of the night? No, the noise seemed to be coming from the middle of the lake. The pitch of the whir lowered as the source apparently moved up the lake. She heard a splash. Was it related to that other sound or was it a restless trout leaping to nibble the moon?

It was all too much to ponder with an exhausted mind. She rested her head back on the pillow and drifted off until the next disturbance. This time it was screams coming from the lake.

"Where's Sarah? Ohmigod I don't see her! STOP!"

"Dammit, what happened, Tamara?"

"She fell overboard. *Stop the boat!*"

Jarod chewed his lip as he continued a few yards before angrily pulling back the throttle and swerving the boat around toward where Tamara believed Sarah fell off.

"*Shit!* Anyone see her? Stop hiding, Sarah! Don't do this to me." He held his cellphone's flashlight over the water.

"Sarah! Where are you? SARAH!" Tamara yelled frantically. "Ohmigod, what if she's drowned already? We have to get help. *HELP!*"

Tommy Knapp jumped into the lake and the rest onboard watched him dive below the illuminated water. He surfaced gulping for air. "See anything?" he asked.

"I'm coming in, too." Mitch slipped off his shoes and dived in next to Tommy.

Kelly heard a loud splash and rose from the couch. From the twist in her gut triggered by their primal cries, she knew this time it was not a dream. She walked over to the screen and looked toward the lake. Moonlight delineated a crowd of shadowy figures shouting as they dangled over the side of a boat drifting in the center of the lake. Another deep splash and she could make out someone swimming away from the boat.

She gasped, and immediately ran into the bedroom, tied on a bathrobe and grabbed her cellphone. With the phone's flashlight on she ran barefoot down the dewy lawn toward the beach. Kelly jogged to the end of the dock and waved the flashlight at the boat. "Hey, do you guys need any help?"

A young woman waved.

"Yes! Sarah fell overboard! We can't find her."

Kelly dialed 911 and told the dispatcher there was a possible drowning in front of her cottage near Thompson's Cove. It didn't take long for both the sheriff's department marine patrol team and the fire department's search and rescue boat to arrive. Within minutes a sheriff's deputy pulled his cruiser into the Cavistons' driveway. He joined Kelly on the dock, asking her about what she'd witnessed.

Meanwhile, the sheriff's deputies ordered everyone back onboard Jarod's boat. They suspected the group had been drinking and didn't want another drowning to occur. When they were all safely aboard, the driver steered his boat alongside Jarod's and two deputies boarded it.

"I'll need the keys, son," a deputy said. "We'll drive you to shore, but then we have to impound this boat as evidence."

Fury ignited within Jarod, but with all these law enforcement personnel so close, he knew he couldn't try to flee with the boat. He tugged the keys out of the ignition and dropped them into the deputy's hand. Jarod folded his pulsing arms and glared at him. The deputy started up the boat and slowly headed for shore, pulling alongside Kelly's dock. She and the deputy who arrived by car tethered the boat and assisted the passengers stepping onto the dock.

"Son, can you tell us where she fell off, right out front here or farther down the lake?"

"I don't know, man. I don't *know*. Everyone was shouting, the music was loud." Jarod pointed toward the rear of the boat. "Sarah was sitting there. On top of the back seat, dangling her legs on the boarding platform. This asshole comes at us. Gotta be doing sixty-five. No lights. Heading down the lake. Passes too close. Kicks up a wicked wake. The waves smack us bad. I turned around to look at the jerk driving the boat. That's when Tamara starts yelling 'Sarah's missing!' Happened somewhere over here. Circled back to see if we could find her. It's been about a half hour now. She hasn't surfaced. Do you think there's even a chance that she's still...?" The rest of his question stuck in his throat and he looked away.

"She was so wasted." Tamara's teeth chattered and a slight shudder rattled her shoulders. "Her long hair kept blowing into her face and the last thing I remember was she was trying to weave it into a side braid to keep the flyaway strands from getting in her eyes. With her hands up like that, and the big bumps from the waves, she must have flopped right over the side of the boat." Her eyes filled with tears, and she daubed them away with her manicured fingertips.

"May I have your name?" the other deputy asked Jarod.

Wait a minute, does this guy think I did this on purpose? He frowned at the deputy.

"Jarod Jensen. Need me to spell it?"

The deputy shook his head. "I'll need to see your driver's license, Mr. Jensen. How much alcohol have you had to drink tonight?"

Jarod dug his license out of his wallet, handed it to the deputy as he squared his chest and looked away. "A beer."

"Only one? I'm going to need to check your BAC anyway." Jarod sighed exaggeratedly as the deputy took a breathalyzer out of his pocket and turned it on. After he slipped a mouthpiece into it and waited a few seconds for it to warm, he handed it to Jarod. "Please blow into this until the device stops beeping." Jarod did as the deputy instructed with his friends watching anxiously. The beeping felt like an eternity, but it lasted mere seconds before it stopped. He handed the device back to the deputy.

"Hmm, it's .05, so you're under the BUI/BWI limit. You're lucky, son. When you're boating, there should always be a designated driver at the helm. It's not worth the risks." Jarod's eyes narrowed and he swallowed back his anger at the unsolicited lecture. His right hand curled into a tight fist. The other deputy turned toward the passengers standing next to the boat. "I'll need to see identification for the rest of you, also." He wrote down all of their information then walked away from the group with the other deputy to confer for a few minutes. The deputies returned and told the passengers they were allowed to call a friend to come and pick them up by car.

Tamara wandered away to sit on the beach and buried her head into her arms, crossed over her knees. She rocked slightly as she sobbed for her missing friend. The rest of the friends walked slowly off the Cavistons' dock, paused to watch the recovery efforts from the shore for a few minutes and then walked arm in arm up to East Lake Road to wait. Jarod patted Tamara's shoulder.

"C'mon. If she's gone, there's nothing we can do here."

The cruel reality of his words felt like a kick to her gut. She stood, rejected his outstretched hand and ran ahead to join the rest of the group. Jarod chewed the corner of his lip as he looked back at the lake. A lone tear traced over his cheekbone.

"Dammit, Sarah!"

***

After an extensive exploration of the waters by the fire department's dive team, the sheriff's marine patrol officer asked if they needed additional assistance. A call was made to the state police to send its sonar-capable scuba unit via helicopter.

Kelly felt helpless as she watched the unfolding scene, noting the moon was setting into a strawberry pink western horizon as dawn brightened over the lake. Back in the house the intensifying reddish glow in the eastern sky lit up Maureen's bedroom, stirring her awake. She rose and parted the curtains to view the dramatic sunrise, then went downstairs to the deck to take a few photos with her cellphone. That's when she noticed her youngest sister standing at the end of the dock and two boats paused in the middle of the lake.

"Hey, what's going on, Kelly?"

She folded her arms and walked back to the lawn to speak with Maureen in a quieter voice.

"I think someone may have drowned. There were screams about an hour ago and I came outside to see what was going on.

These kids were all yelling from the boat. I called the sheriff. The dive team has been searching the water for quite a while."

Maureen placed her hand over her heart.

"Oh how awful. I'll get the binoculars. Maybe we'll be able to see something from here."

Tara heard voices outside the cottage. Why was Kelly walking up from the shore at this hour? She looked toward the lake and saw the boats and the diver-down flag bobbing on the surface. Instantly she knew something bad happened. Her hair was a mess, so she brushed it into a loose ponytail, ran a stick of lip gloss across her lips and threw on a pair of jeans and a tank top. The other two sisters were still dressed in their robes when she ran up the lawn to join them on the deck of the main house. Suddenly a state police helicopter buzzed past the house at treetop level and swept the coves on both sides of the lake before it paused over the scene.

"What's going on?"

"Some girl is missing and may have drowned. Maureen's scanning the water to see if she can see something."

Tara rubbed her shoulders as if she were cold although it was still muggy out.

"What's with the freaky red sky?"

Maureen drew the binoculars from her face and turned to the others, raising her eyebrows.

"Red sky at morning, sailor take warning, or... yikes, maybe it's the curse of the Strawberry Moon?"

That was the moment Kelly recalled the startling dream she'd had of the Seneca brave. Had it been a premonition? Now she felt chilled.

Across the lake a bank of billowing clouds obscured the rim of the setting full moon. They looked like blooming cauliflower florets edged with rosy light. An emergency broadcast system tone blared suddenly on the sheriff's radio, followed by a bulletin issued for a severe thunderstorm watch.

"Great, that's going to delay things if we don't find her soon," one of the divers said to the deputies. His partner surfaced with something in a plastic bag. He handed it quietly to the marine patrol. They raised their eyebrows. Why had a ladies' handgun been stuffed in the bag? The diver found it nestled in a thick patch of seaweed not far from the surface. It was an expensive weapon and appeared to be in excellent condition. No one thought it had been in the water long. Question was, could any of those kids have afforded it?

Chapter Five
Saturday, June 14 ~ 9:00 a.m.

News of the possible drowning rippled fast across the lake. Most learned about it through photographs of the search activity on the lake that were posted on social media. By the time Tara got to work at the winery, she heard a Rochester TV station's breaking news report in the staff room. It was interrupted by an emergency broadcast system bulletin saying a severe thunderstorm warning was issued for the region, including Yates and Steuben counties. Tara wandered out into the tasting room to see if the bus of Canadian tourists had arrived yet. She hoped they'd show before the storm hit. It would be a shame to have to hold the tasting inside, because the patio's balcony afforded one of the most splendid views of Keuka Lake.

"Did you hear the coyotes last night?" her tasting room assistant Marla Russo asked as they prepared for the bus tour.

"No. I was sound asleep all night until early this morning."

"There must have been a big pack along the hilltop, up in that big field my husband nicknamed 'Howland'. It sounded like there were dozens of them baying at the moon. That sound creeps me out. Wonder if they killed something."

"How'd the wedding go last night?"

"Haven't heard anything specific, but the reception was still going strong when I went to bed around eleven. Couldn't sleep much with the howling and yipping. And then there were the coyotes."

Tara laughed.

"We were awakened early today. There was a possible drowning by Thompson's Cove."

"Oh, how awful. Who was it?"

"Looks like it was a DWB—drinking while boating. Some girl fell off a crowded boat."

"If she was drunk, she wouldn't have a chance. There's quite a drop off near that cove."

***

In the vineyards below the winery, the young lovers awoke from their passionate night, minds fuzzy from mixing too much wine and tequila without restraint. He had a numbing headache and his tongue felt cottony. She could barely breathe through her stuffed-up nose and her acidic stomach rebelled against any movement with an immediate queasy response. She rolled over and looked at his face.

Damn. This guy's kinda cute. The last thing she wanted to do was vomit in front of him. She grabbed the trunk of a grapevine as she staggered to her feet and wandered the vineyard row to find a place where she could be ill discreetly. Once purged, she noticed a murder of crows ahead of her shoving each other to get close to something on the ground. They parted at her approach, and seconds later her high-pitched scream flushed the birds, cawing in protest at her intrusion into their midst. The young man raced to her side, looked past her and exclaimed a stream of expletives as he pulled her close to his chest and covered her eyes with his hand so she wouldn't have to see any more of the gruesome scene. He gasped for air as if he'd been punched in the gut, then garnered the strength to direct her down the row, out of the vineyard and back to the road in front of the winery, both of them repeating "Oh, God" all the way. Tara happened to look out the front window at that moment and saw them flag down two of the vineyard workers and gesture excitedly down the hill behind them. The workers raced into the vineyards. Marla walked over to see what she was staring at.

"What's that all about?"

"Dunno. Looks as if they've had an accident or something." The phone rang on the wall behind the tasting bar. It was the main office line, but no one was in there to answer. When it kept ringing, Tara answered. It was Andy Meyers the vineyard manager.

"Hi Andy. You found what? Is he dead? Holy shhhh...! OK, calm down and I'll call 911 for help. The boss is at home. He's probably still sleeping off last night."

Tara hung up and caught her breath. "My God! There's a dead man in the vineyard. That couple outside discovered him."

"Huh? *A dead man?* Who is he? What do you think happened to him? Did he just collapse? Ohmigod, do you think he was murdered? And what were those people doing in the vineyard? Do you think they did it?"

Tara eyed them as she dialed 911 and noticed their rumpled clothes. "Nah. They're wearing wedding reception outfits. Looks like a walk of shame from last night, don't you think? Hello? Hi, this is Tara at Hare Hollow Vineyards. We need someone here right away. A body has been found in our vineyard. An adult male, they said. No idea what happened. Yes, I'll have our vineyard manager meet you by the road." She hung up and left a message on her boss Brendan's answering machine before she called Andy back. "I called 911 and help is coming. How are you guys doing? They said to tell you not to touch anything. One of you needs to come to the road and lead them to the body. OK? I know, Andy. Nothing like this has ever happened here. Just chill, and they'll be here soon to help."

Not too long after, a sheriff's patrol car flew toward the hilltop winery with sirens blaring and lights flashing, arriving just as the bus of Canadian tourists pulled into the parking lot.

"Uh-oh, we have to do a little impromptu distraction here." Tara grabbed a fistful of winery brochures and thrust some at Marla. "Let's assemble our guests on the other side of the bus so we can point out the vineyards in the direction of Bluff Point. Follow me."

"Welcome to Hare Hollow everyone," Tara said with a sunny smile, directing the tourists to gather by her so they faced the spectacular lake view instead of the crime scene activity. "Before you join us in the tasting room, please direct your eyes down the slope from us. Those are the very vineyards where the grapes for our world-famous Riesling wine are grown.

"Three things make this setting perfect for growing Riesling grapes: the lake, which has its own microclimate providing cooler air in summer and warmer air in winter; steep slopes that allow the cold air to flow off the vineyards down to the lake, and a rich glacial soil that provides great drainage. To the left is the seven-hundred-foot high Bluff Point, where the lake splits into its famous Y shape. Water in the left branch of the Y flows south until it meets water in the main branch of the lake flowing north.

Did you know Keuka is the only lake in the world that flows in two directions?"

The tourists murmured about the lake and its beauty, some pausing for selfies. A few wandered around the front of the bus and looked back down the road where the sheriff's cruiser turned. They whispered something as they pointed. Tara immediately engaged them and distracted them to look toward a mansion high above the lake.

"See that home atop the bluff? Near there Seneca Indian chiefs lit bonfires that could be seen from lakes away."

Her distraction worked. As the cruiser cut its siren and maneuvered slowly down the dirt road alongside the southern end of the vineyard, Tara answered questions about the local climate, geology and geography of Keuka Lake. It looked like it could storm soon, so no one complained about the move indoors to see the fermenting tanks, bottling and labeling operations.

Hare Hollow Vineyards was used to hosting large groups and offered several stations within the tasting room for visitors. After their tour Tara led the group into a large back room farthest from the front window. She said this was a special area for private tastings. Conversations grew lively as the tourists assumed they were getting VIP treatment.

Brendan O'Hare, the winery's owner, walked breathlessly through the room as Tara and Marla poured samples of the dry Riesling. He appreciated their wisdom of locating the group away from the commotion outside and mouthed "Thank you" as he walked out the front door to speak with the wedding guests who found the body. They'd been told to remain on the winery's patio by the sheriff's deputy until detectives arrived on the scene.

Not long afterward, another cruiser with flashing red lights raced up the hill to the winery and turned down the dirt road into the vineyards. The driver, Detective First Sergeant Tyrone Kane, ducked his head as he emerged from the car. Once fully upright, he buttoned the suit jacket that barely fit his towering, bulky physique. Kane massaged the top of his aching right shoulder, took a deep breath and strolled across the grassy border with his partner to greet the deputy waiting for him on the scene. He was chatting with two men whom he introduced as vineyard workers. Just beyond them was the dead man lying on his back, head turned toward the lake. As many times as he had seen a deceased person, Detective Kane still winced at the brutal reality of it. He sent up a silent prayer.

"Recognize the guy?" Deputy Corey Martin asked.

"Should I?"

"He's that rock star who just moved into town," a vineyard worker interrupted. "Jeremiah Redfern."

Kane scratched his chin. "Jeremiah Redfern? Are you kiddin' me? How the hell did he end up dead in a Finger Lakes vineyard?" Kane spoke in a softly toned voice that mismatched his massive frame. He tilted his head so he could see the dead man's face lying on its side and winced. "Damn. Yep, that's him. Man, I have most of his albums. After giving us a lifetime of music, you would expect a peaceful retirement. Someone like him doesn't deserve a sad ending like this."

Andy blurted Jeremiah had been scheduled to perform at the wedding reception last night at the winery but never showed. The detective rubbed his brow and looked at the heavens with a pained look on his face.

"Really? A wedding? Aw hell! Well now that's gonna complicate things. We're going to need a list of all the invited guests." Kane let out a deep sigh. "So, who got married?"

"The owner's son Ryan and the daughter of some record producer from LA."

Kane rubbed his shoulder again and then rested his hands on his hips. A swarm of media would be buzzing around the site within hours. He unconsciously began humming Redfern's big hit "Forever Gigi" as he looked at the body, then toward the winery. Slowly he scanned the horizon across the rest of the vineyards, noting the darkening sky to the west.

"He's a high profile victim." Kane took out his cellphone. "I better call the State Police Bureau of Criminal Investigation and request Troop E's Forensic Investigation Unit get down here right away. Storms are coming and we've got to secure the site and gather any evidence we can before they hit. Once the media arrive they'll try to trudge all over the scene."

Kane knew this from experience. The last time he'd handled any case with such a high profile was when a Hollywood actor wrecked his car speeding on West Lake Road after attending a NASCAR race in Watkins Glen. Securing that accident scene was a nightmare, especially when an overly-nosy sports reporter inadvertently compromised evidence on the scene. He was not going to let that happen here.

Kane pulled a pair of black latex gloves from his pocket and as he slipped them on, ordered his assistant Detective Sergeant Mack Hughes to photograph the crime scene already marked with yellow tape by Deputy Martin.

"Is that the weapon under his arm?" Martin asked.

Kane pointed at the body and asked his assistant to photograph all around the deceased before he squatted to gently lifted the arm.

"Hmm. Looks like a microphone."

"So, you think he probably *was* heading toward the reception to sing but he ended up here somehow?"

Kane nodded at Martin as he set the arm back and stood. "Looks like it. Have you noticed any footprints, Corey?"

"Saw just one pair, coming from next to the woods over there."

Recent thunderstorms had softened the soil throughout the vineyard. Kane followed the footprints in the direction the deputy pointed and paused where they stopped. He squatted next to the final print and gazed past it. Grass beyond it was flattened by the force of something. He walked over to where the grass was sparse and squatted again.

"Mack, over here. I need close-ups of these tire tracks." He squinted at the chevron patterns pressed into the dirt. "Too wide for a dirt bike or a motorcycle," he whispered to himself. "Looks like an ATV." He stood and saw the dirt path that led through the woods down to the lake and sighed.

"We'll probably need to expand the perimeter to West Lake Road, you guys."

"I didn't bring that much tape." Deputy Martin scratched his head.

"Better find out whose property lies below here and ask the residents if they've heard an ATV drive through their neighborhood lately."

A little while later they heard a vehicle approach and looked up to see a state police van drive down the road and park behind the cruisers. Three troopers emerged from the vehicle carrying equipment. Kane walked down the vineyard row to greet the female trooper leading them toward the scene.

"Senior Investigator Angela Reilly." She extended her firm handshake to him. "Is the deceased over there?"

"Yes. It's Jeremiah Redfern, the rock star."

"Never heard of him."

Kane winced at her slight toward his childhood idol. That meant she was probably at least twenty years younger than him.

"Severe thunderstorms are heading directly this way. We probably have about forty-five minutes before we lose a good deal of the scene."

"Detective Hughes took some initial photos of the body and its environs. He's over there videotaping some footprints and tire tracks."

"Any weapon found?"

"No. One lone casing is over here on the right. So whoever shot him was probably standing somewhere close to us now."

"Hmm. Could be dealing with a skilled marksman. OK, let's set up the tents," she called out to the two detectives who came with her. "What do we know so far?"

"The body was found by a couple who attended the wedding reception here last night."

"Wait, there was a wedding going on when he was shot?"

"Yes. The vineyard manager over there, name's Andy, told me that Redfern was supposed to sing at the reception."

"How many guests at the wedding?"

"About 300 he said. Fireworks were set off too early. I'm thinking that's when he might have been shot. Easy cover for the noise of the gunshot."

"What was he doing *here?*"

"You got me whistlin'." He smiled but her expression didn't flinch.

"We'll have to interview the guests, bride and groom, caterers and also anyone who was invited but didn't come to the wedding."

"I've already been thinking that. I'd like to set up a command post ASAP out of the way, probably in their parking lot behind the barn. Don't want to disrupt the winery's operations."

Inspector Reilly introduced herself to the vineyard workers, questioned them briefly and then asked them to wait with the others up the hill at the winery. The detectives secured the immediate crime scene, then spread out to photograph and collect every bit of evidence they could find. A slight sparkle on the ground behind where the shooter would have stood caught Kane's eye. It was a tiny pink feather with a few dots of glitter on it. He bent down and picked it up with a tweezer, sealing it into an evidence bag.

Not long afterward, the hearse arrived to transport the deceased to the coroner's office at a local hospital. The driver and his assistant waited silently with the gurney until Investigator Reilly gave the team the go-ahead to remove his body from the scene.

Detective Kane labored to breathe in the oppressive humidity as he walked slowly uphill to where the vineyard workers and couple who discovered the body were waiting by the tasting room. He wiped his sweaty brow. *Gotta get myself back in shape.* An image of his college football team photo drifted into his mind and he sighed quietly. *This is getting ridiculous. I'm too young to be puffing like an old man.*

Kane crossed the road and approached the group gathered on the patio by the tasting room. "Who here found the body?" The vineyard workers pointed at the couple sitting silently at a café table. He greeted them, noting wrinkles and dirt stains on their clothes, especially the woman's lime green sundress. Their pale faces displayed bleak expressions, a clue to him the couple were genuinely distraught by what they'd discovered. Kane smiled gently as he introduced himself and asked for their names and contact information. Then he interviewed each of them privately about what had occurred. After that, he spoke with the two employees.

"OK, thanks for your help, everyone. Here's a card with my phone number if you remember anything else. I'll call if I need more information."

Brendan noticed the detective speaking with the four and walked outside to greet him.

"Hi, I'm the winery's owner, Brendan O'Hare. My son Ryan's wedding was here last night and Mr. Redfern had been hired to sing as a surprise for his wife Esperanza. He'd paid him in advance to perform. So as you can imagine, my son was extremely upset when Redfern was a no-show. What he was doing in the vineyard is a mystery to us all."

"Can your son get us a list of the wedding guests, Mr. O'Hare?"

"Well certainly his in-laws could. Problem is," Brendan paused to look at his watch, "if you want to interview my son, he's already left for his honeymoon in French Polynesia."

Kane chewed his lip, scratched his straight, yellow ochre hair and squinted. "Of course.... Hmm, we *will* need the number of the resort where they're staying. So, Mr. O'Hare, since this is a high-profile case, I'd like to set up a command post on site. I was thinking we could use that parking lot behind the barn."

"The employee parking lot? Of course, whatever you need, Detective Kane."

"A little later today we'll question your staff and any guests still in town. In the meantime, we're going to have to seal off this vineyard to employees and trespassers."

"Absolutely, that is not a problem."

Kane strode back down the hill to the others. Rain sputtered as the team spread out over the immediate area collecting evidence and photographing every inch of the immediate scene. Deputy Martin retrieved some rocks to help stabilize the tent poles as a wind gust stirred through the vineyard suddenly. Thunder crackled and boomed in the distance. Investigator Reilly checked a weather app on her cellphone.

"Storm's just about over us. Let's get everything in the van before it hits."

The troopers and deputies carried their equipment and collected evidence as fast as they could over to the state police vehicle. Kane's cellphone rang. The coroner said he was on his way to the hospital.

"Reilly, I'm leaving now to meet Dr. Lee. Want to ride along?"

She nodded. "Take this evidence back to the lab and begin processing it," she ordered her staff. Kane asked Detective Hughes to hang back with Deputy Martin.

"Call headquarters and let them know we'll be setting up a command post on site. You can discuss the logistics with Mr. O'Hare the owner. He said the employee lot would be fine." Hughes nodded at his boss and joined Martin. Once the two lead detectives left, Martin moved his car to block the top of the vineyard road. A few minutes later the storm hit with a fury. Squall-driven wind whistled through the front door of the winery's tasting room. Tara and Marla tried their best to keep the customers focused on the wines, but it was becoming increasingly difficult with the drumming of the lashing rain on the roof and frequent thunder crashes.

"The sky's so black. Are we under a tornado watch?"

"Nah, this is a typical summer thunderstorm." Tara smiled as she poured their latest vintage of Niagara into the visitor's glass. "Dramatic, but it won't last long."

"Speaking of Niagara...," one of the visitors pointed toward a window. "That gushing gutter reminds me of standing under the Falls." A sudden, blinding flash drew instant thunder. The deafening boom rattled the building, plunging it into darkness.

"Everyone stay calm. Things are about to get old school in here." Tara reached below the counter for a couple of pillar candles and spaced them on the bar. "Anyone have a lighter?"

As soon as the candles were lit, she smiled at the group. "This is pretty cool. How romantic, right? I think this is the perfect moment to try some of our sparkling wine." Their fears were assuaged effortlessly.

The squall line gusted across the lake about the same time the tasting ended. Both power and sunshine returned. As steam rose from the wet road outside, Tara and Marla ushered the visitors into the wine shop. They were ringing up sales from the customers when Andy walked behind them and whispered two words: "Jeremiah Redfern." He made a pretend gun with his fingers and pointed it at his heart. Tara's eyes widened.

"No way!"

Andy nodded. "We'll all be questioned. Cops need the complete guest list from last night."

The two women raised their eyebrows but continued acting calmly toward the visitors. Tara and Marla cheerily helped the Canadian tourists carry their purchases onto the bus. Some of the people hugged them; they'd had such a good time despite the storm. As they waved goodbye to the bus, Tara muttered to Marla, "My face aches from maintaining this fake smile. Damn, I need a drink! My God, can you believe a murder was committed here last night?"

She strode briskly toward Brendan's office to discuss the ramifications of a high profile death on their premises.

"When the news media find out, it will either kill or boost our tasting room traffic." Tara held her hands on her hips as she paced the room. "We probably need to hold an emergency staff meeting, don't you think? I mean, Jeremiah was an international star and he won a few Grammys. I think he was even nominated for an Academy Award for a movie score. Expect big media outlets to show up in droves. Plus, we'll probably have all sorts of fools skulking about the vineyard looking for souvenir evidence... or even his ghost."

Brendan folded his hands calmly and nodded. His demeanor surprised her. *Why isn't he as concerned as I am?*

"Well, Tara, you might have missed your calling as a cop."

"Yeah, I could rock a holster on my hips." Tara laughed as she tossed back her shoulder-length hair. The two smiled briefly but then grew silent as they thought about how this situation could affect their livelihoods.

"I guess we should take it day by day."

Really, that's all he has to say? She raised her eyebrows briefly, squared her shoulders and headed back to the tasting room without saying another word.

Detective Hughes summoned everyone on staff working that day to the command post. They were questioned about their whereabouts the previous night and if they knew Jeremiah Redfern or had any idea why someone would want to kill him. Tara's interview was brief because she had not been on the scene and was able to name two people—her sisters—who were with her at the probable time of the murder.

Around five o'clock Tara rang up the last sale for the day and headed to her car feeling utterly exhausted. Perhaps it was because her day had gotten off to a bizarre start before she'd even arrived at the winery... and then she was so stressed about the tour group. She had nothing to fear about the sheriff's detective questioning her, but it was still unnerving. It wasn't until the moment she unlocked her car that Tara contemplated the chilling fact a killer was on the loose, and that person's victim died down the hill less than half a mile from where her car was now parked.

CHAPTER SIX

Saturday, June 14 ~ 5:30 p.m.

Tara burst through the front door of her sisters' home yelling, "Holy crap! I need a drink."

"What's the matter?" Maureen rose from the couch with alarm.

"Oh, no emergency, Sis. Today's been like a bad horror movie script. Did they find that girl yet?"

"No. Of course they had to stop when the big storm came through. The missing girl's name is Sarah Washington. She's a waitress at The Eggleston."

"*No*, not Sarah! I know her. Oh my God, she was such a nice kid. That's so awful." Tara covered her mouth and shook her head. "Where's Kelly?"

"She's downstairs doing logic puzzles—you know, her favorite go-to distraction when she's stressed."

Tara walked over to the stairs to the lower level.

"Kelly! Get your ass up here. I've gotta tell you two something you won't believe."

"Be right there." Kelly marked the puzzle book with her pen and jogged upstairs to the kitchen. "What's going on? Is everything OK?"

Tara took a bottle of cabernet sauvignon out of the wine rack and opened it as Maureen gathered wine glasses from the cupboard. The two sisters waited with anticipation as she filled all of their glasses and then took a big gulp from her own. Maureen noted her sister's hand was shaking slightly.

"I've gotta sit." Tara draped her lanky body dramatically onto the recliner. "OK, there's not an easy way to say this. A man was found dead in the vineyards this morning. We suspect he was murdered."

"*What?* Murdered? Are you kidding? Who was it?" Maureen set her glass on the coffee table and sat on the couch along with Kelly.

"Where did it happen? Was it during that wedding reception?" Kelly leaned forward in her seat.

"This is so bizarre. You guys won't believe this...." Tara's voice faltered a bit with emotion. "It was Jeremiah Redfern—someone shot him in the heart." Kelly and Maureen gasped as they sank back into the couch. "He was scheduled to play at the wedding reception. Guess Ryan booked him as a surprise for Esperanza."

"How spooky." Kelly looked down and rubbed her brow. "We were talking about him last night."

"It appears to have happened at the bottom of the Riesling vineyard."

"Oh, that's terrible. So close to where you work." Maureen shook her head and reached for her wineglass.

Kelly grew quiet for a moment, gaping at Tara. "Why would someone shoot *him* of all people? And why there? It must have happened during the fireworks, don't you think? No one would have heard the gunshots. Otherwise, we would have heard about this last night. Could the shooter have been related to the wedding party in some way?"

"I think someone said Redfern did know Alejandro, probably through music business connections. On the other hand, there were about three hundred guests there." Tara rubbed her brow.

Kelly's eyes widened. "Wow. That creates a big list of possible suspects. The cops are going to face a big challenge solving this case."

Maureen noticed Tara's hand still trembling. "Were you scared working there today?"

Tara extended the chair leg rest and let out a deep sigh. "I didn't have time to be scared with the tour bus this morning. When the Canadians arrived, Marla and I were trying to distract them from the cop car racing down the vineyard road. Oh, and we lost power during that huge storm. What fun. After they left, Brendan and I discussed how to handle the media if they snoop around the premises. We're having an emergency staff meeting tomorrow morning to discuss it all before we open."

"Good idea," Kelly nodded. "But what if the killer is a staff member?"

Tara stared at the ceiling as possibilities of coworkers who might be capable of committing murder raced through her mind.

"We were all questioned on site today, but geez Louise, that hadn't even occurred to me. Great."

"Oh Tara, keep an eye on everyone's body language," Maureen said. "If you notice anyone not making eye contact, or acting fidgety—even a flushed face might be a sign of either guilt or knowledge of the crime. Also watch to see if anyone distances himself from the others. Oh, and tapping feet are always a sign of nervousness."

"My interview with the detective was pretty quick. Thank heavens I was here with you two last evening."

"So the bride's father is involved in the music industry. Could that be the connection?"

"It could be anyone, Kelly." Maureen looked at her sister sympathetically. "Maybe the realtor who sold Jeremiah his lake house will be questioned. It could even be someone who worked on his new home." Tara took a deep sip from her glass and let out a nervous sigh.

The sisters talked for a good hour and the more they discussed the crime, the more restless Tara became.

"Do you guys want to go out for dinner? I need to do something besides sitting here and dwelling on it."

"Ooh, I have an idea." Maureen opened a weekly paper she'd set on the table and showed an advertisement inside to her sisters. "Here's a new organic café I've wanted to try in Hammondsport called Nearby. Most of the menu is sourced locally. Molly McNamara owns it. Remember when she used to hold those dinners at her house with the wraparound porch?"

"Ohhh, yes! Those meals were great. Sure, I'm up for it." Kelly nodded.

"Could someone else drive? I'm a mess, plus I just belted a glass of wine."

Kelly looked at Tara's empty glass and Maureen's nearly empty glass. She'd only taken a few sips of her own since she was so enthralled with figuring out angles of this crime. She sighed and set her wineglass on the counter.

"Well... it looks like I won the sobriety sweepstakes." Kelly laughed as she picked up her car keys and purse. "OK ladies, let's go."

The day's intermittent showers pushed the humidity past sweltering, but at least there was a slight breeze on the porch of Nearby. Music from the free concert at the bandstand on Shethar Street drifted towards the restaurant as a content crowd milled about.

"Good evening, ladies. Welcome to Nearby. May I get you started with a drink? Tonight we're featuring locally sourced strawberry daiquiris."

The sisters' unified "No!" startled the waitress, so she handed them menus and scurried away to greet the other customers on the porch.

Tara laughed. "Looks like we terrified her."

"We don't need to incur the curse of the strawberry daiquiris." Maureen chuckled as she slipped on reading glasses.

Nearby's creative entrees crafted with local ingredients whetted their appetites and the sisters each ordered something different so they could share. They agreed on one thing: each ordered a cup of the chilled microgreens soup topped with crème fraiche. The restaurant bottled its own organic wine. Tara ordered the driest one on the list, a pinot noir. She was not impressed as soon as she sipped it, but didn't say anything. Pinot grapes were tricky to grow in the Finger Lakes climate. Maureen ordered the Riesling as a safe bet, but Kelly surprised them all when she selected a dessert wine to go with her meal—peach.

Glasses were passed around and they concurred Kelly had made the best choice.

By the time they were sharing a large triangle of raw honey baklava, the outdoor concert ended and the departing crowd swelled onto the sidewalk. They overheard two men talking about Jeremiah Redfern being rubbed out gangland style at Hare Hollow Vineyards. Tara was on the verge of saying something to correct them, but wisely didn't.

"Man, Vinegar Hill was so good," Kelly paused as she watched a man walking a border collie pass by. "Why would Jeremiah leave the band at the peak of its popularity?"

"Bands always seem to have trouble staying together. Creative egos and the craving for adulation collide too often." Maureen shook her head.

"I remember playing *Artistic License* on the stereo until the needle practically dug through the vinyl. They had such a tight rhythm section. I loved how they'd break from hard rock into some seriously funky grooves. They even had a tinge of jazz in their sound... so original."

Kelly sighed and looked at the string of star-shaped solar lights twinkling around the arbor in front of the restaurant's entrance. "Remember how gorgeous Glenn McCann looked in the photo on the *Artistic License* cover? That cobalt blue plaid shirt matched his eyes perfectly."

"Isn't that the album they recorded in Tom Russo's studio in that old mansion on Bluff Point? When was it, back in the mid-'80s?" Maureen turned to Tara. She nodded.

"You're right! I forgot. There were a few big names who recorded there."

"Jeremiah met Tom Russo when they were in college at Rochester," Kelly said. "They reunited in Vinegar Hill, Brooklyn, when the band recorded their first album at Vinyl Buddha. I think it was '68 or so. Tom was the audio engineer there."

"He bought the property on Bluff Point later," Maureen added, "with a little help from his friend... Grandpa Russo. Ha!"

"Tom was such a pothead. Marla told me that back in the '70s her brother-in-law used to have regular shipments of Acapulco Gold dropped by seaplane into Keuka Lake in the middle of the night. He'd row out to retrieve it. Tom used the money he made to help defray costs of his studio."

"Where did the pot come from?"

"Like, duh... Mexico, of course."

Kelly pushed back her chair. "Are you kidding me? Seaplanes dropping pot shipments into Keuka Lake? Wow... how did I miss all of this?"

"You were barely sixteen, Kelly. Tara and I were in college. Didn't Tom get busted eventually on campus in Rochester?"

"No, it was one of his sellers in the late '80s." Tara said. "The guy narced on Tom. Cops showed up at the studio and arrested him. He spent a few years in prison. What an idiot."

"So what's he doing now?"

"Not sure. Marla did mention something about him visiting their farm on the West Side recently. Sounds like he might have moved back to the area a while ago."

They paused to read a poster for a drag show at that new nightclub tucked in the alleyway called Haute Mama's Lounge. "*Tonight: It's fins up for Charlene Da Toona and her star-kissed cast! Featuring rock goddess Grace Sleek.*" A young man cut in front of them and meandered down the small stone path toward the club.

Kelly elbowed Tara and whispered. "Isn't that the guy who was driving the boat Sarah fell off?"

Tara squinted.

"Well now, it does look like Jarod."

"If my girlfriend fell off my boat I think I'd be at home seeking solace with my friends, not going out to party at some nightclub." Maureen sniffed as she continued along the sidewalk. Kelly paused to make sure Jarod went inside Haute Mama's Lounge before joining her sisters.

"Definitely not typical behavior."

The sisters walked to their car as purple lightning flickered deep within a thunderhead in the distance.

"Looks like more storms are coming. Are you going to sleep on the porch again tonight, Kelly?"

She looked at the others and shook her head.

"With a killer on the loose? No way!"

"Hey guys, would you mind if...?" Tara rubbed her arms to ward off a chill only she was feeling.

"Aww, Tara. Of course. Come sleep in the big house tonight. We can have a pajama party." Maureen draped her arm over her sister's shoulder. Tara let out a deep sigh.

"Thanks. I could really use a good night's sleep."

Back home, Kelly drew the blinds to cover the glass doors leading onto the deck. As she did, her thoughts turned to that poor waitress Sarah Washington who slept somewhere in the seaweed-choked depths of Keuka tonight. Would she ever be found?

CHAPTER SEVEN
Sunday, June 15 ~ 6:30 a.m.

A lone kayaker skimmed becalmed water as the pale lemon sunrise bathed the West Side's vineyards in its light. Occasionally the woman in the boat pulled the paddle blades through thick foam and strands of milfoil seaweed churned by last night's violent thunderstorms. Above her the first seagulls of the day patrolled the east shore like sentinels. Songbirds awoke and uttered a few teasing notes from their daytime repertoires. As she steered the kayak down the lake a great blue heron circled above. It delighted her to see it land on a diving platform not far from Thompson's Cove.

She didn't want to frighten the magnificent bird. Pushing against the kayak's course with the paddle, the woman stilled the boat to marvel at the heron's leggy body and its funny kitchen-drain neck. Paused in the Zen-like moment, she heard storm water tumble down the big creek that gushed into the cove. She closed her eyes briefly and inhaled the baby powder scent of a mock orange shrub blooming on shore. A shift in the breeze stirred a slightly fishy odor. The sour smell opened her eyes and she resumed watching the motionless heron.

Something floating in the water beyond it distracted her. *Must be storm debris.* The size of it intrigued her, and as her eyes focused on it, the heron's enormous dark wings unfurled and it leapt suddenly into the air directly toward her head. She ducked and exclaimed, "*Wow!* That was incredible."

Slowly her gaze refocused on the mysterious object in the water. What was it? She steered the boat closer for a better look. The paddle dropped onto the kayak when she raised her hands to cover the gasp coming out of her mouth.

"Help! Ohmigod, ohmigod! Someone, please HELP!" Her screams stirred a chorus of barking dogs from the shore. Screen doors squeaked open and slammed shut behind the people racing toward the shore to see what was the matter.

"Honey, quick," a man bellowed. "Call 911!"

***

The Caviston sisters were driving to early Mass in Penn Yan when a sheriff's cruiser followed by an ambulance and fire rescue SUV whizzed past.

"Where are they rushing to?" Maureen glanced over her shoulder.

Tara looked in the rearview mirror.

"Looks like they turned down East Lake Road. You don't suppose Sarah's body was found."

"Either that or the vineyard killer has struck again."

"Kelly! Don't even...."

After Mass they stopped at Deelight Donut Shop where conversations buzzed with gossip about the murder at the winery. A woman at the booth next to theirs read the Rochester newspaper. Its headline screamed "ROCK STAR FOUND DEAD AT KEUKA WINERY" above photos of Redfern in concert and a brief press conference given by the Sheriff's Department the previous evening at the winery. As Tara stirred two creamers and two packets of sugar into her extra-large coffee, a man approached and tapped her on the shoulder.

"If you guys keep killing off customers, maybe I'll start getting some of your traffic." It was Carl Meade, one of her high school classmates who recently opened a winery across the lake from Hare Hollow.

"Classy as usual, Carl." Tara rolled her eyes and took a big gulp of coffee.

"Wanna hear some interesting gossip?"

Kelly slid over and gestured to Carl to sit next to her. He stared at the box of doughnuts, so she pushed it toward him.

"I heard that rock star who was murdered had been hitting on Sarah Washington late Thursday night at The Eggleston."

Maureen set down the coffee cup in her hand. "You mean the girl who they presumed drowned in the lake?"

"Not presumed anymore. Got a text from an EMS buddy. Her body washed up this morning."

"Oh that's so sad." Kelly widened her eyes at her oldest sister. "Weird, Maureen. This is unfolding just like that Strawberry Moon curse." The loud whir of a grinder pulverizing coffee beans overpowered the end of her sentence.

"So the ambulance we passed this morning must have been heading that way." Tara's fingers tapped the table as she felt a free-floating anxiety unsettle her stomach.

Carl helped himself to the strawberry iced doughnut in the box, and continued talking through chews. "Jimmy Lapp was telling me about it last night at Finian's Pub. He witnessed it. Guess the guy was flirting obviously with Sarah as she served him and his wife dinner on the lakeside deck. The wife got so disgusted she stormed out and walked home alone. She didn't have too far to go to walk off her anger. They own the big new mansion about a mile down the road."

"Ugh, yeah, that monument to excess." Kelly sneered.

"Ha, good one." Carl licked the icing off his fingers before he continued. "Anyway, the guy moves to the bar and is drinking the most expensive bourbon The Eggleston offers. No one paid any attention to him even though he was famous. He was wearing nerdy-looking glasses and a baseball cap low on his forehead that kind of hid his face.

"The band starts playing and this guy is getting annoyed by the quality of the music. Jimmy was there because it was his cousin's band; this was their first gig at The Eggleston. The rock star groans exaggeratedly as if he's in pain from the music. Jimmy admitted they were pretty bad, but hey, give 'em a break. They're just starting out. You know? So Sarah finishes her waitressing shift and sits at the bar next to the guy to have a beer. Her boyfriend Jarod is bartending. The rock star flirts with her, saying she's so pretty she could be a model. Jarod ignores him, trying to keep his cool, then the bar gets overcrowded and he gets distracted. Next thing he knows, the band takes a break and that guy is slow dancing with Sarah by the jukebox in the back room. Jarod sees him get too friendly with his girlfriend, so he yells at the guy to leave her alone. The guy acts as if he didn't hear a single word and keeps dancing. Jarod vaults over the bar and runs up next to them, shoving the rock star in the back.

"'Leave my girlfriend alone!' he yells. Everyone on the dance floor backs away. The rock star's so trashed he doesn't realize the music has stopped. The band takes the stage again and he keeps dancing with Sarah, who by this time is trying to free herself from his grope. Jarod yanks them apart and yells, 'Listen, man! If you don't get the hell out of here now I'll waste you!'"

All three sisters raised their eyebrows.

"And, hello! That moves him to the top of the suspect list." Tara leaned in, "Dum de dum dummm."

"Is Jarod a friend of Ryan O'Hare?" Kelly asked.

"Dunno. It's possible. Interesting background to the story, eh? Anyway, nice to see you girls but I've gotta run. Thanks for the doughnut, Tara." Carl touched her shoulder lightly as he walked away. His gesture made Maureen grin.

"Looks like someone's still got a crush on you."

Tara raised one eyebrow as she squinted with her other eye. "Puhleeze! Wouldn't you know, he took the one doughnut I wanted, too. Grrr."

***

Jarod replayed his last voicemails from Sarah, hung up the phone and pulled his hair from its roots as he doubled over on the couch in his apartment. In his imagination, Sarah was hiding out somewhere until she sorted out their relationship. He didn't believe for a moment that she'd really drowned. She was smart; she'd have figured out a way to get to shore and one day he'd hear from her again. Right?

The sheriff's phone call dashed his dimming hope.

He dragged himself into the kitchen to brew a pot of coffee. When Jarod opened the refrigerator, he remembered he'd used the last of it yesterday.

"Dammit!" He slammed the door so hard the beer bottles inside the door clinked together. What should he do? Who could he talk to at this hour? He grabbed his keys and jogged downstairs to his car.

Despite Jarod's insistent knocking, his mother was slow to answer the front door to her home. Even in his sadness and fury, he noted she did not look well. Her face was redder than the normal ruddiness burned into it from years of heavy drinking. She let Jarod in and didn't say a word, her glazed expression made him wonder if she even recognized him. Sure, he hadn't stopped by for a visit in a while. Maybe she was mad about that, but wasn't this overreacting? He needed her to be strong right now because he was about to fall apart.

"So, Ma," he paused to take a deep breath, "did you already hear the news?"

She looked at Jarod with eyes as wide as if she'd just encountered a coyote. With a quick nod, she walked out to the back patio with the cup of coffee and pack of cigarettes already in her right hand. A Creamsicle-colored cat rubbed past her leg.

Jarod went into the kitchen and poured a full cup of coffee. His hands shook as he drank half of it. *Get a grip, man.* He sunk into the Adirondack chair next to his mother and they both stared ahead at the cold blue water of Seneca Lake.

"It was just an accident, Ma. Cops told me there would be no charges."

The cigarette dropped from her fingers and rolled on the concrete patio.

"Accident! Why would the cops tell *you* that?"

Jarod scratched his head and cleared his throat.

"I was the one driving the boat, Ma." He hung his head, but watched her reaction out of the corner of his eyes. Her face rippled with confusion that shifted to anger and finally some semblance of compassion.

"Son, whatever are you talking about?"

He sat back in the chair and squinted at the sun.

"Sarah's dead, Ma. They found her body in the lake today."

His mother gasped and touched his arm.

"No, no, *no*, Jarod! Tell me, what happened?"

"Our boat hit the wake of some asshole speeding up the lake and she fell overboard. They searched for hours and couldn't find her. Her body washed up this morning."

"When did the accident happen?"

"Middle of the night, yesterday."

His mother rose and walked into the living room. She plopped onto the same place where she'd been sitting on the threadbare couch when Jarod knocked. The morning paper with its solid black headlines about Jeremiah Redfern lay spread open next to an open bottle of whiskey. She grabbed the bottle with trembling hands and tipped it back.

"A little early, don't you think, Ma?"

"Too much bad news. Can't handle it all, son. Jeremiah should have lived at least twenty more years."

Jarod's eyes twitched as he put his hands on his hips.

"What the hell are you talkin' about, *she* should have lived three times twenty years more. Wait, are you getting trashed because of Sarah or some ancient rock star who died?"

She rose to her feet and slapped his face hard.

"You have no idea the impact his music had on my life."

Jarod rubbed his cheek and winced. His nostrils pulled back as his eyes narrowed.

"My girlfriend dies and you're more upset about a total stranger shot dead in a vineyard? What are you... just some sad groupie or have you finally gone completely mental?"

Her flinty face repelled the intensity of his scowl. He shook his head, stormed towards the door and slammed it behind him. The concussion made her jump.

Jarod cried when he got behind the wheel. There must be some way to calm his runaway emotions. He didn't want to get smashed like his mom, but he did know someone who could provide an easy way to soothe this sorrow.

CHAPTER EIGHT
Sunday, June 15 ~ 10:30 a.m.

Tara's heart fluttered when she saw a TV satellite truck parked in the visitors' parking lot as she arrived at Hare Hollow. She figured it was a station from Rochester. When she walked around the side of the truck and saw the network news logo, her pulse quickened. *My God, they must have left New York before dawn to arrive here this early. This is big.*

Hare Hollow's staff gathered inside Brendan's office murmuring rumors they'd heard since Jeremiah's body was found. Several names came up repeatedly as possible suspects. When their boss entered the smallish room with his lawyer, voices cut off mid-sentence. The room's tense atmosphere melded uncomfortably with the overpowering scent of the lawyer's oak moss cologne.

"Thanks everyone for coming in early," Brendan began, "especially if you're not scheduled to work today. I'll get right to the matter at hand. I called this meeting because we needed to update you on what we know so far about the situation and how I want all of you to handle the questions that will most likely arise. Here's what the police have revealed to us so far.

"Jeremiah Redfern was hired to perform at my son Ryan's wedding reception Friday evening as a surprise for his wife Esperanza. He was supposed to arrive in the reception tent while they were reciting their vows. The plan was guests would gradually make their way to the tents for hors d'oeuvres and drinks. At the moment of the wedding toast, the band would begin to play, Mr. Redfern would walk into the tent and sing to the bride and groom. That was the moment when the fireworks were supposed to be set off, not right after the vows were exchanged—as was the case.

"What the police are trying to figure out is why Mr. Redfern was instead at the bottom of the Riesling vineyards. They believe he was probably shot sometime between the marriage vows and the completion of the fireworks display that went off too early. Mr. Redfern was first noticed to be missing right after the ceremony. Ryan went to check if he was ready to perform but the band said Mr. Redfern hadn't arrived yet.

"There is no clear suspect at the moment, so all of us—including myself—must be questioned by the police. If you haven't already, you need to stop by the command post they set up in the staff parking lot after this meeting. They have asked for a list of staff members, so we'll know if you didn't speak with them."

Tara watched to see if anyone was displaying the type of body language Maureen mentioned that would show discomfort with the conversation. Nothing caught her eye. Everyone appeared to be at ease.

"What should we do when the police question us?" a vineyard worker asked.

Brendan looked at his lawyer, Jake Williams, to respond.

"Answer their questions truthfully and to the best of your ability. That said, please don't go telling everyone you know what line of questions the police are asking. One, it could jeopardize their investigation and two, it could inadvertently reflect badly on the winery."

"How are we supposed to handle questions from the media?" Tara asked. "There's already a World Broadcast News satellite truck parked in the visitors' lot."

The staff added concerns in a flurry of questions too fast for Brendan to process.

"What if they try to take our photo without your permission?"

"What do we do if they call us at home?"

"So who set off the fireworks early? Have you contacted the company that handled them to see if they were tampered with by someone?"

"What about the band that guy was supposed to sing with? Did anyone ask if they tried to contact someone when he was a no-show? Was this guy paid up front? If so, find out who cashed the check and you might have the killer."

"If anyone has an idea who committed the crime, do we tell you or do we go right to the sheriff's department?"

"Refer all leads directly to Sheriff Wilson's staff." Brendan turned toward Jake to confirm with a glance that it was the right answer. "Also, the sheriff mentioned something about holding a follow-up press conference this afternoon. I'm not sure if that will be at their command post here or at their headquarters in Bath. As soon as we know the details, we'll share them with the staff."

"That's right," Jake added. "And please, if you see people sneaking around any of the property or vineyards—be they media, tourists or locals—tell them to leave and report it to one of us immediately. The police are prepared to help us with any such situation that might get out of control, due to the celebrity of Mr. Redfern."

"Any more questions?" Brendan scanned the faces of his staff and no one reacted. "OK. We're going to remain open to the public for now and will try to keep business flowing as usual... sorry, pun not intended."

"Uh, one question, Brendan," Andy Meyers asked. "When will we be allowed back in the Riesling vineyard to continue our work?"

"The detectives photographed the immediate crime scene and removed all of the evidence they could before the storm hit, Sheriff Wilson said. They plan to increase the perimeter of the investigation scene from the vineyard's north end service road to the southern entrance, up to and including the top of the vineyard across the road and possibly down to West Lake Road. It could be a few days or possibly longer. Please avoid that vineyard for the time being."

"Great." Andy folded his arms and glared at his boss. "Hope it's not much longer. Some of those vines need a trim. Got to have them looking purty for that new winemaker from Italy, don't you know."

Brendan glared at Andy. This was not the moment to interject his disappointment that Paolo Brigandi had been hired for the position instead of his friend Jack Schultz from Interlaken who had just as much experience. Andy's narrowing eyes returned Brendan's glare, and he folded his arms tightly exposing well-developed biceps under his T-shirt sleeves.

"Are they going to interview all of the wedding guests, too?" Marla asked.

"The police did ask us for a complete list of contacts for the wedding, yes. It will be difficult to question the bride and groom, of course, since they are on their honeymoon for two weeks on a remote island in French Polynesia. Cell service to their island is not reliable, I'm afraid."

Tara noted the right corner of Brendan's mouth tightened and rose slightly when he responded to Marla. It could have been nothing, but the fact she noticed it at all made her think she should mention it to Maureen.

By the time the meeting finished, there were seven satellite trucks in the visitors' parking lot, including that sleazy gossip network Scoop!TV. Brendan went outside and spoke to a sheriff's deputy about the problem. The deputy directed the trucks to park in the lot on the other side of the loading dock, down the hill from their command post. That way they would not block or deter customers. The media outlets complied but their help wasn't needed—the visitors lot was never crowded that afternoon. Too many people, it seemed, were nervous about a possible killer on the loose.

CHAPTER NINE
Monday, June 16 ~ 10:15 a.m.

Kelly sat comfortably on a high back stool behind the counter of The Deckled Edge bookstore as she penciled prices inside newly arrived editions of local author Lou Walter's thriller, *Of The Kings*. Housed within one of the oldest structures in Hammondsport, her store was deeper than its width and its high ceiling and oak walls gave it the air of a collegiate library. A local artist's vibrant pastel drawings of Bluff Point brightened the walls up front. Most of the interior light came from the tall storefront windows, with occasional glow from Arts and Crafts-style sconces and Tiffany-style floor lamps scattered deep within. The sparse lighting imbued the coziness of a home den, a mood enhanced by the Stickley leather chairs tucked in nooks between shelves. The hardwood floors had dried out past their prime, so Kelly hid the groove-worn spots with oriental rugs. A scent of lemon wood polish dangled in the air as Dinah Washington sang "Unforgettable" from the portable turntable next to the sales counter.

Bells tethered to the front door jingled and a tall man wearing a Chicago White Sox baseball cap entered the store. He asked right away if Kelly had any books on grape cultivation. She directed him to a tall bookcase along the far wall. Another customer came in saying he was looking for books about the history of the Finger Lakes. Kelly walked him over to a display near the front window.

"These books are arranged from west to east, in the order of the Finger Lakes. Let me know if you have any questions."

It was a steamy June morning and probably because of that, the store saw few customers so Kelly was able to pay close attention to them. One in particular caught her eye. A woman decked in '60s Mod fashion from her floppy brimmed hat, dayglo orange mini-dress down to a pair of white go-go boots lowered her oversized sunglasses when she entered the store. As she asked where books on 20th Century fashion were, Kelly noticed her white lipstick and heavy black eyeliner, drawn perfectly. She brushed past the man who was interested in grape cultivation and said "Excuse me," in a breathless, Ann Margret-like voice. He looked at the flirting woman's legs for a few seconds, but soon returned to his search. He spent a good forty-five minutes browsing through indexes.

Mod woman and the man looking for Finger Lakes books wandered out, leaving just the grape man in the shop. Kelly looked up from the first edition copy of Thomas Merton's *The Seven Storey Mountain* she was reading to watch the man with the cap. She wasn't quite sure how old he was, but he had long white hair pulled back into a ponytail fed through the back opening of his cap and wore a Hawaiian shirt over a pair of mud-creased jeans. Finally, he turned away from the bookcase and approached her at the counter.

"Would you happen to have any books about old hybrid vines grown in the Finger Lakes? In particular, I'm looking for anything about the noirelle grape."

"Let me check the catalog." Kelly smiled as she clicked on the computer. "Is that spelled n-o-i-r-e-l-l-e?"

He nodded. She did several inventory searches, but nothing came up. "Hmm, there doesn't seem to be anything like that in my collection. I do know a bookseller from Geneva who specializes in books on viticulture. Would you like me to call him now?"

"Thank you, yes. That would be wonderful."

As soon as Kelly got Tim Winston's answering machine she remembered his store was closed on Mondays. She left a message for him to call her and hung up.

"May I have your phone number to give you a call when I hear back from Tim?"

The man locked eyes with hers. Their Paul McCartney-like heavy lids, long black lashes and intensely cobalt blue color mesmerized. He scratched his white goatee with his left hand and Kelly noted the word "Forever" tattooed inside his wrist. She caught her breath.

"Ah... you know, that's OK. I'll be coming through here again next Monday. I'll stop back to see what he said." He smiled broadly at her and she noted his teeth were Hollywood perfect, not the teeth one would expect from the upstate hippie farmer vibe he exuded.

"Sure. Hopefully Tim will be able to help."

"Many thanks." The man gave a quick tip of his brim toward her and disappeared into the blinding white sunlight outside.

"Ohmigod, that tattoo," Kelly whispered as she peeked out the shop window to see which direction he was heading. He got into a green hybrid sedan, drove up Shethar Street and took a left at the stop sign onto Main Street. "That has to be the guy Maureen met at the spa. Hmm, maybe he's an East Side lake resident since he's heading that way." There was something so familiar about his face, yet she couldn't recall him ever being in her store before. Her mind kept processing his features throughout her workday and when she joined her sisters for dinner on the deck that evening, a mental confirmation of his identity surfaced from the depths of her memory.

"Holy Mother of God! I figured out who that guy was in the shop today."

"What guy?" Maureen asked as she handed her the salad.

"This older guy came in looking for books about a grape variety called noirelle. I think he was the client with the tattoos who visited your spa last week, Maureen. I saw 'Forever' tattooed on the underside of his left hand."

"Tall guy, long white hair was it?"

"Yep. There was something about his eyes that looked familiar to me. Hold on a sec." Kelly jumped from her chair and disappeared into the house.

"Did she take a photo on her phone?" Tara asked.

"I guess." They turned toward the sliding glass doors awaiting her return. Kelly came back grinning as she handed an old record album jacket to Maureen.

"Take a look at the guy in this photo, Maureen. Do you think it's him?" She pointed at a young man with dark shoulder-length hair.

Maureen lifted the zebra-striped reading glasses that dangled on a chain around her neck and held the album jacket close so she could study the young man's face.

"He does look like my client, but I'm not positive it's him. Who is that?"

Kelly flipped over the jacket to show her the cover of Vinegar Hill's seminal album *Artistic License*. The photo showed the band members posed casually in front of the Bluff Point mansion that housed the recording studio.

"I think that guy is Glenn McCann."

"What? You mean the guy in the band with Jeremiah Redfern? Let me see." Tara held out her hand.

Maureen handed the album jacket over. Tara scrunched her nose as she squinted at the small photo.

"Whoa! He's not too shabby. If it is him, what do you think he's doing in the area?" She handed the album back to Kelly.

"Who knows?" Her eyes lingered on Glenn's face. *Wow he was handsome.*

"Hmm, odd coincidence." Maureen raised an eyebrow.

"Man, I'd forgotten what a looker he was." Tara whistled as Kelly gawked at the cover photo. "Is he still that good looking?"

"Sure he's a lot older, but *yeah*. Those piercing eyes were what I noticed. Of course the photo was taken decades ago. He'd be close to seventy now."

Tara laughed. "It's weird to think of all these aging rock stars as still being hot, but some really are. Old Jagger still has his swagger."

"Seventy is the new forty, right?" Maureen laughed. "You know, all the massage therapy clients fill out a form and list their occupation and address on it in addition to any health issues before treatment. Tomorrow I'll dig out that guy's form and see what he wrote on it."

"Speaking of all that sort of stuff, remember when you were telling me to watch my coworkers' body language?" Tara asked. Maureen nodded. "What does it mean when one corner of the mouth pulls taut and rises slightly?"

Maureen closed her eyes to better visualize the expression in her mind.

"I think that means contempt for something."

"*Contempt?* Interesting. Now would the facial expression reflect the person's thoughts at the moment or the words being spoken?"

"I believe more emphasis is on the person's thoughts, but I'm not positive. Why? Did you see that on one of the staff member's faces?"

"My boss made that expression when he was discussing the fact his son is honeymooning on a remote island in French Polynesia where he cannot be reached easily for questioning."

"Well now," Kelly said with a slight smile. "That's certainly convenient."

After dinner, something spurred her to go inside and turn on the living room TV. An entertainment news show was on.

"Coming up next, Vinegar Hill band members speak out about mysterious death of their former lead vocalist."

Kelly raced to the sliding glass doors. "Maureen! Tara! Come here. They're going to interview Jeremiah's bandmates!"

The sisters grabbed their wineglasses and crowded onto the couch to listen as former members of Vinegar Hill extended condolences to Jeremiah's widow Angie.

"He was a brilliant writer and performer. What a terrible loss to the music world," drummer Chuck McCummiskey said.

"We'd spoken last week about reuniting on a new recording project he had in the works. I can't believe this... I mean he was just texting me the other day and now...," bass player Will Larsen couldn't continue and wiped tears off his face.

The reporter looked in the camera as she wound up her story. "And as for keyboardist Glenn McCann, with whom Redfern had a notoriously stormy relationship, his whereabouts remain unknown." The camera zoomed in on a photo of Glenn that must have been a couple of decades old and looked vaguely like the man Kelly and Maureen encountered.

Tara, Maureen and Kelly turned toward each other, slack-jawed.

"Do you think we need to tell the police about our suspicions he's here?" Kelly asked.

Someone knocked forcefully on the front door startling the three women.

"Holy crap! Who's that?" Tara cried out.

Maureen could tell the others weren't eager to respond, so she answered the door. A towering middle-aged man nodded at her.

"Good evening, ma'am. I'm Detective Tyrone Kane with the county sheriff's department." He showed Maureen his badge. "I need to speak with a Tara Grande. Is she here?"

"Yes," Maureen responded slowly. "Of course. Let me go get her. Would you like to come in, Detective Kane?"

He nodded and laced his fingers as he waited inside the front door. Though he seemed to be still, his eyes moved constantly observing and noting many details about the interior of the home.

"Tara, a detective is here to see you," Maureen whispered, her eyes wide as she walked into the other room.

Kelly raised her eyebrows as Tara stood from the couch, finger-combed her hair and adjusted her blouse before she neared the door.

"Hi, I'm Tara Grande. May I help you?" She smiled warmly at him; he nodded stone-faced.

"Good evening, Mrs. Grande. I'm Detective Kane with the county sheriff's department. You're employed by Hare Hollow Vineyards, is that correct?"

She nodded.

"I need to ask you a few follow-up questions about the incident at the winery last week. Do you have a moment?"

"Yes, of course." Her face flushed from the illogical fear rising inside that she was a suspect even though there was no possible way she committed the crime. She held her breath as he took out a notepad and flipped it open.

"I want to review the notes Detective Hughes took the other day. Let's start with last Friday evening. Would you repeat your whereabouts from about five o'clock p.m. through midnight?"

"I was here. My two sisters live in this house and the little cottage down the lawn is my actual residence. We had dinner on the deck followed by a little wine tasting of samples from work."

"Just to confirm what you told Detective Hughes, they are Maureen McCarthy—a massage therapist at Ballylough Spa in Penn Yan—and Kelly Caviston—owner of The Deckled Edge bookstore in Hammondsport. Is that correct?" She nodded. "So, Mrs. Grande, you said you were in this house or in the cottage at five o'clock?"

"By then I had closed the tasting room for the day. We shut our doors at quarter to five so we could ensure the parking lot would be clear by the time the wedding caterer's trucks started arriving at five thirty to set up for the wedding."

"Did you come straight home after work?"

"I stopped at the grocery in Penn Yan to buy some hors d'oeuvres to go with the wine—a wedge of brie, a bunch of grapes, a baguette...."

"Would you still have the store receipt to confirm that?"

"Uh," Tara bit her lip as she paused for a few seconds. "Yeah, I think I know where it is."

"And then you came straight home?"

Tara looked at the floor and nodded.

"No other stops?" His eyes focused on her expression like the zoom lens of an SLR camera.

Tara's cheeks reddened again. Were her sisters watching from the other room? Surely they could hear the conversation. Tara shook her head. "Nope."

"So your sisters can confirm you were here from roughly six o'clock through midnight?"

"We were together on the deck drinking wine and watching the wedding fireworks. When they ended, we sat around talking for about an hour. The next day I was expecting a busload of Canadian tourists in the tasting room and I had to get to work early to prepare for their arrival. So I was in bed by eleven."

"I see you weren't asked to work at the wedding reception. Is that correct?"

"Brendan offered me the opportunity, but I declined it because of the scheduled visit from the tourists. The night would have been too late for me. The staff tends to hang around and party once cleanup is done after those events."

"How well do you like your boss, Tara?"

"Brendan?" Her eyes widened slightly. *That's an odd question.* She glanced at the floor again. "There's no problem between us. He lets me do my job and I'm grateful for that. He isn't one of those in your face constantly, meddling bosses."

"So you have free rein to go anywhere you want on that property?"

This was another odd question. Tara balked at responding. *What sort of information does he hope to glean from it? Where is he headed with this line of questioning?* She studied his face. There was something familiar about the way he knit his brow intensely as he waited for her responses.

"I suppose so, as an employee. However, there's so much to do in the tasting room and shop it keeps me too occupied to wander about."

"Ever go on the premises off work hours?"

"Not usually, except when I'm meeting my coworker Marla for dinner or if I forgot something in the office."

"So you went directly from the winery to the grocery and from there straight home."

"Yes," she replied weakly as she glanced at the refrigerator. When she looked back at the detective, a slight smile had stretched across his face. It deepened a darling dimple on his right cheek that seemed incongruous with his hulking six-foot-four, two hundred fifty-pound frame. He scratched his straight, yellow ochre hair and cleared his throat.

"Mrs. Grande, do you know a Michael Connelly?"

Tara's face burned as she looked directly into his heavy-lidded green eyes, and she wished she could turn around to see if her sisters were right there. She couldn't avoid this question.

"Yes. I do."

"Did you see Mr. Connelly at any time on Friday?"

She bit her lip, sighed and hung her head toward the floor.

"Yes."

(As the interrogation proceeded, Maureen and Kelly wrote questions to each other on Kelly's puzzle book in the other room. *When did she reconnect with Mike?* Maureen asked. *Is he even divorced?* Kelly replied.)

"Where did you see Mr. Connelly?"

"He's a woodworker and I stopped by briefly to see a project he finished. He was installing a gorgeous set of hand-carved kitchen cupboards in a cottage on East Lake Road. I was interested in seeing the finished product because one of my freelance interior design clients might like to order something similar."

"And what time was that?"

"Friday. It was on my way home from work."

"Hmm. You said you left the tasting room, went to the grocery in Penn Yan and headed back here. At what point did you visit Mr. Connelly?"

"It was on my way home from the grocery."

"So that cottage is between Penn Yan and here?"

"No. It's farther down the lake, by the Bluff."

"That's going several miles out of the way on your way home, don't you think?"

She looked out the front door as she winced and nodded.

"Do you know who owns the cottage where Mr. Connelly was working?"

"Yes. He told me."

"And that would be…?"

"Jeremiah and Angie Redfern. They weren't there at the time. He said it would be my last opportunity to stop in and take photos of the work."

(Maureen and Kelly clamped their hands over their mouths as their eyes widened toward the other room. *Should we ask her about this when he leaves?* Kelly wrote. Maureen shook her head. *Let's wait to see what she tells us.*)

"Would you be able to show me those photos?"

She nodded. "They're on my phone in the other room. Should I get it now?"

"That won't be necessary. I'll give you my email address so you can send them to me. Did Mr. Connelly ever tell you how long he knew the Redferns or how they met?"

"No. Michael does have a reputation as the best cabinet maker in the Finger Lakes. So they probably got a recommendation from someone."

"Do you have any reason to believe his dealings with the Redferns had gone past a professional client/contractor relationship?"

"Um, not that I recall… although he did say he and Angie discussed Hare Hollow wines once. She is particularly fond of our Lemberger, he said."

When the detective finished asking Tara questions, she tried to lighten the mood a little. She hooked her hands on her hips and tipped her head slightly as she squinted at Detective Kane.

"Say you look familiar to me. Are you from around here?"

He nodded.

"I played defensive end for the Mustangs, Class of '78. They called me Ty-Rex."

Tara laughed as her eyes traced his broad shoulders.

"That sounds familiar. So you were at the high school when I was there. Um, did we date?" She batted her eyes and twirled a strand of her hair.

Det. Kane lowered his eyes and that same, sly smile brought back his dimple.

"No... I think I would have remembered you." He sighed slightly as he folded his notebook and slipped it back into his suit jacket. "Thank you for your time, Mrs. Grande. Don't forget to email me those photos. The address is on my card. Please call me if you recall or learn anything new about the case you think would help our investigation. OK?"

"Will do." Tara took the card which appeared tiny in his enormous hands. She closed the front door and turned around to face the judgmental expressions that would surely be waiting on her sisters' faces. Surprisingly they weren't there. Tara carried the business card over to her phone and emailed the photos as promised to the detective. She poured a tall glass of cabernet sauvignon and walked out on the deck. Her sisters weren't there, either. In the indigo dusk below Tara noticed their shadows sitting on the edge of the dock talking. Of course she knew what they were discussing.

CHAPTER TEN

Tuesday, June 17 ~ 9:07 a.m.

Tim Winston, the bookstore owner in Geneva, responded to Kelly's message shortly after he opened his shop for the day. Yes, he did have an old pamphlet issued from Cornell University about the noirelle grape. He added there was a note inside the pamphlet that said the grape hadn't proved successful growing in the Finger Lakes so most growers ripped the vines out of their vineyards. She wrote the title and price he wanted for it on a piece of paper, tucking it next to the phone for when the man she suspected was Glenn McCann would return to the store.

Kelly got to thinking about her sister's odd admission to the sheriff's detective the night before and what it might mean. Maureen begged Tara to avoid Mike Connelly after learning years ago she was spending time with him again. Mike was married and so was she, but her relationship with Gianni had already dissolved into constant bickering. Both Kelly and Maureen understood the attraction—Mike not only respected her talent, he'd inherited his wealthy family's good looks. His perfectly sun-kissed hair and vibrant wardrobe looked more Palm Beach than upstate New York. They shared a strong interest in good interior design, especially from the Arts and Crafts Movement. He'd found a bungalow on the West Side of Keuka that he thought they should restore together, supposedly so they could flip it. Tara told her sisters she liked to believe he was envisioning it as their future home.

Oh Tara, Kelly sighed. *For someone who spends her life encouraging beauty, why does your life always get so ugly?*

A car alarm warbled between two loud tones right outside the shop and Kelly's thoughts drifted to the relationship between Jeremiah Redfern and Glenn McCann. Why hadn't Glenn come out with a statement on the passing of his former bandmate? It was odd. After all of those years performing together, you'd think he'd express his condolences to the family. What could have possibly been so bad between them that would keep Glenn silent? The bookstore was empty at the moment, so Kelly did a web search of their names and found a reference to a news item from the late '80s she'd forgotten about. By then Jeremiah had left Vinegar Hill and was enjoying huge success as a solo artist. His big hit, "Forever Gigi," had gone platinum in the U.S.

When that happened, the story said, Glenn accused Jeremiah of stealing that song from a notebook of lyrics he'd written that went missing the last time the band recorded together. Interesting, she noted, it was when they were in the studio atop Bluff Point working on *Artistic License*. Jeremiah could not produce any such notebook, and with no copies of his originals, the judge ruled at a meeting between their lawyers that there was failure of proof to proceed with a trial and dismissed Glenn's complaint.

What Kelly now wondered was if he mistrusted Jeremiah so much, why did Glenn return here, where the band recorded its most successful album? Did he move here before or after Jeremiah did? She was also curious why he was researching that particular grape. She sent a text to Maureen: *"Remember to check Glenn's client form @ the spa."* Her sister must have been between appointments because she responded immediately.

"Did. Client went by 'Jay Essbach.' Address & cell # left off. Paid cash."

Kelly laughed. This need for mystery and use of a classical music pun could confirm their suspicions Glenn had been at the spa—and that was before Jeremiah was murdered. Was Glenn aware of Jeremiah's purchase of property within mere miles of where he was living? Had they been in contact at all?

Her thoughts fluttered back to Tara. She hoped she wasn't engaged in some sort of an affair with Mike Connelly, who was still married. Kelly felt he was only using Tara for her skillful design sense, and his attitude of privileged entitlement bugged her. The first time Mike and Tara dated, right before she met Gianni, he dumped her for his future wife who was already expecting their first child. Tara was a magnet for "bad boys."

Did Mike have any connection to Jeremiah's murder, or was it just the odd chance that he had called Tara to consult on his job at the Redfern's house and again take advantage of her skills? Before she worked at the winery, Tara co-owned an interior design firm in Canandaigua called Articulation. Her design school classmate Christophe Aurora handled the choices of color palette and fabric for clients. Tara focused on furnishings and treatments. They were quite successful until Gianni coerced her to give up the work several years after they got married. He wanted her to focus on making their home on Canandaigua Lake spectacular. It was. However, Tara was too much of a social butterfly to be content as a homebody so that situation was doomed to fail. After they dissolved the firm, Tara and Christophe continued frequenting estate sales buying items to sell in his interior design shop. Tara decorated her cottage beautifully, but she rarely entertained her sisters there. Kelly also noted curiously that Tara referred to the house she grew up in as "home" and her own dwelling as "the cottage." In a sense, Tara's life never settled after her divorce.

***

About seven miles north of Hammondsport on the East Side of the lake, a steep road faces the direction where the two branches of Keuka join by the most prominent geographical feature of the lake: Bluff Point. The breathtaking view is unobstructed from a modest hilltop farmhouse alongside the road. The small sign out front reads Jewels of the Lake Winery.

A woman parked her rusty compact car in the farmhouse's long gravel driveway and wept openly as she walked purposefully to the side entrance and opened the door. She set her purse and tote bag on the kitchen table and then went to the sink, wet her hands under the cool water and patted the water on her puffy face. As she daubed her face dry with a paper towel, a man walked in the room.

"Hi Monique," her boss Glenn McCann said as he set an empty coffee mug next to the sink. "I've got a meeting in the business office later this morning, so would you please clean there first today?" She nodded but didn't turn around right away. When she finally did, he noticed her odd expression.

"*Hey*... are you OK?"

She shook her head and burst into tears. Glenn didn't know what to say. He hugged her, then lifted her chin with his hand.

"What's the matter? Why are you so upset, Monique?" She stopped crying long enough to take a deep breath.

"My other boss die. Dey pay me very good money. I clean dere Wednesdays. It very big place, on de lake. I need my money but I feel so bad for de wife. Now he dead, who know if she keep me?" Monique trembled as another wave of sobbing washed over her.

"That's awful. What happened to him?"

Her agitation increased. Glenn tried to steady her with his outstretched arms and whispered "It's OK. Take your time and breathe before you try to speak."

"He... he... somebody... oh, it awful! He been *murdered*!"

Glenn stepped backward as if her words exploded between them.

"What's the name of the man you were working for?"

"He a musician—Mr. Redfern. I guess he famous. I never hear him in Haiti."

"You worked for *Jeremiah*?" Glenn's jaw dropped as he looked down and rubbed his eyebrows. "Since when? How the hell did you get that job?" He squinted at her.

His tone silenced her crying. She tilted her head toward him. Was he angry at her for taking on other clients? Didn't he understand she *had* to have other clients? Although he paid her decently, there was no way she could pay all of her bills on what Glenn gave her.

"He hire me from same agency you did. I start work dere in May." Why was her boss frowning? What was with his change in tone of voice? Should she not have told him she was working in other homes? Now it looked as if he were crying.

"You know Mr. Redfern?" she asked. Glenn nodded as he looked away briefly and sniffled. Monique reached to touch his arm, but he stared back at her with an odd face. She couldn't decipher whether he was upset at the loss of his friend or suspicious of her.

"We were close friends many years ago. I heard he moved here and hadn't had a chance to stop by yet and say 'hello.' He had this notebook of mine he was going to return to me but never had the chance. I'd planned to ask him about it when we got together. I wonder if it's at his new place." He searched her eyes for a flicker of a reaction.

"Dis notebook... what it look like?"

"You'd know it if you saw it. I bought it in Colorado. It has a hand-tooled leather cover that ties shut with a length of rawhide. The cover image is of Mount Evans in the Rockies."

Monique touched her finger to her lower lip.

"You know, Mr. McCann, I see something like dat. *Oui*. He been looking for papers dat been on the piano and ask if I see them. We look all over music studio and living room. Something make me lift piano bench lid. Dat's when I see dat notebook. Mr. Redfern yell at me, so I close bench immediately. I not look anything else dere."

Glenn put his hand over his heart.

"My God! You've *seen* my notebook?"

Monique could not decipher the expression on his face.

"Oh, Monique. If you only knew how long I've been waiting to get that back. Of course being a decent guy, I know he planned to return it to me." Glenn added that in case her loyalty to Jeremiah was stronger than what she felt toward him.

Why was the notebook so important to her boss? He was a bit of a loner and she'd never met any family or friends of his since she got the job here a year ago. Now he looked like he was going to cry again. She wished she could do something for Mr. McCann. He'd been so nice to her and was her favorite housecleaning client. Tomorrow she planned to report to work at the Redferns as usual. Hopefully Angie would let her know if she planned to keep her employed there. If she stayed, she would check that piano bench to see if she could get Mr. McCann's notebook back to him. Wouldn't that be what Mr. Redfern would have wanted her to do for his old friend?

She patted Glenn's hand. "Don't worry, Mr. McCann. *Bondye bon...* God is good."

The corners of Glenn's eyes crinkled as a slight smile brightened his face. From the looks of her expression, Monique bought his performance.

CHAPTER ELEVEN
Wednesday, June 18 ~ 10:00 a.m.

The autopsy confirmed what Detective Kane already knew: this was a homicide, not a suicide. It also suggested whoever shot Jeremiah Redfern knew exactly where to deliver a fatal blow—he'd been felled by one shot to the center of his chest. Once word of the murder got out, the neighboring county's sheriff's department contacted him about the odd coincidence of a handgun found in the lake during the search for Sarah Washington. The two might be linked.

Since the handgun had been put into a plastic bag before it was dropped into the middle of the lake, residue from its recent firing was able to be matched by the State Police Forensic Investigation Unit against that found on the body and the bullet casing found at the scene.

It was an M1911-style pistol and there were two more .45 caliber bullets left in the magazine. Investigators also found a couple of oily fingerprints on the magazine, probably left when it was cleaned. The prints did not match any currently on file with the FBI's Integrated Automated Fingerprint Identification System. When they passed the serial number along to the ATF it matched a gun purchased three years ago in Waco, Texas registered to a Rodolfo Montez of Beverly Hills, California. A check of the address led to a dead end, literally. The smallish residence was foreclosed in 2011 and the mortgagee was a Catriona Glass, whereabouts unknown.

Back in the command post, Detectives Mack Hughes and Reese Bailey checked the name against the long list of wedding guests. Although the surname and hometown matched that of the bride, no one by that name had been invited or was in attendance. To be sure, they contacted the bride's parents who had returned home to California. They assured the investigators there was no one in their family named Rodolfo and they did not know any guests by that name. They had no relatives in Waco, Texas, either.

Data downloaded from Jeremiah's cellphone found at the scene had already been analyzed by the state police's cyber forensics team. They traced the number of the last incoming call—an unlisted number—and were following some pings it was making nearby. By triangulating the signals picked up from cell towers, they were able to determine whoever called Jeremiah that night was in the vicinity of Hammondsport the first couple of days after the murder. However, the person must have turned off the phone or destroyed it because the signal went dead.

In the meantime, the sheriff's department found Jeremiah's car on Sunday when they followed the vineyard path down to where it met West Lake Road. The Jaguar parked off the shoulder a few feet away matched the description and plate number his widow gave them. They towed it to their garage to be checked for fingerprints and any other DNA that could provide clues. Detectives learned the empty cottage across the road had been on the market for over a year. It was being represented by the same firm that sold Jeremiah his lake house, Casa Bella

Realty. The next closest cottages down the road were a good distance away on either side, so no other residents questioned by the detectives were near enough to see Jeremiah or hear an ATV in the area that night.

A comparison of the tire treads from prints left on the scene matched a brand of the vehicle sold at a dealership in Canandaigua. The dealership complied with the request for records of recent sales of the model.

***

Monique took a deep breath as she knocked on the Redferns' front door. It took a while for her boss to answer, and when she did, Angie's disheveled appearance startled Monique. Pizza stains bled into her Japanese silk pajamas and her "bedhead beehive" hair looked like it hadn't been brushed in a few days. Normally her curly hair appeared carefully styled. This morning, bright white roots encroached upon the expensively-dyed merlot strands.

"Oh hell, it's Wednesday already?" Angie squinted at her housekeeper and waved her inside. Monique smelled the pungent scent of bourbon on her boss's breath.

"How are you, Mrs. Redfern?" Monique clasped her hands together as if praying. "I so sorry your husband been murdered." She didn't know whether to hug her. Instead Monique awkwardly thrust into Angie's hand a beautiful bouquet of fragrant Stargazer lilies she'd bought at the grocery on her way to work.

Angie scratched her head as she looked at the bouquet, and handed the flowers back to her maid. "Find a vase for these, will ya hon? Guess I need to take a shower."

Apparently Monique still had a job for now. She didn't let the coldness of Angie's reaction to the flowers bother her. Surely she was still numb from Jeremiah's death.

Monique noticed the new cupboards made by that handsome carpenter were installed since last week. They were beautiful and she let her fingers trace the carved outline of the lake on one door before she searched inside for a vase. She took out a simple cobalt blue glass cylinder, filled it with slightly warm tap water and plunged the trimmed stems inside. Monique looked around the room to see where the flowers would have the cheeriest impact on her employer. If she didn't know better, she'd have thought a burglar ransacked the house. The entire kitchen, dining room and music studio beyond were a mess. A linen blouse lay on the kitchen floor, a stack of doughnut shop coffee cups teetered on the dining room rug and papers were strewn throughout on every bit of counter space. This was going to be a long day of cleaning. She hoped she could get everything done by the end of the day.

Monique decided the flowers would look best in the center of the dining room table, since it was visible from many areas of the house. She set the vase on the glass top just as the table vibrated. Angie had left her cellphone there. A photo of a man in a white fedora with his head tipped (hiding his face) appeared on the screen next to the name "Rodolfo."

Hmm, who is dat man?

Piled dirty dishes crowded the kitchen counter, so that's where Monique began. It took her until past noon to clean her way toward the studio's entrance. She paused in the doorway, blessed herself and whispered a prayer for Jeremiah.

"Sorry this is such an effin' mess! How much longer are you going to be, Monique?" Angie asked as she brushed past her, jingling car keys. Her clean hair was still damp, but it was at least combed and looked much better than before.

"I do this room, master bedroom and bathroom before I done."

"OK, so you'll still be here by the time I get back from town. I'm flying to New York tomorrow for Jeremiah's funeral this weekend and have to pick up a few things."

Monique felt so sorry for Angie. She looked exhausted. It must be difficult to plan a funeral out of town, she thought.

"Don't worry. By time you return, dis home be all clean again. As we say in Haiti: *Piti, piti, wazo fe nich li.* Little by little de bird build it nest."

Angie blinked at Monique, turned to look at the mess around her and let a few tears slip out as she took a deep breath. Suddenly she stretched out her arms and embraced Monique with all her might. Angie's whole body shuddered as she sobbed. Monique patted her back and whispered words of comfort. As suddenly as Angie hugged her she pulled back, wiped the tears from her face and walked out of the house without another word.

Monique could understand the rest of the house being a mess, but what happened in the studio? It looked as if pillows and sheet music and guitar cases and music stands were hurled in some form of combat. Shards of a crystal glass remained on the floor next to a bourbon stain on the wall. Perhaps Angie walked in here after she learned Jeremiah had been murdered and had an outburst of anger because he'd left her to deal with all of this. Who knew? She started picking things up, setting them back in their normal places. When she had stacked a big pile of loose sheet music, she lifted the piano bench to place them inside. Sitting right on top was a leather notebook that matched the description Mr. McCann had given her.

"*Bondye bon.*" Monique blessed herself. She loosened the piece of rawhide and opened it. The pages inside had yellowed with age and lyrics scribbled in blue ballpoint pen soaked through to the other side. She noticed the handwriting was so heavy it felt like Braille on the back of each sheet. There was a folded sheet of paper that fell out from the pages inscribed with lyrics called "For Gigi, My Ever Love." She slid the paper back between the pages, and as she closed the cover, she noticed a frayed backstage pass for a band called Vinegar Hill stuck to the inside.

Monique removed the notebook from the bench, put the pile of gathered sheet music in its place and walked into the kitchen. She slipped Mr. McCann's notebook into her tote, covered it with old rags, and peeked out the front window to make sure Angie had not returned before she resumed the tasks before her.

***

Later that afternoon as Glenn examined growth progress in the new vineyard, tires crunched across the gravel driveway alongside his house. He glanced up from the vinifera scions he'd grafted onto grapevine rootstock and was surprised to see Monique get out of her car and wave at him. What did she want?

"I found it, Mr. McCann! Here you go." She beamed a wide smile as she held out the notebook toward him. Glenn looked all around to see if any cars were passing by, and walked briskly to grab the notebook he hadn't seen in thirty years. He clutched it to his pounding heart and sobbed as if he'd been reunited with a lost loved one. Monique didn't know what to say, he was so broken up by his friend's death apparently he could not even say a word.

"It's OK, Mr. McCann. I let you cry in private. See you Tuesday."

Glenn looked at her and cleared his throat. "Monique, you have given me the most wonderful gift." He pulled her into an embrace and kissed the top of her head.

She had never thought much about Mr. McCann except that he was the easiest client of hers. His kiss though awakened a romantic attraction that may have already been there but she didn't acknowledge until this moment. He blew her another kiss as she pulled out of the driveway. Monique could still feel its warmth throughout the drive home to Geneva.

Glenn poured a shot of Irish whiskey and threw it back. He sat on the couch facing the clear view of the "heart" of Keuka Lake—a shape created where the lake's two branches join below Bluff Point—and cradled the leather notebook, weeping aloud as his trembling fingers traced the leather bas relief Rocky Mountains on its cover.

"Finally. I'm vindicated."

CHAPTER TWELVE

Wednesday, June 18 ~ 4:30 p.m.

A ringtone of the Rolling Stones' "Angie" startled Tom Russo from a 108 proof mezcal stupor. His temples throbbed as he leaned over the couch and fumbled his fingertips toward the phone on the floor, squinting at the daylight peeking between drawn velvet curtains.

"Yeah? Hey, what's up, Ange?" He coughed to clear his parched throat.

"I just realized... it's missing."

"Huh?"

"The notebook's *gone.*"

Tom pulled himself upright and turned on the light on the end table next to the couch. His head throbbed immediately like it had been smacked with a ball-peen hammer. He cringed, letting out a silent yelp.

"Ange, you sure? Did he put it in the safe?"

"Checked already and it's not there. You don't suppose Glenn broke in here somehow when he heard the news."

"Is Glenn even alive? No one's seen him in years."

"Who knows? He'd be the only person who would know what its value is, besides us. Damn, if he gets it back he'll probably sue the estate for royalties."

Tom rubbed his forehead and sighed.

"There goes my new studio," he mumbled.

"Forget that! There goes my retirement. We've gotta get that back."

"Do you think he'll show up at the funeral?"

"If he has the *cojones* to be there, I'll kick them with my stilettos. *Bastard!* I was there the night Glenn accused Jeremiah of stealing his notebook. Glenn was so mad he broke a bottle of whiskey against the fireplace. I was afraid he'd turn around and charge at us with it. Instead he let the bottle drop to the floor and stormed out. Of course Jeremiah *had* taken it, but I didn't know it at the time."

Tom nodded as he rested back against the couch.

"Man, Glenn *always* had a temper. I remember when he found out my cousin Gigi was cheating on him with Jeremiah, back when the group was recording here at Bluff Point. Found him sitting on the floor of the barn in the middle of the night with a bottle of Irish whiskey to his left and a handgun on his lap. I was sure he was gonna blow me away. Guess he went off to his cabin and got drunk with Chuck and Will from the band instead. Never saw him with that gun again, thankfully."

"Oh yeah, I remember that. Earlier that night Jeremiah walked in on the two of us. Glenn *did* fire that gun, but the ceiling took the hit. God! We were all so crazy high back in those days! It's amazing we lasted longer than Jimi and Janis.

"By the way, have you heard from Gigi lately, Tom? Wondering if she's heard the news. I know she's your cousin and all, but man, was she ever a bitch to live with. I remember how she'd use our groceries to cook rigatoni and meatball dinners for the guys, but she never reimbursed us or helped clean the mess after dirtying every pot in the kitchen. It was as if she was the chef and we were kitchen help. You know, I was always nervous to leave my purse in the same room with her. We all suspected she had sticky fingers. Anything was fair game, and including our men. I'm surprised my relationship with Jeremiah survived Gigi. Then that dumb song about her has to go and become his biggest solo hit. We didn't speak for a few months. Jeremiah would have saved us all a lot of hassles and heartbreak if he'd used a different name."

"And not stolen the lyrics."

"Tell me about it!"

"Did Jeremiah love her? Obviously Glenn did, and I think the other two guys may have had feelings for her."

"I don't want to know the answer to that question. She cast unbreakable spells over every man she met." Tom winced when he heard her whimper a little. "So tell me, where is that bitch these days?"

"I think the last anyone in the family heard from her she was living in Sedona with some artist who builds kinetic sculptures." *Did Angie just sigh like she was relieved to hear that?* "We haven't talked in a few years. Man, she could always score some good drugs." He laughed, but when Angie didn't join in, he redirected the conversation. Tom forgot about the time Jeremiah overdosed on one of her deliveries. It was a miracle he made it through alive, and a bigger miracle the press never heard about it.

"So, is there any evidence of a break-in there?"

"Who could tell if there was? Until today the house was trashed. You saw it when you came over to take me to meet the police on Saturday. The previous night Jeremiah and I had a big fight right before he left for that wedding. I was so mad, I threw sheet music and kicked equipment all over his studio," she rubbed her forehead vigorously as she spoke. "Of course the cops came and had to make it even messier when they poked through Jeremiah's belongings. They took his computer, even the printer, for forensic processing. Today our maid came and cleaned everything. She may have unknowingly destroyed evidence of a break-in if there was any."

"That's too bad. Say, didn't Jeremiah mention there was a security camera in the room? He could review the recorded footage from his computer."

"Yep. Cops asked if the camera was connected by Wi-Fi to a computer. That's probably why they took his laptop."

"Well, maybe they will be able to solve this for us."

After they hung up, Angie poured a glass of wine from the bottle Mike Connelly gave her and sat on the oversized leather recliner facing the picture window with a gorgeous view of the lake. She and Jeremiah used to snuggle on this chair during chilly evenings. Since his death, it was the one place in the house where she felt his spirit remained to connect with hers. Angie imagined he was sitting there, his arm draped around her shoulder as he nuzzled her neck.

Her mind returned to the awful moment when the detective made her identify Jeremiah's body in the morgue. Tom held her left hand as she wiped tears away with her right, nodding to the detective. Afterward, the detective drove them to headquarters where he interviewed her alone. His gentle manner was appreciated until he asked about the state of their relationship.

Yes, she'd been seen drinking alone at The Eggleston that night while Jeremiah was already dead in the vineyard. She assured him she was a regular there, and the staff could prove she was sitting on a bar stool at the moment of his death, so she obviously wasn't the murderer. His line of questioning wandered toward would there be any reason why she'd want him dead or would hire someone to kill him, though he never came right out and asked her. Every infidelity Jeremiah committed against her swirled through her memory.

The last image in that awful slideshow zoomed in on the face of that winsome waitress Sarah... no cigarette stained teeth, no crinkles in the corners of her eyes, nothing sagging, nothing dyed, just flawless, natural beauty—the most envious, unreachable kind. Tears streamed her cheeks as she curled into a ball and fell into a deep sleep.

***

Maureen didn't work Wednesdays; on those days she unleashed her culinary creativity to dream up special dinners for her sisters. Seasonal ingredients inspired the structure of each menu. Tonight she planned to grill organic chicken that had been marinating in olive oil, lemon-infused vinegar and herbs picked from her garden. She bought fresh peas at a farm stand on the upper highway that morning and after cooking and chilling them, mixed them into a salad with diced onions, celery, mayonnaise and hard-boiled eggs. For dessert she baked a strawberry rhubarb pie with a vinegar crust to be topped with fresh whipped cream. Kelly offered to pick up a loaf of crusty bread from the bakery on Shethar Street and Tara promised a bottle of the new Pinot Gris from work.

Maureen always cooked with music playing in the background. Typically, she'd listen to the late afternoon jazz show on public radio. Before she started final preparations for this evening's meal, she went to turn on the radio but noticed the old Vinegar Hill album still resting on the coffee table. Her late husband had an enormous collection of vinyl records and had purchased a new turntable, months before the car accident. She hadn't used it since, even though Kelly connected it to the stereo system. What was she waiting for? Cheery sunshine beckoned and a fresh breeze drifted through the screen windows as she lifted the dust cover, set the vinyl on the turntable and clicked it on. She carried the needle arm over to the first track on the album and set it down carefully.

Obviously from the scratchiness of its sound this was a well-loved, often-played album. Vinegar Hill was classified as a rock band, but strong jazz roots flavored their music. Tracks often included guest studio musicians playing tight harmonies on trumpet, saxophone and trombone. Glenn McCann and Jeremiah Redfern shared the duty of lead vocals on most of the tracks. Their songs flashed back many happy memories of Maureen's college years. She sang the title track "Artistic License" as she placed the chicken on the grill. Kelly walked in the house with a loaf of bread, overheard her sister warbling and laughed. She slid open the deck door and waved to Maureen as she tended the grill.

"Man, this music sounds great! What a perfect anthem for a sunny day."

"I'd forgotten how good they were. Makes me think of that guy I was dating from Philadelphia. Remember him, Bo Dwyer?"

"Was he the guy who looked like Frank Zappa?" Kelly asked.

Maureen threw her head back and laughed. "Yes! That was him. His crazy bohemian 'fro stretched as wide as a door frame. Seems like every time I walked into his dorm room this was playing on the stereo."

Tara overheard the conversation as she walked up the lawn toward them.

"*Ohmigod*, did you say Bo Dwyer? Did I ever tell you he hit on me that time you brought him home for Thanksgiving dinner?" Tara walked onto the deck and set a chilled bottle of uncorked Pinot Gris on the table.

Maureen's mouth tightened. She nodded.

"Oh, I knew. Mom saw him try to kiss you and told me to drop him. I was crestfallen, but she was right. What a jerk."

"If I remember correctly, he didn't just try—he succeeded. And you know, he wasn't too bad a kisser, either." Tara filled the three wineglasses on the table as Kelly rolled her eyes at Maureen. She pinched Kelly's arm playfully.

"I guess Sarah's funeral will be held in Penn Yan tomorrow." Kelly picked up her wineglass and paused. "I bet there will be a big...."

"That reminds me," Tara interrupted. "I heard a bit of juicy gossip at work today. Remember what Carl said about Jeremiah hitting on Sarah last Thursday night at The Eggleston? Get this, his wife Angie had been seen there around dinner time Friday night flirting with Jarod, Sarah's boyfriend."

Maureen turned around from the grill to get the marinated chicken waiting to be cooked. "You mean the bartender, the one who threatened Jeremiah?"

Tara nodded as she sipped her wine.

"You don't suppose Jarod was the one who shot him?"

"He would have had a busy night, especially since he was the one driving the boat Sarah fell off," Kelly replied. "Do you think he steered into those waves hoping Sarah would topple into the lake? I heard she was extremely drunk when they got onboard."

Maureen closed her eyes. "Oh, let's hope he isn't that cold hearted."

"Hmm." Tara did the math in her head. "It *is* feasible he could have committed the murder before that boat ride. It's less than a half hour drive from Hare Hollow to The Eggleston. I should know. Marla and I have rushed there to make more than a few happy hours after work. Now by boat...."

The three sisters sipped wine and weighed the possibilities for a few minutes as a wonderful aroma rose from the grilling chicken. Reflections from the setting golden sun shimmered on wave patterns crisscrossing the lake.

"Man that chicken smells good. What did you put on it, Sis?"

Her sister lifted the chicken breasts off the grill with tongs and set them on a serving plate. "Oh, a little of this and that." Tara should have known better than to ask Maureen for the recipe. Everything she cooked was a spur of the moment experiment never to be exactly replicated again.

They sat to dine and as was their tradition, clinked their glasses in salute to the memory of their parents. Maureen, being the eldest, gave their traditional toast,

"To our family and good times always at Keuka Lake."

"Yes, cheers!"

Kelly's mind whirred about what had been discussed, and she changed the subject swiftly.

"No matter what theories are speculated about Jeremiah's murder, I know Glenn McCann didn't do it."

"Really?" Tara asked with a bemused face. "Why not, Kelly?"

"His lyrics are so sensitive. And if that was him in my bookstore, those were not the eyes of a killer."

"So you're an expert on murderers now?" Tara teased.

"I agree with Kelly," Maureen said firmly. "If it was the same man at the spa that day, I'd say he may lean toward neurotic, but definitely not violent."

"The cops questioned more of the staff at the winery today. Everyone's eyeing each other for clues of guilt."

Maureen and Kelly did not make eye contact with Tara. She knew what they were thinking and decided it was time to talk about it.

"Listen, I know you two overheard the detective interview me the other night. For the record, Mike and I are not involved romantically. We've just been discussing a possible business idea."

"Does this mean you'll get back into interior design?"

Tara could not avoid Maureen's directness.

"Possibly."

"Aw, that would be great! I was furious when Gianni pressured you to close your business in Canandaigua."

Tara looked down the lake toward Hare Hollow. "Don't get me wrong, I enjoy my job. But I do miss the full-time design work."

"I hope it works out for you, Sis." Kelly leaned across the table to clink her wineglass with Tara's. "So tell me, what was Jeremiah's house like?"

"To be honest, from what I saw of the kitchen and dining room I wasn't impressed. The designer had no clear style. Of course Mike's cupboards are gorgeous, beautiful hand-carved cherry. The rest of the interior is a mishmash of metal and wood, trying to be both Mid-Century Modern and Arts and Crafts. Ugh, it's not working, kids. Wealth is no guarantee of good taste."

CHAPTER THIRTEEN
Thursday, June 19 ~ 9:15 a.m.

The Rochester newspaper ran a riveting follow-up story on Jeremiah's death. It featured a map of the winery grounds, photos of his widow Angie, the bridal party at Hare Hollow and even the cover photo of *Artistic License* showing Vinegar Hill standing in front of Tom Russo's recording studio on Bluff Point. Maureen read the story as she awaited her first morning massage client at Ballylough. She squinted at the bridesmaids in the photo. They had been at the spa Friday morning for pre-wedding pampering. It wasn't until she read the caption for the wedding party photo that Maureen realized she'd given the bride's own sister a massage. Bits of their conversation drifted back to her, including when Maite Montez said her father had hired a company to film the wedding with a drone camera.

Did they film it, and if so, are the police aware of it? Might there possibly be images of the crime in progress below? Should she call Detective Kane and let him know?

Maureen remembered other things she overheard that day. Maite mentioned that after their massages, the bridesmaids planned to go to the Red & White Ice Cream Parlor to get some strawberry cheesecake ice cream. Esperanza had told them how she and Ryan met in line there one summer when her family rented a West Side cottage near Bluff Point. Ryan ordered a large strawberry cheesecake cone. When he turned around to leave, he brushed into Esperanza who was standing right behind him. Maite said he was so distracted by her beauty that he stopped and stared for a couple of seconds. His ice cream began to melt, the rainbow jimmies slid and the top scoop rolled off the cone onto her flip flops. He was mortified and bent down to clean the ice cream off her perfectly manicured toes, and when he looked into her eyes to apologize, Esperanza said it felt like Prince Charming was about to slide a glass slipper onto her foot. He paid for her ice cream after apologizing profusely and she joined him outside at the covered picnic table where they chatted for about an hour. Before parting they exchanged email addresses, and afterwards they wrote to each other constantly throughout college. He eventually went to visit her at home in Texas. When the family moved to California, Ryan's ardor wasn't deterred.

After the last morning client, Maureen took her break on the shady grounds of the spa out front and sat on a cedar glider bench facing the road. While eating some yogurt, she noticed a line of cars with headlights driving into the cemetery entrance across the street. *Oh dear, it must be Sarah's funeral.* The hearse turned left toward the newest section of the cemetery. Maureen whispered a few silent prayers as she watched the mourners open their car doors and process solemnly to the tent-covered gravesite.

A handsome young man sitting next to Sarah's parents wept openly. Maureen figured it must have been her older brother Colin, a talented singer/rock guitarist based in New York City. Tara had mentioned earlier that Sarah bragged about him one time as she served her dinner at The Eggleston. From the people she could see from across the road, Maureen discerned Jarod was not in attendance. *Did the family ask him to stay away or was it a police order?*

The priest concluded the prayer service and extended his condolences to the immediate family just as another car pulled into the cemetery and climbed the road that went straight ahead instead of turning left. Maureen thought it was odd the car stopped and a woman with sunglasses and wine-red hair got out, walked partly down the hill overlooking the tent and watched everything from behind an old hemlock tree. She waited until the mourners dispersed before approaching the gravesite. The woman looked all around to see if anyone was watching, made an obscene gesture toward the grave and yelled something before walking briskly back to her car.

"My God, what was *that* all about?" It wasn't until Maureen came back into the waiting room of the spa and re-read the Rochester newspaper's story on the death at the winery that she realized who the mysterious woman might have been.

Why was Angie Redfern at the cemetery? Wait until I tell this to Kelly and Tara!

CHAPTER FOURTEEN
Friday, June 20 ~ 12:30 p.m.

During lunch break, Tara overheard some of the vineyard workers out back discussing theories about the murder. They were trying to figure out how someone might have gotten into that part of the Riesling vineyard without being detected by any of the wedding guests.

"I suppose someone could have entered via the old dirt road behind the abandoned homestead, you know the one by the patch of those noirelle vines," the manager said.

Tara spun around toward him. "What type of grapes did you say, Andy?"

"Noirelle. They were an unsuccessful hybrid created at Cornell. Brendan's dad, Martin O'Hare, agreed to plant a few vineyards for them at the insistence of vintner Charles Cormier. You must remember hearing about him—the guy who claimed the future of Finger Lakes wines would be linked to hybrids."

"Did we ever sell wine made with them?"

"We did, but just for a couple years. They weren't big sellers. The winemaker couldn't decide if he wanted to go sweet or dry with the noirelles, and he was never satisfied with the results of his experiments either way."

The news about the abandoned vineyard piqued Tara's curiosity. If it *was* Glenn McCann in Kelly's bookstore researching that grape, and if this were a way to access the Riesling vineyard and not be detected by anyone, might this suggest he was the person who killed Jeremiah?

***

Sheriff Austin Wilson opened the two o'clock press conference at the Hare Hollow command post by introducing the key players on the investigation team. He said the words everyone already knew: "Thank you all for coming. Today we are here to discuss the murder that occurred in the vineyard below this winery on the evening of June thirteenth. As you know, the deceased was musician Jeremiah Anthony Redfern, age sixty-nine, who moved into a home on the East Side of Keuka Lake on May third. Due to the celebrity of this case, I've asked a couple of members from this team to make statements regarding the investigation and then we will take a few brief questions. Senior Investigator Angela Reilly with the New York State Police Troop E will now discuss forensic findings." Detective Kane smiled at her as she stepped before the throng of media extending microphones and focusing video cameras toward the podium.

"Good afternoon. My name is Senior Investigator Angela Reilly, spelled R-E-I-L-L-Y. On the morning of June fourteenth, Detective 1st Sergeant Tyrone Kane of your Sheriff's Department arrived on the scene, assessed the situation of the body found in Hare Hollow's vineyard and since it became clear that the deceased was also a celebrity and this would be a high profile case, he called our Forensic Investigation Unit immediately to assist with recovery and processing of evidence found onsite. Myself and two FIU investigators arrived about a half hour later. We had to work quickly that morning, because a line of severe thunderstorms threatened to compromise the crime scene. Our team set up tents to protect the immediate area and we collected all we could before the storms hit. In tandem with Detective Kane's team from the Sheriff's Department, we continue to investigate the scene actively and for that reason, it remains closed to the public.

"Later on the afternoon of Saturday, June fourteenth, Detective Kane and I were present when County Coroner Doctor Ming Lee performed an autopsy on the deceased's body at the county hospital. The time was thirteen hundred hours Eastern Daylight Saving Time. It was determined Jeremiah Redfern was killed instantly by a single bullet wound delivered to the center of mass in his chest. Doctor Lee estimates the time of death was between nine and ten o'clock p.m. Friday. From the damage done inside the body and the fragments found on the ground below it, we were able to ascertain the bullet used was a .45 caliber and the weapon was a handgun. Since there was an absence of gunpowder residue on the deceased's body and clothing, and considering the angle with which the bullet entered his chest, Doctor Lee ruled out the possibility of a suicide and determined the gun was fired from a distance of no more than thirty feet by the perpetrator. This concurs with the trajectory of the lone bullet casing found on the scene.

"And now Detective Kane will speak about the progress of his investigation."

He smiled again at her as he walked to the podium, but Investigator Reilly breezed past him to stand next to the sheriff. Kane took a deep breath, rubbed the ache in his shoulder and began.

"Good afternoon. My name is Detective First Sergeant Tyrone Kane, spelled K-A-N-E, and I am the senior investigator with the county Sheriff's Department. On the morning of June fourteenth, a 911 call was made to the dispatcher from an employee of Hare Hollow Vineyards saying a body had been found on the premises. Deputy Corey Martin was on patrol and responded immediately. Once he was led to the scene, he called headquarters requesting our help. I arrived shortly after with Detective Sergeant Mack Hughes. After we assessed the scene, as you heard from Investigator Reilly, I called for assistance and we collected as much evidence as we could before the storms hit. Later that afternoon Detective Hughes along with Detective Reese Bailey set up this command post and commenced interviews of the staff.

"Before we left to witness the autopsy, I interviewed the man and woman who discovered the body—James Harrington of Rochester, New York, and Joan Fleming of Bonny Doon, California—and the two winery employees they told, vineyard manager Andrew Meyers and his assistant, Carlos Corea. The staff members told me that on the evening of June thirteenth, the winery hosted the wedding and reception of owner Brendan O'Hare's son, Ryan and his bride, Esperanza Montez. Approximately three hundred guests were in attendance. My team has been conducting ongoing interviews with the deceased's widow, family and friends as well as the entire winery staff, caterers, guests in attendance and the invited who did not show. We have made attempts but have been unable to interview the bride and groom who are on their honeymoon in Fakarava, French Polynesia. We left a message at the resort, but guess they're too distracted to answer the door or phone," he joked, and a few of the reporters chuckled. "They are scheduled to return next week."

"As of today, we are pursuing several leads and invite the public to call headquarters and ask for myself or Detective Hughes if they have any information that would further our investigation."

Kane stepped back and Sheriff Wilson approached the podium once more.

"We'll take a few brief questions. Let's begin with you over there in the yellow shirt."

"Have you found the murder weapon?"

Sheriff Wilson looked at Detective Kane and he stepped forward.

"There was no murder weapon found on the scene."

The sheriff pointed at another reporter.

"We've been told the fireworks at the reception were set off early. Do you believe the murder occurred during the fireworks, and do you think they were set off early to cover up the murder?"

Detective Kane cleared his throat. "To your first question, yes, the murder would have occurred during the fireworks. We're still investigating the second part."

"Sheriff Wilson," a reporter yelled out, "why do you think a rock star was murdered here? Was it a drug deal gone wrong?"

"It's too early in our investigation to comment on any intent, but we continue to explore all possibilities of why the crime was committed. We'll take one more question. You in the back there, with the red shirt."

"Are any of his former bandmates being investigated?"

Detective Kane stepped forward. "I cannot comment on that, but I can assure you every possible lead will be followed. Again, I urge the public to call headquarters with any information that might be useful."

***

After she closed the tasting room and gift shop that day, Tara needed to stop in Hammondsport on the way home to drop off a special order at a liquor store for Brendan. Driving down the hill, she passed the dirt road that led to the old homestead Andy mentioned earlier. She stopped the car, and after thinking for a few moments backed it up slowly. Not a car was visible in either direction and she was out of view from the winery itself.

"Oh, what the heck!" Tara laughed as she turned down the steep road. The car swerved slightly as its tires negotiated the loose gravel. Ahead the abandoned cobblestone homestead was fairly hidden behind an overgrown clump of lilac bushes. Tara parked her car in the grassy driveway, picked up a fallen tree branch for a walking stick in case she encountered a garter snake, and followed the fragrant dame's rocket and wild rose-lined dirt path behind the house that headed down the hill. Sure enough, right along the path was an overgrown vineyard, its posts and wires bending from the weight of unpruned vines. The ground smelled peaty from storm water pooled on the rutted soil. She paused to examine a bunch of grapes that looked fairly healthy though green—a couple of months away from veraison, the time when the fruit ripens and its color changes.

The sound of approaching footsteps startled Tara and she turned around. A tall man wearing a baseball cap with a white ponytail had walked into the vineyard with a pair of pruners in his hands. He looked up and saw her. His expression mirrored the fear within her.

"Who are you?" she blurted as she dropped the stick.

He paused as he narrowed his eyes toward her. "I have the same question."

Tara recognized the haunting blue eyes from the Vinegar Hill album cover. Her heart pounded as she grasped for the courage to respond to someone who was not only a celebrity, but might possibly have committed a murder.

"I'm an employee of this winery." Tara enunciated each word, trying to sound strong as she curled her free hand into a tight fist at her side. "This is private property." He nodded.

"I know. I've leased this vineyard from Brendan."

"Brendan O'Hare? *Really?*" She squinted at his face to see if she could garner any hints of deceit. "Why? Are you going to attempt to make wine with this grape that everyone rejected?"

Glenn stuck the pruner into his back jeans pocket, folded his arms and looked back over his shoulder.

"Why not? I relate well to rejects. Now, are you going to tell me why you're snooping around here?"

What should she say? What should she do? Would he try to hurt her, too? Would anyone hear her screams?

"Excuse me but I have to go make a delivery." Tara brushed past him, holding her breath as she strode quickly toward the safety of her car. Glenn laughed as he tipped the brim of his baseball cap.

"Nice to meet you, whoever you are."

Tara backed out of the driveway and sped up the hill so fast the car wheels churned whorls of dust obscuring her hasty exit.

***

"Oh. My. GOD!" Tara let the screen door slam behind her when she walked in the front door of her sisters' house. "You would not even *believe* what happened at work!"

"I don't know. This is becoming an everyday pronouncement, Tara." Maureen laughed as she leaned against the stove. Kelly rose reluctantly from the couch to join them around the kitchen counter.

"Now what?" she asked.

"Remember that grape Glenn was researching in your bookstore, Kelly? Well I found out today that we have a vineyard of noirelle grapes growing by the old homestead. So after work I decided to take a peek at it. As I was looking at the old vines, someone approached from behind me. You're not going to believe who it was—*Glenn McCann!*"

Kelly looked at her beautiful sister and sighed to herself. She knew too well how this story would be written. Glenn would have already been smitten by Tara's beauty. Every man always was, within mere seconds of meeting her. Yet of the three sisters, Kelly was the one who was a *true* fan of his music.

"Did he have the white ponytail and Chicago White Sox baseball cap?" Maureen asked.

"Oh, yes. I'm certain it was him. The intensity of those blue eyes... *mama mia* they are unmistakable."

"What did he say to you?" Kelly wanted every detail.

"He told me he's leasing the vineyard from Brendan."

Maureen raised her eyebrows. "*Really...* Do the police know?"

Tara shrugged.

"I still don't believe he would shoot Jeremiah, no matter what their disagreement." Kelly folded her arms.

"You have to admit though," Tara looked directly at her younger sister, "this shows he could have been aware of the back entry into the vineyards."

"Does the noirelle vineyard border the Rieslings?"

Tara shook her head at Maureen. "Nope. We have a couple of varieties growing in between them. There is a path way at the bottom of the vineyards however that connects them all."

"Were you scared?" Kelly nibbled a pretzel as she studied her sister's reactions.

"Not too much. He seemed friendly, though he obviously wondered what the heck I was doing there."

Friendly. Hmm, he's already interested in her.

"Any other rumors floating about the winery?" Maureen asked as she turned away and took a cut glass bowl of chicken salad mixed with pecans, red grapes and celery from the refrigerator.

"Nope. Pretty much everyone is still a suspect. Yum, that looks so delicious. May I invite myself to dinner?"

"Of course! Admission is a bottle of wine, though." Maureen dusted the top of the salad with beau monde seasoning and stirred it in.

"There's a Chardonnay chilling in my fridge. And I have a lovely Late Harvest Vignoles to taste later. Be right back."

Tara strode across the lawn to her cottage as the other sisters discussed the murder.

"The clues to this crime are unfolding like a logic puzzle." Kelly gazed out the sliding glass doors toward cumulus cloud puffs drifting over the lake. "I should make a chart of all the suspects to compare what we know so far."

"Who knows, maybe you'll solve the crime before the detectives. You're so good at solving those puzzles."

Kelly nodded at Maureen. "That would be satisfying. I would love to prove Glenn McCann's innocence."

"You don't even know the man and yet you're adamant about his innocence. Why is that?"

"I know the lyrics he's written. Someone with that level of compassion and sensitivity would never commit murder."

Maureen thought of his lyrics she'd been listening to lately as she set a bowl of copper penny carrots on the table. They'd been made from an old recipe that her mother made often for her bridge club parties. "I got the same vibe from him, despite all of his tension. Solving this crime should be our group project. Why don't you go ahead and draw a chart?"

It was a perfect lakeside evening for dining. With the warm honeygold sunlight gleaming against the white deck and the deep blue sky above, it felt like they were in Mykonos, not upstate New York. Tara uncorked the wine, filled their glasses and they held them aloft in their traditional toast. Maureen noticed sunshine illuminating a water skier's slalom spray as he passed by. *Wow, what heavenly light.*

"Oh! I nearly forgot to tell you two. Guess who showed up at Sarah Washington's grave after the service ended there today? Jeremiah's widow! I could see her from across the road during my break. Instead of placing flowers there, she flipped the bird."

"She did? Yikes, that's dark." Tara set her wineglass on the table and leaned toward Maureen. "Are you sure it was her?"

"The woman matched the photo in this morning's paper."

"Well that might confirm Sarah was having an affair with Jeremiah," Kelly said to Maureen. "Perhaps she wandered over to the Redfern's house to," Kelly paused to gesture air quotes, "'pick wildflowers' the afternoon of The Eggleston's staff picnic."

"Ooh, yes! I remember Carl mentioning that. You have to write all of these theories down." Tara brushed Kelly's hand. "I wish I had your smarts for assessing situations and seeing the connecting threads. You're so brilliant."

Maureen nodded.

"I said the same thing to Kelly earlier. Let's chart out what we know."

"OK." Kelly already had a list of possible suspects in mind.

Tara tapped her wineglass. "Don't you think that someone who would give the finger to another's grave has deep-seated anger issues? Why bother? The person's dead. Way to hold a grudge. Hey, has anyone been in your store lately looking for books on voodoo?"

Kelly laughed.

"Hmm, I'll have to look into that."

CHAPTER FIFTEEN

Saturday, June 21 ~ 8:10 a.m.

Maureen's intuition told her to arrive early at the farmers' market before the best local strawberries sold out to the throngs of weekend tourists. Her mother was renowned for her flaky shortcake biscuits recipe. Maureen was suddenly craving them and planned to surprise her sisters with the dessert tonight.

As she browsed green pulp containers overflowing with fully-ripe scarlet berries, she overheard two women who lived on East Lake Road chatting in the checkout line. It was obvious from the conversation they lived near The Eggleston Inn.

"Did you hear about the break-in at the home of that musician who was murdered?"

"No! Did it happen the night he died?"

"They think it was a few days later."

"Oh, someone was probably searching for drugs or something valuable to sell."

"I heard there was a lot of yelling coming from the house the night he died."

"Well, you know what they say," the woman paused as she handed a pint of strawberries to a shy Mennonite girl behind the cash register. "Money can't buy you happiness."

Maureen found herself nodding with the women in line ahead of her. *Why hadn't the break-in been on the news? If it were drugs the burglars wanted, wouldn't they have hit the house before he died or today when his funeral is being held. I bet there's more to the story.*

She handed the pint to the cashier and then noticed the red stains from the berries on her fingertips. Her thoughts went immediately to the curse that had already claimed one victim. Would there be more?

***

Downstate a few hours later, a videographer from a popular TV music network focused his camera in preparation for the live broadcast of Jeremiah Redfern's funeral from a small Presbyterian church in Brooklyn. It was three blocks away from Vinyl Buddha studio where he'd recorded with the band that made him famous as well as cut the album that made him a star solo artist. Outside the studio, mourning fans created an impromptu memorial with bouquets, candles and Vinegar Hill ephemera. Jeremiah's murder stunned the music industry and demand to attend his funeral was so great it was necessary to make it an invitation-only service.

Inside the Gothic church with Tiffany stained-glass windows, a bronze urn holding Jeremiah's ashes sat on an illuminated table in the center of the sanctuary. Large arrangements of white calla lilies and red roses flanked the display. His widow Angie walked up the aisle and sat in the front right pew between their daughter Lauren—an aspiring film actress living in LA—and their son Dean—an alto saxophonist with a jazz trio based in Chicago. Tom Russo, who'd escorted her in, sat in the pew behind Angie. Next to him were the members of Jeremiah's former band Vinegar Hill... except one.

The news anchor for the music network broadcasting from the choir loft noted Glenn McCann had yet to issue any statement on his bandmate's death. She discussed the permanent split between them related to the lawsuit Glenn filed accusing theft of his song "Forever Gigi." Another reporter on the scene questioned the other members of Vinegar Hill, Chuck McCummiskey and Will Larsen, about Glenn's absence when they arrived at the church. They made no direct response but Will turned to walk away and then paused to mumble at the reporter, "You know, everyone grieves differently."

Sitting several rows behind the band was a woman wearing a veiled wide brimmed black hat that hid her identity. Some of the paparazzi speculated she was Tom's cousin Gigi, inspiration for Jeremiah's biggest hit. One curious detail about the mystery woman, though: she wore a big engagement ring and wedding band over the glove on her left hand. As far as anyone knew, Gigi had not married. So who was this woman?

Jeremiah's former backup musicians and singers opened the service with a stirring performance of the gospel hymn "Soon And Very Soon." The pastor walked out, led an opening prayer and read a couple of passages from the Bible, each selected by Angie. After his warm and spiritual tribute to Jeremiah, others were invited to share their cherished memories.

Several people accepted the invitation, including Jeremiah's solo career manager Lou Greenwald, Vinegar Hill's producer—the legendary Nigel Warwick, and PGA Tour champion Robbie Callaghan with whom Jeremiah played in several charity golf tournaments. Their oftentimes profane anecdotes lightened the sorrowful mood considerably, triggering hearty laughs.

When the pastor announced the final comments would be made by Angie and she headed for the altar, the mystery woman gathered her purse and funeral program. The moment Angie blew a kiss toward Jeremiah's coffin, the woman stood and walked the length of the center aisle, her high heels clicking the tile floor all the way to the front vestibule. From the shadows near the police guards at the entrance, a tall man built like a football player watched her walk past, and wrote something in the notebook he had pulled out of his suit jacket pocket. The woman's spicy tuberose perfume lingered in her wake so strongly that he felt like he might sneeze. He said something to the plainclothes police officer standing next to him. The officer nodded at Detective Kane and whispered into the microphone on his lapel. There were so many cameras flashing as the mystery woman passed through the front doors and descended the church steps that it looked like a firefly swarm.

Angie squinted down the aisle, raised both hands, and snorted.

"Leaving so soon? What the hell? Was it something I didn't say?"

The crowd tittered. Angie tossed her thick, unruly curls off her shoulders and grabbed the edges of the podium. She cleared her throat several times before speaking—too much emotion was caught within.

"First of all, your presence here today means the world to our family. Thank you from the depths of our hearts. So... What can I say about Jeremiah?" Angie glanced over at the urn and sighed. "He was an amazing musician, devoted father and not half bad in the sack...." Everyone laughed out loud. "Most importantly, he was truly, *truly*, my best friend." Angie's voice cracked on those last words and she stared at the podium for an uncomfortable minute or two. Her head rose and looked all around the church. "So why the *F* would anyone want to kill him? Uh, sorry Reverend, I did try to censor myself. But it's hard because I have so much ANGER. There he was heading off to a joyous celebration. He was going to sing for a newly wedded couple's first dance. And even though he'd sung that song, 'My Soul Love,' countless times in concert before, a half hour before he left our home he was practicing it. I asked him why bother, no offense to those kids getting married." She coughed as she laughed. "And do you know what he said to me? 'I have to make their moment perfect, dammit.' Oh yeah, he cared that much.

"Jeremiah was such a perfectionist, as most of Vinegar Hill can attest to." She pointed at Chuck and Will. "Right, you guys?" They nodded. "Where's that asshole you guys played with? Hopefully he's rotting in hell." Angie cringed and looked back at the pastor who was rubbing his forehead. "Oops, sorry again, Reverend. You can bring a rock-n-roll chick to church, but cannot make her shut the hell up." She stared at the left side of the church pews where someone laughed out loud, her eyes not focusing on anything. Angie's shoulders straightened suddenly and she brushed her hair out of her eyes once more. "Aw dammit, this is becoming a stream of consciousness and I promised myself I wouldn't do that. Anyway, just wanted to say I loved Jeremiah. Sometimes he made it difficult to do. Beautiful women used to buzz around him like flies on fresh roadkill." She paused and her face reflected anger churning inside for a minute. Angie wiped tears from her face with the back of her hand, and then she shook her head, laughed and twirled strands of her hair in her left hand. "I guess that was an occupational hazard. Right, babe? We got through those tough moments, though. I'm not saying everything was as mellow as a toking yogi—we had more than a few shouting matches that our new lake neighbors surely heard. We'd always make up before the sun rose, though. Nothing more beautiful than make-up sex, am I right, guys?" She coughed and winked at the pastor who sighed, feeling helpless at controlling the moment with the TV cameras aimed at the altar.

"Every day we'd start anew. I'm so... I'm just so furious our time together was shortened by some angry motherfu...."

The pastor coughed loudly and looked heavenward. Angie looked at her feet and giggled.

"Well, you all know what I was going to say. Ah, hell! Sorry, I'm rambling so much here. Listen. If you all can do one thing tonight, go to your stereo—not a stupid smartphone, not a lame-ass computer—I'm talking analog, not effin' *digital*, OK? Play any or all of the vinyl albums you own by Jeremiah. Sit back with a glass of wine, a fine bourbon or whatever makes you mellow." Angie cringed slightly as she imagined the pastor's reaction. "Please just take a few minutes to revel in the genius that was my husband." She blew a kiss toward the urn. "I'll always love ya, babe. Thanks for an unbelievable journey together, for our beautiful kids Dean and Lauren. You left us too soon, babe. Too soon." She shook her head and sobbed. "Dammit!"

Angie wobbled as if she might faint. Tom Russo rushed to the altar, steadied her with his arm and led Angie back to the pew, between her daughter and son. The organist held a microphone up to a portable CD player from which Jeremiah sang his hit 'My Soul Love.' Angie pulled her son and daughter close to her. Hearing Jeremiah's clear tenor voice once again, and the irony of the lyrics he sang, moved everyone within the church to tears.

CHAPTER SIXTEEN
Saturday, June 21 ~ 1:15 p.m.

After the funeral service, Detective Kane studied the crowd outside the church with the police officer who'd assisted him, waiting for opportunities to interview mourners. He thought it was interesting that as soon as the immediate family exited the church, Angie's son and daughter broke away from her.

"Let me know who she talks to," he said to the officer. "I'm going over to chat with the kids."

The pair stood with arms folded against a wrought iron fence that enclosed the church property as they watched the celebrities extend condolences to their mother. They were whispering about something funny when Kane walked over to them.

"Excuse me, I'm Detective Tyrone Kane with the sheriff's department of the county where your father was killed. First, I'd like to extend my deepest sympathy to you both for your loss. I was a big fan of Jeremiah's music." They smiled slightly. "If you'll forgive me, thought I'd take advantage of you both being here to ask a few questions about your family."

Lauren looked at Dean, clasped her hands, and tilted her head toward the detective. "Sure, what do you need to know?"

"Can you describe what his relationship was like with your mother?"

They snickered, and as Dean was about to answer, Lauren interrupted.

"Wait, are you insinuating my mother is a suspect?"

"This is a standard line of questioning, Lauren. We have to look at the wide picture before narrowing in on a suspect or motive."

"Oh. OK. Dean, you were saying...."

He frowned at his sister for dodging an answer, and then Dean opened up about how their home life was anything but the domestic bliss his mother portrayed. When they weren't away at boarding school, their household was always tense. Sometimes after a good fight with their mother, Jeremiah disappeared for a few days.

"We never knew what the mood would be like any given second. Usually mom would start the fights, accusing dad of having an affair."

"Dean!" Lauren hissed. "Respect the dead."

"Well, *was* he having affairs?" Kane asked.

Lauren nibbled the fingernail of her index finger as she tapped her high heel on the sidewalk.

"Yes. There were many. It's what kept their relationship going, I think. They loved each other but they could only stand so much togetherness."

"Yeah, good way to put it, Lauren."

"Any thoughts on who might want to murder your father?"

The siblings glanced at each other. Obviously they'd discussed this subject beforehand.

"Yeah," Dean said, "but we have no evidence. How could we not think it might be Glenn McCann, I mean, after all those awful accusations he made about our father about stealing his music."

"Why would he kill him now after all these years? Do you know if Mr. McCann and your father had been in contact recently, or do you have any idea where he might be?"

Lauren looked back at her mother who was talking with Nigel and Tom on the church steps.

"Not that we know of, right Dean?"

"Nope. I have no clue where Glenn might be now. I think he did spend some time in Europe a while back."

"He has relatives in County Clare, Ireland, and I think his sister lives in Paris. Didn't Mom say they saw him at a concert in Manhattan many years ago?" Dean nodded at her.

"They just saw him from afar. I don't think they spoke."

"Yeah, knowing Dad, he would have punched him in the face if he got close enough. Ha!"

After a few more questions, Kane asked for their contact information and handed them each his business card. Angie saw the transaction.

"Hey, isn't that the cop who interviewed me about Jeremiah?"

Tom turned around and squinted toward Angie's kids.

"Yeah. What's he doing here?"

"Looks like he's digging for family dirt."

"Maybe he has to question all of the immediate family."

"Or maybe he likes to prey on the most vulnerable. He was out of line when he questioned me about our marriage."

Tom chuckled. Angie hit him with her purse.

"I don't need any sarcasm from you today."

He laughed harder.

"C'mon, Tom. I'm the grieving widow."

He turned back and smiled directly at Angie with eyes twinkling. "And oh do you play that role well." She pinched his arm and he yelped.

"C'mon, let's go join the others at the restaurant. I need a bourbon. By the way, who was the broad in the veiled Jackie O hat? Was she on the guest list?"

"Haven't a clue. She must have known someone to get into the church."

"Must be the minister's wife."

Angie laced her arm through Tom's and they headed for the limousine. She glanced back in time to see Lauren whisper something to the detective.

"Hmm, that one's got to be watched," Angie mumbled.

***

Detective Kane cruised up the westbound interstate, heading for home. He was about an hour away from the turnoff for Keuka Lake, but his mind was a great distance away processing the clues he'd gathered regarding the murder of Jeremiah Redfern. From what he found out so far, there were a few strong suspects emerging for who could have killed him:

It could have been Glenn McCann getting even for the legal squabble they'd had years before. Despite their bad blood, it was still suspicious that McCann made no public statement after his bandmate of twenty years was murdered.

It could have been Angie. Her reasons might be furor at his infidelity, desire to access his fortune or an escape route out of a dysfunctional marriage. Her alibi of getting drunk at The

Eggleston did seem to hold up when he questioned employees, though.

It could have been someone hired by either of the above. That might be someone from out of town, such as Waco where the gun was purchased, or someone local such as that cabinet maker, Michael Connelly.

It could have been some sort of drug deal gone wrong. That deal might have involved their friend Tom Russo, a convicted drug felon.

It might have been a spurned lover. Or it might have been the significant other of a lover.

What Kane needed to pursue deeper was if Jeremiah had any connection with that winery or its employees. They would know that property the best. So far, those leads had not advanced the investigation. He was keeping an eye on the vineyard manager Andy Meyers—that guy had as much tension as a shaken bottle of seltzer and it was obvious he had some issues with management. He'd made no effort to hide his fury about Ryan's choice of a new winemaker.

Once Ryan returned from his honeymoon, Kane needed to find out whom he hired to launch those fireworks. No one on staff seemed to have contact information. From what people told Kane, Ryan liked to micromanage things. Did he have something to prove to his father, or father-in-law? Maybe both.

The investigation team found the murder weapon but the fingerprints did not match any known felons. It had been purchased by someone named Rodolfo Montez. Who was that person, and did he have any connection to Jeremiah or Angie? No stray DNA was found in Jeremiah's car.

There was also the new matter of the break-in at the Redferns' home. Was it related to the murder or a chance theft? Angie seemed a bit sketchy defining what was missing. Why would sheet music be valuable to a common thief? Was the person hoping to make money off material possessions of a dead rock star? Or did this lead back to his dispute with Glenn McCann?

Kane's cell phone pinged on the seat next to him. He glanced over in time to see a text from the cop in New York he'd met. "Emailed you the mystery lady pix."

"Great. Now I have to figure out who she is."

CHAPTER SEVENTEEN

Monday, June 23 ~ 10:17 a.m.

Kelly looked up from the counter just as the man with the white ponytail and Chicago White Sox cap returned to her bookstore. She blushed as she greeted him, knowing his true identity.

"Hi there! I have good news for you. I called my friend Tim and he does have a copy of a Cornell pamphlet on the noirelle grape. Would you like me to call him and discuss the price and how to pick it up?"

Glenn smiled broadly. "Fantastic. Yes, please call him."

When Tim answered, Kelly told him the customer who wanted the noirelle pamphlet was in her store. She shared Tim's asking price and Glenn smiled. Yes, he would take it.

"Tim can charge the sale now if you'd like to give him your credit card number and I'll have it here tomorrow for you to pick up." She held out the phone receiver toward him.

The man shook his head. "I know this is asking a lot, but if I paid you the cash, any chance you could pick it up for me. Things are a bit busy in my vineyards right now. I will compensate you extra for your troubles." His piercing eyes and gleaming smile made Kelly disregard how odd and imposing this request was. How could she say "no" if this were Glenn McCann, her childhood idol? Without the slightest bit of hesitation Kelly agreed to the unusual arrangement. The speed with which she accepted it surprised her.

"Um, sure, I can do that. Where should I drop it off?"

"Don't worry. I'll stop in here tomorrow to pick it up. This should cover the cost of the pamphlet and your gas money."

Kelly's eyes widened at the fifty-dollar bill lying on the counter in front of her.

"Oh, sir, that's way too much."

"Not at all. You've been so helpful and your time is money, too. Right...?" he paused with his hand extended to her, waiting for her name.

"Oh, I'm Kelly Caviston."

He held her hand gently and Kelly felt a lightning bolt-like current travel up her fingers across her arm and continue rapidly until it electrified her heart.

"There's something about a beautiful girl with an Irish name." He winked, tipped his cap and left the bookstore.

Darn it. He didn't say his name.

Tim heard the whole exchange on the other end of the phone. He couldn't help but tease her when she returned to their conversation.

"Guessing from your reaction, that couldn't have been a Hamilton. Was it a Grant or a Franklin?"

"Grant," she whispered. "Guess I'll see you later, Tim." Kelly hung up her phone and watched the man walk up the sidewalk to his car. She covered her mouth with her hand as she replayed their conversation in her head.

"Did Glenn McCann just call me 'beautiful'? This is *crazy!*" She laughed as she held the fifty-dollar bill. "I should frame this!" Kelly's face was so flushed from the experience that when a customer walked in right after her little celebratory dance behind the store counter, the woman looked at Kelly and remarked it was such a hot day.

Hot doesn't even begin to describe it.

***

Maureen led one of her monthly massage therapy clients into a treatment room at Ballylough Spa. She dimmed the lights as a small bamboo fountain babbled pleasantly in the corner next to a pillar candle. The gentle scent of lavender and balsam rose in the air, imparting a tranquil mood.

Her client requested a hot stone massage and Maureen had already set the black basalt discs in a warmer. Before Jada disrobed and lay down on the table, Maureen sat with her to assess how she was feeling and how recent events going on in her life had affected her disposition. This gave Maureen clues as to which areas of a client's body might need special focus.

"My right knee has been a bit sore lately. Not sure if it's from gardening or my new high heels. Oh, that reminds me. Monroe and I went to a private invitation wine tasting dinner on our anniversary, June 12. We can't stop raving about it."

"Now that sounds elegant. What was it like?" Maureen asked as she clasped the clipboard to her chest.

"It featured this sumptuous Mediterranean menu, created especially to complement the best aspect of each wine. If we didn't love the bistro over in Naples where it was held, we wouldn't have paid the expensive price, because the name of the Finger Lakes winery was never mentioned. Isn't that odd? The bottles had plain white labels with one-word names on them.

Each type of wine was named after a gemstone. It followed the typical wine tasting order, whites to reds, but we were never told what grapes were used. Instead we sampled Beryl, Pink Quartz, Ruby, Garnet, and for the finale a Topaz dessert wine. And here's what's weird: we were never told where the winery is or who the winemaker is. The lone hint was it's located where you can see the heart of Keuka Lake."

"Ooh, I love a good mystery. Funny, I've never heard of something called the heart of the lake, and I've lived here all of my life. Wonder where it is. What did you think of the wines?"

"They were created by someone who obviously has a sophisticated palate. Each one had undertones of wines we know and love, but we could never agree on which grapes had been used or if they were varietal blends. The Garnet wine was amazing. Our hosts said that hue is prized by winemakers for the difficulty it takes to reach it. Whoever the winemaker is, it's a person with enormous talent."

Jada pulled out her cellphone to show a photo taken by the hostess that she downloaded from the Internet. Monroe had his arm around her as they raised their wineglasses with the rest of the dinner guests. "I remember she couldn't find her phone so she borrowed the sommelier's to take group photos and later posted them on the event's private Facebook page. He was some white-haired, hippie-ish guy—seemed nice but he kept to himself."

Garnet? Maureen recalled Kelly's recent comments about being drawn to anything that color. The coincidence amused her.

"Did anyone figure out where you can see the heart of the lake?"

"Some thought it might be viewed from the West Side, say looking off the patio balcony of Hare Hollow Vineyards. Others mentioned a steep road that comes from the East Side's upper highway down toward the lake."

Maureen wondered whether the outgoing winemaker at Hare Hollow was moonlighting. She'd have to remember to ask Tara later if Andy Meyers mentioned anything like that.

After the initial massage work on her client's back, Maureen opened the warmer and removed the stones. She placed a couple on Jada's back and slowly massaged them into the shoulder muscles.

"So who hosted that wine event?"

"It was this lovely couple from Canandaigua Lake. Do you know Gianni and Luna Grande? He's a lawyer and Luna's a world-famous hand model from Italy. She wore black satin opera gloves all evening. Must say, it added some elegance to the event."

A stone slipped from Maureen's hand and bounced on the tile floor. She held back the profanity that wanted so desperately to be flung. Maureen did not want any negative energy from her sister's ex-husband to invade this therapy session. She took a deep breath, bent down and picked up the stone, laying it on the counter to be cleansed of its negative energy later.

CHAPTER EIGHTEEN

Monday, June 23 ~ 5:08 p.m.

This was a first. After work Kelly drove through Penn Yan and took Pre-Emption Road out of the village heading north toward Geneva to dutifully pick up Glenn's pamphlet. Sure it was a slower route, but the rolling fields of breeze-tossed golden grains and verdant cornstalks with white tassels were some of her favorite views in the area. This route always calmed Kelly, allowing time to think about whatever was on her mind. Right now she was wondering why Glenn McCann had been so mysterious about disclosing his identity to her. Is he fan-phobic? Under witness protection? He seemed pleasant enough in their brief encounters—not timid at all. Glenn obviously did not want his true identity known, to the point of creating the silly pseudonym he used at Ballylough Spa.

About a half hour later Kelly pulled into the long driveway of the bungalow that housed Timothy Winston Booksellers in the city of Geneva, not far from Hobart and William Smith Colleges. Kelly waved at her friend who was talking with a customer in the back and wandered over to peruse the long wall of books arranged by grape varieties. They were broken into three categories: Native, Vinifera and Locally Bred Hybrids, the last having the greatest number of books.

"Excuse me a second," Tim said to his customer. "Be right with you, Kelly. I have the pamphlet waiting at the counter."

She walked over to the glass counter and browsed a collection of antique Finger Lakes vineyards postcards.

"How's business?" she asked when he rung up the sale.

"Not bad, we're starting to see the arrival of a few of the summer people. There's quite an echo in here for a few weeks when the neighborhood empties out after the spring semester."

She handed Tim the fifty-dollar bill and he laughed.

"Well hello, Mr. Grant. Ha! So, is this buyer incapable of crossing village lines? You've never done this for a customer."

"Let's say this one is a tad out of the ordinary." Kelly smiled demurely as she took the change and the bag holding the pamphlet.

"Why, is he a celebrity of some sort?" Her eyelashes fluttered as she paused in the doorway, but Kelly refrained from answering. "Hmmm. Guess the price was right," Tim teased with a wink. He was hoping she'd divulge at least a hint about the buyer.

"You might say priceless."

***

Tonight it was Kelly's turn to make a dramatic entrance at home. Maureen and Tara were sipping prosecco on the deck when she came in.

"You guys will not believe what happened to me today." She took out her cellphone and showed them the photo of the fifty-dollar bill Glenn handed her.

"And you're showing us a photo of President Grant why?" Tara asked.

"Because Glenn McCann gave it to me!" She told them breathlessly about the errand she ran for him and how excited she was to give him the pamphlet tomorrow when he'd show up at the bookstore.

"Boy, he sure knows how to manipulate women." Tara snickered. "Oh, by the way, if he asks for my phone number, please don't give it to him. I'm not in the habit of dispensing it to strangers I meet in abandoned vineyards."

Maureen saw the joy on Kelly's face deflate as fast as a pierced balloon. She knew Tara was teasing, but why steal the moment in the spotlight from her sister? Poor Kelly's self-esteem was low enough when it came to men.

"Speaking of your relationships, Tara," Maureen said tartly to change the mood, "one of my clients today told me about a wine dinner hosted recently by Gianni and Luna."

Tara squinted, as if that small facial gesture could dampen the pain of her failed marriage.

"Oh, *really*? Where was it?"

"Vinelight Bistro, that swanky new restaurant in Naples."

"So was 'Looney' wearing gloves?"

"As a matter of fact, my client mentioned that. She also said the wines were wonderful, though the labels were printed with only the names of various gemstones. No mention of the winery or winemaker they came from. Oh Kelly, one of the wines you'd love. It's called Garnet."

"Really? That's so odd. I rarely use that word, and recently it keeps showing up very specifically in my life." Kelly wondered if it was coincidence or something more as she put her cellphone back in her purse. A strong vein of psychic ability wove its way through the family tree on her mother's side. Did she inherit the gene? Faint premonitions happened to her with some frequency.

Tara flipped her hair as she sat tall in her seat.

"What's odder is Gianni getting involved in the wine industry. Maybe he hasn't gotten over me and this is a way to compete with my success, or get back at me."

Maureen and Kelly looked at each other, knowing what each was thinking: Tara was still struggling with the shocking truth that a man had simply lost interest in her.

"Does he own the winery?" Kelly asked Maureen.

"I don't think so, but I'd surmise he's an investment partner. The one clue about its location is you can see, as she put it, 'the heart of Keuka Lake' from where the wine is made."

Maureen's words conjured in Kelly's mind a view of Keuka Lake as seen from an open field. From the slanting light present in the vision, she figured this was an early summer evening view. She was trying to look for specific clues in the image when Tara interrupted.

"Must be somewhere within view of the Bluff." Tara squinted as she also brought to mind the view of the topography around that part of Keuka Lake. "That's the most likely place where the lake would split into any heart shape."

"I wondered if it was the view from Hare Hollow. Any chance your winemaker or another staff member might be moonlighting?"

"Not that I've heard. And I know most of the gossip. That's an intriguing possibility. I know our vineyard manager is an acquaintance of Gianni's. Plus, Andy gets along better with Brendan than Ryan, our future boss. He's disparaged many of

Ryan's business decisions, such as hiring a new winemaker from Italy. He did that in front of Brendan, too. It's made for some uncomfortable moments."

"Really? Hmmm, a bit of a power struggle there." Maureen tapped her index finger on her chin.

"Why did your client think the wines were so good?" Kelly asked.

"She said they had flavors reminiscent of well-known varieties, but they were different. Everyone had trouble pinpointing the exact grape used."

"That's interesting."

"What are you thinking, Kelly?" Her sisters waited for a response as Kelly thought of the noirelle pamphlet in her car trunk.

"Ah, it's nothing. So what's for dinner, Maureen?"

"I'm making a sweet potato tagine with lemon couscous, and a kale salad with strawberries and roasted almonds."

"Ooh, I have a bottle of Grüner Veltliner chilling in the fridge that would pair wonderfully with that. Let me go get it."

"Is there anything in your refrigerator besides wine?" Kelly asked. Tara paused in the doorway briefly, then grinned.

"Nope!"

Once she was sure Tara was out of hearing range, Kelly smiled at Maureen. "I know what you did just now. Thank you."

"Thought you needed more time to bask in the glow of what happened today. How thrilling for you. Say, I keep forgetting to mention this, but I heard Jeremiah's neighbors gossiping at the market Saturday about a break-in at his home."

"A break-in? There hasn't been anything on the news about this."

"That's what I thought. Why has it been kept so hush-hush?"

"Dunno. Must be Detective Kane is going to keep it on the down low until he determines whether it has anything to do with the murder."

Of course Kelly's thoughts returned to Glenn McCann. Could it be possible this generous, handsome man was also a murderer *and* a thief?

CHAPTER NINETEEN
Tuesday, June 24 ~ 8:03 a.m.

Today was going to be very special. Kelly could feel it. She spent far more time than usual getting ready for work. A halo of heated pink curlers framed her face as she ironed a white cotton skirt and a salmon linen blouse. She slipped the blouse on a hanger and held it next to her face in the bathroom mirror. Its hue brought out the rosiness of her natural complexion. *Good choice.* Kelly even polished a pair of low heels to wear with her outfit. Mascara and eyeshadow—when was the last time she wore *them* to work? She shook her head and chuckled.

Maureen noticed the marked change in the appearance of her youngest sister as Kelly walked upstairs into the kitchen. *She's so excited about Glenn. I haven't seen her so infatuated with someone in ages.* Maureen sipped her first cup of coffee.

"You look quite lovely today, Kelly."

Maureen's words were always genuine, so they brought a big smile to Kelly's face as she opened the door to leave.

"Thanks. Feels a little like I'm going to the prom or something. So silly."

"Not at all," Maureen laughed. "It's not every day you get to wait on a rock star."

"You know it's been so long since I've had anything exciting like this in my life."

Maureen's eyes softened. "You've been in caregiver mode so long, you've done so much for others... I think it's about time you kicked up your heels." Kelly reached over and gave her a hug.

"Thanks, sis. Wish me luck!"

Kelly's "date" was late. Glenn sauntered into the bookstore around half-past eleven that morning. By then she'd gotten over the initial nerves she had as soon as she unlocked the front door, expecting him to show any minute.

"Hello, beautiful." He smiled when she produced the bag with the noirelle grape pamphlet in it. "This is fantastic! I cannot thank you enough for locating this." He fanned through the publication and paused at its table of contents.

"When I was at Tim's bookstore, I was surprised to see how many grape varieties originated in New York State through Cornell's Grapevine Breeding and Genetics program. Funny, but with the amount of Finger Lakes wine I drink you'd think I'd pay closer attention to such things."

He looked up.

"You enjoy wine? What's your favorite type?"

"No fave really, just good wine." Kelly laughed. "I *do* enjoy a dry red, but sometimes there's nothing better than a late harvest vignoles to finish a perfect meal."

Glenn studied Kelly's facial expressions to determine their sincerity before he let down his guard with her.

"Actually, I dabble in winemaking. To me it's creating living art."

"Really? I suspected you did. It makes perfect sense that you relate it to making art. Why are you so drawn to that noirelle grape variety?"

"I bought some personal effects of winemaker Charles Cormier at the sale of his estate when I was visiting here forty years ago. They included a notebook in which he jotted some of his vineyard experiments. He'd had such high hopes for the noirelles because of their winter hardiness. Winemakers had trouble producing any satisfying wine from them, though. They thought the end product was too foxy native grape dominant, you know, that cloying overly grapey taste. I've located one of the last remaining vineyards growing it and am going to try and carry his vision forward. I have a few ideas of how he could have achieved what he was aiming for, and which grapes they should be blended with to give a better result."

"Interesting. Did you study winemaking at U.C. Davis or Cornell?" She knew neither was the case, but it might extend the conversation.

Glenn laughed. "No, I wish. Just a hobbyist at this point. Who knows, maybe I'll turn pro one day."

"Well, cheers then to realizing your dream."

Glenn opened the door to leave but paused and looked back at Kelly. "I'll bring by some of my wine for you to sample. I'd love to get the feedback of a true Finger Lakes wine aficionado."

Kelly tried not to show on her face the delight she felt inside.

"Sure. I'd enjoy that."

"See you again—sooner than later." The warmth of Glenn's radiant smile lingered as he closed the door behind him.

A man walking out of Chefland, a gourmet cooking supplies store across Shethar Street, waved to Glenn. As the man and the woman with him neared, Kelly recognized them: her ex brother-in-law and his new wife.

"Gianni knows Glenn McCann? Coincidence or is he investing in Glenn's winery, too?"

***

Monique arrived at Glenn's house wearing a bright yellow sundress and robin's egg blue clay earrings with a matching necklace.

"Don't you look sunny today." He cleared a pile of papers off the kitchen table. "How are you, Monique?"

"Fine, fine. And you? You still sad for your friend who die?"

Glenn's mouth tightened as he tipped his head slightly.

"Did you go to de funeral in New York?"

He shook his head and looked at the floor.

"You are private person, no? Maybe it better for you mourn him from afar."

"Yes." Glenn's eyes focused on the heart of the lake in the distance as he sighed. "Well, better leave you to your cleaning. I'll be upstairs in the office if you need me." He picked up the pamphlet on the noirelle grapes and climbed the stairs.

Monique smiled as he walked away. She was glad she made an extra effort to dress nicely this morning. He did notice.

As Glenn flipped through the pamphlet and jotted some notes about the noirelle grape's lineage and characteristics, his thoughts drifted to the pretty woman in the bookstore. He should bring by some wine for her today. After all, she *did* go way out of her way to help him. She seemed like someone whom he could trust, too. What variety of his wine would she prefer? The fact she ran a bookstore that featured rare editions made him guess that she'd have an educated palate. She was worthy of his prized Garnet wine.

Hours later he came into the kitchen and walked right past the fresh bouquet of wildflowers Monique arranged carefully in a vase on the counter before she left. He didn't even see her handwritten note next to them saying "Have a nice day." Glenn headed purposefully into the wine storage barn and selected a bottle of the Garnet from the refrigerator and slipped it into a drawstring sack. He opened the refrigerator again to take out some strawberries he'd picked earlier that day from his garden and a block of locally made champagne-flavored cheese. Those were tucked inside a picnic basket with some wine crackers. He paused for a second and grinned as he set the items in his car trunk and then drove down the hill toward Hammondsport.

***

The door bells jingled and distracted Kelly from reading a copy of *Soured Grapes — The Unauthorized Biography of Vinegar Hill*, part of a shipment that arrived a few hours earlier. Kelly's jaw dropped and her face flushed as she flipped over the book quickly and slid it behind a box on the counter.

"Sorry to bother you again—especially right near closing time." Glenn walked over to her and smiled.

"Oh, it's no problem. If you're in the shop before five o'clock we don't leave until your browsing stops." *My God, what is he doing here? Does my hair still look OK from this morning? Man, he does not look his age at all. Oh God, does he notice I'm sweating?*

"Listen, I don't mean to be presumptuous, but any chance you'd be interested in an impromptu wine tasting?"

Her heartbeat fluttered in triplet rhythms. She tried to remain calm and refrain from showing any exhilaration.

"Here? You want me to close early for a wine tasting *here*?" Glenn looked out the window toward his car.

"Well, I had another site close by in mind. I can drive."

Ohmigod... is this some sort of date? Her heart pounded as Kelly stared into those eyes, the same shade as the deep blue waters encircling Bluff Point.

"Um...," she glanced at the clock and saw it was five minutes to five. "Sure, why not. I have to make a quick phone call."

"To your husband?" he asked with an inquisitive smile on his face. He tilted his head as he glanced obviously at her left hand for a telltale wedding band. She fingered the empty spot.

"No. Um, I'm not... can I meet you out front?" She was so flustered by his directness that her arm accidentally knocked the biography of Vinegar Hill onto the floor. *Oh God, I hope he didn't see that.*

Glenn smiled broadly. "Sure, take your time. Sorry. Didn't mean to rush you at closing time."

"OK. Give me two minutes."

The second he stepped outside, Kelly phoned Maureen. She spoke rapidly and sounded slightly out of breath to her sister.

"Hey, I'm meeting a friend for a drink after work. I'll probably eat some leftovers when I get home later."

"Oh, are you and Andrea meeting at the tavern? That sounds like fun."

"No, it's not Andrea. I'll see you later."

"Oh, well who is it?"

Kelly had already hung up by the time Maureen finished her sentence.

What the heck? That was abrupt. Why all the mystery? Maureen's brows drew together as she set her cellphone on the counter. Whatever the details were, something gave her an uneasy feeling Kelly was heading into uncharted territory.

CHAPTER TWENTY
Tuesday, June 24 ~ 5:08 p.m.

Intense golden sunlight blinded Kelly as she looked up the street breathlessly, trying to find Glenn's car.

"Over here," he called out. A car passed between them. As she waited, Kelly inhaled deeply to calm her nerves and then crossed over to smiling Glenn. He opened the car door for her and then returned to the driver's seat, extending his hand.

"Kelly, I'm Glenn by the way."

She was so relieved he told her his real name.

"Nice to meet you." Should she press for his last name, or disclose she knew who he was all along? It was the only logical reason why she'd go off with an otherwise stranger. Her usually perceptive intuition convinced her to remain silent. "So where are we headed, Glenn?"

"You'll see when we get there. It's got the best view of the lake. Mind if I play a little music?"

"No, of course."

He tuned into a satellite FM classical music station and the *Brandenburg Concerto No. 3 in G Major* came on. Kelly giggled as she imagined telling Maureen, *Yes, I won't be home for dinner because I'm driving off with Jay Essbach.*

"Something funny?" He flashed that gorgeous smile and she nearly melted into the car seat.

"Uh, no. Just in a good mood. Lovely music."

He looked toward the water as they passed Champlin Beach. "Strong breeze off the lake today. We should be out sailing."

She smiled at him. *Don't worry, I already feel like I'm flying across the lake.*

Glenn turned up a freshly oiled gravel road a few miles north of Hammondsport. The car climbed steadily around the steep curves, winding through wooded terrain. He didn't say much and the thought did flitter briefly across her overly imaginative mind that maybe he was taking her somewhere to murder her in some gruesome fashion. *Argh, stop thinking crazy,* she assured herself. But the silence became awkward and after a few minutes she decided to break the ice.

"So, Glenn, how long have you lived here?"

"Off and on—sometimes it's been for a couple of months but more recently I'd say about five years straight."

"I'm surprised I haven't met you before."

Glenn looked over the rims of his sunglasses at her. "I guess we'll have to make up for lost time." He grinned as he raised an eyebrow at Kelly, sending her heartbeat on that crazy rhythm once more.

Sure she felt flattered by his flirtation, but Kelly knew someone of his fame would be skilled at smooth-talking anyone to get whatever he needed. As Tara said, the guy was an expert at manipulating people. He'd already gotten her to do two things she'd never done before. *What is he seeking from me now?*

Glenn turned the car left onto a small gravel parking area on the other side of the road. She could see there was a dirt path leading from it through the woods ahead.

"This is it." They got out of the car and he walked around it to open the car trunk. For another fleeting second she thought maybe he had weapons or rope or some other means of killing her and disposing her body inside. As soon as she saw the picnic basket, blanket and wrapped wine bottle she relaxed and smiled. *Wow, I'm going on a picnic with Glenn McCann. Unbelievable!*

At the other side of the woods was a wide field that provided an unblocked panorama of Keuka Lake. Goldfinches chattered happily as they bobbed past, riding the wind currents like a school of fish. The strong northwest breeze tossed clusters of Shasta daisies scattered across the field. Beyond them the field sloped toward the deep blue lake where a rainbow striped Sunfish streaked across the white-capped water. Sunlight illuminated the white pillared mansion atop Bluff Point. Kelly smiled quietly to herself, because that once held the recording studio where Vinegar Hill cut their album *Artistic License*, and here she was having a picnic with their handsome keyboardist, decades later.

"What a spectacular view of the lake. I don't think I've ever been up this hill before."

Glenn walked behind Kelly and placed his left hand on her back, fingers touching her neck as he gently turned her head northward.

"Straight ahead. Do you see it? That's the heart of the lake."

Kelly felt his breath on her neck and the warmth from his body surrounding her. *What is happening?* The teenage crush she'd always felt toward Glenn amplified to an attraction so strong her face flushed as she tilted her head back into the cup of his hand. The contact made her feel slightly dizzy.

"Yes, there it is. I can see it. I had no idea there was such a view." Of course she was lying. Maureen had told her and Tara about this last night. Dark thoughts of Jeremiah's death drifted through her mind. Her eyes moved to take in her field of vision. There were no houses nearby. Not a soul would hear her now should she have to scream for help. She steeled herself to banish the inner distractions from the beautiful moment.

"This view should be on a wine label, don't you think?" Kelly smiled at Glenn and hoped he hadn't noticed a shift in the tone of her voice.

Glenn unrolled the heavy wool blanket he'd tucked under his arm and knelt on it as he pulled the picnic basket close to him. Kelly sat a slight distance away from him that she felt wasn't too far away but at the same time wasn't right on top of him. He stared intensely at her as he uncorked the chilled, label-less bottle of wine and poured it into two glasses set out on top of the picnic basket.

"This is my latest creation called Garnet. I'd love your take on it."

She caught her breath, thinking about how that color kept coming up repeatedly in her life. Had it been some sort of a premonition of this very moment? Kelly knew then that it must have been his wines featured at the dinner Maureen was telling them about. And then she recalled the moment earlier in the day when she saw Glenn talking with Gianni and Luna in the street. OK, that completes the circle. What was her former brother-in-law up to?

Kelly swirled the glass to let oxygen in. The wine's deep, gorgeous hue was indeed gemlike, and when she stuck her nose deep into the wineglass, she smelled a wonderful aroma that was a blend of black cherry and blackberries. When she let a sip of it roll over her tongue there were hints of tobacco, chocolate and even plum flavors. The taste was smooth from its initial sip to the last lingering drop on her tongue and in the middle was the slightest hint of honeyed sweetness that dissipated over its long finish.

Her eyes widened as she looked at Glenn's eager face, watching silently in anticipation of her reaction.

Kelly took another sip, and again the intriguing flow of flavors caught her by surprise; this time undertones of smoky spice.

"What grapes did you use here? Cab Sauv, Shiraz, or is it a blend? It almost tastes like there's even some Grenache or Tempranillo in this."

Glenn raised his right eyebrow. "So you *are* a woman who knows her way around a wineglass."

Kelly laughed. "Runs in the family. My sister works at Hare Hollow...." As soon as the words slipped from her mouth, Kelly regretted them. She knew she'd immediately lost a level of advantage for figuring out the details of Jeremiah's murder. Glenn tilted his head as he studied her face for several seconds as if seeking some clues.

"Yes," he said in a drawn-out tone. "Now I see the resemblance. I believe I may have met your sister recently. She's aggressively nosy. Am I right? Hmm, this small town just shrank even more."

Kelly noted the change in his demeanor and tried to shift the conversation back to the wine.

"This Garnet is superb, Glenn. Are all your wines this good? This isn't a varietal; it's a blend, right?"

Glenn glanced at the lake view for a few seconds and squinted back at her.

"How can I trust that if I answer you truthfully, you won't run off to tell that snooping sister of yours who works for a competing winery?"

Kelly cringed. It also concerned her slightly how swiftly Glenn's mood darkened. Deep furrows dug into his brow, cloaking any remnants of the previous joy on his face. *Well, to be honest, Hare Hollow is his competition.*

"Forget about it. I don't need the details," she chirped. "All I know is this is a true gem of a wine."

There, that got him to smile.

"Can I buy this anywhere? I'd love a case of it."

He shook his head.

"I'm not ready to begin retail sales. Right now the wine is being test marketed to a few specific audiences."

OK, then. Gianni and Luna are helping him. How did their paths cross? Would Glenn feel paranoid if he knew Gianni was her sister's ex?

"Did you grow up here or are you a transplant like myself?" Glenn asked.

"Our family lived... well we still live on the East Side. We're closer to Penn Yan. Where did you come from?" It was killing her not to disclose she knew his identity.

"Good question," he laughed. "My family is originally from Chatham, Massachusetts, out on the elbow of Cape Cod. We moved when I was two to the Bronx, then I lived a couple of decades around Manhattan, a couple in LA, one in the West of Ireland, then back to downstate and now I'm working past five years here. Does that qualify me as being more than a summer person?" She laughed and brushed his hand. He noted how light her touch was and the rosy flush that tinged her cheeks. He locked his eyes on hers, picked up the bowl of ripe, luscious strawberries from the basket and offered them. "These were picked fresh from my garden this morning."

She looked at the fruit and all she could think about was the curse. Glenn held one out to her, and she realized he looked like that Seneca brave in her dream, offering his hand.

Glenn was curious to her frightened reaction. *Why is she hesitating?*

"Don't worry. These are organic. I never use pesticides."

His eyes looked sincere, not threatening in any way. Was it silly she felt superstitious eating them? She cleared her throat.

"Good. I try to buy only organic produce. By the way, do you know the Senecas believe strawberries are a sacred fruit?"

The corner of Glenn's mouth curled into a slight grin and his eyes softened.

"The Senecas are a wise people."

Kelly accepted the strawberry, took a slight breath and as she bit into it noticed Glenn staring at her mouth. Like the wine, the plump berry was garnet red and yielded eagerly its juicy sweetness. The berry dribbled a bit and she wiped away the juice with the back of her hand. When she saw the stain on her hand, again she was reminded of Jeremiah... and yet again, the curse of the Strawberry Moon. She trembled slightly. Kelly hoped he didn't notice. A nagging sense of fear rose in her gut.

"They're at the peak of sweetness, don't you think?" Glenn still stared at her intensely. Her lips parted but she hesitated before she spoke. *Those eyes, are they even a natural hue?*

"Perfection." She chose another, took a bite and a sip of the wine to meld their flavors. *What's next. Is he going to ask me back to his place? Why does he keep staring at my mouth? Is he about to kiss me?*

A soft breeze ruffled her long curls as Glenn shifted his focus to her hair and eyes. His stare lingered and then drifted toward her neck. Though she was flattered—even thrilled by the attention, at the same time it felt unreal and a bit awkward to be examined in this way by a man she'd idolized since she was a teenager. Kelly turned her face toward the heart of the lake to hide her discomfort. He inched toward her on the blanket and his hand brushed her knee.

"Tell me, Kelly, why do books fire your passion?"

Kelly continued to look away shyly as she let her hand run across the soft clover blanketing the ground next to her.

"In a sense they are like what you said about wine—they're living art. Only it's not a sense of being alive biologically, but more a sense of being alive metaphysically in the realm of your imagination." She turned her face back toward him to see his response. Glenn sat back, folded his hands across his knee and nodded, smiling widely.

"You have no idea how much I can dig that philosophy. What's your favorite book?"

She let out a long sigh.

"Ah, that's fairly difficult to answer. There are too many choices and the answer changes every day. I guess at this moment I'd go with a book I was reading last night—*Seamus Heaney Selected Poems 1966-1987*. I love the imagery within his 'Blackberry-Picking.' It conjures vivid memories from my childhood summers on Keuka... those unrushed afternoons spent meandering through hillside brambles, insistent gnats swarming our faces as we maneuvered through the thorns to reach the plumpest berries that yielded no resistance."

"Yes, and then savoring the sweet taste of their sun-warm juice bursting in your mouth when you ate them. Ah, your words paint a vivid picture, Kelly. By chance, would you have that book in stock right now?"

Kelly looked up as she visualized looking at the poetry shelf of the bookstore in her mind.

"Yes, I believe we have two copies in stock."

"Set one aside for me. I'll stop in this week to buy it. I want to know what stirs your passion." Glenn locked his stare on Kelly's eyes as he sipped from his wineglass. She felt another jolt of electricity like the one when their fingers first touched.

Ay-yi-yi, be careful girl. What's going on here? Is he interested or is this wine-induced lust? C'mon, don't be a fool. What does he really want? There must be some agenda behind all of this. Does he need an ally to cover his crime or does he want me to advance the promotion of his wine?

Of course it never occurred to the long-single Kelly that she should relax because Glenn possibly felt the same attraction she did. Instead she was filled with a million investigative-style questions about him, about this moment. Why hadn't he bothered to dye his hair like other members of the band did attempting to conceal the advancement of age? It sounds trivial, but for someone who was a worldwide celebrity at one time, it seemed like a deliberate act of camouflaging himself. Kelly's freely running imagination speculated about the real reason behind Vinegar Hill's breakup. She also thought about the time he spent on Keuka Lake recording their album in Tom's studio. Had their souls passed each other unrecognized on the sidewalks of Penn Yan back then?

Glenn continued talking about the mundane things one encounters living lakeside as she watched the red sun's gentle descent toward the western horizon, glowing liked fanned bonfire embers. The moment felt so surreal because of the ease, yet here she was lounging in a field with a rock star.

Another vision flashed in her mind of him carrying her across the threshold of a small house built on this field. They'd live there forever in fairytale happiness, staring at the heart of the lake. She smiled, and he thought it was of course because of what he was saying.

As the first hint of the evening's dew sweetened the scent of the field around them, Glenn rose and extended his hand to her.

"We better get going before the deer chase us off their land."

She laughed as she stood. The uneven ground beneath her shoes made her stumble slightly into his arms. He steadied Kelly and took her arm as they strolled back to the car. Fireflies glittered deep within the wooded path to his car. She let out a soft sigh and a slight tear at the beauty of the moment. Kelly was unaccustomed to such romantic magic—how did this come to be? She couldn't get that question out of her mind once she was back in her car and driving up the highway toward home.

***

Angie called Tom Russo a few hours after they arrived back home from the airport.

"Hey, Tom. I wanted to say thanks again for helping get through all of this."

"No problem. You know I'm happy to help."

"I have a question. On my tablet's desktop, there's an icon of a little camera. I don't recall noticing it before. Any idea what it might be?"

"Is your antivirus program up to date?"

"Yes. Jeremiah always took care of all the software installations or upgrades for me."

"He installed it on your laptop?"

"Yes."

"Is there any title under the icon?"

"Phantom."

"Hmm," Tom paused, "hey, isn't that the brand of security camera you have?"

"Let me check." Angie wandered into the studio and looked at the camera in the far corner. She saw the named embossed on the side. "Yeah, that's it. Phantom."

"So he must have installed the Wi-Fi program on your tablet, too, but didn't tell you. Click on the icon and see what happens."

Angie waited as a new screen popped up. "It wants a password. Great."

"Try his birthdate."

"Nope."

"His social security number?"

She typed it in. "Also nope." They spent about twenty minutes trying to figure out what Jeremiah might have used."

"Nothing's working. I've tried all of the dates that were important in his career. I tried Gigi's middle name, Violet. His birthday, your birthday and even typed in the kids' birthdays."

"Hmm, he must have gone for something that would be his last choice on earth. Ha, something like Glenn McCann."

"Why didn't I think of that? What the hell. Give me a sec." She set down her cellphone and typed in the name of her late husband's former bandmate. At first she put it in all lowercase. Then she capitalized the G and M. Finally, she added 86 after his name, the year the band broke up. Tom heard coarse laughter.

"Did it work? Did you unlock it?"

"That sad bastard always felt guilty about the breakup. Well, looky here. There's a bunch of videos. Hmm, now let's see where the files are for the dates when Glenn's notebook could have gone missing. It's lucky we figured out the password now, Tom. I remember he said once these videos are automatically deleted after three weeks. I'm pretty sure I saw it in the piano bench the night before Jeremiah's death. We only need to review the Friday through Wednesday tapes. Want to come over and watch them with me?"

"Sure. Give me a few and I'll be there."

Tom hung up the phone and looked at his watch, hoping this task wouldn't take too long. He had to get home by two the next morning so he could make the predesignated package pickup on time.

When he arrived, Angie opened the door and stood there with a pint glass filled with bourbon on the rocks. He didn't need a drink. Tom lit a joint as they sat next to Jeremiah's laptop computer on the dining room table.

"Look, Ange. If you hover the cursor over this icon, you can see frame by frame. It will let us scan the footage until we see something of interest."

"Cool. OK, let's start with the recordings from that Friday evening after Jeremiah was murdered." Angie wasn't happy to see herself cursing her late husband after he left. In the video, she stands in the middle of the studio yelling and throwing things around as she mentioned Sarah's name. In a moment of chilling calm after her unleashed rage, she pauses by the window and says "I wish you were dead, you cheating bastard."

Tom snorted. "Whoa, Ange. Angry much? This video should be deleted. It could make you the No. 1 suspect in his death. How much are you going to pay me to keep quiet?"

Her eyes narrowed as she gripped the glass of bourbon. "Oh, I know ways to insist you keep quiet. Expecting any deliveries soon?" Tom raised an eyebrow, but resumed the dopey expression on his face.

"Whoa, that was some evil face, Ange. Dude, you wouldn't even...," he laughed.

"Well, the cops have probably already seen this and that's why they put that detective on my trail. Remind me to keep looking in my rearview mirror."

It was obvious no one had been in the Redferns' house much in that time, so they fast-forwarded through the videos.

"Wait, who's that?" Angie paused the video. In the frame, Tom appears briefly in the doorway holding something. "What's that in your hands?"

"One of the drones Rodolfo Montez uses for deliveries. It ran out of battery power and crashed into my boat last Tuesday night when I was near your dock. Remember when I stopped by to have you take a look at the cut on my arm?"

"Kind of. You made a special delivery that night, right?"

Tom and Rodolfo could always be counted on to reduce the pain in her life with their various assortments of illegal drugs. To her she wasn't really an addict. She knew where she could get the proper prescription for what ailed her at any particular moment. Angie fast forwarded past the scenes where she popped some pills in her mouth and emptied another tall glass of bourbon. The videos were monotonous. Most of the time there was no traffic in the studio.

"Look, there's Monique cleaning the room." Tom pointed at the screen. "You know I could listen to that woman talk all day. It's like music, that Haitian accent of hers. I love the way she says anything like 'It beautiful day, no?' or 'Would you like a drink of water, Mr. Tom' or.... Whoa there, pause the video a second, Ange. What's she doing in the piano bench?"

Angie and Tom moved close to the tablet screen.

"Did you see that? Did you just *see* that? Monique took the notebook! Of all people.... What did she do that for?"

"Maybe she thought the leather cover was valuable? Have you checked your jewelry lately? Or your handgun collection?"

Angie's hand felt her earlobes to see if her diamond earrings were still dangling from them.

"Guess I'd better do an inventory. She's supposed to clean the house tomorrow. I think I have to show her this video. Holy crap! I'm shocked. And here that woman hugged me when I started to cry about Jeremiah's murder. She's been playing me all of this time? Wow!"

Tom looked at his watch. It was half past one in the morning.

"Hey. Gotta run, Ange. Do you want me to stop by tomorrow when you confront Monique?"

"Sure. That would be good."

"What time should I get here?"

"Let's have her clean the house and almost finish before we speak with her. How about three-ish?"

"Deal. See you then."

***

Tom drove home to his cottage, walked to the beach and crossed the dock. The evening was cooling from the recent heat spell and he considered running back inside to get a jacket, but didn't. There was little time to spare so he lowered his bass boat from the lift into the water, revved the engine and steered it toward the middle of the lake. He cut the engine at the designated spot, miles away from the sheriff's lake patrol post, and turned off the boat lights.

The crescent moon set hours ago, leaving him surrounded by total blackness. Tom opened an app on his cellphone that served as a beacon of his location to the only other person with that app, and that person was also tuned in at the moment. As he drifted on the dark lake he could hear the whirring of the approaching drone. It released the plastic bags it was clutching above his boat and the cargo landed right at Tom's feet.

"Perfect!"

Tom started the engine and sped away without the boat lights turned on. As he passed Thompson's Cove near the Cavistons' property, he pushed the throttle all the way forward. The engine roared and woke Kelly who was sleeping in her bedroom with the screened windows open.

Her heart pounded as she lifted herself off the bed, walked over to the window and peered out at the yard nearby. *What was that noise? Is someone out there?* Kelly held her breath slightly when it occurred to her that maybe Glenn had followed her home and was now crouching in the woods trying to figure out how he could break in and attack her. She shook her dark thoughts away and walked back to the bed, letting her head return slowly to the pillow, attuned to every sound outside until sleep overcame her.

CHAPTER TWENTY-ONE
Wednesday, June 25 ~ 11:25 a.m.

"What the...?" The text message popped up on Colin Washington's cellphone, startling him. It was from that woman his late sister had met at The Eggleston Inn. Sarah told him Angie Redfern helped promote young musicians like himself. She was messaging him through a social networking website to see if he was still in town and would he be interested in meeting her tonight for a drink to discuss his music. Colin was thrilled. He knew she had tons of music industry contacts who could advance his career.

"Sure, that would be awesome," he replied. "Where?"

"Haute Mama's, Hammondsport, in the alley btw Shethar & Lake streets."

"Time?"

"9ish. Meet you outside."

"K"

***

As she unpacked a shipment of books in the back room of the bookstore, Kelly replayed the impromptu date with Glenn last evening in her mind. It felt like one of those soft focus moments in a chick flick. How did she get cast in a film like that? After a few moments of recollected bliss, Kelly's mind drifted to her reaction to that mysterious noise she heard in the middle of the night. *If my mind can move so easily to negative thoughts about Glenn, what is my subconscious trying to tell me? Should I fear him?*

Kelly felt as though she'd approached every encounter with him cautiously enough. Last evening though there were a couple of moments when she felt vulnerable in his presence. If he had kissed her when they were looking at the heart of the lake, how far would her runaway emotions have taken the moment? It frightened her how swiftly she could abandon common sense when the prospect of romance, especially this unexpected encounter with a celebrity like Glenn McCann, could be imagined as a true possibility. She feared her tender heart was an easy mark for him. Kelly felt like she knew him, but was that the public persona crafted by public relations over the decades, or was she picking up a true sense of his character?

***

Angie paced her bedroom. Why hadn't Tom returned her phone calls? Monique was in the house and she needed to confront her about the missing notebook. She decided she couldn't wait for him to show up. Monique did not appear to be a person who'd be prone to violence, so all she had to do was ask her if she took it.

Angie waited until Monique came into the studio to dust.

"Monique, I have to apologize for the mess this room was when you had to clean it last week. You did a great job."

"No problem, Mrs. Redfern. I hope it help you."

"Do you remember seeing Jeremiah's sheet music scattered all over the floor? Where did you put those papers when you picked them up?"

"In de piano bench. Dat OK?"

"Would you get them for me, please?"

Had Angie noticed the notebook was gone? Monique's hand shook slightly as she opened the bench lid. "See, all dere."

Angie walked over and rifled through the papers.

"Hmm." She put her finger on her mouth and looked from the bench directly into Monique's eyes. "Didn't Jeremiah keep that old leather notebook in here?"

"I not see it dere. You see it?"

"Did you place it somewhere?"

Monique stared empathetically at her employer.

"You very tired, Mrs. Redfern. I get you some water?"

"I'm perfectly fine," she replied tersely. "But did you see...?" Her cellphone rang. It was Tom. He'd been hiding out at his brother's house on the West Side after he saw a sheriff's car pull out of his driveway when he returned home after the drug pickup. Angie yelled at him for being so careless, her free hand gesturing angrily as she stomped off to her bedroom, slammed the door and continued shouting at Tom.

"What do you mean he was in your driveway at that hour? Do you think he suspects you in Jeremiah's death? Oh, Tom. How could you be so careless?"

Monique couldn't help but overhear the shouting as she tried to finish her tasks. The intensity made her stomach queasy. She forced herself to focus on her work so she could leave before Angie got off the phone and brought up Glenn's notebook again. Her slender hands worked in a flurry, dusting, drying dishes, folding linens and putting all away. As she tossed the last of the dirty paper towels into the trash and picked up her tote bag to leave, she heard Angie's bedroom door open.

Monique let herself out the front door as quietly as she could, ran to open her car door and backed out of the driveway. She glanced in the rearview mirror just as Angie walked onto the porch steps with a glass of bourbon in hand, glaring toward her.

***

Ryan and Esperanza were all smiles when they returned to the winery after their honeymoon.

"Tell me all about Fakarava!" Tara greeted them warmly as they walked through the tasting room. "Was Polynesia as breathtaking as the photos I've seen of it?" Her eyes were drawn to the double-stranded black pearl necklace adorning Esperanza's neck. "Ohmigod, are those Tahitian black pearls?"

Esperanza beamed as she pulled the necklace up for Tara to examine. "Ryan bought them for me as a wedding gift."

"They're exquisite. You married quite a gem." Tara winked at Ryan.

"No, I married a pearl of a woman." Ryan squeezed his wife's hand. Brendan entered the room and motioned for his son to come over. He whispered something in Ryan's ear. Tara looked up every once in a while from her conversation with Esperanza and noted a growing look of alarm on Ryan's face. Did she hear him mention the Montez name? Ryan replied tersely to his father that his wife wouldn't have any reason to lie to him. Was there trouble in marital paradise already?

***

A copy of the Seamus Heaney poetry collection Kelly promised Glenn sat on the counter tucked within a brown paper bag silkscreened with The Deckled Edge logo. Traffic within the bookstore was dead for most of the day. School wasn't over and "the summer people" hadn't moved back fully into their cottages yet. Kelly sipped a lavender Earl Grey tea while she read *Soured Grapes,* waiting to close the shop for the day. Lil' Jimmy Capone, who wrote the unauthorized biography, was a studio technician who was ever-present since the beginnings of the band Vinegar Hill. He even went on their tours in the U.S. and Europe, doubling as a roadie.

Of course she knew the group got its start in the heyday of the "sex & drugs & rock & roll" era, but Kelly was still a bit startled to read how excessively her favorite band embraced all those tour vices. If Capone was telling the truth, and that was questionable because he added too many sketchy, macho anecdotes about himself, the band was stoned out of its collective minds when they recorded most of their early big hits. He wrote Glenn was particularly fond of psychedelics and would sometimes wander naked in the woods reciting lyrics-in-progress to the trees. If Glenn heard a leaf rustle, he took that as confirmation the universe thought his words were right. The list of women he'd slept with at the time was like a Who's Who of rock stars on that same music scene. Capone used the initials of each woman's name, but it was obvious to her whom he was referencing with JJ, GS and SN.

"Glenn was from a wealthy family and had exceptional taste in wine," Capone wrote. "He always used expensive wine as an aphrodisiac to loosen up the chicks he wanted to bed." Her jaw dropped and she closed the book and stashed it in the counter drawer.

"*Holy Christmas,*" she whispered aloud.

Bells jingled above the front door. Kelly turned to see Glenn walk in clutching a wrapped wine bottle. He flashed his brilliant white toothy grin at her as he set the bottle on the counter.

"For your private collection, but you must promise me you'll never share an ounce with anyone else." He handed her the bottle of Garnet. She suspected it was intentional when his fingers grazed hers. Kelly laughed nervously. He was dressed casually in a weathered sage green T-shirt and overalls.

"Here's that book of Heaney's poetry you wanted." She slid the bag between them. Glenn opened the book and flipped through the pages of the hardcover.

"Excellent. What do I owe you?"

"Nothing." She glanced at the patterns on the oriental rug, then back at his face. "It's on the house."

"Really?" Her shy smile delighted him. "You're being too generous, Kelly."

"Well, so are you."

He smiled. "Listen, do you have any dinner plans?"

Kelly took a breath to speak but not a word would come out, she was so nervous. Her palms began sweating on the wood counter as she shook her head.

"How does an evening of food, wine and poetry strike you?"

He said "evening," she noted. Kelly inhaled another soft breath... "Sounds perfectly wonderful."

"I'll stop by that bistro on the corner to order some takeout. Meet you back here at closing time." He glanced at his wrist. "Hmm, guess I left my watch at home. My phone's been missing for about two weeks now, too. Ah well. We'll figure it out. After all, does anybody *really* know what time it is?"

She turned on her cellphone and said softly, "It's four-thirty."

"OK, see you in a half hour." As soon as he disappeared out the door her stomach rolled like the Cyclone at Coney Island. Kelly could hardly breathe. Did this mean she had *another* date with Glenn McCann? *Holy Mother of God!* Kelly took the money from the cash register and put it into the safe in the back office, turned off the computer and shut off the interior lights.

Her sister Maureen responded coyly when Kelly phoned and said she was going out once again after work: "So when do we get to meet *him*?"

"Oh, gotta go, he's back already," Kelly whispered.

"So our suspicions are correct?" Maureen laughed. Kelly knew her sister must have already been theorizing who this new man is.

"Grrr, I can't get anything past you guys." Kelly laughed. "I'll fill you in on all the details later."

CHAPTER TWENTY-TWO
Wednesday, June 25 ~ 5:01 p.m.

Deputy Corey Martin tailed the green hybrid sedan from the moment it pulled out of the side road near Hare Hollow's vineyards to where it was parked on Shethar Street in Hammondsport. He saw the driver enter The Deckled Edge and ran a check of the license plate. It came up registered to Glenn Edward McCann, 9100 Coyne Springs Road, Hammondsport. The name sounded vaguely familiar. He called Detective Kane who happened to be interviewing Ryan and Brendan O'Hare at the winery. Kane stood from the table and wandered over to a corner of the room.

"Got an ID on that car I was telling you about, Ty. Registered to a Glenn McCann from Hammondsport."

"Wait. Say that name again."

"Last name's McCann, first is Glenn."

"Holy crap! Glenn McCann's living here too?"

"Who *is* he? The name sounds familiar."

"He was the keyboard player in Jeremiah Redfern's band."

"Did I overhear you mention my friend Glenn McCann?" Brendan interrupted. "Nice fella. He's leasing the old noirelle vineyards we abandoned several years ago. Thinks he can make good wine with those grapes. What's up, is he in some sort of trouble?"

Kane rubbed his brow, sighed and looked directly at Brendan. "Did he ever happen to mention he was a musician, that he played in the band Vinegar Hill with Jeremiah Redfern, or that they broke up when he accused the deceased of stealing his lyrics?"

Brendan's eyes widened, then he frowned. "No, but I remember that band. Come to think of it, he does look like a guy in the band, but a heck of a lot older. I wasn't much into their music. Preferred Southern rock, myself. Marshall Tucker, Skynyrd, Allman Brothers... you know, kind of a ramblin' man."

Ryan planted his face in his open right palm and sighed.

"What's he doing now, Corey?" Kane asked.

"He got back into his car. Now the owner of that bookstore is locking up and... wait, she got into the car with him. What do you want me to do?"

"She *did*? Follow them."

By the time Deputy Martin hung up, Glenn had already pulled away from the curb. Martin started to follow the green car, but was cut off by two Mennonite horse carriages clomping past. When he finally made it to the intersection with Main Street, Glenn's car vanished from sight.

***

After several miles, Glenn turned onto Lower East Lake Road from the highway and headed toward the lake shore. Right before a sumac-choked dead end, he turned onto a long gravel path toward a tiny house overlooking a point. A sense of déjà vu overwhelmed Kelly—she recognized the house from the vision she'd had back in the field.

They got out, crossed the lawn and walked toward the steps.

"Are those solar panels on the roof?"

Glenn figured Kelly would notice. "Yep. The exterior is made from one hundred percent recycled materials, too. This structure leaves a small footprint on Mother Earth."

She had been drawn to the concept of the tiny house movement, but wasn't sure if she could embrace it fully. Once he opened the door and she saw the sparse interior, it was obvious to Kelly this was not where he lived. The cramped space was more like a playhouse where he came to write music, especially because the side facing the lake was dominated by windows. She paused in the kitchen to appreciate his view of Keuka Lake. A massive maple tree overshadowed the left side of the property and its leafy lower branches obscured some of the shore. There were two askew "eyes" on the tree's trunk where limbs had been severed by the elements years ago. It gave the tree a slightly trippy feel as if it were watching them. She laughed to herself because it reminded her of the tales of Glenn's LSD use in *Soured Grapes*. Had he talked naked to this tree? Straight across the lake the land rose into steep vineyards. To the right, looking northward toward Bluff Point, was a flattened view of the "heart of the lake."

Glenn set the food on an antique enamel-top table next to the kitchen window, slid off his baseball cap and hung it on a coat hook by the door. He fluffed his shoulder length hair out as he carried the book back to the far room. She looked around the cleverly designed, space-efficient kitchen. A knife block had been built into the cabinets above the refrigerator. To the right stood a narrow vertical wine rack. Wooden blinds were built into the back window and could be pulled down like a garage door for privacy. Below the window was a small counter with a sink basin. She noticed he used the same brand of organic lavender hand soap she did. That made her smile. A narrow stove snuggled against the left side of the sink counter. Vertical shelves crowded next to that. A few books rested on the upper shelf, seashells on the lowest and a handmade porcelain pot with a celadon glaze, a bamboo whisk and a tin of matcha tea sat in the middle. Behind it was a box of crystalized ginger and a tub of Medjool dates.

Glenn returned and opened the refrigerator to get a chilled, unlabeled bottle of wine. When the door closed, Kelly noticed a magnet holding a business card for that Hammondsport nightclub, Haute Mama's Lounge. *Hmm, does he go there for the live music or the occasional drag shows? Why would he go there if he was such a stud, as Jimmy Capone claimed?*

"Did you build this cottage?"

Glenn laughed.

"No, I have a friend from Texas who creates these to your own specs. My home is elsewhere. This is where I allow the magic in." His smile dazzled in the reflected lake light pouring into the kitchen.

As for the rest of the house, there was a small open area down the hall Kelly suspected was his music space. It was barely wide enough to accommodate the electronic keyboard facing the window, an office chair and a pair of headphones resting next to hand-written sheet music on a stand. Across the room was a small closet and bathroom. Beyond that an open door led to a room with a wall of windows over a bed. As soon as she noticed it, a knot of dread twisted in her stomach.

Glenn set out the *Piatta di Amore* tapas special he'd ordered from the bistro and uncorked the wine. He poured their glasses full, raised an eyebrow playfully and dipped his finger into the one closest to him, letting the wine dribble from it into his mouth. She laughed and while her mouth was open he did the same to her.

"Quick, what variety of grape is it?" he asked. She was startled both by his overt gesture and being put on the spot, so she lifted her wineglass to her lips for a true taste. He watched every micro-expression on her face to see if he could figure out if she liked it.

"It's sweeter than a Riesling, but there's not as much residual sugar as Diamond, and the mouth feel is heavier than a typical Valvin Muscat. Hmm, I'm not sure what it is, but I like it... a lot. Are you going to tell me what it is?"

Glenn shook his head and grinned. "Proprietary info. You know, you have some serious wine chops, Kelly." He raised his wineglass and clinked hers. "Care for a nibble?" He pushed the plate toward her. "We have honey-fried oysters, roasted figs drizzled with balsamic vinegar, asparagus wrapped with asiago cheese and prosciutto, plus bourbon-candied almonds."

The "dinner," she noted, was a selection of tapas made with ingredients to set the mood for *amore*. There were no utensils so she'd have to use her hands. After considering her choices, the oysters seemed like the least messy option. He pushed his hair behind his ears as he watched her bite the delicately breaded shellfish, its soft bellied interior released a brine carrying the flavor of a salty ocean breeze.

"Mmm," she sighed, "that was amazingly good."

Glenn smiled and ever so slightly licked his lips.

"Excellent choice."

Kelly was too nervous to return his stare and glanced away. She noticed there were no seats in the kitchen. The only seating options were the lone chair in the music space or the bed in the far room. He saw her looking toward the bedroom.

"What are you thinking?" he asked in a lower voice that she felt resonate against her.

Her eyes widened. Was he reading her thoughts? She grabbed another oyster.

"Wow, these are some of the best oysters I've had." Her voice rose from alto to soprano. Kelly heard how nervous she sounded and chased the rest of the oyster with a gulp of wine.

"Have another." His eyebrow rose slightly as did the corner of his mouth. Kelly took a deep breath to calm herself as the palpable intensity rose between them. *Why isn't he eating?* He stepped toward her, propping his arm against the refrigerator behind her and his voice dropped to a whisper. "Do you know what would make this moment? You should read aloud that poem of Heaney's you love so much. Let me get the book."

Glenn walked the short hallway into the bedroom. He paused in the doorway to open the book and scan the contents.

"Kelly, would you come here for a second? I have a question." She walked slowly toward him. *What's he up to?* He showed her the table of contents. "What was the name again of the poem you liked?"

"'Blackberry Picking.'"

"Yes, I see it. Stand right there and I'll lie down here and close my eyes. I want to visualize every word." He set his wineglass on the floor, then laid back on the bed, knees crooked over the edge and hands propped behind his head.

This is weird... what the heck? Did I ever think a couple of weeks ago I'd be in a situation like this with Glenn McCann? The gorgeous rock star I desired from my youth, the man who is one degree of separation from Jimi and Janis and.... Ohmigod this is so bizarre!

She stood with wineglass in one hand and the book in the other, reading the poem aloud. Although Kelly felt nervous, she paced her recitation and tried to capture each nuance of meter as Heaney intended. Glenn opened his eyes slowly and smiled when she finished.

"I knew you'd read it well. I could feel the poet's passion in every word. Now I know why you love this poem. The imagery is so vivid, the metaphors of unfulfilled desire so obvious." He sat up, smiled and raised his eyebrow slightly as he patted the space on the bed next to him. "Sit here for a second."

Kelly froze. Though immensely attracted to him, she was not emotionally ready for anything physical with him. This was all happening too fast.

Glenn took the book gently from her hands and set it on the bed. He kissed each hand and interlaced his fingers with hers. She stared into his seductive, heavy-lidded eyes. *Uh-oh, this could get dangerous real fast.* Her pulse quickened. *Maybe I should admit this situation is too uncomfortable.* She bit her lip.

"Please, Kelly. Let's savor Heaney's words for a few moments together."

Against her better judgement, she sat.

"Kelly. May I place my hand on your heart?"

She didn't know what to say. *Hmm, this is getting a tad Jim Morrison-y.* Kelly stifled a nervous giggle.

"Um, I guess...."

The moment Glenn's hand touched her, she *pinged*. It was a text message alert on her cellphone. Glenn frowned. Kelly pulled the phone out of her pocket to mute the sound. That's when she saw the pop-up message from Tara. *"Police are looking for you."* Her hands trembled as she clicked off her phone. She could feel her pounding heart in her ears. *Crap! Why would they be looking for me? What should I do? What if Glenn is the prime suspect in Jeremiah's murder? Am I in danger? Will I get entangled in the investigation or be considered an accessory?* Kelly's intuitive fight or flight sense screamed within her.

"Glenn, I need to go."

"Why, what's happened?" He rubbed her back.

"Family emergency. That was my sister."

"Can I drop you off somewhere?"

"Just take me to my car."

"Wouldn't it be quicker to bring you home?"

She felt the phone vibrate in her hand and turned it over.

"Detectives are here, want to question you."

Kelly did not want Glenn to see where she lived.

"No! Please just take me to my car back in Hammondsport."

"Yes, of course, but first... may I get a quick hug?"

There was no time to dally, especially with someone who might possibly be a murder suspect. *Why do the police want to question me? It has to be something connected to Glenn.*

"Umm maybe we should just," and before she could say anything else he hugged her harder than she was expecting. His long fingers cupped the back of her head as he buried his nose into her long hair. As he tilted his face to kiss her, Kelly pushed him away.

"*No, I can't!*"

Glenn's stunned face reflected his surprise at her unexpected rejection. He released his hold on her immediately and backed away, hands in the air. The gesture reminded Kelly of a surrendering criminal.

"Hey, whoa, I'm truly sorry. My bad. Thought we were both digging this vibe happening between us. Did I turn you off in some way?"

She studied his confused face and it did seem to reflect genuine remorse.

"No, of course not. Sorry, my sister's message was urgent and I didn't want to...."

"Let things get out of control?" His face relaxed into a mellow Hollywood actor-like smile. "Listen, Kelly, that's cool. I can dig it. No problem. I shouldn't have pushed... man, I thought maybe we both wanted...." His hands pointed back and forth between them. "Aw hell, let's get you back to your car." He kissed the top of her head in a fatherly gesture—*how awkward*—and put his hand on her shoulder as they walked out of the house.

They approached his car in silence and he opened her door for her, unaware of the drone that had just launched from the dead end nearby and was hovering above the treetops, filming their departure. As Glenn crossed around to the other side of the car, Kelly felt tears well in her eyes. She didn't know whether to be afraid or happy, embarrassed or concerned.

"Now I realize what's going on." Glenn fastened his seatbelt and turned toward her with a soulful look. "It's obvious you haven't been with a man in a while. Don't worry, Kelly. We can take this slowly. You let me know when you're ready."

She winced. *Ouch! Does he assume getting me into his bed is a done deal?*

"Oh, when I'm ready I'll definitely have my people call your people," she whispered sarcastically toward the window.

He backed out of the driveway and headed toward Hammondsport. The drone shadowed their journey from a good distance above.

Neither Kelly nor Glenn spoke during the drive back to her bookstore. As she opened the car door to get out, they looked into each other's eyes briefly.

"Thanks for the book, Kelly. I'm really grateful you turned me on... to Heaney's work." His grin made her uncomfortable.

"Um, I'm glad. Thank you for the wine and the delicious tapas. Hey, I'm so sorry that...." She stopped mid-sentence when a sheriff's cruiser drove up next to them. Glenn followed the line from the shocked look on her face to the subject of her fear.

"What the hell is this all about?" Glenn muttered. He looked back at her, still clinging to the open car door. "Did *you* do this?" he asked in a sudden accusatory tone.

"Of course not. I don't know what *this* is."

Detective Kane approached the car slowly.

"Mr. McCann, I'd like to ask you a few questions. Would you please step out of the car?"

Glenn glanced at Kelly, whose terrified face soon traced with tears.

"So you knew who I was all along?" he asked in a whisper.

"Ma'am, come with me please." Detective Hughes led Kelly a little way down the block, across from The Deckled Edge. Kelly looked over her shoulder at Glenn as he was being questioned. The angry look in his eyes sent chills through her.

Ohmigod, he thinks I turned him in.

CHAPTER TWENTY-THREE
Wednesday, June 25 ~ 6:45 p.m.

They were questioned separately for several minutes. Detective Kane asked Glenn when the last time he spoke with Jeremiah was.

"It's been years, man," Glenn snarled. "Why would I call that thief?"

"Why do you say he was a thief? What did he steal?"

"My artistic property. There was a whole legal dispute about it. Look it up. He got a platinum record thanks to the lyrics he stole from a song I wrote."

"How long ago was that?"

"In 1986. You must know the song, 'Forever Gigi.' The lyrics were in a notebook he stole out of my room when we were recording an album together."

Kane winced. If that really happened, he could imagine why Glenn's anger simmered so close to the surface.

"Did the court rule in your favor?"

"Never made it to court," Glenn clenched his fists on his legs. "Because no one could find the notebook, the judge threw out my case. Twenty years-worth of lyrics I wrote for future songs just gone, man, *gone*."

"Did anyone ever find the notebook?"

Glenn looked at his feet and the tone of his voice changed.

"No... I don't believe so."

"Do you own a handgun, Mr. McCann?"

Glenn's eyes widened.

"Not anymore."

"Why not?"

"It was stolen. Years ago."

"You seem to lose a lot of things, Mr. McCann? How long ago did that happen?"

Glenn rubbed his forehead. "Around the same time I lost the notebook. We were in a recording studio here at the mansion on top of Bluff Point cutting an album. Our fame was growing crazy around that time, we had no privacy. The chicks were everywhere, man. Some of the groupies following us had fathers and boyfriends who were overly protective. That gets you feeling paranoid. I asked my cousin in the military what would be a good choice for personal protection. He got me a Glock 17 through some connections he had.

"We were in the midst of recording at Bluff Point and I'd met this beautiful local girl named Gigi Russo—she was the studio owner's cousin. Jeremiah was jealous of our romance for some reason. It was ludicrous because he had Angie, and trust me, she was a real looker back then. He told me my relationship with Gigi was affecting the band's music. Secretly, I learned later, he was sleeping with Gigi but wouldn't admit it. Anyway, I used to keep the gun on my nightstand in our cabin at the studio. Woke one morning and it was gone. I'm pretty sure Jeremiah stole that, too."

"Hmm, so that's where 'Forever Gigi' came from. Did Jeremiah know how to use a gun?"

"Oh, both he and Angie collected guns. He used to tease her and call her 'Angie Oakley' back when they were dating."

"When was that?"

"Around the same time."

"So his widow knows her way around a gun."

"She has way better aim than I ever did."

Kane squinted at Glenn for a few seconds.

"Why were you on Hare Hollow Vineyard's property today?"

"Pruning grapevines I'm leasing from Brendan O'Hare. You can ask him about our agreement. We drew up a contract, he'd have the paperwork."

"Have you ever wandered off that immediate property into the nearby vineyards?"

Glenn folded his arms.

"What are you insinuating? Listen, I didn't kill Jeremiah Redfern. Sure, I hated the guy for what he did to me, but I would *never* kill another human being."

The intensity of his reply struck the detective as sincere. He considered mentioning Rodolfo Montez and asking if they knew each other, or if he'd ever been to Waco, Texas. That might leak out information proprietary to the murder case too soon. Instead he asked, "Have you ever met or recorded music with Alejandro Montez?"

"No, though I would have liked to. The guy's known for producing quality music."

"One final question for now, were you aware Mr. Redfern had moved to the area?"

"No. I wasn't. It didn't surprise me to hear it after he was murdered. Our time spent recording at Tom Russo's studio was incredibly inspiring in a creative sense. I mean, man, how could you not dig that view from the Bluff. We all said at the time we wished we lived here rather than LA."

Kane smiled. He appreciated the genuine nod toward his home turf.

"Would you please give me your phone number and address in case I need to follow up with more questions?"

"I can give you the number for my cellphone, but it's been missing for a couple weeks."

"Missing? Did Jeremiah take that too?"

Glenn could have given a snarky reply back to Kane, but opted for honesty. "Blame it on being in my late sixties, but I can't seem to find it anywhere. It's probably buried in a mess of paperwork at my house." Glenn gave him the number anyway as well as his address.

"Thank you for your cooperation, Mr. McCann. And if I may say a few words here off the record, I have to let you know what a big influence your music was on mine. Really loved your song 'Prove Me Wrong' on *Artistic License*."

"Cool, man. Glad you dug our sound. What's your axe?"

"I played a Strat, just like Jeremiah. And, by the way, bad blood aside... I'm deeply sorry for your loss."

The detective's sincerity moved Glenn and his eyes watered. He spread his palm across his heart and lowered his head, then returned to his car.

At the end of his interview with Kelly, Detective Hughes got back into the cruiser with Kane and pulled away. Kelly stood there, looking like a child just abandoned in the middle of Times Square. Glenn drove toward her, she waved slightly and he pulled the car over. He gestured for her to walk around to the driver's side window.

"Hey, love, everything's cool. Sorry I was such a jackass."

Kelly shoved her hands into the back pockets of her pants as she scrutinized his expression. He seemed upbeat. Was it all a case of misunderstanding?

"Guess someone saw me wandering around the noirelle vineyards at Hare Hollow today and thought I might be a suspect in Jeremiah Redfern's murder. All's straightened out now. I apologize for jumping to conclusions about you."

"Of course I eventually realized you're Glenn McCann. I was always a big fan of your music and even saw you in concert years ago. Sorry I didn't let on I knew who you were, but since you were so careful not to divulge your last name I wanted to respect your privacy."

"To be honest, I knew you recognized me. You did a lousy job of hiding the copy of *Soured Grapes* in the bookstore. By the way, FYI, Lil' Jimmy Capone is a delusional wannabe. That's all I'm going to say."

Kelly covered her face with her hand and laughed briefly, then stood awkwardly in the silence between them, not sure if Glenn wanted to say more or if she should just walk to her car and get home as soon as possible. He took her hand and kissed it gently.

"I'm sorry if I frightened you in any way today. You are simply lovely, Kelly. I hope we can continue this conversation we've begun."

She studied his face. Even after all of this she felt an irresistible attraction toward him. Kelly wished he'd just kiss her like he was going to do back at his cottage, but she was too intimidated by his fame to initiate it. Instead she smiled and crossed the street to her car. As she waited for the car to warm up, she thought about everything that happened. She wanted to believe so completely Glenn had no involvement in Jeremiah's death. What would it take to convince her?

CHAPTER TWENTY-FOUR
Wednesday, June 25 ~ 7:30 p.m.

Maureen and Tara waited restlessly on the couch for their sister to come home. When they heard Kelly's car pull up, they rose immediately to greet her at the front door.

"Are you OK?" Tara asked. "What did the cops want? Did that guy you are seeing try to hurt you?"

Kelly shook her head and breezed past them. She tossed her purse on the counter, crossed the living room and opened the sliding door to the porch. A chilly northwest breeze blew in from the steel gray lake as she leaned against the railing. Maureen walked out with a glass of wine and placed it in her younger sister's hand. She noticed a tear resting on Kelly's cheek.

"Tell us what happened."

"Oh it's the usual scenario, following the same sad old script. I meet a fascinating man, there's a true romantic spark between us, and then he gets yanked out of my life. Usually it's by another woman. In this case, however, it's my own common sense barring the door to a possible relationship. He's genuinely interested, but does he only want a fling?"

"Who is he?" Tara asked as she joined them on the porch.

Kelly covered her face for a few seconds and let her hands slip to her chin.

"Glenn McCann."

Tara folded her arms and smiled broadly. "Whoa! Are you kidding me? You go, sis!"

Kelly's mouth smiled faintly at the rare compliment from her beautiful sister.

Maureen's reaction differed greatly. She bit her lip as she studied her sister. How far had the "relationship" gone between her and the rock star? Poor Kelly was not as experienced with men as they were. Her vulnerability made her an easy mark for a lothario on the prowl.

"What did the police want?" Maureen asked.

"They questioned us separately, so I'm not sure exactly what Glenn was asked. He was dropping me off in Hammondsport when they pulled up alongside his car. Glenn did mention someone reported he'd been hanging around the noirelle vineyards at Hare Hollow."

Tara put her hands up. "Hey, it wasn't me." Kelly studied her face before continuing.

"The detective wanted details about our relationship and he asked how long I've known Glenn. Felt like saying 'since I was a teenager' but I knew that wasn't what he was asking."

Maureen smiled briefly before continuing.

"So Glenn McCann is interested in you? Wow, Kelly. What are you going to do about it? Did he get your number?"

"Oh... he has my number, but not for my phone. Phew." She fanned her face with her hand. "This evening was crazy intense with him. We were sampling some of his wine—he's an amazing winemaker by the way—and then...."

"Ohmigod, Kelly. Did you two fool around?" Tara guffawed, as if such a thing would be unbelievable. Part of Kelly wanted to lie to Tara and say yes, they'd had mind-blowing sex. She knew Tara would know otherwise by reading her expression, so she told her the truth.

"Not quite. We shared sort of a trippy, Jim Morrison moment. I'd rather not share the details if you don't mind."

Tara fiddled with her dangling earring, and Kelly knew that was something she'd do when her mind was awhirl, trying to work out a solution to a problem she faced. This time it was how she could get Kelly to spill all the details of her celebrity tryst.

"Tell us, Kelly. Do you think Glenn is guilty?"

Kelly looked at the hazy sky for a few seconds and turned back toward Maureen.

"With all my heart, and in my gut, I believe he is innocent."

"Hmm... well, trust those feelings then." Maureen patted her back. If Kelly felt this so strongly she was probably correct. She sensed her younger sister had clear intuition. Tara showed more exuberance.

"Well, if this develops into anything, he's lucky to have you. After all, you're beautiful, funny and the brainiest person I know. How could he not be utterly smitten?"

Kelly blinked at Tara. Did she really utter those words? She couldn't help but smile after that compliment from left field.

"Back to Jeremiah's murder. If we can cross off Glenn, who else does that leave as a suspect?" Tara asked as she tapped her manicured fingernails on her wineglass. "Weren't you going to make a logic chart of the top suspects, Kelly?"

She tapped her finger on her lips. "You know, I forgot about that. That would be fun. Get out some snacks, refill my wine and I'll go get some paper."

***

The two detectives returned to headquarters and transcribed the interviews they'd had with Glenn and Kelly. Hughes agreed with Kane's assertion that neither person was involved in the murder, though they still might be valuable in solving the case. After Glenn told Kane about Angie's gun skills, he decided he'd swing by her cottage to have a follow-up discussion about how she was doing (and possibly glean a few more clues about her husband's death). Her car was pulling onto the highway as he neared, so he did a U-turn and followed her towards Hammondsport. Where was she going at quarter to nine on a Wednesday night? It struck him as odd given her recent loss.

Once she arrived in the village, Angie turned up an alley between Lake and Shethar streets and followed it to a parking lot next to Haute Mama's Lounge. Kane paused his car in the alleyway and waited to see where she'd go.

A man in his early twenties approached her, Angie hugged him, and they went inside the club. *Naw, this can't be. Had she been having an affair with this kid while Jeremiah was still alive?* A car pulled up behind him so he had no choice but to turn into the parking lot. He found a space at the end of the lot, farthest from any illumination by the nightclub's neon sign. Kane backed his car into the space so he faced Angie's car and would see when she left the club.

Inside the club it was karaoke night. A shy copy machine repairman from Prattsburgh warbled Lady Gaga's "Bad Romance" in an alien-sounding falsetto. Angie cringed at the bartender as she bought a craft beer for Colin and a double bourbon for herself. She led Colin over to a table in a far corner where she made a brief amount of small talk, asking him how he got involved in music and then began discussing the loss of his sister. When the moment was right she launched into her pitch.

"Listen, Colin, my business partner and I are about to open a state-of-the-art recording studio here on the lake. We're looking for the next big thing in talent, and I have to say that I was impressed with the CD of your music Sarah gave my husband."

The mention of his sister's name again made Colin's eyes well with tears, and when he spoke, his voice cracked slightly from emotion.

"You really think I could be the next big thing?"

Angie reached across the table and touched his hand. "Honey, my husband was a multimillion-dollar recording star. I probably know a thing or two about the business, don't ya think?" She laughed so hard it set off a coughing fit. "So here's the deal. You've got a soulful rock vibe going on, Colin. It reminds me of Jimi a bit."

"Whoa, Hendrix?"

Angie nodded as she drained the bourbon from her glass and waved at the bartender. "Two more," she mouthed to him.

"Is there any other Jimi in the universe, darling? And I should know because we partied once, after a gig at the Fillmore East. Now since we will be able to offer you the highest standard of recording, it's going to cost a little more...," she paused to see how the young man would react. His thoughts were miles away imagining what it was like to party with Hendrix. "But don't worry, there are ways we could get around that. My lawyer can draw up a contract in which we'll get only forty-nine cents of every dollar your songs earn. Does that sound fair enough?" She could tell math was not this kid's strong point.

As Colin listened blank-faced to her deal making, a drag queen dressed like the lead singer of Jefferson Airplane snarled at the scenario from offstage. Grace Sleek, as she was known, had witnessed enough of Angie's "talent searches" to know it wasn't making music she was after. She was sick and tired of seeing her sponge off the talents of others. *How dare that bitch take advantage of another man!* Grace clomped off the stage and headed straight toward their booth, interrupting Angie's pitch to grab the young man's hand.

"I need someone to sing with me." Colin laughed nervously and shrugged at Angie, but the drag queen's hand was so strong he was yanked out of the booth and onto the stage.

"My new friend is going to help me sing my biggest hit," Grace said as the karaoke monitor began to roll through the lyrics to Jefferson Airplane's "Somebody to Love." Colin blended moody indie rock harmony with her lead vocals effortlessly, giving the impromptu version a softer vibe. Grace exaggerated singing the chorus, acting as if every weighted word was being sung to Angie. Oh, she picked up the message all right and began tapping her fingernails noisily on the table. *What was this drag queen's problem?* Angie's eyes twitched as if she hadn't had any sleep in days. She drained her glass of bourbon and took out her cellphone to snap a photo of Grace. Angie texted it to Tom and asked, "Who is this jerk?"

Once the duet finished, Moan Jett jumped onstage, shoved Grace aside and sneered, "Go ask Alice, hon. Now I know why your singing has a bad reputation." She sneered as she slung an electric guitar around her neck. "Time for some serious rock 'n' roll!" Grace slunk into the shadows of the back room, simmering from the public dissing. Colin rejoined Angie who applauded with the rest of the audience as he sat down.

"Sorry about that. Whoa, that chick was crazy!"

Angie tilted her head, her face twisted in a look of quizzical disbelief that this kid didn't seem to understand he'd been singing with a man. "Listen, it's too loud to talk here. Want to come over to my house and see Jeremiah's music studio? I'll let you play his Strat."

"No way. Awesome! I'd love to."

Angie exited the nightclub with the young man.

"Follow me," she yelled to him.

"What's she up to?" Kane waited for both cars to exit the lot and followed. When she turned left on the highway heading back toward Penn Yan and eventually turned down the lake road near her home, he figured out what was about to happen. He couldn't stomach walking in on that.

"I guess my questions can wait until tomorrow."

CHAPTER TWENTY-FIVE
Thursday, June 26 ~ 11:30 a.m.

Angie begged Tom to stop in Penn Yan for coffee before their meeting with the group financing his new recording studio. She was barely awake when he arrived to pick her up and needed to jumpstart her brain. As they turned off the West Side highway toward the top of the bluff, memories of Jeremiah and the outrageous times they all spent together at Tom's former studio flooded his mind. He chuckled.

"What?" Angie winced; her hangover made it hurt to speak.

"Do you remember when that punk Johnny Stryker showed up early for his recording session after Vinegar Hill's? I can still see him snarling as he rode his motorcycle through the mansion. The moment when Glenn stepped out of the vocal booth and saw Johnny steering toward him, Gigi hugging him from behind.... Man, I thought he was going to kill him."

"Glenn's temper always frightened me." Angie swigged her coffee.

"Do you think it's possible he shot Jeremiah?"

"Not after what they learned from the autopsy." Angie snorted. "If his aim is as good as his lovemaking, there's no way he took Jeremiah out with a single shot."

Tom nearly drove off the country road.

"Wait, how did I miss you two were seriously an item?"

"We were never an item. We met next to the bottle of bourbon Jeremiah left in the living room one night when he ran off with Forever Gigi to her friend's cottage in Branchport. Misery loves convenient company."

Tom snickered. "So he was a lousy...."

"Well, I was trashed and he was high, so maybe I should cut him some slack."

"You wild thang, Angie. How come we never, you know...."

Angie rolled her eyes. "Please, Tom, I have *some* standards."

He winced from the bite of her words but his good-natured grin soon returned. Their conversations were always like this.

"Looks like they beat us here. Man, it's going to be weird walking inside that place again."

Ryan and Esperanza O'Hare, her father Alejandro Montez and some people Tom didn't recognize stood next to their cars at the end of the long driveway.

"Don't make any commitments today, Tom. OK? Let 'em sweat a bit before you agree to something that might be out of our price range."

"Yes, Mother." Tom gave her a playful look of disdain.

"And that's why we never slept together, 'son.' Don't get sassy with me, Thomas. Remember I'm bankrolling half of your dream here."

"How could I forget," he muttered out of the side of his mouth as he emerged from the car, pushed his sunglasses up like a headband for his unruly hair and walked toward his possible future co-investors.

"Tom Russo?" a man asked as he approached with his hand extended. "Hi, we haven't met yet. I'm Gianni Grande, the attorney for the O'Hares and Mr. Montez in our negotiations. This is my wife, Luna."

Angie noticed how pale Tom's face turned suddenly. Why didn't he shake the woman's extended, gloved hand? He was speechless and that was a rare occurrence. Tom always had a quick-fire quip at the ready. What was the matter with him? She didn't want him to blow this contract deal. Angie elbowed Tom in the side and his hand stretched out immediately to greet Luna's.

"Nice to meet...."

Angie elbowed him again.

"...You, Luna. This is my friend, Angie."

Luna tipped her wide, tortoise shell sunglasses to get a better look at Angie's face as they shook hands. Angie noted her skin was freakishly pale, bluish and translucent like skim milk. The heavy eyeliner she wore and the way her hair was twisted into a shiny-sleek topknot bun invoked a vision of Audrey Hepburn. Even though her hand was gloved, Angie got a chill from it when they made contact. Something about this woman was downright spooky.

Gianni extended his hand to Angie. "Mrs. Redfern? You might not remember me, but I represented Casa Bella Realty when they sold you your lakeside home."

Angie squinted at him. He did look a little familiar, but she was still distracted wondering why Tom was reacting so strangely to Luna. Did he fall suddenly under the spell of her mysteriousness? *Men are so weird.* She looked back at her old friend and studied the odd expression on his face. Those eyes were wider than she'd ever seen, and the whites were visible around the irises. No, this was not attraction. This was fear. Even Luna's husband seemed to pick up the odd vibe.

"What, do you two know each other already?" Gianni asked. His wife smiled.

"Oh, I feel like we do. I've heard so much praise of Tom's studio skills. My father is a big fan of the recordings made at the previous studio here."

"What's your father's name?" Angie asked.

"Ignazio Fracasetti."

Angie's face went ashen.

"Oh. Have you heard of him?" Luna asked with a slight smile. "He bought a lot of property in New York City when our family moved here from Sicily in the '60s. His office was in the Vinegar Hill section of Brooklyn."

A wave of dread rolled across Angie's gut. She wanted to flee the scene with Tom, but he stood frozen with his own fear. *Figures this spooky woman would be the spawn of Iggy.*

Many years ago Iggy Fracasetti, the former landlord of the building that housed Vinyl Buddha recording studio who was briefly the manager of the band, bailed her and Jeremiah out of a big debt incurred when he left Vinegar Hill to pursue his solo career. He'd demanded a percent of Jeremiah's royalties from "Forever Gigi" as payment. When the song rocketed the Top 40 charts, Jeremiah kept delaying payments to Iggy saying he was busy on tour. Then one night during a gig in Germany as Jeremiah walked off stage for intermission, a beefy arm lunged from the shadows and stopped him. It was Iggy's henchman and his fist blackened Jeremiah's eye seconds later after he yelled, "Pay the damn bill, *capisce*?" The show went on, thanks to Angie applying some makeup on his bruised face before he slipped on a pair of sunglasses. Jeremiah told the audience they were needed to protect his eyes from the glare of the spotlights. He wired Iggy a payment as soon as he woke the next day.

Now Angie was wondering if Iggy was involved in the background of this deal. How would he have heard about the plan? Did Luna know about their connection and the money they once owed her father? Or, was Iggy friends with the newlyweds from Hare Hollow Vineyards? Might that explain why Jeremiah was murdered there? Could she trust any of these people? She tried to go back over the details in her mind of how plans for this deal came about. Who tipped off Tom originally last December that the mansion might be on the market? Had Jeremiah ever mentioned the name? Surely he would have discussed that person with Tom. She'd have to remember to ask him after their meeting.

As Angie recalled Jeremiah telling her, soon after they moved to town in early May, he joined Tom at a private wine tasting at Hare Hollow arranged his cousin Marla. That's where they met Ryan and Esperanza. Jeremiah said the topic of music came up and Ryan was bragging about his vintage 1961 Gibson Les Paul Custom electric guitar.

"How could you not dig that third humbucker?" Jeremiah said casually, waiting for his reaction.

Ryan raised an eyebrow.

"You know guitars?"

Tom guffawed and elbowed Jeremiah.

"Yeah, I have a few axes around the house including one of those and a 1960 Les Paul Standard."

Ryan's eyes widened. "No way! That's awesome! How much did you pay for that, a couple hundred grand?"

"Nah, got a great deal on it... through my old buddy, Eric Clapton."

That name was all Jeremiah needed to drop. As soon as he mentioned they were trying to secure funding to rebuy Tom's former studio, Ryan said, "My fiancée and I have been exploring investment opportunities around here. We'd be happy to discuss being part of that investment. In fact, her father is a record producer in LA. Do you know Alejandro Montez?"

"You mean the guy who founded Stellar Records? Uh yeah, I kind of know him," Jeremiah grinned at Tom. "They own a smaller record label called Quasar. I recorded a little hit for them. Ever hear of 'My Soul Love'?"

Esperanza's eyes widened as she gaped at Jeremiah.

"That's *your* song? Ohmigod! Wait, you're Jeremiah Redfern! Oh wow, that's like the most romantic song ever. I have it as my ringtone. So you're a friend of my father?"

Tom snorted, incurring a swift elbow to his side from Jeremiah.

"Yes, we've met."

Ryan raised his hands and smiled broadly. "Well that seals the deal. Give me your number and I'll see if he'd like to get on board with this." Tom patted Jeremiah's shoulder as he wrote his phone number on a slip of paper for Ryan.

Esperanza left the room to refill the cheese and crackers tray. The moment she was gone, Ryan leaned toward Jeremiah and whispered, "Say, do you ever play weddings?"

Jeremiah drained his wineglass. "Not usually."

"How about a big wedding with members of the music industry present? All I'd ask is for a couple of songs, including 'My Soul Love,' as a surprise for Esperanza. Name your price." Jeremiah ignored the alert expression on Tom's face.

"Let me get back to you, Ryan."

When they walked out of the wine tasting toward their car in the parking lot, Tom gave Jeremiah a high five.

"Looks like we're going to be back full time in the record business, brother. Oh, and nice job scoring the wedding reception gig."

One phone call led to another and here they were, months later, preparing to carry on Jeremiah's dream of purchasing the mansion and signing the contract for the management of the recording studio there. Tom amassed a sizeable amount of cash mainly through his distribution of drugs for Rodolfo, and though Angie benefitted from their alliance, his side business was a concern to her. From the frequent phone calls Tom made to him, she assumed Rodolfo would be a silent partner in this deal. So far they'd only chatted on the phone a few times. Angie considered whether she'd need to officially meet him before Tom inked this deal.

The group walked down the long driveway approaching the back of the mansion. Built in the Jeffersonian classicism style, the mansion weathered centuries of storms as it stood exposed to the elements atop Bluff Point. Instead of taking the first door they encountered, that led directly into the den and kitchen, the group crossed the lawn toward the house's front side facing the lake. They paused on the porch under the pillared portico of the two-story home. It offered breathtaking views of the confluence of the east and west branches of Keuka Lake. Although she'd spent a lot of time there back in the '80s, Angie noted for the first time that this perspective of the lake formed the shape of an upside-down heart. She snorted to herself. *Hmm, that's appropriate.*

Tom recalled a vivid memory of Jeremiah standing one night on the balcony above them, strung out on something, wailing away on his Stratocaster after their recording session. He'd dragged his amp outside with him and cranked the reverb and the volume. Unsuspecting cottage residents surrounding the Bluff must have wondered if a UFO was landing on that otherwise still spring evening. Tom recalled wishing tape had been rolling at that moment because Jeremiah's riffs were brilliant. It was some of the best playing he'd ever heard.

The real estate agent unlocked the French door entrance off the porch and they walked into the empty main room. A lot of renovation had been done to the interior after the house was left in deplorable shape when Tom lost the property due to his drug bust. Since then all of the hardwood floors had been polished back to their original beauty. The cracked enormous picture windows were replaced and re-grouted. Fresh cream-toned paint brightened the interior that had once been a hideous shade of violet Tom applied to invoke a purple haze vibe.

Something made Angie look up. She grimaced at the bullet graze which still dented the whitewashed cathedral ceiling. Immediately she replayed in her mind the events that led to the incident on that evening back in the mid-'80s. She'd been lying on the couch entwined in Glenn's arms sleeping off the shots of bourbon they'd shared before Jeremiah returned from his tryst with Gigi. He was furious when he walked in the room and saw his bandmate with his girlfriend in such a compromising position. The couple hollered at each other. When Jeremiah pulled his hand back to slap her, they heard a loud pop and the vase on the far table shattered into smithereens. Angie and Jeremiah turned toward the sound. They saw Glenn standing there with his handgun pointed at Jeremiah.

"That was just a warning. You lay one hand on Angie and I'll blow you away, man."

"Not cool, Glenn. Put away that gun."

"Ha! You know what's not cool? Slapping your lady! And what's worse? Cheating on her with your best friend's girl!"

"Oh, but it's OK for you to screw my girl? Shut up, Glenn. You're just jealous because Gigi wants me more than you."

Glenn charged at Jeremiah with his finger on the trigger of the pointed gun. Angie shrieked yet she was able to squeeze herself into the middle of their scrum and wrest the weapon from Glenn's hands. When she grabbed it though, Glenn's finger squeezed against the trigger and a bullet fired at the ceiling sending a small shower of plaster onto Jeremiah's head. The other band members heard the ruckus and raced downstairs from the second-floor studio where they had been mixing the album's final track. Chuck and Will managed to separate all three and get everyone calmed enough so no further flare-ups occurred that night.

Angie recalled the intense mutual hate reflected on the faces of both men in the heat of that moment and rubbed the chill away from her arms. In that instance, yes, Glenn could have killed her husband. Instead, the blowup initiated the slow demise of Vinegar Hill later that year. The jealousy and animosity was bad enough. Once the trust among the men was obliterated by the theft of Glenn's notebook, the relationship was irreparable. She never knew why Jeremiah bothered to steal Glenn's work—he had plenty of talent of his own though Glenn did have the reputation as the band's songwriter. That must have always bugged him.

The tour for the completed album *Artistic License* was as tense as watching a high-wire act walk between skyscrapers during a gale. Glenn spent most of his time in the back of the bus and never chatted with the crew or his bandmates unless it was necessary. He was finished with Gigi. Any lingering spark from the brief fling with Angie had been extinguished that night, too, so Glenn would find refuge when he needed it in the warm arms of eager groupies. That's when Angie's hate for Glenn began to build. She knew they just had a fling, but in her heart she felt a connection spark with his mysterious soul. Was he capable of caring about anyone except himself?

"Has this room and the rest of the house been rewired?" Tom asked the real estate agent, interrupting Angie from her mental journey into the past.

"Of course. Until the previous owner moved in there were no circuit breakers installed. It's now updated to current code."

Tom rubbed his chin as he glanced around. He pointed toward the back of the massive room. "That's where I'd like to install the digital rig. Last time I made the mistake of setting up our massive analog 60-track console upstairs. I imagine the main mixing will be done here instead. We could turn the open space upstairs into sound booths for vocals and special effects."

Ryan nodded. "Will you go Mac or PC for your rig?"

As Tom humored him and let the kid toss around as many terms as he could, trying to sound like he knew something about recording music, Angie watched the dynamics of the rest of the group. Alejandro walked away to tour the first floor with Luna. Angie was glad to have her out of the room, but she wondered if those two had a past connection also. Luna's silent presence was enough to unnerve her. Esperanza chatted animatedly with that lawyer married to Luna about where to find the best flights to the South Pacific. What was it going to be like working with all of these parties? When she, Jeremiah and Tom had discussed reopening the studio, she didn't envision the management team being so crowded. How involved would this Luna be? Angie had intended to be a silent partner in supporting her old friend Tom. Now she feared Iggy would come after her finances if he knew she was connected with the deal. She wondered if Jeremiah paid him everything he owed? It irritated her Iggy was still drawing royalties from 'Forever Gigi.' The long reach of Iggy was something Tom must fear, too. But at the moment, he seemed oblivious, distracted by tech talk posturing with Ryan.

After touring the rooms upstairs, the real estate agent opened the door at the end of the hallway and ushered them onto the second floor balcony. Since Angie was one of the first of the guests to walk through the door, she ended up standing closest to the railing. The real estate agent waited until everyone was on the balcony and then described the breathtaking view before them. She explained that since this was one of the highest points in the Finger Lakes, the Seneca Indians who first settled there centuries ago held the land in great regard. They called it

Ogoyago—land between waters. Bonfires were lit from this prominent point to send signals to clans in surrounding areas.

"Legend even has it," she said pointing toward a stone wall that arced below the mansion, "that several Seneca chiefs are buried right down there." The guests moved closer to the balcony's edge and leaned to get a better view. Angie felt Luna's shoulder pressing against her back.

"Don't get too close to the edge," Luna whispered. "We don't want any accidents happening." The threatening monotone of Luna's voice confirmed Angie's fears about Iggy's involvement. She wanted to scream from the terror building inside her. Could the nearly two-hundred-year-old structure nailed against the mansion's façade hold all these people? She gripped the railing as Luna's elbow pressed into her back. The whole view before her began to twirl, her stomach churned. Angie closed her eyes and asked Jeremiah to help get her out of the situation soon.

Tom turned to his left and noticed Angie's pallor. She looked like she was about to faint. Were the lingering memories of Jeremiah getting too much for her?

"Hey, Ange, you OK?" he asked as he stepped between Luna and his friend. Tom slipped his arm around Angie, drawing her toward his chest. She rested her head in the crook of his arm and whimpered slightly. Luna heard the soft cry and a slight smile curved the corner of her mouth.

CHAPTER TWENTY-SIX

Thursday, June 26 ~ 1:45 p.m.

Tara just finished a wine tasting and was heading for the
break room to relax a bit when she ran into Ryan, Esperanza and
Alejandro. They were gathering in Brendan's office, just back
from their meeting at the mansion. Ryan paused.

"Question, Tara: Are you related to a Gianni Grande?"

Tara put her hands on her hips and frowned.

"Who's asking?"

Ryan snorted at her gruffness.

"I am. We're working together on an investment deal."

"Well, that'd be your first mistake—trusting my ex-
husband."

All the happy vibes from Ryan's important meeting drained
from his face.

"What do you mean, mistake? Is he a crook or something?"

Tara looked at her boss's son and realized he was being
earnest with her. She knew it was wrong to pass on her personal
judgement of Gianni and frighten Ryan.

"Aw, just kidding. He's quite a good lawyer."

Ryan didn't act convinced.

"What deal are you getting involved in with him?"

"This guy wants to open a recording studio for major artists
on top of Bluff Point. There were two guys involved initially, but

one of them was that singer who was supposed to perform at our wedding reception, Jeremiah Redfern."

Tara's eyes widened.

"Who's the other partner?"

"His name is Tom...."

"Not Russo!" Tara snorted. "That'd be your second mistake."

"Yeah, it *is* Tom Russo. Why? What's the matter with *him*?"

"Um, for starters he used to have a little dope delivery business on Keuka Lake back in the '80s."

"*Really?* How funny. Maybe he was polishing his entrepreneurial skills. Ha! Did he ever get arrested?"

Tara laughed. "Heck yeah! He even did a little bit of time in prison. Listen, if you want the scoop on him, speak with Marla. He's her brother-in-law. She'll be frank with you."

"Oh, she is? I didn't know that. Thanks for the tip. I'll have a chat with her. Say, your ex-husband's new wife seems to know a lot about the music industry."

Boom. Tara felt a jolt of seething anger clench her jaw. *Gianni didn't want me to have a career, but he lets this chickie do whatever she wants?* She unclenched her teeth and took a breath before responding.

"Looney? I mean, Luna? She does? That's weird. I thought she didn't have much free time, you know, being a hand model is such *demanding* work."

Ryan chuckled.

"I guess her father bought a lot of property in Brooklyn when he arrived in the U.S. from Sicily, including many properties in the Vinegar Hill area. He owned the property where Tom worked for another recording studio, Vinyl Buddha."

Tara scrunched her nose as she considered the implications of Ryan's words. What were the odds of Gianni's wife having a possible connection to Jeremiah Redfern and Vinegar Hill?

***

Chicken marsala bubbled in the oven filling the house with a savory sherry aroma. As they waited for dinner, Kelly unfurled the chart she drew of suspects in Jeremiah's murder across the dining room table. Maureen pored over the logical connections it showed. In the left hand vertical column, Kelly listed the current suspects. Across the top, in a horizontal line, she added names of key players to check off if the suspect knew them—Jeremiah, Angie, Jarod and Sarah. Also included on that top line were possible reasons for committing the murder—money, revenge, jealousy, and other. The suspects included Glenn, Angie, Ryan, Esperanza, Alejandro, Jarod, Andy Meyers and Other.

Tara leaned over the chart when she walked into the house after work.

"May I suggest you add a couple of names to the suspects, Kelly?"

"Sure. Who are they?"

"Tom Russo... plus Looney and Gianni."

"Huh? Why would *they* be possible suspects?"

"Well get this. I was talking with Ryan today and he told me he's thinking of investing in a new recording studio Tom wants to open in that mansion on Bluff Point. Guess who was there at the meeting they had today? Gianni and Luna!"

"What were they doing there?"

"Gianni is their lawyer for the deal. That's understandable. He's done work for plenty of celebrities and a few bands from

Buffalo that achieved nationwide success. Here's the part you'll find as fascinating as I did. Guess Luna's father is some bigwig landlord in New York City, especially the borough of Brooklyn. Ryan said his purchases include, and I quote, 'many properties in the Vinegar Hill area.' Kelly, what was the name of the studio where Vinegar Hill recorded in Brooklyn?"

"Vinyl Buddha. Why?"

"Yes, that's it! Her father owned that property, too."

Kelly pushed her chair back from the table, wood floor squeaking under the legs.

"Get out!" She covered her mouth with her hand.

"Didn't you tell me once that Luna's father is Sicilian?" Maureen asked. When Tara nodded, she hummed the theme song to *The Godfather*.

"Whoa, this is getting crazy twisted." Kelly traced her finger across the chart. "Did I tell you Gianni and Luna apparently know Glenn McCann, too?"

"Whaaaat? Tell me more," Tara said as she sat next to Kelly.

"When Glenn left my store after stopping in to pick up the pamphlet about noirelle grapes, Gianni called out to him as he was crossing the street. Luna was with him and as I watched from inside the store, it was apparent to me from their lively conversation that Glenn knew them both well."

"Why am I hearing this for the first time, Kelly?" Tara's eyes were wide, but Maureen's grew even wider.

"Ohmigod! The dinner that my client was talking about with the great wine, especially the one colored like a garnet gem—you don't suppose the winemaker that night was Glenn, do you?" As soon as the words slipped from Maureen's mouth, Kelly jumped from the table and dashed into her bedroom. Tara and Maureen looked at each other.

"What's with her? Is she upset you mentioned Glenn?"

"Don't know why she would be."

Kelly returned to the kitchen with an unlabeled bottle of wine in her hands.

"Feast your eyes on this evidence. It's is a bottle of Glenn's Garnet wine that he gave me after we tasted it on the evening when we went on a little picnic to see the heart of the lake."

"The heart of the lake, that's what my spa client Jada was talking about. Where is it, Kelly?"

"You can see it from the hills on the East Side, below the bluff." Kelly set the bottle on the table. "I have to say this is an amazing work of winemaking. He was so mysterious about it. I couldn't figure out what grape was used and he wouldn't say if it was a blend or one variety."

"Yes, I recall Jada saying they were closemouthed about the details of the wines and that they also couldn't figure out what grapes had been used."

Tara rubbed her brow. What was Gianni involved in now? Had her ex conspired with Glenn to have Jeremiah killed for some reason? He'd never do that. Would he? More likely, it was a mob hit ordered by Luna's father for some reason.

The three sisters examined Kelly's chart of the possible suspects and filled in the blanks, placing a dot where any positive connection could be made between a suspect and one of the key players or a reason for committing the crime. When they had gone through all of the names of the suspects, they sat back to take a look at the chart. It was covered with ink.

"So our murderer is somewhere under all those dots. We've got to connect them to one person."

The three sisters leaned their elbows on the table, chins held up by their palms.

A loud knock on the door startled them.

"Is the answer on the other side of that door? Dum dee dum-dum!" Maureen said in her best Joe Friday voice. "No need to rush to the door, girls. I'll answer it."

Tara glanced at her watch.

"Why would anyone be stopping by now?"

All eyes focused on the front door.

"Detective Kane, how nice to see you again. What can I do for you?"

"Good evening, Mrs. McCarthy." He looked past her toward the table where Tara and Kelly sat. He noticed Kelly immediately leaned forward to cover something on the table with her arms. *That's odd.* Tara sat back in the chair and folded her arms tightly across her chest. She was obviously unhappy to see him. Something was up here and he'd arrived at the perfect moment of surprise.

Kane was used to such things happening. While studying anthropology at Colgate, he became fascinated by symbolism and omens found in Native American culture. Many years ago at the Genundowa Festival in Hammondsport, a Seneca woman read his totem. She told him the presence of the cricket in it gave him a strong sense of intuition, good communication skills, the knowledge of when to get out of a dangerous situation and great focus. Right now he was counting on his cricket senses to learn as much as he could about the moment right in front of him.

How would he be able to get these women to "sing" out the details he needed?

"Mind if I come in and speak with you and your sisters?"

Maureen smiled broadly at him, turned toward them with wide eyes and clenched teeth as she waved in the detective. "C'mon in."

"Hi Tara, Kelly...." He walked right over to the table. Kane noted the label-less bottle of unopened wine and the lack of glasses on the table. "How is everyone tonight? Smells like something delicious is cooking for dinner. Don't worry, I won't take too much of your time." As they smiled weakly at him, he let his eyes glance at the table and saw the chart partly covered by Kelly's arms.

"Oh, I see someone's a fan of logic problems." He pointed at the chart.

Kelly's eyes brightened. "Yes I love them. These two prefer crosswords, which you think I would prefer too since I run a bookstore." As she spoke she gestured with her hands revealing more of the chart. Kane noticed some familiar names on the chart. What the heck were they doing?

"That's a big bottle of wine. Hope I didn't interrupt your happy hour."

"Not at all. Would you like a glass?" Tara asked. "Oh, like duh, you can't. You're on duty."

"Is it red or white wine? Looks homemade. Did you girls bottle it?"

"It's red wine. Nope, we wish we had those skills. Kelly's boyfriend gave it to her. It's from his vineyards." When her sister kicked her under the table, Tara yelped.

"It's a wine called Garnet made by my *friend*."

"Oh, you mean Glenn McCann?" Kane smiled wide enough to deepen his right dimple. It worked. Kelly frowned as she folded her arms and he was able to view the whole chart they were working on.

"Hmm, I see Glenn's name is on this chart." He scratched his chin. "What exactly is this for, ladies?"

Maureen sat back at the table and motioned for the detective to sit in the chair next to her. "You should thank us. We're trying to solve Jeremiah's murder case for you. It's fascinated us all so much."

"You're kidding me! Ha! Let me take a look at this and see if you have something I don't." The detective scanned the list of suspects. "You've got Angie, Tom, Jarod, et cetera. Not a bad start. Hmm, I even see your ex-husband, Tara. So this other box would be for names such as yours?" Kelly and Tara stared at each other. "Ha-ha... gotcha!" That made Maureen laugh. "I don't see Michael Connelly on this list, Tara." She winced.

Kelly pulled a slip of notepaper from underneath the chart.

"Here are some tips we've gotten from various sources. The night before the murder, Jarod and Jeremiah got into a big fight over Sarah at The Eggleston."

"That came from my school classmate." Tara pointed at the dot connecting Jeremiah and Jarod on the chart. "His friend witnessed it."

"Yep. We knew about it. Thanks."

Kelly continued.

"Friday night Angie was flirting with Jarod at the bar there. It was around happy hour and she was already trashed."

Kane nodded. Tara sat back and narrowed her eyes.

"Did you know Glenn has leased some old vineyards on the Hare Hollow property. I heard it directly from him."

Kane glanced from Tara to Kelly and noted she frowned slightly at her older sister.

"Yup. Brendan confirmed."

"OK, I have two tips for you, and one I know you won't know about."

Kane grinned widely at Maureen and Kelly noticed his charming dimples.

"Bring it at me." He gestured toward himself.

"First, I gave Esperanza's sister a massage the morning of the wedding. Maite told me that their father hired a wedding video company to fly a drone over the ceremony. Since the fireworks went off early, I bet it might have caught the flash from the gun."

Kane bit the corner of his lip slightly as he nodded.

"And your second tip is...."

"I watched the graveside service for Sarah from the glider bench out in front of the spa. A woman with curly red hair much like Angie's approached the grave after everyone left. She raised her middle finger toward the grave and yelled something."

"Did she walk or drive into the cemetery?"

"Drove. Some sort of sporty car, black."

Kane knew that description matched Angie's vehicle. He shifted the conversation swiftly so they wouldn't dwell on those two tips he didn't know.

"Would you ladies be able to explain why Luna Grande is on the list? I hope it's not because she married your ex-husband."

Tara tipped her head and sneered slightly before speaking. "Sorry, not that shallow. It's because Ryan O'Hare told me that her father owned property in Vinegar Hill, Brooklyn, including the building that housed Vinyl Buddha, where Tom Russo was an audio engineer."

"So Luna's father should be on this chart then, right? What's his name?" They shrugged at Kane. He jotted a few notes and sat back in his chair to process the new bits of information. They watched his expressions carefully, looking for the raise of an eyebrow or the slightest of smirks. He gave them nothing.

I'd never want to play poker against this guy, Maureen thought.

"Not bad work for amateurs." He winked at Kelly and she laughed. "By the way, do any of you ladies know a Monique Toussaint?"

"Why, should we?" Tara asked.

"Well she is connected to at least three of the suspects on your list."

"Are you going to tell us who, or do we have to guess? Because you *know* we will be able to wheedle it out of you." Kelly uncrossed her arms and grinned.

"She's a cleaning lady."

"Wait, Monique you said? I think I may know her." Tara and Kelly turned toward Maureen.

"How?"

"One of the cleaning ladies at the spa is named Monique. Is the woman you're thinking of black, from New Orleans?"

"Actually she's from Haiti," Kane corrected gently.

"Oh yes, that explains her accent."

"How is she regarded there?"

"I've never heard a negative word about her. She's always friendly and appears to be hardworking. Why?"

"So there have been no complaints about her taking anything that wasn't hers?"

Maureen shook her head. "I've never heard anything negative about her. Frankly, I'd be surprised if she ever committed a theft."

"Do you have a name of a supervisor I could question?"

"Absolutely, Thresa Byrne. She's the owner."

"Great. I knew you ladies could help me. Oh, Kelly, one more question. Have you ever been inside Glenn McCann's house?"

Maureen and Tara couldn't wait to hear this response. So far Kelly had dispensed precious few details about her two dates with Glenn.

Kelly shook her head.

"That means not yet," Tara laughed as she brushed the detective's arm playfully. He paused from writing in his notebook and glared at Tara. His intensity unnerved her and she bit her lower lip as she looked away.

"Where exactly have you gone on your dates with Mr. McCann?"

Kelly blushed. This seemed like too personal of a line of questions. Was this information of any real value to his investigation? His focus on her reaction unnerved her. It was like a border collie staring down a field full of wayward sheep. She sighed and spilled the details of the locations of her romantic interludes with Glenn McCann.

"He has property on Lower East Lake Road? Hmm. Do you know what the address is?"

"No. It's somewhere south of Bluff Point. The road turns into a dead end that you can't see from the main road because it's overcrowded with sumacs there. The property is right next to a small point. He's got one of those tiny houses on the land used as a cottage and it's next to a big old maple tree. There are two big faux eyes on the limbs where branches were removed years ago. If you were tripping on drugs, you'd probably think the tree was staring at you. He did tell me that he has another home at the lake, and I'd assume it's on the East Side. My guess is there might be vineyards on the property."

Kelly continued describing the interior of the cottage. Kane rubbed his chin as he processed what she discussed.

"OK. This has been a big help. Thanks very much for your time, ladies. I'll be in touch if I have any more questions. Now I know I gave one of these to Tara." He dealt out his business card to the others. "Kelly and Maureen, please, if you have any more tips, don't hesitate to call or email me. Your keen curiosity and observation skills could be a big help to solving this case."

"Listen, Detective," Tara smiled, "if you ever want to do a quality wine tasting, come and visit me at Hare Hollow sometime." Kane blushed and his dimples reappeared as he waved goodbye.

Maureen and Kelly shook their heads. *Really, Tara, you're flirting with this detective now?* A pang of jealousy stung Kelly. Detective Kane seemed truly a nice guy, lacking the emotional baggage Glenn lugged around. Oh well. What was still ahead with her relationship with Glenn? If he were vindicated in this crime, perhaps something serious could still develop between them. You never know, right?

Outside in the driveway Kane paused for several minutes in his parked car as he jotted notes about every new fact he gleaned from their conversation, and then started the engine.

"Man, those women are sharp. I ought to put them on the payroll."

CHAPTER TWENTY-SEVEN
Friday, June 27 ~ 2:50 p.m.

A woman with long chestnut hair wearing a floral mini-dress stepped out of her car, looked all around her to make sure no one was watching and walked from the driveway to the front door of Glenn's cottage on Lower East Lake Road. She slipped a tool out of her fringed suede purse and jimmied open the front door. The empty tapas takeout carton sat on the kitchen counter where Glenn had left it the other night. As soon as the woman saw the receipt for "The Piatta di Amore Assortment" sitting next to a wine cork, she upended the carton in a fit of fury.

"Bastard!"

She rushed down the short hallway and brushed away the long bangs covering her eyes with one hand so she could get a better view of the disturbed bed linens.

"How could you? Doesn't our relationship mean *anything*, Glenn?"

The woman grabbed a piece of paper sitting on the music stand in the hallway space and wrote something in big letters on it before racing out of the house sobbing. The paper drifted to the floor in the breeze following her wake.

***

Later that afternoon Glenn visited the indoor shooting range off the highway in Barrington and showed his membership

ID to the attendant. He paid the rental fee for a Beretta and headed for the farthest lane in the range. After putting on safety glasses, inserting some ear plugs and then covering them with ear muffs, he carefully removed the pistol from its bag, pointing it down the lane with his trigger finger alongside the outside of the gun. Glenn loaded the gun and set it on the counter facing away from him, then hit the button to his left that moved the paper target down the range lane from him.

Before he could pick up the handgun, Glenn heard someone shout his name. It was that young bartender, Jarod, from The Eggleston Inn.

"Hey man," Jarod called out as he approached him. "What's goin' on? Thought I saw your car out there. It's been a long time since you've been here."

"Hey brother." Glenn shook Jarod's hand as he patted his shoulder. "What's happenin'?"

"Been keeping sort of a low profile these days. Don't know if you heard about the accident involving my girlfriend, but she fell off my boat and drowned."

Glenn winced both in sympathy and at the odd manner in which Jarod mentioned it. "Yeah, I did. Very sorry for your loss, man. How are you doing? That had to be a nightmare." Glenn was curious as to why Jarod's face showed no hint of sorrow, his eyes squinting as if he'd just woken up. It was odd.

"Well, I haven't been charged with anything. Passed the Breathalyzer test, too. I was worried they'd charge me with manslaughter or something." He rubbed his nose with the back of his hand, grinned oddly and patted Glenn's shoulder. "Well, that's nothing you know anything about. Am I right?" Jarod pretended to shoot Glenn with "pistol hands" and winked as he stepped away laughing.

Is he implying something? What a weird kid.

Glenn gawked at Jarod; he'd paused mid-step to send a text message before going over to the first lane to begin his session. The door to the range opened and another man walked in. Glenn turned back to face his lane, but out of the corner of his eye noticed the guy approaching him wore a blue baseball cap with a mustang on it, baggy jeans and a Santana T-shirt. He stood tall with broad shoulders like a football player's. The man took the lane midway between the two men.

After firing a few rounds, Glenn glanced over his shoulder as the man in the middle lane prepared for his session. He recognized his face—it was that detective who questioned him yesterday. Glenn moved behind the lane divider and hoped the detective hadn't seen him.

As the paper target moved to the back of Detective Kane's lane, he donned a leather glove to hold the pistol. Glenn couldn't help but notice how tiny the weapon looked in his enormous hand. Jarod was distracted, shooting the heart of his target to shreds and didn't see the pink pearl-handled gun Kane aimed straight ahead. Both men noticed immediately, however, when Kane hit the center bullseye with a single shot, removed the spare ammunition from the gun and packed it up to leave.

"Whoa, dude, what's that you were firing?" Jarod asked.

"Just a gun I found floating in the lake." Kane stepped away from his lane and looked quickly from Jarod to Glenn to see if they had any reaction. And they did. The dimple returned with the detective's smile as he walked out of the range. He waved to the attendant on his way out.

"Thanks for the tip, 'cuz. I'll be back later to review your video."

Kane locked the decoy gun back in its case, got in his car and followed the narrow gravel drive from the parking lot down the hill. He made a left onto the highway, heading toward the area south of Bluff Point. After looking up the various branches of Lower East Lake Road on satellite maps online, he focused on three possible sites for the property where Glenn's cottage stood. The first turnoff was the closest to The Eggleston Inn and not far past the tip of Bluff Point. As soon as he turned down the narrow lane, he knew it wasn't the right location because there was little vegetation at the end of the road. Kelly specifically mentioned the overgrown sumac, so he backed up the road and continued to the next turnoff. That led to a flat area near a cove but it was lined with mobile homes. He turned around in a driveway and was startled when a slobbering fang-baring mastiff lunged at his car, its leash scraping against the car bumper.

"Holy crap! Why the heck would anyone need a dog that big," he yelped and sped away.

As he searched for the third site, Kane noticed an unmarked road out of the corner of his eye. The only clue for the turnoff was a wooden stake wrapped with yellow caution tape flapping in the breeze. Someone had jammed it into the ground right next to the road. A tractor trailer tailgated his car, forcing him to continue on, so Kane turned left at the next major intersection and made a U-turn. He didn't see the turnoff marker again until he passed it. Once more he turned around, but this time he drove a bit under the speed limit so he could see the yellow tape. He noticed it just in time and turned sharply, then followed the steep drive to its completion next to a dark dead end. Kane wrote down the mailbox number for the property to the left of Glenn's. After all of that effort, it was apparent that the tiny house below had no sign of activity so he headed back up the road with plans to return at a later time.

***

The weird, unexpected encounter with the detective at the shooting range unsettled Glenn. Had that little show been put on to intimidate him? Or was it to freak out Jarod? That kid looked like he was flying in the stratosphere from some sort of pharmaceuticals. Why was the detective firing a ladies' handgun? Did the detective still suspect him in Jeremiah's murder? He must. Why else would he do that? Glenn wanted to pack some things from both his lakeside cottage and his home in case they might be construed as incriminating evidence.

Yesterday he brought the notebook Jeremiah had stolen to the cottage. There, with the gnarled maple tree and Keuka Lake for his audience, Glenn sang all of those songs for the first time in years. He was so in the zone of creating and playing music he forgot to eat. After taking a long nap, he left for home to get something for dinner because the food leftover from his visit with Kelly spoiled and he threw it out. For some reason he left the container on the table. It wasn't until the middle of the night that Glenn woke up and freaked out slightly when he realized he'd left the notebook in the cottage lying on his bed.

As he approached the turnoff to his cottage, Glenn saw a car he didn't recognize waiting to pull out. He couldn't stop and wait there—the shoulder was too small for a car—so he continued on, planning to turn down the next entrance to the lake road and double back. However, when Glenn passed right by the car sitting at the turnoff, he recognized Detective Kane behind the wheel.

Glenn ducked low in his seat and hit the gas. *Damn! What's he doing there?* Had the detective been snooping around his cottage already? *Crap, what do I do?* Did the detective see him drive past and was he following him now? Glenn sat higher in the car seat and looked in the rearview mirror. Behind him was a minivan and a tractor trailer. He didn't want to take any chances. As soon as a left-hand turn came, Glenn took it and sped up the steep road until he hit the road parallel to the highway. From there he raced down the back roads to his home on Coyne Springs Road. Before making the turn into his driveway, Glenn checked the rearview mirror. All was clear. He parked the car at the far end of the driveway so any view of it from the road was partially blocked by the house.

Glenn sprinted into his house and packed a few things into a box—spare ammunition he'd brought home from the range, angry diaries written after Jeremiah's "Forever Gigi" raced up the pop charts, and a few letters Angie wrote him after the band broke up. He struggled with ideas of where to store them safely.

Sometimes it's better to hide things in plain sight.

For some reason, he thought about Kelly as he packed the box. She has a genuine kind heart. Perhaps he could persuade her to hide the box for him or even stash it in her bookstore. He could bring her another bottle of wine as a bribe, or another takeout of the bistro's tapas. She seemed to enjoy that.

He stashed the box in his car trunk and headed back toward the cottage. *Hopefully that detective should be gone from the area by now. I'll run in and grab the lyrics notebook.* Glenn pushed the key in the lock and the door handle opened without twisting it. Had he left the studio unlocked? Or, did that detective break in? He held his breath as he walked toward the bedroom. Phew! The notebook was still there. When he grabbed it into his arms, he saw a piece of legal paper lying on the floor. Glenn figured it was a random sheet of old lyrics. He flipped it over. Written in large letters with a felt marker was the message: *"Don't ever cross me. Keep your eyes on the skies, lover boy."*

His thoughts turned immediately to Angie. She used that phrase "Don't ever cross me" often. What was she referencing though? And wait a minute, if Angie did break in here, why didn't she take the notebook? Or, was this something from Tom Russo? Maybe he'd found out about the fling he'd had with Angie back when they recorded at Bluff Point. It was obvious to him that Tom long carried feelings for Angie. Damn, he didn't have time for yet another mystery. After he made sure the cottage door was locked, Glenn ran back to the car, opened the trunk and set the notebook in the box. He sped away toward Hammondsport, glancing nervously in the rear view mirror to see if that detective's car was pursuing him. Had he only tilted the mirror toward the sky, he would have seen a drone following his every turn.

Kelly was still in the shop when he parked across the street. Glenn was so nervous that she might notice him, he got out of the car swiftly and forgot to lock it. He crossed the street farther down, and made his way into his favorite bistro.

When she heard the bells on the bookstore's front door ring Kelly was shocked to see Glenn there with a box in his arms.

"The clock in the bistro said it was wine o'clock when I left. I'd say your store hours are over for today and you need some refreshment from Bacchus accompanied with tapas."

She laughed and shook her head.

"You are one persistent tapas pusher."

"Guilty as charged." Glenn set the bag of takeout cartons from the restaurant on the counter and bent down to set the box on the floor before taking out the bottle of Topaz.

"Since I'm waving a flag of truce today, thought I should accompany it with some of my white wine. I think you'll appreciate its complexity."

"Nice. You do know my weaknesses."

"Such as honey-fried oysters?" He lifted an eyebrow playfully.

Zing! Kelly felt that electric attraction again when his cobalt blue eyes locked on hers, followed by the familiar twist in the pit of her stomach.

"Babe, do you have any glasses or a corkscrew. I forgot to pack them."

"I have a couple of extra classy coffee mugs in the break room. And there may even be a corkscrew in there. I'll go check."

"Please, nothing but the classiest mugs for my wine." Glenn laughed.

As soon as Kelly was out of sight, Glenn slid the box filled with items he wanted to hide into the storage closet right behind the counter. He closed the door but didn't realize the box hadn't been pushed in far enough. That left the door slightly ajar. He spread out a couple of napkins and opened the takeout containers. The bistro included only one plate and fork. That was fine with him. It provided an opportunity to share the repast more intimately and he was feeling suddenly turned on by what they could find for dessert in the back room.

"Found it!" Kelly returned cheerfully with two rinsed mugs. Glenn took the corkscrew from her hand but did not pull away immediately when his fingers touched hers. Kelly took a soft breath and bit her lower lip slightly as she waited for him to pull the cork out of the bottle. *She's as turned on as I am.* He tugged it out teasingly, never losing eye contact with her. The cork made a juicy pop. He tipped the bottle toward the coffee mugs and filled them halfway. Together they sloshed the wine in their mugs to aerate it. She sipped a little.

If honey-gold October sunlight could be bottled, this must be what it tastes like. It's a bouquet of floral and peach on the nose, fruit forward in the mouth, a velvety luscious mouth feel. She tipped her head back, exposing the curve of her long neck.

"Ahhhh, that's so good."

He picked up a crisp warm oyster, held it to her mouth to nibble, and once she'd swallowed it followed by a good sip of wine, he set his wineglass down to offer her a ganache drenched strawberry. She took a bite and he popped the rest of it into his own mouth.

"You're so beautiful," he purred as he cupped her face with his long, elegant fingers and kissed Kelly with an ardor she didn't expect. He stroked the long curls of her hair, leaned close to her ear and whispered that with her permission, he'd love a tour of the office.

The old Kelly would have giggled nervously at Glenn as if he was joking. Not this Kelly. After locking the front door, she followed Glenn eagerly as he led with his arm around her waist toward the back room.

Outside on Shethar Street, car tires skidded to a stop right in front of the bookstore. Three loud pops exploded with the simultaneous crashing cymbal-like sound of bullets breaking the front window into smithereens. Glenn knocked Kelly onto the floor to protect her. The car screeched away.

Detective Kane was in the midst of a property records search for Glenn's lakeside studio when the 911 call came into headquarters about a drive-by shooting in Hammondsport. Detective Hughes looked up from his desk.

"Isn't that the address of Kelly Caviston's bookstore?"

Kane scratched his forehead as he waited for the dispatcher to repeat the address.

"Damn. I was making some progress on this case, too." Kane looked back at his computer as the deed for Glenn's lakeside property came on his screen. He'd purchased it through Casa Bella Realty. He clicked on the link, then the website's About page. "Hmm. Mack, have you heard anyone in this investigation mention an Ignazio Fracasetti?"

He shook his head. "That's a new one. Should I add him to the list?"

Kane sighed. They had plenty of suspects and motives in Jeremiah's murder case. What they lacked was one clear lead. He grabbed his car keys. "Let's go!"

A couple of deputies and Detective Reese Bailey from the sheriff's department were already on the scene when they arrived, photographing the bookstore inside and out, interviewing witnesses for a car description, looking for the bullet casings on the street and examining the tire skids out front. Kane called back to headquarters.

"Be advised, witnesses to the shooting said they saw an older model, two-door white sedan with out of state plates— possibly Michigan or Minnesota they said, the vehicle moved fast away from the scene. Appeared to be two suspects in the vehicle, both male. Driver looked to be in his twenties. Shooter was about the same age wearing a strawberry pink long wig. Last seen heading toward West Lake Road. This could possibly be related to the murder investigation since a bandmate of that victim was at the bookstore at the time of the shooting."

Kelly shivered in Glenn's arms as they were questioned by Hughes near the back of the store. Kane stood inside the front door and surveyed the entire scene as the all-points bulletin went out on the radio. He was listening to the response chatter about possible sightings of the vehicle, while at the same time looked around for anything that might seem out of place inside the store. Obviously there was glass all over the floor by the front window. He noticed a light on in the back office. Since the incident was at closing time, why had anyone been in there? Even from across the store he could see the open bottle of wine and a corner of a takeout food container.

Hmm, perhaps Kelly and Glenn's relationship has progressed further than I realized. He folded his arms and sighed quietly. *They seem like a mismatch. Kelly has an innocent air about her and doesn't give off the typical groupie vibe. She seems too classy for that. Glenn's real slick though, and somehow he's convinced this intelligent woman to trust him. Maybe she's just lonely?*

His eyes continued scanning the room in a counterclockwise direction. It was then he noticed the closet door behind the cash register was slightly ajar. He'd never even noticed that door on his previous shopping visits there. Just a couple of months ago he'd been in the store browsing and found a great book on Seneca mythology. Kelly wouldn't remember him though because he paid cash for it and since it was his day off he was wearing jeans, a wool cap and winter coat.

"All cars on patrol, please be advised. Caller reports a white sedan, matching the description of the vehicle being sought in the Hammondsport incident, just drove across her field," the dispatcher said on Kane's radio. *"Caller lives in Urbana above Hare Hollow Vineyards. Says there's a dirt road at the end of her property, and the vehicle was likely taking a shortcut to reach it. The road leads directly into the state forestland."*

Kane raised his eyebrow. The fleeing suspects must be familiar with that area. This could definitely be linked to the murder. Hughes was busy interviewing Glenn and Kelly, so Kane quietly opened the closet door. Office supplies lined the shelves. As he reached to pull the string to turn on the light inside, his foot kicked something.

"Well, what have we here?" he whispered as he knelt and opened the box containing everything Glenn had tried to hide from the police. As soon as he saw the tooled leather notebook and opened it to find song lyrics, he suspected it was the one Angie reported missing from her home. Kane stood and turned off the closet light, pushing the box forward with his shoe so he could close the door without making a sound. Hughes was still interviewing the others, so he walked over to chat.

"Kelly, I doubt anyone would have any reason to shoot at someone as lovely as you. Glenn, however, I'd be a bit concerned. One of your bandmates has already been killed. Now there's been an apparent attempt on your life."

Even though he said that, he knew the shooting was probably meant as a warning. From the shards remaining in the window frame and the graze on the ceiling, he suspected the gunman aimed high intentionally.

"Any idea who might want to harm you? Any problems with the other two bandmates? Anything you're trying to hide?" As the detective asked the last question, he looked over his shoulder toward the closet where the box was hidden. Glenn's palms began to sweat as he thought about what the detective would suspect if he found the box. He detested this man who seemed hell-bent on linking him to Jeremiah's murder.

"Of course not. I'm as clueless as you are about this." Glenn knew saying he was "clueless" would irk the detective. He was right. Kane walked to the front door and gestured to Detective Bailey outside.

"Take these two into your car and stay with them," Kane barked. His tone surprised everyone. Was he angry at them about something? "Mack and I will finish gathering the evidence here." His face softened as he turned toward Kelly.

"You'll want to call someone as soon as possible to come down here and board up this window. Teddy Toner has a glass repair shop outside of Bath. I know he does great work."

She stared ahead blankly as her fingers traced the elbows of her folded arms. "Thanks for the recommendation."

"We'll take you to headquarters in a little while to discuss further what happened here." As soon as Bailey walked outside with Glenn and Kelly, Kane brought Hughes over to the closet, opened the door and pointed at the box on the floor.

"Take a peek inside."

When Hughes lifted the box flap and saw the tooled leather notebook he looked up immediately at Kane.

"Is this the one that Angie reported missing? You don't think Kelly stole...."

"Of course not. I've never even noticed this closet door here before. It's never open. Today it was ajar. And look at the back office from here. See the little seduction tableau?"

Detective Hughes snorted. "Oh, yeah. All that's missing is candlelight. But why here? Why wouldn't he take her back to that tiny cottage on the lake or even his home?"

"My guess is he needed to dump the contents of this box fast. Who would suspect a box of stolen goods would be stashed in Kelly Caviston's friendly little bookstore?"

"I don't get what she sees in that guy. He's got to be about twenty years older. She doesn't strike me as a gold-digger."

Kane bit his lip as his eyes drifted to the office.

"Of course not. Maybe it's his fame that's the attraction, but that feels out of character for her."

"You know what a guy once said to my sister? Never stand too close to a band at a concert. You'll fall for any guy on stage, no matter how ugly he is."

"Ha! So it's that old bad boy musician mystique?"

"Probably." Hughes crossed the room and snooped around the office. He sniffed the bottle of wine and opened the tapas takeout box.

"Well looky here... he brought her oysters. Ha!"

Detective Kane wanted to laugh, but he felt sick. This smooth rock star was setting up Kelly for seduction, when actually Glenn was trying to use her to dump incriminating evidence against himself here. Kane took out a pair of latex gloves from his jacket and slipped them on. Hughes came back over and photographed each step as his boss removed the contents of the box. As soon as they saw the ammunition they looked at each other.

"Same caliber bullets as the ones found in the murder weapon. Not sure if they're the same make."

"Should we take this into headquarters?"

"You know what, let me return these items into the box. I'd like you to go and fetch Kelly from the car so we can see her reaction to what he did here. If she acts as shocked as I suspect, then maybe she will share any other bits of damning evidence that she's been holding back because she's interested in the guy. And while you're at it, have Bailey go ahead and take Mr. McCann into headquarters."

"Sounds like a plan, chief. I'll be back in a few."

He didn't really want to, but Kane wandered back into the office and examined the seduction scenario Glenn created. He lifted up a fig drenched in balsamic vinegar and sniffed it. Kane cringed and set it down. His hands curled into fists at his sides as his right eye twitched. A warm flush spread up his neck to his cheeks. The pain in his right shoulder returned and as he rubbed it, Kane noticed what looked like old family photos on the wall. One was a black-and-white photo of a couple standing on a dock and by the clothes they wore, he guessed it was taken in the '40s. He figured they were Kelly's parents, and he smiled softly when he saw her father held a tenor saxophone in his left hand. His own father played the drums. Music was in their genetics. The way Kelly's father looked adoringly at her mother brought a sense of sadness to Kane. That generation seemed to have better luck finding decent partners. He hadn't met a woman in a couple years he would seriously consider dating.

Truth is, last time he was in this store buying the book of Seneca mythology... he actually went in the store because he thought Kelly was so pretty. In their brief, pleasant conversation, she spoke like an intellectual. Kane suspected that if he told her he was a cop she wouldn't be interested. If they'd met under different circumstances, and he told her he was an anthropology major in college, he might have had a chance.

Kane realized he was readying her for a fall of sorts, that is, realizing what a cad this Glenn McCann was. He felt bad she'd find out this way, but he also needed to cross her off his suspect list for good. Would Kelly hate him if she found her name on that list?

Detective Hughes and Kelly returned to find Kane sitting behind the counter reading a rare book he pulled from the shelves about the Iroquois Confederacy. Kelly laughed.

"Hey. You read it, you buy it," she teased.

"I may just do that. I'm especially interested in the Senecas." He smiled genuinely at her, and noticed she was much more at ease than the last time he saw her. *God, she's beautiful.*

"You wanted to speak with me about something?"

He gestured for the two of them to come over by the closet.

"Kelly, would you please tell us what you store in here."

She looked at the two detectives' faces and scratched her head.

"Uh, supplies I can't fit in the office out back. Register tape. Scissors. Bags. Wrapping paper and bows. Scotch tape. Why?"

"Would you please show us?"

Kelly was afraid to open the door. *Is there a body in there? Did the shooter leave something threatening inside?* She did as he asked, opening the door and pulling the cord to the light.

"See, office supplies."

"What's in the box on the floor?" Hughes asked.

Kelly's surprised look gave Kane the first confirmation it was indeed Glenn who left the box there. She did something Kane hadn't done though. She looked for a label on the box, and when she rotated, they were all surprised to Glenn McCann's home address printed on it.

"What the heck is this?" she asked as she knelt and lifted the flaps. "I never saw this here before."

"Allow me." Kane slipped on the latex gloves and reopened the box. He pulled out the items, let her gaze at each one, and then set the item on the counter.

"Could you open that?" Kelly asked when Kane lifted the leather-bound notebook. "Those look like song lyrics." Kane flipped briefly through the pages for her and a sheet that had been folded in half fell to the floor. He set down the notebook and bent to pick up the piece of paper. When he opened it, Kelly gasped.

"Ohmigod! Those are the lyrics Jeremiah must have stolen for his hit song 'Forever Gigi.' He changed the title from 'For Gigi My Ever Love,' apparently. But look! These are practically the exact lyrics Glenn wrote. Do you know what this is? It's evidence that would have won Glenn back the rights and royalties to that song. This is huge!"

Kane watched every facial clue that came across Kelly's mouth and eyes. *Yes, she was being sincere about this. And no, she obviously did not have anything to do with the theft of these or Jeremiah's death.* Should he proceed to show her the rest of the contents of the box? His own attraction toward Kelly complicated the moment. *Is it selfish to dash her feelings toward Glenn?* His police sense took over and canceled those thoughts. *No. This is right. She needs to know the truth about him. There might be the slightest thing she saw or overheard that could help me break this case.*

Next Kane removed the diaries Glenn wrote after the band's breakup. He happened to flip open one to a page where the words "I could KILL Jeremiah for what he's done to me" were printed and retraced with heavy pressure.

"Whoa, that's intense. You have to realize how betrayed he was feeling at the moment though, right Detective Kane?" When Kelly looked into his eyes, he noticed for the first time they were the same peridot green as the clear shoreline waters of Keuka Lake. He also noticed the faint freckles that dotted the bridge of her nose. And when she smiled, he felt a brief urge to kiss her delicate lips.

"This doesn't prove he killed Jeremiah, right?" Kelly's eyes now reflected her concern.

"I agree, Kelly. They enhance his possible motive. That is all. But... why are these here?" He removed the rest of the items in the box to expose the box of bullets. Kelly touched her throat as she caught her breath, then covered her mouth with her hands.

"What? He owns a gun? Are these the same type that...?"

She looked at the detective for a clue as to what this discovery meant, but he never changed his expression.

"Ohmigod! What an idiot I've been! How could I have trusted him? What if he planned to shoot me? Whoa, I'm a bit dizzy. Let me sit."

Hughes brought over a chair from the back office. Kelly sat and buried her face in her hands, shaking visibly. The two detectives raised their eyebrows and backed away slightly. Once she regained composure, her hands slid to her sides, but soon she became angry when she realized what Glenn had done. A few hours earlier she had restocked the paper bags in that closet. The box was not there. That meant he must have brought it with him to dump there so he would not be caught.

"Wait, I remember. When he walked in this afternoon he *was* carrying a box. But he took the wine and food out of it. I didn't notice anything else in it. So he brought that stuff as a ruse...." Her words trailed off as she looked back at the office. *What would have occurred there if the shooting hadn't happened?* She shivered.

"Men are such *jerks!*" Her words stung. Detective Kane cleared the emotion caught in the back of his throat. "Not all of us are," he said softly and left her alone.

Kelly shut her eyes tight, scowling as her thoughts slipped into a daydream. She was at Finian's Pub and the bartender came over with a tall drink adorned with a strawberry in his hand. *This is from the fella over there.* She turned and saw Glenn sitting in a booth, waving. Only it wasn't the current Glenn. It was the rock star Glenn from that night decades ago in Rochester. She lifted the glass to her mouth, and noticed a few pieces of glitter stuck to the condensation on the glass. Glenn stared seductively at her, as he had in the moment in his cottage bedroom. Kelly took a deep sip and instantly coughed and spit out the liquid: it was pure *vinegar*. All she could hear was the coarse laughter of Glenn and the bartender. She opened her eyes with an expression reflecting inner pain conjured by the daydream.

Kane could not read Kelly's emotions at this moment. *Was she now mad at him? Damn, maybe he'd gone too far with this stunt. Or, was she understandably furious about what Glenn had done today?*

"We don't need to question you anymore. Would you like Detective Hughes to follow you home, Kelly?"

"Please."

"Listen, why don't I call Teddy and have him come over right now to cover the broken windows for you. That way you won't have to worry about all of this. OK?"

Kelly nodded. "Thank you."

His heart panged at witnessing how broken up she was about this news. If his instincts were right, though, he knew she was resilient and would heal from this betrayal. Would her heart remain hardened though?

CHAPTER TWENTY-EIGHT
Friday, June 27 ~ 7:00 p.m.

The team finished processing the crime scene as Teddy Toner arrived with tools to board up the bookstore's windows.

"What a mess." Teddy hung his thumbs on his tool belt as he inspected the jagged edges of glass poking out of the large window frames. "I'll get this covered for now and can get the replacement in by Monday or Tuesday."

"Thanks, bud." Kane joined him as they stared at the mess. "Those two were lucky not to be hit by flying glass."

"You're not kiddin'. Where do I send the bill, Ty? This address?"

"Yes. The owner's name is Kelly Caviston. The poor woman, she's pretty traumatized by all of this."

"Join the club. Stuff like this never happens here."

Kane patted Teddy's back as he headed off to the cruiser where Hughes was putting the evidence in the trunk. One deputy remained to keep watch on the scene until the business could be secured for the night.

Kane fastened his seatbelt amid more chatter over the radio. The shooters abandoned the stolen vehicle in the state forest. Bullet casings matching the evidence at the bookstore were discovered in the back seat. A K9 unit arrived and began searching the woods. The dispatcher mentioned a family from

Michigan who were renting a cottage in Pulteney reported their car was stolen. The plates on the abandoned car matched their vehicle.

"The average tourist wouldn't know about that side entrance into the forest. Sounds like there's definitely a local connection to this, Mack."

"I agree. No one breezing through would be familiar with all those back roads. You'd have to be pretty lucky to discover a state forest on your getaway."

Back at headquarters, Glenn glowered because he was being detained without being charged for anything. Detective Bailey had been put in charge of staying with him. He could sense the rising tension in Glenn and wondered if it meant they had the murderer of Jeremiah Redfern.

"How much longer do I have to stay here?" Glenn tapped his fingers on the arms of his chair.

"Not sure, but Detective Kane wanted you to hang on until he got back from the scene. He has a few questions for you."

"About what?"

"Well I would imagine it would be if there was anyone you know of who would be mad enough to try to kill you today."

Glenn looked visibly relieved this would be the line of questioning. He tapped his foot nervously on the floor. Bailey's radio came alive with the sound of dogs barking excitedly. One of the deputies giving chase to the suspects called in.

"We followed the suspects' trail to a creek in the woods. It goes cold right there. We've been up and down this path and the scent is nowhere else. Wonder if they had a canoe or something waiting here for a getaway. Should we remain on the scene?"

The front door opened and Detective Hughes walked in. He waved at the deputy behind the desk and joined Bailey and Glenn.

"Let's go into this room for a brief chat." He opened the door next to Glenn and flicked on the light.

"So where's Detective Kane?"

"I'm coming, you guys. Hold on a second." Kane asked the deputy behind the desk to turn on the video camera in the interrogation room. A few moments later he walked in the room carrying the box Glenn stashed in the bookstore closet and set it on the floor.

All of the color drained from Glenn's face as Kane sat across from him.

"Thanks for your patience, Mr. McCann. Sorry to keep you waiting so long. The bookstore was a real mess. So anything I can get you to drink before we begin? Water? A cup of coffee? Sorry, but we left your bottle of wine back at the bookstore."

Glenn's face reddened and he shook his head.

"Let's get started. This afternoon you stopped in at The Deckled Edge to visit the owner, Kelly Caviston. Is that correct?"

"Yes."

"Describe your relationship with Miss Caviston for us."

Hughes curled the edge of his mouth slightly as he watched his boss. If as he suspected, Kane was attracted to Kelly, this confirmed it. This was a question that didn't need to be asked.

"Why do you need to know?" Glenn asked, his foot tapping the floor again.

"We're trying to set up the background of your visit and see if there could be any possible reasons that contributed to someone shooting out the store's windows. It's routine questioning, Mr. McCann."

Glenn shrugged. "We're friends, that's all."

"Thanks. Now what time did you arrive at the store?"

"It was a few minutes before five o'clock."

"And did you know the store closed at that time?"

"Yes."

"What was the purpose of your visit?"

"I wanted to have a chat with her. It's easier when there are no customers in the store, you know."

"So were you there to shoot the breeze or did you bring her anything?"

Glenn knew this line of questioning was leading directly to the box. It would be brought up inevitably. How could he get around the fact that he planned to hide his stuff there?

"No, I brought her a bottle of my wine and some takeout from the bistro down the street. I know she likes their food."

"So were you planning a picnic in the bookstore?"

"Nah, maybe just a little *happy* hour." The innuendo behind Glenn's smile irked Kane. He wanted to punch him.

Kane turned to his side and lifted the box from the floor, setting it on the table so the side with the address label would be facing Glenn.

"Recognize this box, Mr. McCann?"

"Yes. It's what I carried the wine and food in when I arrived at the bookstore."

"Were you aware this box was not empty?"

"Yes. There are some of my personal belongings in there."

"Why did you bother to bring them in the store?"

Glenn had to think quickly. "I'd stopped home and picked these up to bring to my studio on the lake. I was heading there after meeting with Kelly."

"Why not leave them in the trunk of your car?"

Glenn folded his hands on his lap, turned his head and sneered at Kane. "Well, you know, things get stolen from me with regular frequency."

Kane set his right elbow on the table and curled his hand under his chin as he leaned toward Glenn. "Tell me, I know you're in your late-sixties, but was the takeout food container that large you couldn't hold it in one hand and the wine bottle in the other? Plus, weren't you afraid of spilling food from the takeout container on the contents of the box?"

Glenn looked down at the table. What should he say?

"Funny thing is," Kane paused as he slipped on the latex gloves and pulled the leather bound notebook out of the box, "this looks exactly like what Angie Redfern said was stolen from the music studio in her house after her husband's death."

Glenn leapt out of his seat and pointed a finger at the notebook.

"Well, that bastard husband of hers stole it from me years ago! He got a hit song from my lyrics in that book and I have never been given credit or received royalties for their usage."

Now that he had fully riled Glenn, Kane decided not to press him on how he got the notebook back. Instead he pulled out the box of bullets.

"You know what else is funny, this is the same caliber of bullet that was used to kill your former bandmate, who you just accused of being a thief."

"I DID NOT KILL HIM! The *reason* I was hiding the box in Kelly's store was that I thought these items might be used to frame me for a murder I *didn't* commit. DAMMIT!" Glenn collapsed back into his chair. "I'm so SICK of being punished for making the mistake years ago of recording music with Jeremiah Redfern. I'm telling you the ABSOLUTE truth. I DID NOT KILL HIM!" Glenn covered his face with his open palms and groaned angrily.

Kane gestured toward Hughes and he took the box of evidence out of the room. He pointed at Bailey, then the door. The detective understood and left the room.

Once Glenn regained his composure, Kane patted his shoulder.

"Listen, Mr. McCann, you may not believe this but I don't believe you killed Jeremiah Redfern."

Glenn slunk back in his chair and exhaled deeply.

"I do think the murderer is an acquaintance of yours and is possibly the same person behind the shooting this afternoon. I'll have Detective Bailey drive you back to your car now and you're free to go home. Please, for your own safety, let me know if you receive any threats, hear anything that might lead us to the killer or remember any details that you want to share with us. Especially if you can think of anyone who might be carrying a grudge against you." He slid his business card across the table.

"Thank you." Glenn's face remained stony and solemn as he took the card.

Glenn inhaled the breeze off the lake deeply once he stepped outside the detective's car and headed for his own. He could not wait to get back home and pour a full glass of Irish whiskey. His mind was a-whir with racing thoughts, and maybe that's why he did not seem to notice the car was unlocked. As he pulled the seat belt over to fasten it and start the car, his eyes caught something glimmering from the floor of the passenger seat.

"Is that my phone? What the...?"

Glenn unbuckled so he could lean over and pick up the oblong object with his trembling hand. It was indeed his cellphone. Had it always been there? After dropping on the floor did it slide under the seat a few weeks ago, and then it reappeared earlier today—propelled forward perhaps when he braked the car coming down his steep hill? Glenn wiped the dirt off, slid it into his jeans pocket and noticed the passenger side door was unlocked. Was this evidence planted while he was at headquarters in an effort to convict him? He glanced in the back seat to make sure no one was there. Kane had asked for a call if anything unusual happened. He'd told Glenn he didn't think he was the murderer. Was it better to leave things alone, or should he go back into the station? Or was that what Detective Kane wanted?

Glenn re-buckled the seat belt and pulled away from the curb. He knew there must be other evidence Detective Kane had for solving this case. This phone wasn't necessary, right? However, Glenn did plan to review the call records on the phone once he got home.

***

Kane picked up the pizza he'd ordered and a six pack of porter on his way home from work. He owned a small Cape Cod house situated in a tree-lined neighborhood about eight miles away in Bath. Kane tossed his keys on the small stand in the foyer and walked past four small landscapes he'd painted that adorned the walls of the living room. They were some of his favorite views throughout the county.

His eyes happened to focus next on the photo of his parents hung on the kitchen wall. The photo was taken before his father left to join U.S. Army troops fighting the enemy in the Pacific during World War II. It immediately reminded him of that photo of Kelly's parents in the bookstore.

Kane pulled the cap off a bottle of porter and pulled out a slice of the fried Spam and pineapple pizza he got from Moretti's. It was something he suggested once after a trip to Hawaii, and the owner eventually put it on the menu. Kane didn't bother to sit or grab a napkin—he ate standing next to the kitchen counter.

"Mmm, tasty Spam," he murmured between bites.

His thoughts drifted back to Hammondsport, wandering through Kelly's bookstore looking for evidence. This case had been a surreal experience for him. He'd grown up to Vinegar Hill's music and when he was a kid he aspired to be a rock star like Jeremiah. That was the year his parents bought him a Stratocaster electric guitar for Christmas. It was the exact same color as Jeremiah's. Kane loved jamming on the guitar, and was even in a rock band for a few years in high school, but the demands of playing football soon made him quit and eventually stop playing music altogether.

After eating a couple slices of pizza, Kane opened another porter. He went into the den and passed by that old guitar. He grinned, picked up the Strat and slung the vintage '70s woven strap around his neck. An old pick was still tucked in by the tuning pegs. He slipped it out, fingered a D7 chord and began strumming. The metal strings pressed sharply into his fingertips. It felt like knives cutting him when he tried sliding that chord formation up the fretboard. Kane hammered the notes for a climbing D scale across all six strings. Even without amplification, his playing sounded lame. There was little life in the old strings and they desperately needed to be tuned. He sighed and set the guitar back into its stand.

Though he'd stopped playing music, Kane still enjoyed singing. His coworkers bought him a karaoke machine as a surprise for Christmas a few years ago, and it was plugged in next to the couch by the opposite wall. He flicked it on and inserted a Vinegar Hill album from the pile of CDs he'd been listening to lately. The neighbors' house was about thirty feet away, so he cranked the air conditioner to create muffling background noise before he picked up the microphone and began harmonizing with Jeremiah and the band.

Man, this music still sounds great. He shuffled through each song on the album. For some reason Glenn McCann's lyrics brought to mind the life of a professional musician. *How tough it must be waking up in a different city every morning and spending so much time away from your family.*

Though his parents were both deceased, Kane had a sister in Branchport and a brother in Binghamton, so at least it was easy enough to get together with them. They didn't do that often, though. His siblings both had families—their children were now having children. He loved being an uncle to his nieces and nephews, but somedays he ached for the family of his own he never got to have.

Oh, he was close once. There was a serious girlfriend to whom he nearly proposed, but before he got the chance she moved west suddenly some twenty-four years ago and never told him why. Surprisingly, Kane wasn't bitter after that loss, but he was wary of getting too involved with someone unless he felt sure about the relationship. From time to time, he'd wonder what their married life might have been like. Where was she now? Did she ever think of him?

He picked out another disc of music and popped it in. This was *Karaoke King's Mega Hits of the '80s* and the first song on it was Jeremiah Redfern's "Forever Gigi."

"God, what are the odds." Kane shook his head and laughed, then he picked up the microphone and sang.

"We're just starting out, babe,

"But you know when it's real.

"I want you to be my forever, Gigi.

"I haven't a doubt,

"Our love's a big deal.

"Please be my forever, Gigi.

"When I looked into those green eyes, and

"Really saw you that first time...."

His jaw slackened—all he could think of was Kelly Caviston. Kane's voice cracked and he dropped the microphone. He flicked off the karaoke machine, wandered back into the kitchen and opened another bottle of porter.

"Man, my life sucks." He sunk himself onto a kitchen stool and rubbed his aching shoulder.

***

The Caviston sisters spoke in low voices on the deck. Their neighbors weren't too close by, but after what happened earlier that day at Kelly's bookstore they were all feeling a bit paranoid.

"You need to wait until at least Monday to reopen." Maureen patted Kelly's arm gently.

"But will that make whoever shot at us feel like they won?"

"Who cares? You need at least a few days to relax, Kelly. Do you need some more wine?"

Without hesitation Kelly held out her glass.

"Do you have a good security camera in the store?" Tara asked.

"Phhbbt! I have decent locks on the doors. Never felt the need for more than that because the store is so small. And it's in cozy little Hammondsport, for God's sake!"

"The person must have been after Glenn. If I were you, I'd have no further contact with that man." Maureen's motherly tone did not offend Kelly.

"Oh, you don't have to worry. He's *dead* to me."

Tara laughed. "You sound like some of Gianni's relatives." They laughed until they noticed the sudden change in Kelly's expression.

"My God, I could have been killed or maimed today. What the hell's going on with the world?" She rubbed her arms as if she were chilled. Actually, she was but it had nothing to do with the temperature. It had everything to do with the realization of how Glenn had used her.

Tara saw a red light out of the corner of her eye, turned and squinted toward the treetops to see it better. There were four lights total and whatever it was in the sky was stationary. *Obviously not a jet.*

"Turn around you guys. What's that above the trees over there? A helicopter?" The other sisters looked behind them at the red lights hovering over their neighbor's property.

"Listen." Maureen shushed them. "Do you hear a noise?"

"Weird! That sounds like the whirring I heard the night Sarah drowned, before there was a big splash in the lake."

"Really, Kelly? What do you suppose it is?"

"You heard a splash? Ha! Wonder if it was another pot drop for Tom Russo."

The object moved closer to their house.

"Is that thing coming at us?" Tara grabbed the bottle of wine.

"Ohmigod! I bet it's one of those drone cameras and someone is spying on us. Run inside!"

They grabbed their glasses and the snacks as the drone lowered toward the Caviston home.

"Draw the curtains!" Maureen told Tara once she made it through the sliding glass doors. They cowered against a wall in the dining room away from the windows.

"Duck! It's by the window over the sink!" Kelly yelled.

The sisters scrambled onto the floor and crawled behind the kitchen counter. "Anyone have a cellphone?" Kelly asked as she took out Detective Kane's business card from her purse. Tara pulled hers from her jeans pocket and handed it to Kelly. She dialed his number as fast as she could, but it went right to his voicemail.

"So much for 'Call me anytime.'" Kelly sighed she waited for the beep to leave a message.

Miles away in a pizza-induced dream, Kane meandered through the deep woods with a flashlight. He'd borrowed a K9 unit German shepherd and they were searching the state forest for clues on the disappearance of his ex-girlfriend. The smell of wood smoke led them to a clearing where a Spam pizza cooked on a griddle over a bonfire. A pitcher of strawberry daiquiris and a Strat were left on a red wool picnic blanket. *Hmm, someone's been here recently.*

CHAPTER TWENTY-NINE

Saturday, June 28 ~ 9:12 a.m.

He tossed his flowing hair back and strummed the concert's final fierce chord. The frenzied crowd screamed for more until a sudden, high-pitched yip from the dachshund next door pulled Kane off stage. He opened a sleepy eye toward the alarm clock.

"You've gotta be kiddin' me. I haven't slept this long in forever." Kane rolled his legs over the side of the bed, his feet hit the floor in one smooth motion and they kept moving toward the hallway. He was supposed to meet his cousin Lee in an hour to have a look at the gun range's security videos from the other day.

"Must... have... caffeine...," Kane said in a Frankenstein voice as he filled the coffee pot with water and poured it in the brewer. The rich scent of roasted Colombian beans filled the kitchen as the dark liquid drizzled from the filter. Kane scrolled messages left on his phone while he waited. He opened the one left by Kelly immediately. The fear he heard in Kelly's voice made him feel especially bad for not hearing and responding to her message before now. *Why would a drone buzz her house? This must be related to the mayhem earlier.* When he returned her call it went straight to voicemail.

"Hey, Kelly. This is Detective Kane. Right now it's about nine-thirty on Saturday morning. I'm sorry that I just found your message from last night. Hope all is OK, but if it's not, please call me back immediately. I have a meeting I need to go to, so unless I hear otherwise I'll stop by your house on the way back."

It was ten thirty when Kane drove into the gun range parking lot. Lee welcomed him at the door and then they huddled in the office by the computer to watch the video replay of the suspects' reactions to his arrival at the range. The conversation with Glenn the day before convinced Kane he was not the killer, so instead he concentrated on Jarod, taking careful note of his body language.

"Whoa, did you see Jarod do a double take when you held up the gun?" Lee asked.

"Do you think it was because he recognized it or because I was shooting a ladies' pistol?"

"Who knows? I want to show you some video from about a half an hour later. Hold on a sec while I fast forward. OK, now. There, do you recognize that woman?"

Kane squinted at the screen. A woman wearing a floral mini-dress and fringed boots sashayed into the room and took the lane between the two men. As she removed the pistol from her purse, she tossed back her long wavy brown hair with bangs that covered her eyebrows. Her exaggerated eye makeup suggested she was some sort of entertainer.

Glenn finished his target practice, and when he headed to the checkout counter the woman in the middle lane touched his arm and he paused to chat with her. As they spoke she kept tossing her hair back and touched his arm again.

"Look like she's into him, don't you think, Ty?"

"Can you zoom in on these images?"

"Yep. I have to pause the video though. Where should I?"

"Rewind back to where she first flips her hair. There. Zoom in on her arm."

Lee fiddled with the video controls until they focused on a clear image of the woman's arm. They studied the image for a few minutes.

"What are we looking for, Ty?"

"Look at her wrist. It's kind of large for a woman."

His cousin squinted at the frozen video frame and nodded. He let the video continue and paused it a few seconds later when Kane pointed at the screen.

"There! Look at her neck. Is that an Adam's apple?"

"What are you saying?"

"She's likely a he."

"Really? You think?"

"Play the video and watch closely the body language."

As they continued theorizing, the woman on the screen grabbed Glenn's arm and leaned in to try and kiss his cheek. Glenn pulled back from her as he turned his face away and walked quickly toward the exit. Lee paused the video and looked at Kane.

"Kinda looks like he doesn't know her well right there, but she wants to change that. He just wants to get the heck away from her." He resumed the video.

Jarod waved goodbye as Glenn passed him. Once he was out the door, Jarod went over to the woman in the middle lane. They chatted and laughed as if they knew each other well.

"By the way," Lee turned away from the screen to look at his cousin and continued, "I heard Jarod got a new job."

"Did he get fired from The Eggleston?" Kane kept watching the interactions between Jarod and the woman.

"Not outright, but they suggested he look for work elsewhere, so he's bartending now at a small nightclub in Hammondsport."

"What's the name of the place?"

"It's some new place in the alleyway behind Shethar Street."

Kane recalled that's where Angie led him the night she met up with that young man. As he pondered what the nature of their relationship was, he noticed the woman in the video reach into her purse and pull out a plastic bag filled with what looked like small pills. Jarod looked all around the room before he grabbed the bag and slid it casually inside his hoodie jacket.

"Dude! Did you see that?"

"Well, well now. Things just got interesting. I'm going to have to bring this to headquarters, Lee."

"Glad I could be of help, cuz."

***

"Let me apologize, Kelly. I didn't hear your message until this morning." Detective Kane put his hand over his heart as he spoke to her through the front screen door. "I feel so bad, especially after what you went through yesterday."

Kelly's arms crisscrossed her chest as she squinted from the bright sunlight behind him and tried to discern his sincerity.

"So why *didn't* you answer? Did you have a big date last night or something?"

He detected more than a little acidity in her greeting.

"As a matter of fact I did. And she was one gorgeous...," he paused for a second to see her reaction before he continued,

"...six pack. I hope my neighbors weren't too frightened by my karaoke singing."

Kelly studied his face. Was he kidding?

"You, singing karaoke? I've gotta hear about this. C'mon in."

Maureen made white chicken chili before she left for work and put it in the crockpot to simmer all day. The melding aromas of onions, peppers and cumin in a bath of melting pepper-jack cheese taunted Kane's empty stomach.

"Man, it smells so good in here." He lifted the crockpot lid for a good sniff before he pulled out a chair and sat at the kitchen table. "So before you tell me about last night, let me ask how you are doing. You had a big scare yesterday."

Kelly nodded as she stared toward the far corner.

"It's like I'm drowning in a churning sea of confusion. To be honest, I don't really know how I'm doing." She looked back toward Kane, her eyes lingering on his. He wanted to grab her in his arms and hug her, not in a romantic way, more like a fatherly protective way.

"Yesterday was such a nightmare." She leaned over the table and rubbed her forehead. "Any progress on the shooter?"

"They located the getaway car and a K9 unit searched for them, but the trail went cold. We're pretty sure that whoever these people are, they're local. They knew how to cover up their trail quickly."

"So they're still out there?"

Kane nodded.

"When are you going to reopen the store? We can have a patrol pass by a couple of times in the day."

"Probably Monday. I'll see how I feel that day."

"Good. Don't let them bully you out of business. So what was this about a drone last night?"

"The three of us were sitting on the deck having some wine. I was still pretty freaked out and my sisters were trying to calm my nerves. Tara looked up and noticed a light above the neighbor's trees. As soon as she mentioned it, the lights came at us. We ran inside, and the next thing we knew it was right outside the kitchen window over there."

Why was someone trying to intimidate Kelly and her sisters? Kane scratched his chin. *Was this about Jeremiah's death, or was it a threat about a different issue?*

"Have you had any disputes with anyone in the past couple of months? Any customers upset at the store? Are your neighbors mad at you about anything?"

Kelly thought for a few minutes, tapping her fingers on the tabletop. "No, all is fine with the neighbors. Nothing memorable at work except Glenn's arrival there."

"I'm going to visit your neighbors and see if they saw anything last night. Give me a call if you see the slightest thing out of the ordinary either here or back at the store. And I promise to leave my phone on." Kane stood and headed for the door. "Please be sure to keep all your doors locked, too. And if you have air conditioning, turn it on at night so you can lock your windows on the ground floor."

Kelly waved goodbye, then locked the door. She leaned her back against it and wished one of her other sisters were with her. They couldn't return home soon enough.

CHAPTER THIRTY
Sunday, June 29 ~ 1:25 p.m.

Her unknown caller ringtone stirred Angie from sleep. "Who the hell's this now?" She held the cellphone close to her eyes so she could focus on the incoming number. Angie shrugged and answered it.

"Yeah? Who's this?"

Gianni was not amused.

"This is your future business partner, Mrs. Redfern. Gianni Grande."

His stern tone made her bolt upright in the bed. "Gianni, of course, how's my favorite lawyer this morning?"

"You mean this afternoon, don't you?"

She looked at her watch. It was nearly one-thirty.

"Oh, I was working on something so intently here I hadn't realized it was already the afternoon." She picked up the glass that was filled with bourbon when she went to her bedroom last night and drained the last drops.

"I have some good news. The owners have accepted our offer on the mansion. We're going to meet at the bank tomorrow afternoon at three to sign the papers. Are you available?"

"Damn straight I am! Woohoo, this is wonderful. Have you spoken with Tom yet?"

"No, I was contacting the major investors first."

Angie winced at the slight toward Tom. That stung.

"Would you mind if I called him? I'd like to tell him the great news."

"Sure, that will be fine. See you tomorrow afternoon at three."

Angie wrapped her robe around her silk pajamas as she made her way into the kitchen. She opened the refrigerator and took out a bottle of champagne she had been chilling to celebrate when the property sale was made. As she pulled two flutes from the cupboards, she paused to admire the craftsmanship and traced the carving of Keuka Lake on the door.

"I *really* need to celebrate this news." Angie stuck the champagne bottle into a silver bucket and emptied a couple of ice trays around it. She sent a text message and went off to take a quick shower and get dressed.

By the time there was a knock on the front door forty-five minutes later, she'd slunk into a scarlet halter-topped sundress, slid on matching mule high heels, fastened on a pair of dangling bohemian earrings and tamed her unruly hair. Angie paused in front of the mirror to feather her hair and adjusted the dress's plunging neckline.

"Hmm. Not too shabby for a sixty-something." She opened the front door and flashed a mischievous grin.

"Woah! Hello there, foxy lady. Um, your message sounded urgent. Is there a problem with my work?"

Angie opened the screen door, grabbed Michael Connelly's hand and pulled him into the kitchen. He couldn't tell if she was angry, so he was holding his breath as she stopped in front of the cabinets he'd built for her. Then he saw the champagne bucket.

"What's going on, love?" He smiled in expectation that it was good, not bad news.

"I need to celebrate something today, and I could think of no better person to share the moment with than you."

He blinked, tilted his head and grinned at her. This was not expected. "Define share." His voice lowered softly.

"Well, we have this for starters." Angie grabbed his arms and wrapped them around her waist, leaning in for a kiss. When she felt his soft kisses descending her neck she sighed, "Ahhhh, just like old times."

Michael Connelly was the second person Angie met in town, thanks to her realtor. Their mutual attraction was immediate and they took advantage of every moment they could to spend time together when Jeremiah wasn't home. Shortly before Jeremiah died, it appeared Michael's wife suspected something was going on between them, and she demanded he spend more time with their family. Michael wasn't a fool. He knew his wealthy wife was his steady paycheck. That didn't mean he couldn't explore what it was like to have a dalliance with a rock star's wife.

***

When Angie phoned Tom with the news earlier, he wanted to thank her in person. After they hung up, he drove into town to buy a bouquet of long-stemmed roses and headed straight for Angie's place. He thought nothing of it when he saw Michael Connelly's car in the driveway. It seemed like he was always working on some carpentry need. When Angie didn't respond to his knock on the door, he figured she was on the phone with the investors.

He felt overjoyed when he saw the champagne bottle poking out of the ice bucket. *Yes, let's truly celebrate!* It took him a few seconds to realize it was already open. Tom peeked out the sliding glass doors to the deck, but Angie wasn't there. *She must be in her room.* He headed down the long hallway. When he entered the studio, there were discarded scarlet high heels and a pair of men's jeans on the floor. He heard the laughter coming from behind the bedroom door. The amorous tone of Angie's whispers sickened Tom. He threw the roses in the garbage as he headed out the front door.

Michael Connelly? Are you kidding me? How long has this been going on? Aren't you supposed to be in mourning, Ange? Tom slammed the front door behind him as he headed back to his car. Angie heard the concussion and pushed Michael away.

"What was that? Did that sound like a gun?"

CHAPTER THIRTY-ONE
Monday, June 30 ~ 8:59 a.m.

Monique felt nervous, unsure where the referral had come for the job she was to start with a new client this morning. Until now she had never worked this far up the West Side of Keuka Lake. It would be fun exploring the shops and neighborhood around Graceful Creative in Branchport. A well-dressed man answered her knock on the front door promptly.

"Good morning, Ms. Monique Toussaint. What a melodic name. Makes me want to break into sonnng!" He gestured widely and bowed, opening the door for her to enter. "Welcome. I am Mr. Montez." She detected a slight accent and her eyes were drawn to his beautiful long black hair tied neatly with a strip of velvet. "This is my office. Let me give you a tour and show you where you'll be working." Monique noticed his citrusy cologne filled the entire space and lingered on her hand. She felt a strong urge to sneeze and pinched her nose as he turned away.

The walls within the office glowed from its coral hued paint. On her right, two potted palm trees arced next to a low window sill crowded with jade and kalanchoe plants. Across the room a series of photo portraits of The Beatles with simple white mats and silver frames hung on the wall behind the reception desk. Monique raised her eyebrow when she noticed a porcelain

Yellow Submarine and a Paul McCartney bobble head figurine on the desktop.

"Now follow me up these steps. This is the bathroom on the left. It's important this be given plenty of attention because my clients also use it. Across the hall is a kitchenette with the coffee maker. You may help yourself to two cups on every work shift. Finally, down this hallway is my personal office space. Do not go inside to clean this unless the door is already opened. I do some photography work back there and if the door is closed it means something is in progress in the dark room. Now, any questions?"

"Where's de mop, vacuum?"

"Of course, darling. All of those items are in the closet in the hallway, next to the bathroom."

"You want me start now?"

"Absolutely. You can work from the front to the back of the building. Oh, and I intend to pay you double what Glenn is paying you."

Monique's smile was so wide it brightened the room.

"Oh, Mr. McCann tell you about me?"

"Yes, you could say that. I would imagine his house is tidy anyway because his everyday appearance is fastidious."

"Fas...?"

"Not to worry, darling. If you work for him that's good enough for me. Well now, I have some work to prepare for a client in the office. Please let her in when she arrives."

"Yes, Mr. Montez."

"It's Rodolfo, dear. I despise formality among my staff."

Monique smiled, but where were the rest of the staff? *Dis will be interesting.*

***

A sweeping pink brimmed hat emerged from the Cadillac parked in front of Graceful Creative. It matched perfectly the sundress and gloves Luna Grande wore as she walked up to the front door and rang the buzzer. She looked surprised when Monique unlocked the door.

"Oh, is Rodolfo not here?"

Monique smiled and waved her in. "*Oui*, he here. You sit, I let him know you arrive."

Luna eyed Monique's sundress and matching flats as she sat. "I'm sorry, I hadn't realized he was seeing anyone."

That made Monique giggle and cover her mouth with her hands. She smiled and shook her head at Luna. "I am Monique, de cleaning lady. What your name, Madame?" The woman did not extend her hand.

"Luna Grande."

"Pretty name. Nice to meet you."

Monique ascended the three short steps and walked down the carpeted hallway to Rodolfo's office. She noticed the door was ajar. Should she knock or call out to him? Monique did both, knocking lightly as she opened the door a bit more to whisper her message.

"Rodolfo, Luna Grande here now."

He looked up from his desk. "Great, I'll meet with her in the front office. Did you clean the bathroom yet?"

"No. I still clean office."

"OK, for now why don't you do a quick swish and dry to the bathroom counter. Move onto the kitchen afterwards so we won't be disturbed."

"As you wish." Monique's eyes were drawn to a large, sepia photo portrait on the wall. It took a few seconds before she recognized it was Glenn. The photo had been taken when he was much younger. That smile took her breath. She covered her mouth with her hands and smiled. Rodolfo noticed her staring.

"Oh, yes, that. It's some work I did early in my photography career when I lived in New York."

Monique could not stop staring at Glenn's gorgeous feathered hair and bright eyes framed with long lashes. He was stunningly handsome.

"Darling... the bathroom awaits your talents." He made a brushing away gesture with his hand. Monique blushed as she backed out of the room quickly. When she returned to the front office Luna was talking loudly on her cellphone.

"Meet you at the restaurant in an hour? But I'm still at the salon. Did you forget I was getting my hair done?" Luna hung up as Monique lifted her bucket of cleaning supplies from the floor next to the desk.

"Husbands... they're the worst kind of nags, right?"

Monique didn't know how to respond, so she smiled slightly and disappeared up the carpeted stairs. From behind the closed bathroom door she could hear Rodolfo give Luna an exuberant greeting, as if they were best friends. It was her normal work ethic to shut out conversations within earshot. Today though, Monique couldn't help but hear the woman ask him about the video he'd taken of her husband's ex-wife and sisters.

"I'll bring up the video for review, Luna, but it doesn't look as though Gianni was with them. There is no extra car in their driveway, either."

"Where is he disappearing to at night? I've hired another private investigator to follow him when he works in Rochester. Gianni is cheating on me with someone, I *know* it."

***

Kelly was in the back of the store discussing books about sailing with a customer, so she didn't notice when Detective Kane walked in. He picked up a book from the new arrivals rack as he waited for her to be free to chat. After a few minutes, she returned to the counter and he set the book back in the display, but before he could greet her the door swung open and the woman he recognized from the gun range video walked in.

"Hello dear. I'm back!"

Kane noted the familiarity between Kelly and this customer, and planned to ask her later how she knew the woman.

"Listen, I need a birthday present for a special friend. He's really into winemaking. Do you have any suggestions for a book specifically about the Finger Lakes wine region?"

Kelly was about to answer the woman when she looked over and noticed Kane standing by the front window. She smiled at him, which made the woman at the counter turn around and glance at the detective.

"Mmm, he's cute," she purred to Kelly. "There's something about a man with broad shoulders, right?" Kelly couldn't help but grin at her.

"I have a book that is a history of the first winemakers around Keuka Lake. It has some great photos in it, plus excerpts from the diaries of a couple of winemakers in the Nineteenth Century."

"Sounds perfectly boring. He'll adore it!"

Kelly laughed as she retrieved the book from the shelf. The woman took out her wallet to pay with cash and looked past Kelly at the bulletin board next to the store entrance.

"Dear, would you mind if I pinned a flyer here for a show I'm part of on the Fourth of July?"

"Not at all. That space is for all of the community to use. There are plenty of pushpins stuck in the corkboard. Help yourself."

"You're a peach!" The woman pulled the flyer out of her oversized pocketbook, posted it on the board and turned to look at Kane. "Have a look, handsome." She tapped her long manicured finger on the board, and waved goodbye with a jingle of the thin metal bangles on her wrist.

The other customer asked Kelly a question about vintage pulp fiction paperbacks as Kane walked over to read the flyer pinned to the board. Once that customer left, Kane approached the counter.

"How does it feel to be back?" he asked.

"I admit, I get nervous any time I peek out the door and see a car slowing out front to pull into a parking space. It will be good to get that window replaced this afternoon. It scares me to think who might be on the other side of those pieces of plywood."

"We're keeping an eye on the place. Don't worry. Say, who was that drag queen just in here?"

"Drag queen?" Kelly tilted her head. "What are you talking about?"

"You know, the guy who posted that flyer on the bulletin board just now."

"That was a guy? Really? Get out! She's... I guess I mean *he's* been in here a lot lately."

Kane unpinned the flyer and handed it to Kelly. "See?"

Kelly read the pink paper. *Haute Mama's Independence Day Rockin' Rollin' Fireworks Party, Friday, July 4th, 10 p.m. Red, White & YOU!* Two drag queens posed with sparklers as they blew kisses to the camera. The caption below the photo read *Your hostesses, Grace Sleek and Moan Jett!*

"He goes by the name Grace?" Kelly shook her head. "All this time I thought he was a she. Now I'm confused."

"Do you recall if she, *he*, has been in here when Glenn was?"

Kelly looked toward the ceiling scratched by flying glass the other day. "You know, she might have been a few weeks ago. Wait a minute. She bought a book for her winemaker friend. Oh crap... was it for Glenn?"

"Anything is possible. Did he use a credit card?"

Kelly shook her head. "No. Cash of course. Maybe you need to go to that performance Friday and see if Glenn shows."

"Uh, I'm not going in there alone. Care to join me, fellow sleuth?"

Kelly laughed. "Ha-ha! That would be very interesting. Sure, why not."

"Great, I've gotta run. Just wanted to make sure you're OK. Knew you would be. You strong Irish girls don't take any guff."

"Damn straight! Thanks, Detective Kane."

He grinned as he looked at the floor for a few seconds, then his eyes rose to meet hers.

"You know, it's all right if you just call me Ty."

Her eyes sparkled back at his.

"OK. Then it's bye, Ty. Hmm, that sounds like a blender drink. Better not be made with redrum!"

Kane was happy to see a mischievous spark in her that he hadn't noticed yet during the investigation. Kelly was still smiling a half hour after he left. For a person with a relatively tame life, she'd lived through more in one month than the past couple of decades. *That Ty, now there's a good man.*

Kane got into his car and glanced back through the book store door toward Kelly. He adjusted his rear view mirror and looked briefly at his own reflection, running his fingers across his chin.

"Whaddya know, old man," he whispered. "You may have gotten yourself a date."

CHAPTER THIRTY-TWO
Monday, June 30 ~ 2:47 p.m.

The parties involved in the sale of the Bluff Point estate started gathering at Wine Country Trust on Main Street in Penn Yan. Tom planned originally to carpool with Angie to the bank, but called her to say something came up and he needed to meet her there. Angie wasn't thrilled about the arrangement, especially since she was his benefactor in the deal. She hoped Tom would be waiting at the bank for her, because she did not want to encounter creepy Luna alone.

Ryan and Esperanza walked up to the bank entrance at the same time Angie did. They planned to wait for Esperanza's father outside, so Angie lingered with them in casual conversation to avoid going inside alone. A sleek black Ferrari pulled to the curb. Gianni let Luna out and drove off to park the car behind the bank. They all exchanged pleasantries except Angie who remained quiet and pretended to read her text messages while the others made small talk. *Where are you Tom?*

Luna sidled next to Angie and raised her head so her eyes could be seen under the wide hat brim.

"Isn't it wonderful we're going to be in business together? I hope we become best friends," she touched Angie's arm with her gloved hand. It felt like it weighed fifty pounds. *Do I really want to become entangled with Iggy's family again? Did Luna tell him about the deal yet?* Of course Luna didn't need her father's money. She was one of the top hand models in the country and Gianni surely pulled in at least a six-figure income from his high-profile clients. *Hopefully she's doing this without her father's involvement.*

Tom crossed the street and joined them on the sidewalk. He gave a warm hello to everyone and leaned in quickly to kiss Angie's left cheek.

"So, how are those cabinets working out for you, Ange? You know, now that they've been re-screwed."

She raised her eyebrows. *How did he find out about yesterday? Did Michael blab to him? Oh crap.*

"Want to grab a bite to eat after this?" she whispered to Tom. He smiled and folded his arms.

"Oh, maybe, but only if you're sure you have some free time for *me* on your calendar."

The others were oblivious to the sarcasm woven into Tom's banter.

"Need a hug?" she asked.

"Nope, I'm fine. Eyes are wide open now." He gestured with two fingers from his eyes toward her.

She fluffed her hair as if the gesture made her impervious to his stare. *Why can't we remain good friends, as we've always been. If I ever slept with you, Tom, this whole deal would fall apart. I need you as a friend, not a lover. How the hell did you find out about me and Michael?*

Alejandro arrived last in a rented Escalade and greeted everyone cheerfully. When everyone was seated within the boardroom, the lawyers discussed what was about to take place.

Once final questions were answered, each of investment parties took turns signing the document.

"Ladies and gentlemen," Gianni beamed, "you are now the proud owners of the property on top of Bluff Point, the future home of Keuka View Studios."

Tom folded his hands on the meeting table and rested his chin on them.

"Wow. Things just got real. OK, when can we move in?"

The lawyer for the former owners of the property handed Tom a set of keys.

"Whenever you'd like, Mr. Russo."

Had this been last week, Tom would have grabbed Angie in that moment and planted a juicy kiss on her mouth. After what happened with Michael Connelly, though, Tom felt all alone in his moment of joy. Angie stroked his back.

"Hey, my friend. We did it," she purred. "Jeremiah would be so proud of you."

Her sexy voice simultaneously drove him wild yet made him sad. "I'm ready anytime you are Tom to begin setting things up."

He turned his head so he could see her face. It did appear to reflect a conciliatory tone toward him. He sighed, pushed his chair back and stretched his arms behind his back.

"Been a total pleasure, all. I'm off to start working on our studio."

He was the first to leave the boardroom and he scooted into the open elevator door before it closed. Rodolfo answered the phone as soon as Tom dialed his number.

"Yes, I can express a package. Want me to land it on the upper balcony?"

Tom laughed. "Wow, you're a regular Chuck Yeager at flying that thing. Nah, a package isn't necessary. I just need a little self-medication for tonight."

"I have some errands later. Want me to stop by your place?"

"Sure. If I'm not there put them under the lid of the barbecue grill."

"Congratulations, my handsome amigo. Hope you have abundant success with this new studio."

"Thanks, bro!"

It was apparently too much effort for delicate Luna to walk into the parking lot with Gianni, so she stood outside the bank and took out her cellphone to make a call. When a man answered she said, "The property deal is done."

He sighed. "I guess it's on to the next phase of our plan."

"Soon, my darling. Soon! Our wines will be winning international awards."

"My darling Luna, you're a gem!"

***

Angie craved munchies. She hadn't admitted it to herself yet, but this transaction brought back all sorts of tough emotions entwined with memories of Jeremiah. For the first time since right after his death, she was overcome by a sense of true loss. Others may have judged her for not playing a traditional grieving widow role, but their relationship had been quite stormy over the years. Angie first felt a sense of peace when she received the awful news. Of course no one witnessed her crying jags at home, they only saw the flinty demeanor she displayed to the world.

Jeremiah would have gotten a kick out of this. He would be thrilled to know we completed his dream. Right now the only thing that could bring her consolation was scoring a few bags of chocolates. She drove a couple of blocks over to the grocery and made her way to the sweets aisle. As Angie perused the choices in front of her, she heard a familiar voice talking low. At the end of the aisle stood a man with a white ponytail and Chicago White Sox baseball cap talking on a cellphone. She squinted at the very familiar profile. *Nooo! It can't be. Am I freakin' hallucinating?* Angie placed her palm over her pounding heart. The man disappeared toward the meat department. She grabbed two bags of mini candy bars and tiptoed to the end of the aisle where he'd been. Angie peered around the potato chip display to her left, looking down the aisle beyond the meat cases to the bakery and produce section. He wasn't there. She looked over her right shoulder toward the dairy cases. Not there, either.

"Crap! He's the last person on earth I want to see now," she whispered to herself.

"Angie?"

The voice behind her startled Angie so much she flailed her arms and dropped the bags of candy. Tom bent to pick them up.

"Somehow I knew you'd be seeking chocolate."

She grabbed his arm and the look of terror in her eyes alarmed him.

"Ohmigod, Tom. Glenn McCann is here!"

"Huh?"

"Glenn! I saw him talking on his phone seconds ago. Right here, on this spot."

"Wait. Glenn McCann just happened to be in a grocery in Penn Yan right after we signed this deal? What are the chances...? You're positive it was him?"

"Yes! That voice is unmistakable. His hair is long and white now, tied in a ponytail. He was wearing that damn baseball cap Gigi gave him years ago."

"Holy crap! Is he still in the store?"

"Dunno. Let's check the next aisle. Hold my arm, Tom."

The two searched the entire grocery together, but Glenn could not be found. Tom ushered Angie into the express checkout lane.

"Whoo, I need a drink." Angie winked at the cashier. He laughed.

"I'll buy you one at the cantina in the alley after I get out of work at five. Can you hold on until then?" He made her smile and she blew him a kiss.

"You're a doll, handsome, but I've gotta roll."

Tom carried the grocery bag to her car.

"I can offer you more than a drink if you need one, Angie. You know, mother's little helper...."

"You're a lifesaver, baby. I'm so freakin' shaken by this. Can you follow me home, Tom?"

***

Rodolfo Montez left the office and drove toward Hammondsport. He plugged in his phone and switched it to speaker function. Then he dialed Monique's number.

"Hello darling, it's your new boss Rodolfo."

Monique could not imagine why he was calling. Had he been unhappy with her work this morning? She was afraid to hear what words would follow next.

"Hello, Mr. Montez. How are you?" She tried to sound as pleasant as possible and hide the fear within.

"Listen, I'm heading over to Glenn's house right now and I want to leave him a little gift. He said something about having errands to run when we spoke earlier. I'm super busy right now, so if he's not there, do you know where he keeps his spare key to get inside. I need to leave this on his kitchen counter."

She was so relieved he wasn't calling to fire her.

"Oh, yes, dat key is under de planter on front porch."

"Thanks, darling. Oh, and your work is marvelous. My friend remarked to me how clean the place looked after you left."

"I so glad you happy. Have nice day, Mr. Montez."

"You, too, sweetie." He clicked off the phone and looked in the rear view mirror at his freshly tweezed eyebrows. "Well now, Glenn. Time for a gentle reminder." Rodolfo tilted his head back like a wolf and laughed. The sound had an almost howl at the beginning and raised a few octaves before ending in a hiss.

CHAPTER THIRTY-THREE
Tuesday, July 1 ~ 8:59 a.m.

Glenn's curiosity nagged at him. After delaying the inevitable, he finally had a few clear moments to take a look at his phone to figure out where it had been. He was almost afraid to check through the history once he turned it on, lest it might be tied to Jeremiah's death. As he feared, the top number dialed was one he did not recognize. The time and date corresponded with the approximate time on Friday the thirteenth when Jeremiah was murdered. Was someone trying to frame him? He wanted to dial that number to see who would pick up, but figured if the police had Jeremiah's phone, they could trace the call back to him. That would not be smart.

Right below that call was one made about a half hour earlier to another number he did not recognize. He copied the number on a slip of paper and opened a web browser to do a reverse lookup. Of course it was conveniently a cellphone number, so it wasn't listed. If he dialed it, the person might know he had his phone again. He didn't want to add any danger to his life, but he knew that phone number could somehow be a clue to Jeremiah's murder.

Creaking noises came from the kitchen. Glenn looked at the phone's screen. It was nine. *Monique must be here to clean the house. Oh, wait a sec... I could get her to call the number on the phone and pretend it was a wrong number. She lives in Geneva, so the call wouldn't be linked to this place.*

He walked the stairs calmly and greeted Monique with the warmth of an old friend.

"Don't you look like a ray of sunshine today in that yellow dress." Glenn shone his wide, dazzling smile at her. It took Monique's breath.

"Thank you, Mr. McCann." She touched the heart locket on her necklace. "How are you dis day?"

"It's going to be a great one. Don't you agree?"

She smiled and set her tote bag on the floor by the door.

"Say, before you get started, love, would you be able to help me with a little mystery."

He say 'love'? Ô mon Dieu! Anisa been right about me wearing dis dress to get attention. Monique leaned on the island in the middle of the kitchen and twirled the string of clay beads dangling from her right ear.

"I like mystery, Mr. McCann."

"Monique, darling, please call me Glenn. We are good friends by now."

The look from his sparkling eyes made her wobbly inside. Did lighting that love intention candle Anisa gave her work? Her face flushed as she responded.

"Yes, Mr. Glenn."

"I'm so embarrassed, but someone called me on my phone and did not leave a name. It was a message for me to return the call. The phone number must be new, because I don't recognize it. This could be one of my wine clients, so I would like to be able to return the call and act as if I knew who was calling. You know, to sound as professional as possible. After all, this person might have been calling to invest in my winery."

"Yes, Mr..... I mean Glenn. It important look professional."

He touched her elbow with his warm hand and looked directly into her amber brown eyes.

"I knew I could count on you, because you understand what being professional is all about."

Ô mon Dieu! Please, do not let me faint. Let me be strong. I will prove my love.

"What I must do, Glenn?"

He handed her a piece of paper with the phone number.

"Dial this and pretend you are calling a friend. When it is obviously a wrong number, ask the name of the person and apologize. If the person asks what number you were dialing, repeat this number but change the last two digits. OK? Would you be able to do that for me?"

"Yes, Glenn. Anything for you." Monique took her cellphone out and dialed the number. It barely rang before an exasperated woman answered without looking to see who was calling.

"Rodolfo, is that you?" the woman asked.

Monique was stunned to hear the name of her other boss. She didn't know what to say and looked at Glenn. He thought she was overcome by nervousness.

"Go on, ask for your friend," he mouthed at her with a smile.

"Hello, Anisa?"

The now fully awake woman paused on the other end. This was her "other" phone used for secret business transactions and a handful of people had access to it—not even her husband. She did not recognize this caller.

"Whom are you calling?" she asked.

"Dis not my friend Anisa's number?"

"Do I sound like your friend Anisa?"

Monique looked at Glenn. She could tell that he was desperate for her to come through for him.

"Who dis?"

The woman laughed before replying, "Who are *you*? How did you get this number? It's unlisted. Are you a friend of Rodolfo's?"

"I sorry lady, must misdial. I thought dis Anisa's number."

She said "lady," Glenn noted. He began to run through a list of possibilities of women who might have taken his phone.

The woman replayed Monique's voice in her head. That was a distinct accent and she recalled where she'd heard it recently.

"You know your voice sounds familiar. Did I just meet you? Are you Rodolfo's cleaning lady?"

Monique freaked out and hung up.

"What's the matter? What happened?"

"I think I know dis woman."

"Great! Tell me."

"She friend of my other boss; you know, de one you recommend me to."

"Huh?"

"Mr. Montez. Rodolfo. I start work for him yesterday."

"*What?*"

"How come you not know that?"

"You've gotta be kidding me. First Jeremiah and now you're working for Rodolfo? He's in town? *Here*? How did you ever meet...?"

"You not get de gift he left yesterday?"

"Left where? Here? He *knows* where I live?"

"Yes. He ask where spare key is. Listen, I tell him because you good friends."

"YOU WHAT? Oh crap, Monique! We were acquaintances many, many years ago but since then I've kept him at a distance. He's an odd duck—sort of a stalker type. What he's doing here now at Keuka Lake? Are you telling me he may have been inside this house yesterday?"

"I sorry, Glenn. I get confuse. He say you good friends."

"Dammit! I hope the key is still there." Glenn brushed past Monique and ran out to the front porch. He lifted the barrel planter and was happy to see the spare key was still where he'd left it. Glenn stuffed it in his pocket and returned to the kitchen where Monique was sobbing. He wrapped his arms around her from behind and gave her a gentle hug.

"Don't worry, Monique. The key was there. I'm sorry this guy manipulated you. He's a master at that." She snuffled and he picked up a box of tissues and handed it to her.

"Mr. McCann, I so sorry. It my weakness, trust people too much." Her words made Glenn's eyes well with tears.

"That's one of my weaknesses, too."

He took a deep breath. So apparently Rodolfo had not gotten into his house. Now back to the phone call.

"Monique, you said the woman on the phone was a friend of Rodolfo's. Can you describe her to me?"

"She wealthy lady. Clothes and jewelry expensive. She wear big hat—like you wear to church Sunday. And she wear gloves—dey match de hat."

"Gloves you said?"

"*Oui*, long gloves."

"Dammit. Oh, God...." Glenn rubbed his forehead, sat on the couch in the other room and stared out toward Keuka Lake.

"You know dis lady?"

Glenn set his elbows on his knees and sunk his face into the palms of his hands. He didn't say a word for a couple minutes. His reaction puzzled Monique. How did he know this woman? Was it a bad thing she called him?

"Listen, Monique, why don't you skip today. Don't worry, I'll pay you. I need to be alone right now."

She bit her lip. "You fire me now for dis?"

He looked up finally and shook his head.

"No. You didn't know better. Don't worry. I have to process all of this. Promise me you won't mention this to Rodolfo."

Her eyes watered slightly as she bent to grab her tote.

"I so sorry. Never want to upset you, Glenn."

"Please don't worry, Monique. You have helped me more than you can imagine. I'll see you next week."

When he heard her start her car, Glenn locked the door and collapsed back onto the couch facing the lake.

"Luna is a friend of Rodolfo's? And whoever had my phone... possibly Jeremiah's killer... knows her?" He grabbed the cellphone and shut it off.

Glenn felt like he'd been kicked in the stomach with a steel-toed boot. *How will this affect the future of my winery? I was counting on her financial support. Dammit!* His hands began to shake. He looked at his watch. It wasn't even ten yet. *Who cares, I need some whiskey.*

He walked over to the bar in the dining room and reached for the bottle. When Glenn tried to unscrew the cap, he noticed it didn't budge. The bottle hadn't been opened yet. He could have sworn that it had been opened and there was only a third of the bottle left. Had he finished it recently and forgotten he bought a new one? Glenn had been under too much stress lately. He held the bottle out so he could have a good look at it. There was something odd on the label. He saw a red glitter heart sticker adhered to the label over the letters "Tulla" and an X drawn over the "or" in the rest of the brand name.

Is this some sort of puzzle? What does "heart me dew" mean? Is that supposed to be some weird sort of leprechaun language? Wait, does the heart represent the word love? Love me dew?

Glenn exclaimed, "Oh! I get it. That Beatles' song... it's 'Love Me Do.'" He laughed, but his smile recoiled immediately into a cringe when he realized the person who left the bottle there must have been Rodolfo. When they'd first met in Brooklyn back in the '60s, Rodolfo wore his hair exactly like Paul McCartney's and wore one of those thin tailored mod suits. He was Beatles obsessed... until he fell for Glenn.

"He did get in here. Dammit!" Glenn's eyes darted wildly around the room. *Where else did Rodolfo leave his mark in this house?*

***

Luna called Rodolfo immediately after Monique hung up.

"Hello, darling! How are you today?" he purred.

"Why did you give your cleaning lady my private number?"

"I have no idea what you are talking about, dear."

"That woman I met at your office yesterday... she just called me. Said she was trying to reach her friend Anisa, but was it you snooping on me?"

"Well, darling, I'm not in the habit of dispensing your number to every Jack and Jill. It was probably a misdialed number. Maybe she didn't have a telephone back in Haiti and is still getting used to the whole dialing thing."

"I doubt it. She called me on purpose. Why? Was she checking to see if I was home so she and her friends could break into my house and steal my jewelry?"

"How would she have gotten your address from an unlisted number? Stop behaving like little Miss Polly Paranoid. I can assure you there was no way she could have gotten it from me. My cellphone was in my pocket the entire time she cleaned here yesterday."

After Rodolfo hung up, he thought of one possible way Monique could have gotten that number. It would mean she must have broken into Glenn's car and found his phone. Perhaps she *was* a thief.

CHAPTER THIRTY-FOUR
Wednesday, July 2 ~ 10:00 a.m.

With all of the uproar lately, Monique had forgotten about the confrontation with Angie the last time she cleaned her house. She took a deep breath and knocked on the front door. There was no response, so she peeked in the garage window. Angie's car was there. Monique returned to the front porch and knocked again. After about five minutes of waiting on the steps, Angie opened the door as she held a cellphone to her ear.

"Tom and I are heading over this afternoon." She waved Monique inside as she kept talking, "I was wondering if you'd like to meet us there. The place needs some storage units and other cupboards in the office. Are you up for it, Michael?" Monique grimaced when she heard Angie make a sexy growl toward the phone. *Guess the widow is done crying.*

Monique noted a big difference in Angie's mood. What caused the sudden shift? She was fully dressed, with makeup and her hair styled pretty. Her smile toward her when she opened the door felt sincere and welcoming. Angie looked and acted much happier than back when Monique had her initial interview with her. What changed?

Several minutes later Angie hung up the phone.

"Oh, Monique, several of my friends are visiting from LA and New York for the weekend. Would you please make sure there are fresh linens on the beds in the four guest rooms? Also, we'll all be swimming at some point. If you could tidy the cabana by the lower deck, I'd appreciate it. You can let yourself out when you're finished. I have to meet Tom at the new studio this afternoon."

Monique tilted her head. What did her boss mean?

"That's right, I haven't had a chance to tell you yet. We're so excited! We've purchased the old estate at the top of Bluff Point and are returning it to a recording studio."

"Dat big mansion you can see from highway?"

"That's the one. Tom owned it back in the '80s. It's where Jeremiah's former band recorded their last album. We're having a housewarming party on the Fourth there after nine. If you're free you may come with a guest."

Monique folded her hands over her heart. "*Oui*, Mrs. Redfern." Her exuberance shifted to empathy. "I sorry your husband not share dis moment." She tilted her head at Angie.

"It was one of the reasons we moved here. Tom told us he'd heard the mansion might be going back on the market. He missed his days of recording music. Jeremiah was working on some new material he was hoping to record. It was a rock opera based on the life of a firefighter he knew from Brooklyn who died on September 11th. I have all of the lyrics he'd written so far—he was nearly done—and we hope to find a decent collaborator who can finish them using the score Jeremiah already began."

"Dis be wonderful tribute to him, Angie."

Her boss's eyes narrowed suddenly. "Oh, and by the way, speaking of lyrics, did you happen to see...?" Her cellphone rang and Angie saw it was from Tom. She answered it right away.

"Thanks for getting back to me. Listen, I spoke with the carpenter about the layout for the studio and... yes, it is Michael... no, this shouldn't be a problem, Tom. Listen, if we are truly going to be business partners you have to trust me." Her hands waved in the air as she listened to Tom yelling at her from the other end of the call. "I know, I know. It won't happen again. Listen, Tom, you might not believe it but a woman my age has certain needs that must...." Angie looked at Monique who was drinking in every word, wide-eyed. Angie walked down the hall to her bedroom. "Well maybe this *IS* how I'm processing my grief, Dr. Phil!" Her voice trailed off behind the closed door.

Monique resumed her cleaning tasks quietly. Hopefully Tom would distract Angie enough so she could get another day's work in before Angie brought up that notebook again. Ugh, she seemed to be in the middle of messes wherever she worked. Monique looked forward to her work shift tomorrow at the spa, because at least that would be peaceful.

***

Detective Kane was heading up the West Side of Keuka Lake to an appointment in Penn Yan when he got a text message from Investigator Angela Reilly of the State Police. He pulled the car over to read it.

"Unlisted # woke up. Brief pings from Penn Yan on Mon, Wayne on Tues. Still @ Keuka vicinity. Appears to be off now. Will continue to monitor & advise."

***

The last person Maureen expected to see waiting when she walked out to the spa's lobby to greet her appointment was Detective Kane.

"Well now, to what do I owe the honor of your visit, Detective?"

"I heard you were the best massage therapist in town."

"Oh, you're legitimately here for a walk-in session?"

"My right shoulder is a mess. Chronic football injury, exacerbated by yard work I did recently. Thought you might be able to help."

"What type of yard work?"

"Dividing a big clump of hostas. I wedged a pitchfork between them, then tried to yank them apart by hand. Think I might have pulled something."

"You like to garden?" Maureen smiled at the incongruous image of this burly detective on his hands and knees, tending plants gently. "OK, well let's get working on that. I see you've filled out the paperwork, so follow me."

They walked down the hall to Maureen's room. Kane felt slightly anxious, because he'd never been to a massage therapist before and wasn't sure about the protocol. He noticed immediately a pleasant scent in the room. The lights were low and flute music mingled with ocean waves played softly on the stereo.

Maureen had him sit in a chair to the side as she reviewed his questionnaire. His health looked to be good except for that shoulder issue.

"Would you like me to use the hot stones on that shoulder?"

"What are they?"

"Flat stones that are warmed and gently massaged into the muscles."

"Sure, if you think it could help."

"Trust me, it will make a huge difference."

"Great."

"OK, I'll step out while you disrobe. When you're ready, get under these sheets on the table and lie on your stomach with your face nested at the head of the table here."

"Uh, I've never done this before. Do I take everything off?"

"Not to worry. I'm used to seeing naked men and women. If you prefer, you can leave your underwear on. Whatever you feel comfortable doing is fine."

Now he felt embarrassed. Maureen left and he stripped to his boxers. Should he drop them, too? He couldn't bring himself to—it would be too weird, so he left them on and slipped his body between the sheets on the massage table.

When Maureen began the treatment, she picked up a strong vibe of sadness coming from Kane. As was the case with other clients, she asked a few questions gently that revealed what was going on. By the end of the session, she knew he held a profound loneliness since his parents were gone and his siblings were miles away. He'd never been married although he had a close call a couple of decades ago. She also gleaned some information on his interests, such as anthropology and Native American mythology, that confirmed something she'd been thinking about for a while: he was a bit like her sister Kelly. *Now wouldn't they make a good match?*

Maureen wasn't the only one prying out information. Kane found out Monique worked there on Thursdays. To be truthful, she was the main reason why he stopped by. He also learned more about the day Maureen gave massages to several members of the O'Hare/Montez bridal party.

As she focused on his upper arm below his aching shoulder, he asked if she'd ever met Angie, Tom, Jarod or heard of that nightclub Haute Mama's.

"Jarod helped install the gazebo in back of the spa, but that was when he was employed by the hardware store. I haven't had any contact with him since."

"Tell me, how come both of your sisters have connections to the suspects in this case and you seem to be squeaky clean? No skeletons in your closet? C'mon, Maureen. Fess up!"

"Well, my actual name is Miss Scarlet and I'm seeing a man I met in the library named Col. Mustard, and for some reason he always carries a wrench in his hand."

"Ha! I suspected as much." He laughed and lifted his face so he could see her eyes. "One last question: how do you like the new wife of Tara's ex?"

He noticed a dramatic change in her expression.

"I've met her only a few times. Something about her gives me the chills. She has the dark charisma of Morticia from *The Addams Family*."

"Ha! Yeah... I could see that."

"OK, ready for the hot stones?"

"Bring 'em on." The warmth of the stones and her gentle push and pull on his shoulder muscles brought a slight twinge of discomfort that was soon replaced by a sensation of total relaxation. He felt the stress he was carrying slip through his fingers and dissipate. She asked him to turn over so she could work on his front side. By the time Maureen had worked her way to his neck and begun craniosacral therapy, he could barely keep awake.

When she was done, she leaned over his face and whispered, "You should now be totally relaxed. Stay here as long as necessary before you get dressed."

Maureen was texting Kelly when Kane emerged from the room about ten minutes later.

"I have to apologize. I fell asleep for a few minutes."

She nodded. "Not to worry. We always build in extra time for our clients to relax post treatment. Now remember to drink plenty of water the rest of the day, and avoid alcohol."

"Don't need it. I haven't been this mellow since I was a baby. Thanks, Maureen. You're a true artist."

"Listen, now that you know all of us so well, why don't you come over for dinner some night. If that wouldn't be problematic for your investigation."

The thought of making additional plans to see Kelly off duty was very appealing. "That sounds great. I'd love to."

"Well, what are you doing on the Fourth?"

He hemmed and hawed because he'd been invited to his work partner Reese's barbecue that day. Plus, he'd planned already with Kelly to check out the drag show at Haute Mama's later that night.

"Hmm, what time on the Fourth?"

"We have a cocktail hour around five, followed by a dinner buffet and dessert by the bonfire so we can watch the fireworks."

That would work, and it wouldn't affect the plans he had with Kelly later that evening.

"Sure, what can I bring?"

"Yourself. I hope you can relax and just enjoy the evening."

He laughed. "I'd look forward to that very much."

CHAPTER THIRTY-FIVE

Thursday, July 3 ~ 5:35 a.m.

A blanket of steel blue clouds parted just enough for Jarod's mother to see the first fiery rays of the sunrise. She'd stretched out a foam yoga mat on the concrete patio and sat in a lotus position facing east, hands resting on her knees in a healing mudra. Meditation centered her rambling thoughts, and it had been an invaluable tool over the decades as she tried to sort all of the messy relationships in her life. This morning though her zazen practice could not quiet the stormy thoughts, the waves of overwhelming guilt centering on her son.

For a brief moment she thought about dipping into the whiskey bottle sitting on the coffee table, mere feet away from her. There was something about the intensity of the carmine red sunlight that made her shake her head.

"No. It's time to tell him the truth."

The moment she spoke the words aloud a sense of peace rose within. She went inside and got a notepad and pen, fixed a cup of coffee, grabbed her cigarettes and returned to the patio. Within the hugging "arms" of the cedar wood Adirondack chair, she mustered the courage to write a note to Jarod. In this quiet moment she would have the clarity of thought that would be hard to raise in a direct confrontation. Her son's temper would not intimidate her from saying everything that needed to be said.

"Dear Jarod," she began, "It's time to tell you about your father." Once she allowed herself to begin the process, words flowed easily. She tried to infuse her note with love and gentleness. It was hard to revisit why she and his father never married before she moved west, but nothing was edited. The truth spilled out in black ink all over the paper that she signed with hearts and flowers, folded gently and inserted into a pink envelope. She grabbed her car keys and drove to his apartment.

On the short drive from Dresden to Penn Yan, she rehearsed what she would say to him. Was it better to explain why she wrote it down first or should she just hand it to him? *Give me a sign, universe!* At that moment she noticed a dead opossum at the side of the road. She remembered that was a sign in Native American totems to lay low. When she arrived at his apartment and noticed his car was gone, her gut told her that this was an opportunity to slip the note in the mail slot next to his door and escape without disturbing the peace of his neighborhood or within her soul.

***

"Guess who might join our bonfire soiree tomorrow night, Kelly?" Maureen asked a few hours later as she was packing a lunch to bring to work.

"Who?"

"Detective Kane," she answered, looking to see what her sister's reaction was. Kelly didn't show much of a response though. "I invited him when he stopped by the spa yesterday for a treatment on his shoulder."

"How can he do that? Wouldn't it be a conflict with him working on the case and all?"

"Well, I take it he's ruled all of us out. Otherwise...."

"Unless he's hoping one of us will slip and provide him with some information. Isn't this a little sneaky on his part?" Kelly was cool with their prior plans for later that evening because it was at a different site. But to grant him free access to their home? That made her uncomfortable. Was Kane hoping to glean something more from them?

"He didn't invite himself," Maureen blurted. "I picked up a sadness around him during his session and thought it would be a nice gesture. That's all; there's no ulterior motive."

Oh dear, I didn't want to bring in any negative energy in regard to Detective Kane. She needed to shift the mood quickly so Kelly wouldn't brood over this.

"Oh and in case you are wondering, it's boxers."

Kelly lowered the newspaper and glared at her sister.

"I don't recall asking about that." She took a sip of coffee.

"Ahh, but you were thinking about it. Right? I would have wagered ten bucks on briefs. Always preferred men in boxers."

Kelly blushed. "Maureen! I can't believe we're discussing Detective Kane's underwear preference."

Of course that was the moment Tara walked through the door.

"Briefs! Has to be. And can a girl buy a cup of coffee here? I forgot to stop by the grocery last night."

Maureen poured a mugful and handed it to Tara, shaking her head.

"Nope, boxers."

"Really? Ooh, suddenly I'm seeing the detective in a sexier light."

"You guys, please. I'm trying to digest my granola here."

"Oh, Kelly. We could run with that... but it's early." Tara loved teasing her younger sister. She tapped the newspaper in her sister's hands. "Speaking of briefs, did you read the one on the business page about the old Chauncey Mansion on Bluff Point being officially sold? Keuka View Studios is expected to open later this summer."

"Oh, I'm glad to hear that." Maureen rinsed her coffee mug in the sink. "Hopefully those new owners will bring it back to its former beauty. It's been heartbreaking to see it deteriorating."

"Did you know the mansion is haunted?" Kelly set down the newspaper and folded her arms across it. "I sell a book at the store that lists all of the well-known haunted places in the Finger Lakes. According to the section on the Chauncey Mansion, one of the previous owners was shot on the balcony by a business partner who accused him of betrayal. The book claims no grass will grow on the spot where his body fell."

Maureen cringed.

"Ooh, before the new tenants move in, someone needs to cleanse that space intensely with sage."

"Of course it's haunted... by a living ghost, Looney."

"Taraaaaa!" Maureen teased.

"Ciao, bellas," Tara said in a singsong tone as she set her mug on the counter. "Gotta run!"

"Bye," Maureen waved as her sister whizzed past. Kelly stared at the unwashed mug Tara left behind.

"You know, sometimes it feels like we're her hired help."

More dark moods gathered around her little sister—she'd been through so much lately. Maureen picked up her car keys and lunch, then opened the front door. She paused and grinned back at Kelly.

"To be precise, they were plaid. Royal Stewart tartan. Buh-bye…!"

***

A little after ten that morning, Detective Kane returned to Ballylough Spa and asked to speak with Maureen when she was free. He didn't have to wait long.

"You're back for more?" she asked, eyebrows raised in fake shock.

"Two things—I won't take too much of your time. First of all, I have to thank you for the work on my shoulder. I noticed a huge improvement today on my range of motion."

"Any soreness?"

"A little, but what amazed me was how loose the muscles feel."

"I told you those stones work miracles."

"Second, I've been told I make an authentic pecan pie. Do any of you have nut allergies, or will that be OK to bring to your party?"

Maureen was impressed. *He gardens and bakes pies?*

"Are you kidding, I love a good pecan pie. Sounds great!"

Monique entered the lobby with a feather duster. She smiled at the man in the nice suit. Was he Miss Maureen's boyfriend? When he turned to speak to her, she was pleasantly surprised.

"Excuse me, are you Monique Toussaint?"

She reacted with surprise that he knew her name. Monique and smiled a bit warily.

"*Oui.*"

He smiled back and showed his badge. "Hi, I'm Detective Kane with the county Sheriff's Department. Would you mind if I asked you a few questions?"

The feather duster in Monique's hand trembled slightly and Maureen noticed the look of fear in her eyes.

"No." She stared at the hardwood floor. "It is no problem."

"Maureen, is there a room where I could have a private chat with Miss Toussaint?"

"Absolutely." She led them into a small break room next to the restrooms. "I'll let my boss know what's going on."

As she backed out of the room, Maureen felt many emotions. Mainly she felt bad for Monique in the way she'd been "ambushed" by Kane. This woman was not guilty of Jeremiah's murder. She was sure. Maureen also felt a slight resentment toward him. Had he been using her yesterday so he could ease in here to corner Monique?

Inside the break room, Kane tried gently to put Monique at ease.

"Need a glass of water before we begin?" She shook her head. "OK, I have just a couple of brief questions. You work for several people around Keuka Lake. I was wondering what you could tell me about your job at the Redferns' home."

Monique gripped the armrests of her chair. She knew she had sinned in a way by taking that notebook from Angie's house. However, it originally belonged to Glenn, so she was helping Jeremiah by returning it to him. Had Angie reported her to the police for this? She said a prayer to God for guidance. Her father told her to be always truthful, because her character was one of her most valuable possessions.

"I take de notebook!" she blurted. Kane never flinched and continued asking about visitors to the Redferns' house. She was stunned by his lack of a reaction. Had he not heard her?

"Listen," she interrupted, "my other boss Mr. McCann tell me about dat notebook. He been very upset Mr. Redfern not return it before he die. I find it when I clean studio. Dat room look like some hurricane come through. Papers, plates, coffee mugs and wineglasses... dey are all over dis place. It a mess!"

"Wait, what day did you see the room like that?"

"Tuesday after Mr. Redfern been murdered."

"Really. And the house was still a mess like that?"

"Messiest place is studio."

"Did you ask Mrs. Redfern what had happened in there?"

"No. She still in pajamas and her hair not be comb, her face so sad...."

"Have you ever found evidence of drug use when you cleaned these rooms?"

Monique looked at the floor. "I not judge people I work for. I clean dere messes."

"Ever find a marijuana joint, an empty narcotics bottle or booze bottles."

"OK, Detective Kane, yes, yes, de bottles, de weed. Everything go in garbage."

"Is Angie on the phone a lot?"

"Her phone always ring. Many times it Mr. Russo, sometimes de carpenter. One time come a call from Mr. Rodolfo...." Monique paused. She'd forgotten about that message on Angie's phone. Did Angie know her new boss, too?

Kane noticed she looked distracted.

"Who's Rodolfo?"

"Might be dis man I know. I just get new job at Graceful Creative on West Side. My boss Mr. Rodolfo Montez."

Kane tried to not show that he recognized at that name. Of course the gun used to shoot Jeremiah was registered to a man by that name in Texas.

"What's the address of Graceful Creative, Monique?"

He wrote her reply, flipped his notebook closed and smiled at Monique.

"Thank you, Miss Toussaint. You have been helpful. Keep up the great work."

She was so astonished that she hadn't been charged with stealing Glenn's notebook she stood and hugged the detective. Her gesture startled him, but Kane smiled as he opened the door to leave.

"Have a nice day."

***

Kane pulled into the parking lot of Graceful Creative and decided to knock, even though it looked closed and there wasn't a car in the parking lot. A woman with long chestnut bangs peeking out under a denim cap that matched her mini-dress and go-go boots answered.

"Well hello there, sweet thang," she purred. "Have we met?"

"Hi, is Mr. Montez in?"

The woman squinted at him, eyeing his whole body. Kane squirmed slightly under her stare.

"No, I'm sure we've never met. I'd remember those broad shoulders." She paused for a wink at him, and her face shifted slightly. "Sorry, Rodolfo's not here right now. He should be back in a few hours. Anything I can help you with?" She tilted her head, twirled her pink feather earrings and batted extravagant fake eyelashes at him.

"Did I almost meet you at The Deckled Edge the other day? Wasn't it you who put up a flyer about the show at Haute Mama's Lounge?"

"Ooh, you saw it. Wonderful! Please tell all of your handsome friends about it."

"Are you in the show?"

"Maybe. You'll have to show up and see. Tell them Catriona sent you and you won't be charged the cover."

Kane noted the size of her wrist as her hand held the door open.

"I should bring my friend Glenn. He'd enjoy it." Kane walked toward his car knowing he'd tossed a little firecracker at the "woman" in the doorway.

"Wait, I don't even know your name to tell Rodolfo when he returns."

"Don't worry. I'll stop back when I get a chance. Maybe I'll see you tomorrow."

He pulled out of the parking lot and turned on an oldies radio station just as that funky song "Heart Pumper" by Vinegar Hill started to play. Kane cranked the volume.

"Well, well, well," he said. "It appears the mysterious handgun-toting Rodolfo Montez *is* a drag queen."

***

Michael Connelly dropped by Hare Hollow around noon to discuss a future renovation project with Ryan O'Hare. He figured Tara would be working, so when his meeting was over, he jumped in back of a line of tourists piling into the tasting room. Tara was busy handing out wineglasses and the list of what they would be tasting. She didn't notice Michael until reaching the end of the bar. Tara raised an eyebrow and grinned, pretending they didn't know each other.

"So we'll start off with the white wines, going from driest to sweetest. First off we have a Grüner Veltliner that has less than 0.1 percent residual sugar. You'll notice it has an enticing balance of minerality and spice."

"Oh, yes, extremely enticing." Michael playfully raised his eyebrows and flashed his toothy smile.

Tara laughed and continued. "This wine pairs perfectly with so many foods. We had it last month at a luncheon with some roasted asparagus and a strawberry chicken salad. It even tasted great with the lemon tarts we had for dessert."

"Oh, I'd love the recipe for that strawberry chicken salad," a woman said. "I would have never paired those two tastes."

"Sure, remind me in the gift shop and I can get it from my sister over the phone."

"I'd like the recipe for that dessert, please. Nothing tastes better than a juicy tart."

Everyone raised an eyebrow as they turned toward Michael who hid his grin behind his raised glass of wine. Tara glared at him and continued.

"Now we'll try the chardonnay. This has been aged in oak for three months to enhance the malolactic fermentation. Afterwards it was transferred into an aluminum tank. There is a bit of buttery mouth feel, but not too much. I think the winemaker achieved a delicate balance here."

Michael started to make another off-color comment but Tara threw a bar rag at him before he could utter it.

By the end of the tasting she was exhausted trying to keep his mischief at bay.

"What's your problem? Are you trying to get me fired?" she hissed at him while the tourists wandered towards the gift shop.

"Fired? No. Fired up? Yes."

She shook her head. "You're incorrigible."

"Guilty as charged. So anyway, I've got a new gig in the 'hood."

"Huh?"

"That's musician-speak."

"I know, so...?"

"I'm helping to build a recording studio."

Tara figured immediately it was Angie's project. "That sounds cool. Where is it?"

"The old Chauncey Mansion—it's being turned back into a studio by Tom Russo and Angie Redfern."

"Oh, I read the business brief about it in the paper this morning. You know my ex is a partner in that studio."

Michael cringed. "Gianni is? Angie didn't happen to mention that."

Something about the way he dropped Angie's name in an intimate tone annoyed Tara. Michael loved associating with celebrities and hinting that he was privy to their private circle.

"Tom hopes to record some artists there later this month. So I have a lot of work to do."

I bet a lot of the work will be with Angie, Tara thought. *He's probably already slept with her.* She sighed a little to herself.

Michael is one gorgeous specimen of the male sex. Too bad he's the male equivalent of plutonium. Too much exposure to him is poison.

"What are you doing for the Fourth?" he asked.

"You know, the old family bonfire on the shore thing. Lighting flares to create the ring of fire around the lake, like the Senecas did."

"I bet that's fun."

"Are you and your wife doing anything?"

He winced.

"Nah, she's visiting her folks with the kids in Grosse Pointe. I'm going to be working at the mansion. Angie said something about having a little get-together there with some music industry friends. I imagine the view of fireworks from that balcony is amazing."

"Take my advice, Michael—don't go on that balcony. It's haunted."

"Haunted? Ha. Says who?"

"Kelly read it in a book. It was in the late 1800s. A man was shot on the balcony and fell to his death. Grass still won't grow where his body landed."

"Hmm." He studied her expression to see if she was being truthful. "You know I don't really believe in ghosts. Well, gotta run. Have fun tomorrow."

Tara waved goodbye and muttered, "Yeah, you say you don't believe in ghosts, but I bet you'll remember that story if you step on the balcony with Looney."

CHAPTER THIRTY-SIX
Friday, July 4 ~ 12:40 a.m.

Sarah's death cracked open the inner armor guarding Jarod's insecurities. He'd always been a scrapper, exuding the fierceness of a cornered badger as a way to fend off bullying and criticisms that haunted him throughout his youth. Now, though, he felt utterly vulnerable and hated it. His buddy Mitch invited him to stay at his place for a few days to calm down, and that helped, but he couldn't take one minute more of his slobbering bulldog and the odor of its urine that infused every inch of his old house, especially the couch where Jarod now lay.

"Nothin' personal man, but I need to sleep in my own bed tonight."

Mitch held a glowing joint in his hand and nodded before he took another hit.

"Whatever, man. *Mi casa es siempre tu casa,* bro."

Jarod noticed an odd tingling in his hand as he gripped the steering wheel driving home. When he extended his hand with the keys in them to unlock the door, his hand shook. *I've gotta eat something.* He pushed the door open and thought about walking over to the grocery to get something he could nuke to eat, but then his eyes noticed the pink envelope on the floor.

"What the hell is this?" Immediately he thought of Sarah's friend Tamara. She'd been especially concerned about him lately, leaving nice messages on his phone. Was this some sort of invitation from her? He'd always liked blondes and wondered how long he should wait before asking Tamara out without possibly offending her. He imagined ways they could comfort each other and smiled. Jarod slid his finger eagerly under the envelope's flap and pulled out the note. His expression changed when he recognized the handwriting as his mother's. Jarod sat on the couch to read it and as he progressed, agitation escalated within him. More than a few neighbors heard his livid screams followed by sobbing shrieks and then the weighty silence after his fist punched through glass.

***

Although she went to bed early, Kelly had yet to fall asleep. Just when she first drifted off, noise from a distant M80 firecracker woke her and she feared someone was shooting at the house.

"I guess this is what post-traumatic stress disorder is like." She got out of bed and wandered wearily into the dark kitchen. As per her order to her sisters, shades were drawn on every kitchen window so no drone camera could peer in at them. She followed the light cast by the stove clock and turned on the faucet to get a drink of water. Car lights coming up the lake road illuminated the window shades and dimmed as they drove past. The clock said three thirty. Who would be driving down the lake road at this hour?

A car door closed, and she heard footsteps coming up her drive. Kelly hid behind the refrigerator so there was no way whoever was approaching could see her shadow. Her heartbeat throbbed through her fingertips pressed against the cold metal.

Was this person going to try and break in? If so, where could she hide next?

Footsteps creaked on the wooden porch. *Ohmigod.* The person clicked the handle on the storm door and opened it, squeaking slightly. *Oh crap, someone's about to break in here.* She dropped to her hands and knees and scooted behind the couch. There was some sort of scuffling noise against the lower part of the front door. The storm door closed, and then she heard the person step off the porch and run up the driveway.

Did that person set a bomb against the door? Ohmigod I have to get to Maureen and warn her. Kelly scrambled across the floor and pulled herself upright so she could run up the carpeted steps. She opened Maureen's door and crouched next to her sister.

"Maureen," she whispered breathlessly, "wake up! Maureen... *please*, you have to wake up."

Her sister snuffled and turned her head away from Kelly.

"Maureen." She shook her sister gently. "It's me, Kelly."

Maureen opened her eyes slightly, but her lids soon dropped and she let out another snore.

"Maureen!"

This time her sister heard her and sat up.

"What's going on? Did someone die? Why are you on the floor?"

"There's a prowler outside the house. The person fiddled with the storm doorknob and left. There might be an explosive set against the front door."

Maureen's jaw dropped and her heart pounded as she thought for a few seconds about what they should do.

"Was the person near the deck at all?"

"No, out front."

A car door closed and they heard the vehicle drive past their house heading down the road.

"What should we do, Maureen?"

She got out of bed and peered out her bedroom window. A nearly half moon outside shed some light on the yard, but she did not see any person there.

"What time is it?"

"It's almost four."

"Why don't we wait until dawn and then go outside and see what's on the porch. If the door is booby-trapped, we'll see it."

"OK." Kelly let go of the curtains and stood by the window, not knowing what to do.

"C'mon, let's hide under the bed covers."

"Maureen, why do you think someone is trying to hurt me?" She folded back the blankets next to Maureen and lay down.

"Either the person suspects you know something about the murder, or the person doesn't want you to get involved with Glenn McCann. That's something I happen to agree with Kelly, by the way."

"Don't worry. I'm so over him."

"Really? You can honestly say that if he showed up here on the deck one moonlit night with a keyboard and began singing to you, it wouldn't persuade you at all to get involved with him."

"Nope, I wouldn't buy it. Guess I'm getting too cynical."

"Nah, you're wising up. The best men tend to be slightly invisible. You know, they're always right in front of us but we have to open our eyes and notice them there."

For some reason, that made Kelly think of Detective Kane. After a few minutes she turned to her sister.

"Were they really Royal Stewart tartan?"

Maureen laughed heartily.

"Yes, my dear. Perhaps he's descended from kings."

They half slept, half listened to every noise outside until the first rays of dawn warmed the opposite hills of Keuka Lake.

"You awake now, Kelly?" Maureen asked.

"Mmph, yeah."

"Let's go see what we're dealing with downstairs."

Kelly nodded and yawned as she stood from the bed. They tiptoed downstairs and then peered out the window next to the front door.

"See anything?"

Kelly smushed her face against the closed window. "No, the angle is all wrong from this vantage point."

"Let's go out by the deck and walk around to the front of the house." They slid on flip-flops, unlocked the sliding glass door and stepped onto the deck. After scanning the yard for anything out of the norm they walked the steep stairs leading to the yard. A heavy dew weighed on the grass, wetting the hems of their pajamas.

"Brrr. It's a bit chilly this morning." Maureen folded her arms as she led Kelly to the front yard.

"The storm door is propped open. See that?" Kelly pointed toward the porch.

"Whoa, this is weird. Who would be doing this to us?"

They stepped closer, looking over their shoulders to see if anyone was watching. Once they were within a few steps of the porch, they could see what was nestled between the storm door and the front door. It was a plastic jug.

"Do you think it's filled with explosives?" Kelly asked.

"There seems to be some label on it." Maureen squinted so she could read the letters better. "It looks like it says vinegar."

"Vinegar? Why would anyone leave a bottle of vinegar on our porch?" Kelly walked right over to the bottle and saw it had its original seal on it. Yes, this did appear to be just a bottle of white vinegar. She was afraid to touch the bottle with her hand, so she gently pushed it away with her flip flop. The bottle turned slightly, and she saw a big black X had been crossed over the word vinegar on the front label.

"Someone doesn't want us near vinegar," Maureen said.

"Vinegar Hill!" Kelly shivered as soon as the words slipped her tongue. "Translation: stay away from Glenn. I wonder if he has a spurned lover stalking him."

"If you get a phone message asking 'Play "Misty" for me,' run away as fast as you can." Maureen cringed.

"Why would someone go to all of this bother at three in the morning? It's so bizarre."

"I don't know. We better call Detective Kane before he comes over later."

***

Kelly went to bed in her own room and recalled the weird vision of Glenn buying her a glass of vinegar at Finian's. Had that been some sort of premonition? It all made her quite weary, and finally she did fall sound asleep. Her imagination replayed the previous dream of the Seneca brave coming ashore with his canoe. This time though she felt his icy hand actually grab hers, and when she looked up in shock at his face, Kelly realized the brave was Jarod. She screamed, but since he was now pushing her underwater, no words were intelligible.

Delicious aromas wafting out of the kitchen around eleven eventually woke Kelly from her terrifying dreams. After a few good yawns and arm stretches, she wandered upstairs to see what Maureen was cooking. Cupcakes baked in red, white and blue paper cups crowded the dining room table. Corn pudding browned in the oven as Maureen stirred a slow cooker filled with pulled pork.

"Man, I feel like such a slacker." Kelly poured a cup of cold coffee and warmed it in the microwave. "How many people are coming tonight?"

"Spoke with Kevin. He said they'll have to skip it. Andrea isn't doing so well now that Conor's graduated. You know how she struggles with depression. Guess Aidan is starting basketball camp soon, too. They hope to rent a cottage on Skaneateles later in the summer before Conor leaves for Buff State."

"None of our other Kennedy cousins are around?"

"Nope. Tom's family is driving across the country to Yellowstone. Chris and her husband are on Cape Cod for a wedding. Erin is spending the holiday in Manhattan with her fiancé."

"Aw, I'm going to miss all of those guys. They always make the party a little edgy."

"Tara invited Christophe and a couple of her coworkers, also Marla is coming with her hubby and kids. There's also a new winemaker from Italy hired by Brendan who arrived this week. Guess he and his brother will be joining us."

Kelly laughed. "I bet he's on Tara's radar already."

"She did say he was easy on the eyes. Oh, and a couple people from the spa will be coming, Paul, Rita and Monique."

"Isn't she the cleaning lady Detective Kane was asking you about?"

"Yes. She's had a rough go of it lately. I thought it would be nice to treat her to a real Fourth celebration."

"Great. Glad Marla is bringing her kids. That means I get to play with sparklers later."

Maureen opened the lid of the slow cooker to stir the pulled pork. The timer on the oven went off, and she put on some mitts to take out the pan of corn pudding. The beeping noise reminded Kelly of the prowler's visit.

"What did Kane say about the vinegar bottle?"

"He wasn't too concerned about it since it had the original seal. He said to leave it off to the side on the porch and one of the deputies will pick it up for fingerprint testing. The guy came by about an hour ago."

"So, did Kane confirm he'll be here for the party?" Kelly asked as she started reading the paper.

Maureen tried to show the least amount of reaction she could, but she knew this question meant Kelly was intrigued with him.

"Yes, and he's bringing a pecan pie."

"He bakes pie?"

"Yes. Claims it's his signature dessert."

"Well now, that's unexpected." Kelly smiled briefly, and then sipped her coffee and unfolded the newspaper on her lap. The story she read didn't grab her attention. Instead Kelly's thoughts drifted off to an image of Kane wearing an apron as he took the pecan pie out of the oven. The apron tied in the back over his Royal Stewart plaid boxer shorts.

CHAPTER THIRTY-SEVEN
Friday, July 4 ~ 11:45 a.m.

Across the lake, hammers and drills played spirited percussion within the new home of Keuka View Studios. Michael Connelly and his crew didn't mind working on the holiday, because Angie promised them double pay. She wanted to get the place "rock-and-rollin' as soon as possible."

Tom sat on a brand new adjustable chair in the studio's office space as he called musician friends all over the country to let them know what was going on. Angie, accompanied by the interior designer recommended by Gianni—Christophe Aurora, walked through the upstairs of the mansion to discuss choices of paint colors and window treatments. Christophe told her he was heading over to Keuka anyway today, so it worked out fine with his schedule to have a spontaneous meetup.

"Now the paint on this hallway leading to the balcony doors needs to be much brighter. You don't want depressed musicians here."

"Yes, you're right about the walls, Christophe. I'd love it if the ceiling were painted midnight blue with some fluffy clouds near the edges and glow-in-the-dark stars forming summer constellations directly overhead."

Christophe raised an eyebrow as he looked at the plain white ceiling and sighed softly to himself.

"And why would you love that?"

"Well, I want it to be a reminder to all that Jeremiah is looking down from heaven on their creativity. If they need inspiration, all they have to do is look up."

Oh dear God, why do I attract all of the New-Agers? Christophe raised an eyebrow as he tapped a finger sporting an onyx ring on his cheek. "Ummm... kay... I guess we can do that. Perhaps we should drift toward the cornflower blue shades used in European cathedrals. Anything darker will frankly amp the dismal."

"Want to see the view from up here?" Angie led him down the hall and unlocked the balcony door. When they stepped out, Christophe could not help but exclaim about the beautiful view.

"Well, darling, this is worth the purchase price. Look at all of the hilltops you can see from here. This is like a view from a soaring eagle cam." He outstretched his arms and leaned against the wrought iron railing.

"Don't get too close to that edge." Angie shielded her eyes. "I can't watch. Let's go back inside and discuss the wall treatments in the recording booths."

Christophe was curious as to why she led him onto the balcony if she had such a fear of it.

"Do heights freak you out, Angie?"

"Not usually, but I get threatening vibes from the balcony."

Oh great, and she's a psychic, too. I'm going to need a tall drink as soon as I get to Tara's party.

"Plus, I have some dark memories of my late husband associated with that balcony."

"Really? So you've been here before?" *Hopefully in this life.*

"Tom owned this mansion a few decades ago. My husband's band Vinegar Hill recorded here back in the '80s."

Christophe shuddered and brushed her arm gently. "The '80s...*Quelle horreur*! Just had a flashback to my Flock of Seagulls hairstyle and shoulder-padded jackets."

Angie laughed. "Ha!"

"Why did Tom give up this place?"

"Oh, he didn't want to, Christophe. But he couldn't run the studio from his prison cell."

Christophe snorted. "Tom's a felon?"

"Oh, yeah. He used to run drugs from Mexico to the campuses near the Finger Lakes. Planes regularly dropped shipments in the middle of the lake and he'd recover them."

"How exotic! Sounds like an episode of *Magnum P.I.*"

"If only he looked like Tom Selleck...."

Their laughter drifted downstairs where Michael and Tom discussed shelving options for his office. Someone knocked on the back door.

"Helloooo? Anyone here?" a woman's voice called out.

Michael answered the door and was surprised to see a woman with a wide brimmed red hat and long gloves that matched her sundress standing next to a distinguished looking older man.

"May I help you?" he asked.

Luna felt an instant attraction to his Hollywood good looks, that roguish grin and dimple, that unruly black hair and sapphire eyes.

"Hello, should I know you?" she purred.

"I'm Michael, the carpenter. And you are...?"

Luna's eyes immediately settled upon his brawny arms exposed by the sleeveless shirt he wore. She noted a slight glisten of sweat on his weight-sculpted biceps.

"I'm Luna Grande, this is my father, Ignazio. We're here to see Tom and Angie. My husband and I are co-owners here."

The realization she was Gianni's wife drained all the flirty warmth Michael had exuded.

"Oh, forgive my ignorance. Please come in. Tom is in the office and Angie's upstairs with the interior designer."

"Great, she called Christophe already? You'll love him. He's a genius. C'mon, Dad, let's go surprise Tom."

Her father hoped his past interactions with Tom and Angie would have no effect on their relationship with his daughter. She was truly interested in developing her business skills and Iggy could not have been prouder.

Tom's feet were on his desk and he was chatting with a rapper he'd met in Buffalo who was a client of Gianni Grande's. Michael coughed in the doorway.

"Hey, Tom. Luna and her father are here to see you."

Tom swung his legs off the desk and onto the floor.

"Listen, Jimarcus, catch ya later. Got a meeting here at the studio. Look forward to you guys checking us out in August. Stay cool, bro."

Tom stood and smiled warmly at Luna.

"Wow, don't you look beautiful today." They air kissed, and then Tom's eyes locked with Iggy's for the first time since he was arrested.

"Uhhh... Mr. Fracasetti, to what do I owe this honor?" Tom hoped he'd sounded sincere enough.

"Hello, Thomas. Long time no see. I trust you've been keeping yourself on the right side of the law."

Tom winced. He'd forgotten what an imposing figure Iggy was. Even thirty years older he towered above Tom, his hair was thick as a teenager's and he had hands bigger than Tom's feet. As they shook, Iggy squeezed Tom's hand so tightly he had difficulty not yelping.

"Isn't it wonderful you two are reuniting after all these years?"

"We share many memories. Some good, some... not so good." Iggy spoke in an intimidating monotone.

Tom tried to act cool with the uncomfortable situation.

"We're so grateful your daughter is graciously helping us pursue this new dream."

Iggy liked that and patted Luna's back.

"Yeah, she's got a good head for business. Guess it's a genetic thing, ha-ha." His genial expression shifted swiftly. "So what's your plan, Tom? When do you guys expect to be in the black?"

This guy rattled him so much Tom's mind went blank. He gawked at Iggy. Luna knew firsthand how intimidating her father was, so she spoke.

"They made a presentation to us a couple of weeks ago and have a detailed timetable," she assured her father.

Tom smiled at Luna, grateful he wouldn't look like a complete idiot in front of her father.

"Yes, we are working on booking the acts right now. Our plan is to finish the renovations that would affect the studios themselves by the end of this month. I just got off the phone with a rapper from Buffalo who has booked some recording time here in August. We have other artists scheduled in September, October and January of next year. Angie's recruiting some new local talent, too."

"OK. Promising start." Iggy rubbed the two-inch wide gold watch on his wrist. "You're gonna need to have this place booked at least two full weeks of every month, I'd guess, to stay ahead of the mortgage and utilities."

Tom hadn't done his math yet, but that sounded about right.

Voices neared from the stairwell.

"Perhaps we could riff a bit of blue from the ceiling upstairs on the molding downstairs, Christophe. Don't you think?" Angie paused on the bottom step when she saw the four people standing in Tom's office. "What the hell is he doing here? Dammit, I don't want to see that man."

"Whom are you talking about, Angie?"

"The older man in the office. He had his goons beat up Jeremiah when he was on tour in Germany."

"Wow, you know people with goons? I'm totes impressed."

Angie snarled. "Oh, you're hilarious... *not*. Listen. We have to get out of here before he sees us. I don't want to have to speak with...."

"Hey, Angie," Tom called out. "Look who came to visit. You remember Iggy Fracasetti don't you?"

"Dammit!" she muttered through a clenched smile to Christophe as she strode across the large room toward the office. "Iggy, what a pleasure to see you. How have you been?"

Iggy kissed both cheeks and grabbed her hands, holding them out. "You're looking good, babe. What's your secret?"

"Yoga. And bourbon. Pretty much yoga and bourbon, ha-ha." She noticed the frown on Luna's face. "I'm kidding of course. I run on the lake road and have a Pilates instructor come to the house."

Michael raised his eyebrows and grinned at her, way out of view of Luna and Iggy.

Luna and Christophe air kissed. "I'm so glad you're on board with this project. I know you will turn this space into something dreamy."

"This is still a great location for a studio." Iggy looked around the space before his eyes focused on Angie's. "Sounds like Tom is doing a good job booking the acts to record here. What will be your job title?"

Angie glanced at Tom as her palms began to sweat.

"I'm primarily an investor, but I'm volunteering my time now to help with interior design and planning events. I've also been grooming local talent as future recording artists here."

"Speaking of special events, Gianni and I will be here tonight for the fireworks party. How many others are coming?"

"We're expecting around seventy-five people. Those who can't book hotel rooms will be camping over by the cabin. It will be sort of Woodstocky." Angie clasped her hands and forced as warm a smile as she could, turning to Iggy. "Since you're in town, will you be joining us also, Iggy?"

"Perhaps. I have to see what the wife has planned for us."

"Are you two living here now?"

"Antoinette and I have been staying with Gianni and Luna on Canandaigua Lake. We'll be heading back to Italy to our place on Lake Como shortly."

"Ahh, well, hopefully we'll get to see you tonight, but if not have a nice summer in Italy."

"Yeah, you know though, it *would* be fun to come here tonight and reminisce about old times with you, Angie." He winked as he eyed her trim figure overtly. Tom and Michael both caught the gesture and it startled them. "Oh, and by the way, I'm terribly sorry about Jeremiah." He took her hand and kissed it gently. As she felt the weight of the gold-laden hand clutching hers, Angie wondered if he'd put a hit on Jeremiah. It felt like a gesture Don Corleone would have made in *The Godfather*.

The stress of the moment was too much for her. Angie burst into tears and ran back upstairs. Christophe didn't know what to do, so he followed.

"His death was such a shock," Tom said solemnly. Michael nodded.

"Why did you have to go and make her cry, Daddy?"

Iggy looked away from her toward Tom's desk, his hands clenched into fists. "I didn't mean nuthin' by it. I was being genuine."

"Hmm. Well, we'll see you tonight, Tom." Before Luna left the office she turned back and looked right into Michael's eyes. "And will you be there also, Mr. Connelly?"

"Yeah, I plan to," he gave her a megawatt smile. "Looking forward to the party."

They let themselves out. Tom looked at Michael who had an odd expression on his face.

"What's the matter, bro?"

"I don't recall fully introducing myself to them. How did she know my last name?"

"Dude, nothing is a secret to the Fracasettis. They have eyes and ears everywhere."

Michael grimaced.

"I'll be sure to keep that in mind."

***

Glenn spent part of the morning installing an inside lock onto the front door of his house. He feared Rodolfo made a copy of his key to come and go at any time of day. When he went to the hardware store earlier that day, Glenn also bought a couple of solar motion detector lights and a small security camera. For crying out loud, he'd felt safer living in the band's seedy Vinegar Hill apartment in Brooklyn than he did here at this moment.

While Glenn labored, his mind drifted back to the year when Vinegar Hill was touring the U.S. and Iggy Fracasetti was their manager. He'd been Vinyl Buddha's landlord and used to drop by during the recording sessions. Although Iggy played drums with a fair to middlin' jazz trio in Greenwich Village, he longed to try his hand at rock-n-roll. He'd wander into the studio after a recording session and jam with the band. His laid back attitude made Jeremiah comfortable enough to discuss the band's future. Somehow Iggy convinced Jeremiah he should manage the tour one year. To show his commitment to the idea, Iggy purchased an old Greyhound bus and had a friend gut the interior and build it into something similar to a recreational vehicle for Vinegar Hill. Jeremiah was impressed by his efforts and convinced the band it sounded like a good deal.

Glenn hated those days of riding that bus. There were six guys living in cramped conditions. It smelled liked a dank locker room most of the time, even though the bus driver attempted to mask the smell with patchouli oil. Trying to sleep in his upper bunk bed was useless—the shocks were so bad on the bus that every bump in the road felt like a body slam from a WWF wrestler.

They'd arrive at their destination feeling as if they hadn't slept at all. After the roadies dragged the giant cases of equipment out of the tractor trailers and set them up in the venue, the band had to run through sound checks.

"Checking, 1... 2... 3.... Sibilant esssss," Glenn would yawn into his microphone as Tom and another audio engineer adjusted levels. They'd run through a couple of tunes from the set list and once Tom felt things sounded good enough, everyone took a break to grab dinner backstage. Later on the band members wised up and added specific food and beverage requests to their contract rider. Before that, they'd typically find cold pizza or some oily submarine sandwiches with indigestible fatty cold cuts. At least there would usually be a big bowl of M&Ms. For some reason, Chuck the drummer would eat only the red ones. He convinced everyone that they tasted better. Soon they all did it and added a request for "red only" to the rider. Glenn smiled at that memory. Sometimes those concerts would be fueled by red M&Ms and whiskey alone.

After sound checks, the musicians wandered off to the dressing rooms to prepare for the show. That's when they'd first assess the local groupies they'd hook up with later in the evening. The girls hung around the place as casually as if they were employees. The scent of Jovan musk perfume lingered in the hallways after security eventually shooed them outside. Those groupies knew the band's schedule better than the guys did. It was as if they had a sixth sense for where Vinegar Hill would be at all times.

Once the band got notice it was fifteen minutes to show time, they'd gather slowly to watch the crowd from backstage with guitars and drumsticks in hand. Glenn could survey the crowd quickly and get a feel for how the performance would go. Sometimes it was their faces that gave him a clue, other times it was what they were wearing. The trippier they looked, and the thicker the pot smoke haze in the venue, the more likely it would be they would extend their solos and end up doing a three-hours plus gig. Those usually became the brilliant performances of bootleg-recorders' dreams.

Glenn smiled as he remembered those magical moments when the houselights cut off and Vinegar Hill walked onstage led by a roadie's flashlight. The crowd responded immediately with cheers and shrill two-fingered whistles. A red spotlight widened on Will as he'd pluck the first three notes of a bassline for eight bars, followed by Chuck adding a rhythm on snare, cymbal and cowbell for eight more. By then the crowd would be clapping, sometimes stomping their feet. Jeremiah would play a crisp $C7(^\sharp 9)$ chord followed by funky scratch strumming. After eight bars of that, Glenn's hands stretched across the organ keyboard playing a downward chord progression beginning with $D^\sharp$. When he'd hit the bottom, Jeremiah wailed on his Strat and started singing the first verse to "Artistic License." *Boom!* The crowd would *explode* with frenetic energy.

That moment—that initial unbridled jubilation—*that* was what made all the drudgery of traveling and life on the road bearable. In that moment, Glenn and his brother musicians merged into a single soul emitting this amazing force of energy that pulsed through the crowd. They didn't have to talk or signal each other about the direction they were heading. Instinctively, each knew and understood. It was such a difficult thing to explain to interviewers, the palpable sensation of their spirits truly melding into this vast, deep groove of their music. There was no chemical that could ever mimic this high. None! In those moments, Glenn felt more alive than in any other experiences of his life.

He missed that high. Glenn explored all sorts of new interests once he left the industry, but none—not even the art of winemaking—could top what he shared with his brothers onstage.

A profound sadness overcame Glenn. *Dammit, Jeremiah. Why did you have to cross the deep trust we shared? Despite all the bad blood, I still miss you, brother. What I would give to be nineteen again, back in that tiny apartment in Brooklyn, jammin' 'til four in the morning.* Glenn wept without trying to stem his tears. Finally, he had to stop and grab a paper towel to wipe his nose. He stood sniffling for a few seconds as he thought about Jeremiah's hit, "Forever Gigi." He looked heavenward.

"Really, bro, you had to take my rock lyrics and turn them into a power ballad. *Seriously?* Man, that's what hurt me the most!" His words made Glenn laugh. He rubbed his eyes. "Life is so freakin' strange sometimes."

He closed his eyes and was transported immediately back on stage with Vinegar Hill. Jeremiah did not like to break long for an intermission, so they would play for two straight hours before taking one. If anyone felt like his energy was slipping, he would double nod toward Jake the roadie. He'd slip an upper into a small cup of water and hand it to him at the end of a song.

Once they were done with that performance, a different sort of show began. Before the band's first tour, Glenn had never seen so many men with diamond rings sporting foxy women on each arm. Soon they didn't even notice them. Groupies swarmed backstage with local bigwigs or friends of Iggy. They were relentless in their conquest attempts, and wouldn't leave the dressing rooms until they had to be dragged out by the roadies.

When the band eventually stumbled outside toward the bus, they'd see earnest fans who'd been waiting patiently for autographs or to have a photograph taken with them. They'd have to get their acts together, look sober as they forced smiles and made pleasant talk like, "Hey man, that's so cool you have an exact replica of the guitar I played on our third album."

Before they'd go back to the bus, Iggy climbed onboard to do a groupie purge. The bus driver had a difficult time saying 'no' to their come-ons, and he'd often be found in the back bunks with one or two of them.

"Joe, you moron! This one looks like she's not even in high school. Get the hell off our bus, chickie!" Iggy would yell. Some managers might have fired Joe, but Iggy knew it was his one perk of the job. As long as he didn't break any laws, he'd keep Joe on staff. The guy was an excellent driver.

Glenn recalled lying in his bunk after those exhausting nights, wishing he'd been a banker or a teacher, some sort of a career with a normal family life and weekends off. It was funny, all the rest of society thought the rock-n-roll lifestyle was a nonstop glam fest of fame, fortune and sex. They never considered all of the personal, emotional sacrifices band members had to make to maintain their careers.

He thought of course about Chuck's son Devin. The kid had been a star pitcher on his Little League team. Once he reached high school, he led the team to the state championship and won. Devin earned an athletic scholarship to Mississippi State and was courted right from college to play on a minor league team. Amazing accomplishments, but it must have hurt Devin that his father missed every single one of his games.

Glenn winced when he recalled the night they were playing a gig in Oklahoma City. Chuck was antsy because he wanted to get to a bar as soon as the show was over to catch his son in his first game with the majors. He'd been called up as a relief pitcher for the Kansas City Royals in their home game against the Texas Rangers. The audience was so enthusiastic that night, however, that Vinegar Hill played three encores. By the time everything was packed up, Chuck raced across the street from the venue to a sports bar where he saw the crowd reacting to his son's winning pitch on the TV. He never got to see the replay because Iggy yelled to him they were waiting for him to get his ass on the bus. It was a long, silent ride to Phoenix that night.

Chuck's wife Andrea often joked she was a tour widow. In their divorce she cited her husband's life on the road as the main reason their marriage unraveled.

Glenn sighed, tightened the final screw in the lock, and stood back to see if it was straight. His thoughts drifted back to the afternoon in the field with Kelly. What a lovely moment that was. Now she was a fine woman—naturally beautiful, intelligent and sexy, too. He wished he hadn't come on so strong to her so soon. She needed to be tended to patiently and gently, like a fine wine. *Will she ever be able to trust me again?*

A knock on the side door startled him. Glenn peeked out the window and saw Monique's car in the driveway. He unlocked the door and smiled to see her dressed in red, white and blue.

"Well hello there, Monique. Aren't you a star-spangled banner of happiness."

"Happy Fourth of July, Glenn." He smiled at the ease with which she finally called him by his name. She held out a plate covered in plastic wrap.

"I make you dessert. Dis recipe come from my country, *pain patate,* sweet potato pudding."

"How kind of you, Monique. I'm sure it's delicious." He took the plate and let the screen door close between them as he went to set it on the kitchen counter. She was disappointed. The gift would have given her a chance to come inside the house and chat with her handsome boss on his day off. Maybe he knew she was interested.

"I make several and have some left over. I think you would enjoy." She hoped her explanation covered her overt gesture.

"Do I need to do anything special with it?" he asked when he returned to the doorway.

"Keep it chilled. When you want, warm in de oven, 350 degrees. Just few minute. Taste good with coconut ice cream."

"Thank you for thinking of me, that was so kind."

I always do. She smiled sweetly at him. "I go to two parties today, so there is extra."

"That sounds like fun." She noticed that his expression did not match his words.

"First at Maureen's house, then I go to Mrs. Redfern's recording studio."

"Her *what*?"

Monique noted a slightly angry tone in his voice.

"She and Mr. Tom open new studio in mansion on Bluff Point. You know dat place?"

Glenn's face reddened. "Of course I do." He looked away, "I know that place well." *Hmm, Luna neglected to mention that important detail of the property purchase when she called.* Now he was angry. "Tell me, Monique, when does that party start?"

"It begin at nine. She say, 'bring guest.' Would you be mine? I can pick you up on way dere." Monique was a little surprised she felt emboldened to invite him.

"Yes!" He replied so swiftly it stunned them both.

"OK! Good, good. I pick you up at nine. Bye-bye, Glenn." Monique was so ecstatic at his answer and so nervous he might change his mind, that when she started the car she put it in forward, not reverse. She slammed on the brakes, waved sheepishly, and pulled out of the driveway.

Glenn walked over to the living room window and stared at the heart of the lake as his thoughts drifted. Why didn't Luna mention the property she was investing in—on which they planned to eventually relocate his winery—was to be the future site of Tom Russo's studio? It made him question Luna's motives. Was she truly in love with him, or, was this some bizarre backhanded plan from Angie to crush him after he'd rejected her advances years ago after the court case?

CHAPTER THIRTY-EIGHT
Friday, July 4 ~ 3:17 p.m.

Detective Kane pulled a fragrant bourbon pecan pie out of the oven just as Detective Reese Bailey called.

"Hey, I know it's our day off, but I overheard an interesting conversation in the grocery earlier and didn't want to forget to pass it along. Esperanza O'Hare was ahead of me in line and the cashier asked how her wedding went. She mentioned they'd just watched the finalized video of the fireworks and reception. 'If you ever need drone videography, check out Graceful Creative,' she said."

"And... boom! That connects Rodolfo to the wedding. We definitely need to get a copy of that video now. It might have Jeremiah's murder on it."

"That's what I thought. So when are you bringing your ass over here to my party. Mack has already drunk too much beer and he's boring everyone to death with his deer hunting stories."

"Ha-ha! Be there shortly. Hitting your party first, but I have another one to go to around dinner time."

"OK. I'll keep the ribs warm for you. See you soon, bro."

***

"Why haven't I heard from him?" Jarod's mom knew that by now he must have read her note. Maybe he just didn't know what to say. She decided to go to him instead of waiting any longer for a response. It felt as if she couldn't breathe when she arrived at his apartment—her heart pounded wildly, but both sensations faded when she saw his car was still missing from his driveway. Had he even been home to read the note? It would still be on the floor if he hadn't. Perhaps she could see it if she peeked through the mail slot.

She tiptoed up the steps and looked around before she crouched by the slot. Propping it open with her left hand, she tilted her head until she could see the floor below. Nothing was there. He must have gotten it. She bent down just a bit more and looked in from a different angle to be sure. Wait. There was something pink a little bit away. She caught her breath and her heart fluttered when she saw white shreds of paper next to the open envelope.

"Oh no!"

She caught herself as she stumbled backwards on the porch. Since she'd yet to hear from him, her first concern was he might have taken out any rage he felt from the news on her parents. Her fear magnified as she sped down the winding country roads on the West Side of the lake to their home in Branchport. People milled about the sidewalks after the firemen's parade and chicken barbecue, waiting for the fireworks to begin at ten. The crowd slowed her arrival at her parents' Main Street home. She exhaled the moment she saw them sitting safely on the front porch, completely relaxed as they watched the festivities.

They offered her a cold beer, and she sat down waiting for the appropriate time to ask if Jarod had been by. Instead her father dropped a different sort of bombshell.

"Did you read the news about your cousin Tom?"

She shook her head. "Haven't been reading the paper lately. There's too much bad news." Her mother stopped fanning her face and pointed at her.

"You've got that right, dear."

"Anyways," her father interrupted, "he just repurchased Chauncey Mansion on top of Bluff Point."

"He did? Why?"

"He's opening another recording studio. Guess they're having some sort of big shindig there tonight. Chet told me Tom stopped in for a fireworks permit. Already seen a couple of limos pass by today."

"Wonder what celebrities will be there?"

Their words piqued her curiosity. She recalled the famous crowd that used to hang out at Tom's recording studio. Oh, the memories! Her fearful thoughts of Jarod's anger faded as she disappeared into her imagination, picturing what outfit she could pull together from her closet so that she wouldn't stand out when she crashed Tom's party tonight.

***

Tara walked into the kitchen with a case of wine a couple hours later and plopped it on the counter. Kelly looked up from the red velvet cupcakes she was icing and smiled.

"Hey, sis."

"Yum, my fave." Tara walked over and swirled her finger into the bowl of cream cheese frosting.

"Eww, c'mon. Get your finger out of there."

Tara growled playfully.

"Anyone here yet?"

"Only Monique. Maureen took her down to the beach."

"So that woman cleans both Glenn and Angie's homes? I'd like to ask her a few questions."

"I imagine she knows a lot about both of them, probably more than we'd ever want to know."

"Yeah, Kelly, like does Glenn wear boxers or briefs?"

"Argh, stop with that talk. Detective Kane will be here today."

"Will you kill me if I play some Rod Stewart on the stereo when he arrives?"

"Yes. And in regard to Glenn, probably the answer is neither."

"Still livin' the rock star dream... he wishes. Ha! Anyway, I was excited at first by the news he was dating you, but both Maureen and I are happy to hear you've moved on. Never trust a guy who moves too fast. I know of what I speak. Been burned way too many times."

Kelly smiled. Even though Tara exuded a carefree vibe, beneath that exterior she was just as vulnerable as everyone else.

"You know what? I think Gianni was a fool to let you go."

Tara scrunched her nose. Her unresolved pain from their breakup still burned within.

"Onward to handsomer, *younger* men, right?" Tara took a deep breath, fluffed her hair and walked onto the deck.

The afternoon brightened although a determined breeze frothed whitecaps upon the water. A sudden gust whistled through the screen door, spinning paper plates and napkins airborne off the snack table outside. Kelly rescued and anchored them with the red and blue glass votive candle holders that were part of the centerpiece.

"I hope this wind dies down by the time everyone gets here."

A knock on the front door, made them both turn around.

"Hello, is this where the party with all the cute babes is?"

Tara's face brightened to see Michael Connelly at the door.

"Michael?" She looked back swiftly to see her sister's reaction. "Happy Fourth of July, what a nice surprise." He kissed her cheek as he walked through the doorway.

Kelly fought back a frown. *What's he doing here? Why would Tara invite him?*

"Hey, I was just in the neighborhood and thought I'd pop in before I head off to my other party."

"Oh, lucky me. I'm so honored."

Kelly snorted at Tara's sarcasm.

"Here, I brought you a bottle of wine. I hear Hare Hollow is pretty good stuff."

That softened Tara's expression until she recognized the bottle was one she'd given to Michael the evening she'd met him at the Redfern's lakeside home. *Seriously, he's re-gifting the wine I gave him? What a chump!*

"Hello, Kelly. How are you these days?"

"Fine," she replied curtly. "Nice you could crash our party."

"Ow," he laughed, winking at Tara. He never did warm to Kelly.

Tara opened his wine and poured two glasses.

"Care for some of this Cabernet Sauvignon?"

Kelly shook her head. "No thanks. Wine makes me do dumb things."

Tara responded to her sister's glare with a sharp pinch on her arm as she passed.

"Let's go out on the deck, Michael. Shall we?"

They sat at the table shaded by a wide umbrella and clinked their glasses. Maureen walked back up the long, sloping lawn toward them with Monique. Their conversation was about life in Haiti and Maureen was asking her specifically about spices used in their cuisine. When she glanced up and saw Tara chatting with Michael Connelly, she couldn't help herself.

"Oh Lord, what's *he* doing here?"

Monique looked toward the deck at the handsome man laughing with Tara. Maureen was surprised by the grimace on her face.

"Dat's Mr. Connelly de carpenter? You know him? He your friend?"

"No, he's an old friend of my sister. How do you know him?"

"He work for my boss, Angie Redfern."

"So I heard."

"Many bad feelings between him and Mr. Redfern. So much tension. Felt like it choking you."

"Hmm, I wonder what their mutual anger was about."

"That waitress who drown—she return Mr. Redfern's glasses one time. He forget dem at bar. Michael removing old kitchen cupboards and whistle at her. She hug him like a boyfriend. Mr. Redfern not very happy when he see dat. After she left, he stomp around house, slam doors."

"Sounds like Jeremiah was pretty jealous. Did Angie suspect he was interested in Sarah?"

"Ha! She too busy flirting with dat Sarah's boyfriend, Jarod. He come by with boat when Mr. Redfern not there. She wear dis tiny bikini." Monique grimaced.

Now it was Maureen's turn to cringe. "Sounds like it was an anything goes sort of household. That's pretty creepy."

Monique made the sign of the cross.

"*Ô mon Dieu*... She my boss. If I not need de money...."

Michael took a sip of wine as he glanced at the two women nearing the deck.

"Is that Monique, Angie's cleaning lady? What's she doing here?"

"Maureen knows her from the spa. She works there on Thursdays."

"Hmm, I've never run into her anywhere else." Michael stopped talking until the others reached the deck.

"Monique, don't you look beautiful and so patriotic." He stood and kissed her cheek. Tara frowned, which of course Maureen saw. She knew that meant feelings leftover from their disastrous affair still simmered. Monique blushed at his overt gesture.

"Thank you, Mr. Connelly."

Kelly witnessed a bit of what was going on and decided to join the group on the deck.

"I hope you brought your appetites. We have a ton of food inside."

I forgot the music, she reminded herself and turned on the classic hits FM radio station. The conversations spiked in volume as waves of guests arrived and crowded the deck. Marla Russo arrived with her husband and brood of kids, who immediately fell in the lake fully clothed and had to change into the bathing suits she wisely brought along. Upstairs, Tara held court with several men, including the new winemaker from Italy and Michael. Maureen and Monique were having a heart to heart about real life conditions in Haiti after the devastating earthquake a few years ago. Kelly put herself in charge of introducing guests, keeping an eye on the children playing on the beach and refreshing everyone's beverage.

She was in the kitchen pouring two iced teas when a voice at the door interrupted her, "Did someone here order pecan pie?"

Kelly looked at the screen door and saw Detective Kane standing there with a big grin on his face. He wore a blue oxford shirt with the sleeves rolled and a pair of jeans. His hair looked fuller than when he was on the job (maybe he'd used hair product in it) and she noticed a faint scent of woodsy cologne.

"You know, I've heard men like pie." She opened the screen door and welcomed him inside.

"It's all true," he laughed. Kelly noted the artistic pattern he'd created with pecans around the rim.

"Are those candied pecans?"

"Good eye. Maybe you should join our team in the great battle between good and not so good pie."

She laughed. Who knew Detective Kane had a silly side?

"My cape is ready. Sign me up, Detective Kane."

"Please, Kelly. I'm off the clock. Seriously, like I said before, it's okay to call me Ty." He looked past her toward the deck filled with people. "Sounds like you have a big crowd out there."

"Once the sun finally came out, throngs arrived. What can I get you to drink, Ty? Wine? Beer? Other?"

"Well I had a beer over at Reese's, so I'll stick to that."

"They're in the cooler on the porch, next to the buffet table. Fill your plate while I get a server knife for the pie. Make sure you get some of Maureen's pulled pork. It's made with bourbon, a recipe she got from a chef in Louisiana."

Kane patted his stomach. "Oh, yeah, I'm all over that." He waited at the door for her, scanning the buffet outside overflowing with summer salads and side dishes. "What did you make, Kelly?"

"I assisted my sister by frosting one of her desserts. They're at the end of the table—red velvet cupcakes."

"Man, my favorite. You're killing me."

"They're my mother's favorite cupcake, too."

"Looks delicious. Is she here?"

Kelly looked at the food and shook her head. "No, both my parents have been gone for some time. There was so much love in this home, and it remains, that sometimes it feels as if they're still here."

"I bet they were wonderful people, Kelly. How could they not remain with you all in spirit?"

The tone of tenderness in his words resonated within her. Kelly's hand spread across her heart. "Thank you, Ty. C'mon outside, I'll introduce you around."

Rod Stewart's song "Maggie May" came on the radio the moment they stepped onto the deck. Tara laughed so loudly everyone turned to look at her, and then they saw Kelly and Kane. Monique shrank in her chair a bit, hoping the detective wouldn't notice her. Michael turned around in what seemed like slow motion, noticed Kane, and quickly looked back wide-eyed toward Tara. Kelly noticed the reactions. Of course, so did Kane.

"Hmm, interesting guest list today," he whispered.

"Well, Monique was invited. Michael's a crasher. I never trusted that guy."

"And for a good reason. Your spidey sense is well-tuned."

She studied his expression for clues. "Is Tara in any danger?"

He looked over at the crowd surrounding her. "Nah, she can handle him."

"Well, she needs to prove something to herself after Gianni divorced her."

"Hmm, another winner. Say, what's your opinion of his new wife?"

Kelly smiled slightly and squinted toward the lake before looking back at Kane.

"There's a reason why we all call her Looney. I want to run over to her and peel those damn gloves off. When they are off, she's always massaging cream into her hands. They look dead to me. Creepy."

The radio DJ announced what was coming up next on his playlist. "Where were you when our next song became a hit? Here's the late Jeremiah Redfern's unforgettable love ballad, 'Forever Gigi.'"

It was funny, but despite the fact that loud conversations were tucked in each corner of the deck and patio, every voice hushed when his song came on. It felt like a moment of silence being offered for the dead. A few seconds later the conversations slowly increased in volume until they were so loud you could barely hear Jeremiah's voice.

More guests arrived over the next half hour and soon the crowd spilled onto the lawn. Marla and her husband were engrossed in a conversation with another guest about the coyote population on the West Side. Meanwhile their children splashed each other in the lake.

"Hey, is anyone watching those kids?" Kane asked.

"Nope. They were supposed to let us know if they went in again. Wanna play lifeguard?"

Kane put his empty paper plate in the trash, grabbed another beer and one of Kelly's cupcakes.

"Let's go."

Michael watched the two stroll toward the beach.

"So what's with your sister cozying to that cop, Tara? Did she sic him on me?"

"She's involved with someone else. I doubt she had him come after you. He was being a good cop and checking out all of the connections to Jeremiah. You *were* working in their house. Right?"

"Someone else? Who's she seeing? A librarian?"

"Nope, she's been dating a rock star." Tara grinned and walked over to greet some new arrivals at the party. Michael squinted toward Kelly and the cop, wondering whom Tara was referring to when she said that. As far as he knew, Jeremiah had been the only rock star in town.

Kane demonstrated proper stone skipping technique to Marla's oldest boy.

"First, you have to find a quality stone—one that is flat, round and uniformly smooth, like this." Kelly smiled as she watched the two compare stones and noticed how patient Kane was in showing the boy the right wrist action needed to get the most skips per stone. *He would have made a great dad. What a shame*. Later, she and Kane scoured the beach for dried twigs to add to the bonfire pit. A large, rotted willow branch fell during the Memorial Day storm, and Kelly had it sawed into thick chunks and stored in the shed for today. The two carried them across the beach and neatly deposited them in a pile next to the bonfire pit.

Kelly watched him assemble a pyramid of logs and kindling.

"Ty... If I tell you something, do you promise you won't laugh at me?"

Kane shoved two fistfuls of dried leaves under the crossed logs, wiped his hands together to get the debris off, and then sat down on the grassy edge of the beach next to Kelly.

"I will laugh only *with* you, never at you, Kelly."

She tipped her head down and smiled. "OK, here goes. My mother's family line has a bit of psychic ability. Nothing as strong as those clairvoyants on TV. We have random bouts of very intense intuition. Mom told me my great aunt actually had visions from time to time." Kelly looked up at his face. He was still listening intently, and there was no look of judgment. "For me, the ability manifests itself in my dreams. Ty, I think I know who murdered Jeremiah Redfern."

Kane raised his eyebrows and leaned toward her to whisper. "Who did it?"

"OK, it might be impossible given the other circumstances of that night, but I believe it was Jarod Jensen."

His eyebrows raised as he parted his lips to speak, but no words came to mind.

"You see, I've had this repeated dream about that Seneca legend of the curse of the Strawberry Moon. Are you familiar with it?" Kane smiled and nodded, turning toward her fully in anticipation of her explanation. "Well last night after that weird episode with the vinegar bottle, I finally fell into a deep sleep. This time when the Seneca brave came ashore dragging the canoe, he reached out and grabbed my hand. His fingers were icy, and it startled me so that I looked right into his eyes. That's when I realized he had Jarod's face."

Marla's kids started horsing around with the Cavistons' row boat, and they picked that exact moment to drag the aluminum boat over the shale stone beach. The noise startled both Kane and Kelly. Once they caught their breath, both of them laughed so hard they shook. Slowly Kane's face turned serious.

"Hmm, aside from that confirmation by the universe just now, I will keep your theory in mind."

She studied his reaction.

"You think it's someone else, don't you?"

He tried to shift the topic. "Are you trying to read my mind right now, because if you are, I am not one of the people driving the clown cars in the Penn Yan parade." It worked. She laughed and their conversation switched to memories of the Fourth of July celebrations past.

As the sun set, the Cavistons' remaining guests gathered along the beach. Some relaxed on the cement steps, others on the assortment of plastic chairs they'd set out earlier. A few people sat at the end of the dock and dangled their feet in the warm lake. Tara went to refresh her glass of wine in the kitchen and Michael followed. The house was empty, so he had no qualms about grabbing her from behind, turning her around and locking her into a passionate embrace. She knew he was bad news. Even Maureen had warned her about Michael in several heart-to-heart conversations on the deck.

The Fourth of July always reminded Tara of her ex-husband though. It was the day years ago when they met at a jazz festival on Seneca Lake. She fell instantly for Gianni's black, feathered "Serpico" hair. His Aramis cologne lingered on her hands after they were introduced. They'd sat next to each other on the lawn and had such intense conversations she was sure she didn't hear a note of music that night. All she heard and felt was his rich vibrato voice resonating against her heart. *Ohmigod he was gorgeous.*

Tonight she was missing Gianni something fierce. *How could he have abandoned me for that ghoulish wisp of a woman? Does she ever smile? I bet he hasn't had nearly the fun with her that we shared in the good days. When did the good days turn bad? What was it that made him lose interest in me? I look damn good for a woman of fifty-six. So what if I'm allergic to housekeeping. I've still got so much more class than Looney.*

Yes, Michael picked the perfect moment for his amorous advance on Tara. She needed to be reminded of the beauty she possessed, of her allure to men, and desperately needed some loving caresses.

"Any empty bedrooms around here?" he whispered as he pressed her against the stove. She let out a schoolgirl giggle.

A voice cleared behind them.

"Tara, do you know where the matches are?"

Michael's arms went limp and he backed away from an embarrassed Tara.

"I'll catch you later, Tara." Michael never turned around.

"Take care," Kane called out as the screen door slammed behind Michael as he fled toward his car. Tara covered her face with her hands.

"The matches are in the far drawer."

"Thanks, uh... sorry to interrupt."

She appreciated that he just took them and went back to the beach. *God I hope he doesn't tell Kelly. I don't need her judgmental comments.* Tara filled her wineglass, ran her fingers through her hair and went down to the beach to join the others.

Kane handed the matchbook to Kelly and she ignited the bonfire. Maureen rounded up Marla's children to distribute already lit sparklers and instructed them to toss the burned out metal rods into the bucket of water when they were done. Kane lit the road flares and planted the fiery sticks along the shore. Firecrackers crackled in the distance across the lake. One of the neighbors lit a Roman candle and everyone oohed at the fountain of pretty colors erupting from it.

"Need another beer?" Kelly asked Kane.

"Nope. I'm fine. What a perfect Fourth of July."

"I know. It usually rains a bit."

"Actually... I was talking about the company." He smiled slightly as he drew on the beach with a twig. Kelly looked away and grinned. *What is happening here?*

A spectacular golden chrysanthemum firework exploded across the lake, prompting some guests to spontaneously croon "God Bless America." Everyone joined in and sang robustly every patriotic song that came to mind. When they ran out of those songs, Marla began singing old TV show theme songs. The sisters were grateful the vibe was so happy and everyone seemed to be genuinely enjoying the free show.

Monique glanced at her watch and felt a sudden flash of warmth across her face. It was time to leave and pick up Glenn. She stood to say thanks and farewell to Maureen who'd been so gracious to her.

"I must go. Mrs. Redfern expect me at her party."

"Where's that?" Maureen asked Monique.

"Bluff Point, her new studio. Many celebrities will be dere." Her eyes danced as she flashed a full grin.

Tara and Kane both tuned their attention to this conversation. And when Monique added she was giving her other boss a lift to the party as a surprise to Angie, Kelly nearly dropped her glass of wine.

"Bye, everyone. Thanks for lovely time."

"Be careful driving, Monique." Maureen waved.

Monique's departure gave tacit approval to the others who wanted to head home that they could leave without offending the hostesses. By the time the flares reduced to flat piles of white ashes by the shore, it was down to Kane, Kelly, Tara, Maureen and two of her coworkers.

"Should I put another log on the fire?" Kelly asked.

Maureen's friends stood to leave. "Well, we have to head home. Thanks for a great time, Mo."

"I'm so glad you two could join us. I'll walk back to the house with you."

Kelly poked the bonfire with a stick. "Well, since this is pretty much embers now, guess I'll fill the bucket with some water and douse it."

While she dredged the old aluminum bucket in the lake and put out the fire, her sister watched Kane's expression toward Kelly. *Oh yeah, he's interested.*

"So Ty, were you ever married?" Tara asked. She was more interested in Kelly's reaction to the question than his. He shook his head.

"Nope."

"Why not?"

"Tara!" Kelly hissed. "That's none of our business."

Kane's face turned wistful.

"Years ago there was a local girl who I wanted to marry. She left town before there was a chance to propose."

"Where did she go?"

"Not sure. It was as if she'd vanished into thin air. Her friend told me she headed west. I recall her wanting to spend some time in Taos. That's where she probably ended up. Her parents didn't even know her location. At least, that's what they told me. I always pictured us living here with three sons."

"Ever Google her?"

Kelly shook her head. *Let it go, Tara. It's obviously a painful subject for him.*

"Yeah," he sighed. "Found one reference to her name on a cat rescue chat group based in Salt Lake City. Pretty sure it was her because she had seven cats when we dated."

"*Seven* cats?" Tara struggled to maintain her composure. She tittered briefly, then erupted into full-blown belly laughs. Kane frowned at first, but her hilarity was so infectious he couldn't help but join in. Poor Kelly tried to display the empathy she felt for him, but also dissolved into uncontrollable guffaws.

"Oh, Ty...." Tara tried to catch her breath long enough to speak. "You could have been a cat herder instead of a cop." That set them careening again into fits of laughter.

"Could you see me in my cruiser, hanging out the window with a lasso in my hand, calling 'Here, kitty-kitty.'"

They laughed so loudly that someone on the opposite shore yelled, "What the hell's so funny?" Tara wiped her humor-induced tears away and eventually calmed down.

"So what's the deal with this party tonight at the mansion on the bluff?" Kane folded his arms. "I heard some rumors about the guest list that it includes well-known music biz types. What have you heard?"

"Well my ex will be there apparently."

"Ah, so you have a true connection to the festivities. I'd love to see who shows up. The timing of all this is intriguing. Think you could stomach crashing their party?"

Tara put her hands on her hips.

"Yeah. Definitely. I'd like to see Looney's face when she sees me there. Hey Kelly, wanna crash Angie's party with us?"

Tara's use of "us" bugged Kelly, but secretly she was intrigued to know if Glenn might appear there.

"Hey, why not? I'd love to see the inside of that place and chill with a celebrity or two."

"Will Maureen want to join us?" Kane asked as he helped Kelly rake the bonfire to make sure it was extinguished.

"Maybe. She might be too tired, though. She's been prepping for this party for days."

They picked up empty bottles and glasses and walked the long slope to the house.

"Great party, everyone." Maureen spooned leftover pulled pork into a plastic container. "Definitely one of our best."

"Are you game for a little adventure?" Tara asked. Their wide grins mystified Maureen.

"Why... what's up?"

"We're in the mood to crash a party. Wanna come?"

"Where? You mean Angie's soiree? Won't Gianni be there?"

"So what. We have a big strong detective with us. He won't mess with me." Tara slipped her arm through Kane's. Kelly refused to let Tara get the upper hand with him, so she grabbed Kane's other arm.

"Or me!"

Maureen snorted.

"Why not? Give me a couple minutes, kids." She went upstairs to her bedroom and returned wearing a new blouse and pair of sparkly earrings. "OK! Off to reckless adventure!"

As they headed for Kane's car, he dropped back and whispered to Kelly, "Don't worry. I haven't forgotten about our other planned adventure." He felt his phone vibrate and took it out to read a text from Investigator Reilly.

"Been monitoring the ping again. Live, right now. Signal is moving from Wayne toward Hammondsport. Are you available if we close in?"

Kane frowned at the text, and looked at the women waiting next to his car. He hoped nothing would come up until after this spying adventure. Then again, they were strong women and he figured they could handle it if they had to be left somewhere until he could come back and get them.

"Yes."

CHAPTER THIRTY-NINE
Friday, July 4 ~ 10:07 p.m.

Grace Sleek peeked around the curtain at Haute Mama's. Two men sipped margaritas quietly in the audience waiting for the Firecracker Drag Show to begin. She looked at her Peter Max watch. It was after ten. Where was Glenn? He'd agreed to stop by when she invited him at the gun range. Was he standing her up?

Moan Jett sneered at her. "Stop pacing. You're gonna wear out the heels of your Frye boots, my little fringe queen."

"He promised he'd be here. The front table is reserved for him. I planned this to be such a special night, hoping it would remind him of our backstage antics at Woodstock."

"Snap out of it, girlfriend. He was probably tripping on brown acid when you hooked up. That guy's too rural granola for me."

"Lil' Miss Leather's suddenly a love expert?"

"Listen you b...."

Mitch arrived at the stage door entrance, walked over to Grace and whispered something in her ear. She flared her nostrils and cut him off mid-sentence with a raise of her hand.

"That whore is throwing a party tonight? Are you sure he went? He'd have to be a fool to walk in there."

"I waited outside his house like you asked. Some black woman arrived and he got in her car. Followed them all the way up Bluff Point to the mansion. There are tons of people there, too. I think I saw one of the guys from Journey."

"Don't utter a single word." He paused for a dramatic breath. "There's yet *another* woman?"

Grace fluttered her false eyelashes and feigned a swoon. Once she collected herself, she clomped off the stage to mope in the dressing room. Dyan Cannondaigua walked by in white overall hot pants with Miss Skinny Atlas, dressed as a body-building beauty queen. Judy Carland paused at the mirror to adjust the automobile fin shoulder pads on her red sparkling dress.

"The show will have to go on without me. I can't deal with this utter affront to who I am. Where's Jarod? He was supposed to be here."

"Haven't heard from him since he left my apartment early this morning. Should I call him? What do you want me to do?" Mitch asked as he looked at his reflection in the lighted mirror.

"I'm not going to sit around waiting for either of them to show. The show must go on without me. Drive me back to my office. I'm in the mood for a night flight. It's time to teach that bitch a lesson."

***

"Look at all the cars already." Kelly leaned her head out the car window to get a better view as Kane neared the old Chauncey Mansion. She could hear the bassline of Talking Heads' "Psycho Killer" pulsing from the DJ's stereo. "We're going to have to walk a mile to get there."

"Isn't there a path in the woods by the old observatory below that will bring us to the house?" Tara asked. "We could park on the side of the road there. It might even be closer than parking way back here."

"And you know about this path how?" Maureen teased.

"We used to drink in those woods."

"I should have known. Ha! Anyone have a flashlight?"

"No, but there's the light on my cellphone. I don't see any place to park here. How do I get to that observatory, Tara?" Kane asked.

"Keep driving past the mansion, and follow the curve in the road. There's another lower road to the observatory itself. Don't bother going down there; park along the shoulder above it. It's right near the path through the woods."

"Well, you promised me adventure." Maureen laughed, but she hoped she'd be able to walk OK through the woods. Kane assessed her situation as soon as they got out of the car. He extended his arm.

"May I have the pleasure of escorting you to the party?"

What a gracious and kind man. Oh Kelly, you'd be smart to fall for this one.

Tara led them up the path using the light from her own cellphone. The route was well worn; she figured it must still be a drinking spot. Lights gleaming from the mansion's balcony could be seen beyond the edge of the woods. "We're almost there, you guys." Tara strode fearlessly into the clearing, then paused for everyone to cross the field to her. A short distance away a stone wall about three feet high blocked their path.

"Oh dear, how do we get over that?" Maureen asked. They looked toward areas where light spilled from the mansion's windows illuminating the grounds.

"Over to our right," Kane pointed. "It looks like the wall ends a few feet from the tree line. If everyone can see well enough from the glow of the house lights, we should turn off our phones. Don't want to give a warning of our surprise arrival." Just as he went to shut down his phone, Kane got another text from Investigator Reilly.

"Pings stationary from top of Bluff Point. Sending cars to check area around Chauncey Mansion."

Kane's eyes widened. Should he send the women back to the car for their safety? If there were a killer on the loose here, he did not want the sisters to be out of his sight. Yet after that text, he couldn't leave the scene.

"Ladies, a heads up. I may have to put on my detective cap this evening."

"Was that a message related to the investigation?" Kelly asked.

"Let's just say now I *have* to go inside this party. Wanted to warn you things might get a little exciting. Would you rather wait in the car?"

"No freakin' way would we miss this." Tara breezed past him.

"We need a code phrase. If I turn to you and say 'moonshine,' that means I want you all to head back to my car and wait there. *Immediately.* Can we agree on that?" They gave him a thumbs up. He texted back to Reilly, *"Already on the scene. Party under way. Moving in."*

"I'm not letting go of you, Ty." Maureen tightened her grip on his arm.

"Nor I you," he laughed. "OK, here we go."

As the DJ morphed "Rock the Casbah" into "Groove Is in the Heart," distant conversations emerged from the background noises.

"When do the fireworks begin?" one guest asked.

"Angie said something about eleven."

The four paused by the side of the house.

"Uh-oh. Look up. Have the paparazzi caught wind of this?" Tara pointed toward the south lawn of the mansion as lights approached in the sky.

"Hey, maybe we'll make it into *People* magazine. Ready for your close-up?" Maureen laughed.

"That's not a helicopter." Kane put his hands on his hips as he squinted at the form moving toward them in the dark.

"He's right. It looks like the drone that buzzed our house."

Tara squinted at it. "Dayum, Kelly. Is that thing still following us?"

Kane led everyone behind a lilac bush next to the house. They watched the drone buzz the mansion.

"Phew! That thing gives me the creeps," Kelly whispered.

"Who's flying it?" Maureen asked.

They heard a whirring noise approaching.

"Oh, God! Did it see us move behind this bush?"

Kane noted the fear in Kelly's voice. "I doubt it. Relax. We'll be fine here."

"Look, it's hovering next to the balcony. That's bold." Tara parted the lilac bush leaves so they could see better.

It didn't take long for the guests to notice the peeping drone. Someone let Angie know about it, and thanks to the bourbon she'd been drinking, she strode angrily onto the balcony, set her glass on the railing and raised the middle fingers of both hands toward the drone.

"How's that for a photo shoot, you damn parasites! Oh wow, look at Jeremiah's widow, so drunk and distraught that she doesn't give a sh...." Angie stumbled toward the railing, and a strong arm circled her waist before she tumbled over. It was dark so she couldn't see who the man was. Once he brought her inside though, she stared at him with one eye squinted until she recognized him as the man who'd been in the grocery.

"What the hell? Lookin' a bit older, but is it really *you*? Dammit! Who let you in here, Glenn McCann?"

He turned toward Monique and whispered, "Close that balcony door," and then sat Angie on a couch in the hallway.

"Are you OK, Ange?"

"Am I OK? Am I *effin'* OK? Fine question coming from you, *murderer*."

The DJ stopped for a break and everyone upstairs stared at the noisy pair encountering each other, face-to-face for the first time in decades. Their voices even carried outside.

"Was that Angie screaming?" Tara whispered. "My God, they must all be trashed."

"Things are definitely getting interesting in there. I bet no one would notice us now. Let's go around to the back entrance." He gestured for them to follow.

"But what about that drone?"

"It won't notice us, Kelly. Not with all the drama upstairs."

They snuck forward behind the lilac bush and the shrubs beyond it until they found a clearing. It was a short jog around the corner of the mansion into the back entrance.

"OK, on the count of three, make a dash for it."

A man wearing dress slacks, white shirt and bow tie guarded the door. His brawny arms enfolded a clipboard to his chest.

"May I have your names?" Kane took out his detective badge and flashed it at him. The guard's eyes widened.

"Mrs. Redfern asked me to do some surveillance of the guests, related to her husband's murder. We won't be long." Kane pushed the Caviston sisters past him into the mansion. They were greeted immediately by the catering staff who handed each sister a champagne flute and offered them bacon-wrapped scallops or duck-filled jalapeño poppers. Kane nodded and they each took something so they would blend in with the crowd.

"Twelve o'clock high, Tara." She heeded Maureen's warning and looked directly across the room where Luna stood chatting with Ryan. She turned so Luna couldn't see her face.

"Where's Esperanza? I wouldn't leave my husband alone with that witch for a second."

The shouting increased on the second floor. Tom, who'd been chatting with some members of a band from Buffalo he hoped to record, excused himself and ran up the stairs, two at a time. When he reached the landing he yelled.

"What the... who invited you, McCann?"

Kelly turned her head immediately toward the commotion.

"Uh-oh, sounds like things are going to get a bit rough up there," Kane whispered to her.

"Are you going to play the cop card again?"

"Not unless I have to."

Outside an orange Volkswagen Beetle covered with daisy stickers approached the mansion. Cars choked the shoulders narrowing the route to a single lane and spilled into the driveway ahead. The driver knew an alternate path to the mansion, however, and backed up to a spot where it was easy to cross the shoulder onto the property. She parked the Beetle behind a water pump shed, fluffed the high tease of her long hair and headed toward the mansion. A pair of eyes watched her from a darkened car as she entered a side door. The DJ had just pumped up the volume with Prince's "Let's Go Crazy," but everyone downstairs could still hear Tom shouting at Glenn.

"Chill out, man. For your information, I just saved Angie from falling off the balcony. Some paparazzo is buzzing a drone out there."

"You still haven't answered my question. Who invited you here?" Tom jabbed his finger into Glenn's chest.

"I heard you were setting up the studio again and wanted to stop by and wish you two luck."

Tom winced from a pang of wanting to believe his former friend was sincere.

"He just wants to jump my bones, Tom." Angie held out her glass of bourbon as if saying "cheers" to them and laughed.

"You sonofa...!" Tom lunged for Glenn's throat and put a chokehold on him. Luna heard the screaming and ran upstairs.

"Let him go, Tom!" she yelled as other guests screamed. Tom was afraid Luna would say something to her father Iggy and released his grip immediately. "Glenn, are you OK?" Luna put her arm around him as he bent over to get some air.

Angie squinted, and right now she was seeing two Glenns, two Lunas.

"Well looky here. When did you two get cozy?"

"All righty then, I just got called into work." Kane inhaled deeply, then turned toward Kelly. "Wish me luck."

"Please be careful, Ty." Something instinctive made her lean in and kiss his cheek. Her impulsive gesture startled Kane as much as herself, but he acted unflustered by it. "OK, stay put you guys. Be right back."

"Yell if you need our help, Ty." He nodded at Maureen.

The grandfather clock in the downstairs living room chimed eleven times. A thunderous bang outside rattled the mansion.

"Ah hell, here come the freakin' fireworks." Angie left the fighting men and staggered toward the balcony door. "C'mon everyone. The show's just begun." Monique was afraid she might really fall over the railing this time, and held the door closed as Angie tried to open it.

"Monique? Wait a minute... is it Wednesday already? What're you doin' here?" Angie wobbled toward her.

"Dis is your party. Remember? You invite me."

"Oh, yeah. Forgive me, oops! I might be a little drunk at the moment."

"A little?" Monique lowered her eyes and grinned.

Angie glanced past her and saw a tall man break up a fist fight newly erupting between Tom and Glenn. It was someone she didn't recognize, maybe one of Iggy's goons. *Aw hell, I hope that bastard isn't here.*

Kane and another guest successfully separated Tom and Glenn, then he called headquarters for backup. Party guests paid little attention to the drama and spilled onto the balcony to watch the fireworks show right outside.

"Hey Monique, who did you say you came with?"

She looked toward Glenn sitting on a couch with Luna, still simmering from the fight. "With my other boss. Dat's him."

Angie tilted her head toward the man Monique pointed at and stumbled into her slightly as she turned around quickly. She poked her maid's arm.

"What the hell? You *work* for that monster?"

"Glenn is not bad man; he a very kind boss."

Angie staggered backwards and paused to slurp more bourbon from her glass.

"Not a bad man? *Really*? Sorry to burst your bubble dearie, but that man killed my husband."

"No, he would never kill him."

"How do you know?"

"I just do."

"Ha! Has he bedded you, too? Get in line, honey. That jerk's a murderer and you're a thief. It's a match made in effin' heaven."

Monique folded her arms and frowned.

"You very drunk now, Angie."

"Oh yeah? Tell me, Saint Monique, what *did* you do with that notebook you stole from my house."

"I not steal. As we say, *Tanbou prete pa janm fè bon dans...* a borrowed drum never make good dancing. I gave dis notebook back to de true owner."

"You did whaaaaat?" Angie screamed. "Why you little...." Angie grabbed Monique's hair and yanked hard.

"Help!" Monique screamed.

Down in the basement of the mansion, a waiting hand hovered over the circuit breaker box for the perfect moment.

Boom! The hand flipped the main breaker and every mansion light turned off and the DJ's booth went silent. Some laughed, thinking it was part of the fireworks show. Not the Cavistons.

"I've got a bad feeling about this." Kelly could barely make out her sisters from the faint glow of a distant candle.

"Let's get out of here. This is too creepy." Tara saw the back entrance light up from the continuing fireworks outside. "Follow me you guys."

"What about Ty, though. Shouldn't we wait for him to come downstairs?" Kelly winced as another firework boomed outside.

"He'll find us outside. I'm sure he's capable of taking care of himself."

The fight between Monique and Angie spilled out onto the balcony where guests oohed at the fireworks. Loud, repeated explosions covered the sound of the women fighting.

In the meantime, Luna grabbed Glenn's hand and led him downstairs in the dark. She rushed him outside to safety and then paused to throw her arms around him. Luna kissed Glenn with an intensity that made the three Caviston sisters hiding nearby drop their jaws and gasp aloud.

"Why you little whore!" a deep voice hissed from behind them all.

The sisters' eyes turned toward the woman who emerged from the driveway pointing a handgun at Luna and Glenn.

"Step away from my man! Now, sugar!"

Luna released her arms from Glenn's neck and turned to face the woman dressed like a Vogue fashion spread from 1969, from her Day-Glo mini-dress to her fringed boots. The woman brushed back the long bangs shading her eyes.

"If I can't have you, my love, no one can." She raised a handgun and aimed at him.

"Hey, I recognize you." Glenn stared. "Didn't we meet at…?"

A giant chrysanthemum firework exploded directly above them as a hulking body emerged from the shadows and knocked Grace Sleek to the ground. Kane rolled over and grabbed her handgun before she could.

"Hands above your head, Miss." Kane patted her down.

Kelly didn't know which direction to watch. There was so much going on it was confusing. She was mainly drawn to observing the body language between Luna and Glenn while Kane was arresting this woman.

"Are you alright, love?" Kelly heard Glenn whisper to Luna. Her jaw dropped even farther. Had these two been an item while she thought she was dating Glenn? And where was Gianni during all of this?

The sound of approaching screams drew their attention toward the back doorway. Monique zipped past them, Angie chasing after her with a fireplace poker.

"Come back here you little thief!"

Glenn managed to subdue Angie by grabbing her from behind. He squeezed her fist until it released the poker. She spun around and slapped his face.

"You bastard! You used your freakin' cleaning lady to spy on us so you could get your precious notebook back. Hope you're happy you have it back now, even though it's covered in Jeremiah's blood."

"Now that it's back in my possession, I plan to sue your ass and get the rights to royalties he earned with my stolen lyrics!"

Luna turned from Angie and Glenn's ruckus toward the fleeing woman. *Is that who I think it is?* Luna yelled to get her attention.

"Hey, wait! Aren't you Rodolfo's cleaning lady?"

"Yes, she is," said the handcuffed woman who'd just threatened her. Luna squinted back.

"How would you know?"

She lifted a cuffed hand slowly and tugged at her long hair. The fall slid off. Now it was Glenn's turn to squint.

"Holy crap! Rodolfo, is that *you?*"

Angie gawked at him and snorted. "Wait, you're Tom's friend Rodolfo? Whaddya know. He never said you were a drag queen." Rodolfo sneered as he returned the wig to his head.

"Oh honey, you wish you looked this good." He continued his previous conversation, ignoring Luna's gaping mouth. "Yes, Glenn. It's me. Remember when I took that photo of you and the rest of Vinegar Hill, right on the lawn over there."

"Of course, man. I always dug your photos of us. You have a great talent." Glenn spoke calmly, hoping compliments would soothe Rodolfo's agitation.

"Why thank you."

Luna didn't know what to say. "Why do you need to do all of this, Ro? Isn't the money from Graceful Creative enough? I mean, I could help you out. As Glenn said, you do beautiful work."

"I don't need your help or your faux pity, Luna. This is simply who I am."

"How long have you been in town, man? Wished I would have known. We could have done lunch or something." Glenn tried to sound as convincing as he could though he was actually freaked out by confronting his longtime stalker.

"Oh, honey. I would have loved that. If you only knew...."

"Are you guys taking all of this in," Tara whispered to her sisters.

"Someone pass the popcorn." Maureen couldn't help herself and laughed aloud. Glenn and Rodolfo turned toward the sound.

"*Kelly?* What are you doing here?"

She cringed. What now? Should she come out from the shadows and say hello to him?

"Hey, who invited you bitches?" Angie pointed toward the sisters. "Do I even know you?"

Monique grimaced as she waved shyly at Maureen.

Another explosion sounded, but this time it came from a gun at close range, not a firework. A bullet whistled past their heads and shattered part of the window sill behind them.

"Everyone down!" Kane yelled, pulling Rodolfo behind him.

"Who's shooting?" Angie whispered.

"Haven't a clue. That was too close, though." Glenn cowered when a bottle rocket whistled in the distance.

Angie staggered to her feet a few seconds later and groaned toward the shadowy figure nearing. Kane didn't want Rodolfo to get away, yet he didn't want Angie injured.

"Get down, *now*! You'll get shot," he hissed.

"Jarod hon, is that you?" The face of the approaching man was nearly visible. She reached out to hug Jarod, but he froze in his footsteps.

"Angie, I'm sorry," he replied in an emotionless tone. "But I have to do something."

"What Jarod, what is it?"

He raised his handgun at her.

"NO! Stop it, Son. Put that gun down. *Now!*" A woman with long hair emerged from the shadows with pleading hands stretched toward him. Jarod looked toward his mother. He rubbed his eyes and tried to focus on her face. *What's she doing here and why is she dressed like Janis Joplin?*

"Who the hell are you?" Angie squinted at her. "Are you Jarod's mom?"

The woman looked away from her son. It had been years since she'd seen Angie, but despite the toll of age she easily recognized Jeremiah's widow. Emotions swirled inside. Her hands shook... oh how she needed a stiff drink. Before she mustered strength to answer she took a deep breath.

"Yes, I am."

Jarod scratched the side of his face with the handgun. He paced like a toddler that needed to pee. "Ma, I have to tell you something. I don't know how to... it's just, I didn't realize that... but I needed the cash... to buy our house... and then Sarah died... I never would have... but he was already dead in my mind."

She tipped her head to the side as she looked as his distraught face. This odd behavior meant Jarod probably read her note, but what was he trying to say?

Tom walked out the back door and saw the commotion.

"Oh, please! What's going on now?" He stopped his approach the minute Jarod pointed his handgun at him.

"Whoa! Chill, man." Everyone turned around.

"Hi, cousin."

It was a familiar voice Tom hadn't heard in decades. He gawked at the woman with the long hair wearing a flowing blouse, hip hugger bell bottoms and a peace sign pendant on a chain. The recognition of who she was made him stagger backwards, like a cowboy shot in a western.

"My God. *Gigi?* Is that you?"

Angie hissed at their surprise reunion. "Holy effin A. The bad karma just keeps rollin' in."

Glenn's arm slipped immediately from Luna's shoulders. He neared the woman slowly, hands over his mouth and then stretched both arms toward her for a hug.

"Gigi... Oh, I can't believe it. It's really you. My God, I thought I'd never see you again," he whispered as he buried his face in her long gray hair. He swayed his body against hers gently as if they were slow dancing to music only they could hear. She wanted to hug him back with all of her might, but Jarod was watching and the look on his face was terrifying.

"Wait, Ma... you know Glenn?" Jarod squinted painfully as if he were experiencing an excruciating migraine.

"Of course she knows him. She slept with the whole band and everyone else who recorded here. Well whaddya know. We meet again, Gigi." Angie sounded suddenly sober as she folded her arms. "Where have you been whored up, I mean holed up, all these years?"

Jarod swung back toward Angie. "Shut up, or I'll blow you away, too."

Gigi pushed Glenn away. "Too? What do you mean by 'too'?"

Jarod scuffed the ground with his foot, then pushed his hands against his temples as if his head were ready to explode.

He started that pacing again, like a prizefighter, hand still clutching the handgun.

Gigi thought he looked insane. Sure Jarod was prone to angry moods, but she never saw anything like this. He must be high. But what's he on?

"Ma... I'm really sorry. I didn't know... I never would have... if only you'd told me sooner... like I said, I needed the cash and Rodolfo hired me to...."

Rodolfo tapped a finger in front of his lips, hoping Jarod would see him and stop talking. It was too late. Could he make a break for it while this drama unfolded? Kane's firm hand grabbed his shoulder.

"Don't even think about it," he whispered.

It took a few seconds before Gigi processed what her son was trying to say. When she realized what he'd done, she gasped, flailed her arms and groaned like a wounded mother bear before she collapsed into a squat on the ground, lacing fingers behind her head and rocking as she sobbed.

"Can someone just tell me what the hell is going on?" Angie gestured with her hands toward the heavens.

"I KILLED YOUR HUSBAND! I KILLED MY FATHER! ARE YOU HAPPY NOW!" He lifted his finger toward the trigger.

At that very moment Kane's coworkers Detective Reese Bailey and Deputy Corey Martin tackled Jarod before he could shoot Angie. Bailey wrested the gun from Jarod's hands as Martin snapped a pair of handcuffs on his wrists.

Those witnessing the moment gawked in stunned silence. Tom grabbed Angie into a big hug. She closed her eyes tightly as she sobbed so hard her entire body shuddered into his embrace.

No one spoke as the cops gave Jarod the Miranda warning before walking him away from the scene. As if on cue, the moment the police drove away everyone made a deep sigh. Kelly turned, wide-eyed to her sisters.

"You guys, I had a premonition it was him. In the vision, I saw his face on that Seneca Indian from the curse of the Strawberry Moon."

The sisters raised their eyebrows at each other.

"As if we needed to be freaked out any further tonight, Kelly." Tara exhaled as she placed her hand over her heart. "My God!"

Now Glenn understood why Gigi abandoned him about twenty-five years ago. Jeremiah must have gotten her pregnant and she couldn't bear to tell either man. He took her hand tenderly and raised it to his lips.

"I wish you had told me you were pregnant. It wouldn't have mattered. We could have raised your son together."

Gigi smiled faintly at the thought of what her life might have been like, but worries over the difficult road ahead crowded her mind.

"I better go with Jarod." She pulled away and released her fingers from his, giving Glenn one last heartbreaking glance.

CHAPTER FORTY
Saturday, July 5 ~ 12:25 a.m.

The two sheriff's deputies tucked zombie-like Jarod and a defiant Rodolfo into their cruiser. When Inspector Reilly arrived on the scene, she and Kane searched Jarod's car. They found some more guns and a drone in the trunk.

"Get his cellphone from him, Kane." They checked its phone number against the one that had made the call to Jeremiah. It didn't match.

"So an accomplice is still here among this crowd?" Kane looked back toward the mansion where four troopers remained on guard. Reilly sent a text back to headquarters to see if the pinging had moved. *Still live from that stationary position,* the reply came seconds later.

"Let's get everyone back inside." Reilly surveyed the guests milling about the lawn. "We'll interview a few people, then I'll call the number and see where it rings."

They herded the guests into the main room on the mansion's first floor. Tom went downstairs to check out the circuit breaker and saw the electricity had simply been shut off. *Gigi, you always were such a trickster.* He switched it back on and joined the others.

"Well, we might as well make ourselves comfortable." Maureen plopped onto an oversized couch and her sisters nestled next to her. Tara tapped her foot for a few minutes, stood and wandered over to the buffet. She poured a glass of wine. "Anyone else want something?" Kelly and Maureen shook their heads. It was probably the exhaustion of preparing for the party they'd hosted earlier, but Maureen soon fell asleep. Tara wandered around looking for Michael and finally found him near the kitchen chatting with some pretty brunette as he held a plastic bag of ice on his face. His eyes widened as she approached.

"Hey, Tara. That's some ex you have."

"What do you mean? Gianni did that?"

"Doesn't want me hanging around you."

She blinked, paused, then sauntered away silently. *Gianni, the man who abandoned me... defended my honor tonight?*

Glenn and Luna whispered across the room from Kelly. It sickened her to hear their cozy conversation on top of witnessing his emotional reaction earlier to Gigi. How many women was he seeing at one time? He felt as distant to her now as he did that night his magical rock star presence passed her after the concert in Rochester. Kelly slipped away upstairs where she wouldn't be subjected to the sound of their intimate tones anymore.

She wandered past the rooms that were formerly used as studios. Which one of these was where Glenn recorded his vocal track for her favorite Vinegar Hill song, "I Need Your Truth"? Her intuition led her to the middle room, and she opened its door. The ceiling still had the original foam acoustic panels from when Tom owned the place. She imagined where the grand piano and microphone would have been set up. If she closed her eyes, she could hear Glenn playing those lush chords with bittersweet harmonies that sounded so beautiful though his lyrics were so sad. Yes, the emotion of that song was what she felt at the moment. Had she been an absolute fool, or could a rock star truly have felt something briefly for her? She sat cross-legged on the floor, hoping to absorb any residual vibes from the band's recording sessions. Before long she fell asleep.

It had been a long, crazy night and she had another brief, disturbing dream about Jarod which woke her up. Kelly wandered farther down the hallway and opened the door to the balcony. A couple of party guests talked quietly in the corner about the album they hoped to record here. She tiptoed past and went to the railing that offered a spectacular view of Keuka Lake. The faintest hint of light on the eastern horizon brightened the indigo black sky. *What time is it?* she wondered. She took out her phone. *Six minutes to four in the morning? Man, when will this end?*

One of the sheriff's deputies opened the balcony door.

"We need to ask you all some questions. Will you please join me downstairs?"

Kelly followed him and saw Maureen was now awake on the couch sitting next to Tara and... Gianni!

"Hey, have you guys been questioned yet?"

Maureen shook her head. "Looks like we're next."

A deputy waved Gianni into Tom's office and Kelly took his spot on the couch.

"Man, what a night! So where's Glenn?"

Tara draped her arm around her sister. "His phone rang, that woman state trooper walked over, whispered something and took him away to be interviewed."

"Whoa. Maybe he *was* involved? So what's with Gianni?"

Tara tightened her mouth then released it into an unbridled grin as she shrugged.

Oh, Tara... I can't even go there. Kelly shook her head.

It was nearly six in the morning before the sisters had been interviewed and Kane returned looking surprisingly upbeat.

"Thanks for your patience. Ready to head home?" he asked.

"So, did Jarod say more?" Maureen asked.

"As a matter of fact, he did without any prodding. He was so high he came right out and confessed repeatedly that he killed Jeremiah. It's a matter now of sorting out the reason why and who assisted him."

They walked out the main entrance beneath the balcony and headed down the lawn toward the stone wall.

"Look, there are lights in the old sanitarium." Maureen pointed across the lake. "Naomi from work said some guy from the state of Washington bought the property and intends to restore it and reopen the water-cure spa there."

"Will that cut into your business?" Tara asked.

"I hope not. The type of fresh air and water cures they used to do there were highly controversial. There was a similar spa at the south end of Skaneateles Lake. Lots of prominent people from writers to politicians went there in the late 1800s."

"Hmm, sounds like a great story there."

"Hey you guys; can you hold on for a second?"

They turned around to see what Kelly wanted.

"Ty, would you be able to take a photo of us right here. I think this is the exact spot where Rodolfo took the photo for the Vinegar Hill album cover."

"You're right, Kelly. The mansion was above them, slightly at an angle."

Kelly handed her cellphone to Kane.

"OK everyone. Act like it's nineteen eighty-six." They each struck a pose with rock star attitude. Kane laughed so hard he could barely steady the camera.

"Here you go. I took a few so you can choose the best one for your upcoming album's *Rolling Stone* review."

"May we have a better future than Vinegar Hill." Maureen draped her arm around Tara's shoulder.

Kane caught Kelly looking back at the mansion, a wistful expression on her face. He knew she was still wondering what might have been with Glenn McCann. Witnessing the moment wrenched his heart.

CHAPTER FORTY-ONE
Tuesday, June 2 ~ 7:00 a.m.

The waitress hugged three menus as the Caviston sisters followed her to a table in the back of The Rowdy Rooster diner in Penn Yan. A patron was reading the Rochester paper. Kelly noted the headline: "Jensen sentenced to 22 years in rock star's murder."

"Look who's here," Maureen whispered as they neared a booth where Detective Kane and his partners Reese Bailey and Mack Hughes were eating breakfast.

"Howdy, stranger." Tara tapped Kane's shoulder. He looked up and a wide smile brightened his face.

"Look, the whole crew is here! Haven't seen you all in the same place since last year. How are you, ladies?"

"What the heck are you eating, Ty?" Maureen pointed at his plate. Bailey folded his arms across the tabletop and nodded at the buckwheat pancakes towering next to a fried Spam omelet.

"My friend here's a growing boy. He can't live without his weekly ration of tasty Spam." Bailey grinned at Kane.

"Hey, stop with the Spam hate already."

"We've got to get you off processed foods, Ty. C'mon over for dinner sometime. Take a walk on the wild foods side."

"I would love to, Maureen."

Hughes turned to her.

"And I bet I know what he wants for dessert."

Kane kicked his shin under the table as Kelly looked away and smiled shyly. Hughes watched the exchange carefully.

Oh yeah, something's definitely still there.

Several minutes later while the women sipped coffee waiting for their breakfast orders, the three detectives stood to leave.

"I'll catch up with you guys later." Kane wandered over and put his hands on the empty chair next to Kelly. "Mind if I join you?"

"Please. Have a seat."

"That was quite a party we crashed last time we were all together. Nothing like being involuntary extras in solving a murder case."

"I've been busy casting my role in the film version. Thinking Scarlett Johansson would be able best to portray the subtleties of my character." Maureen and Kelly raised their eyebrows at Tara.

"In your dreams, sis. Ha!"

Kane caught Kelly's eye as the others teased back and forth.

"Thanks for all your tips, by the way. I loved the logic chart process, but that intuition of yours... spooky. FYI, I was pretty sure it was Rodolfo."

"In a way, we were both right. Jarod followed Rodolfo's plan." She leaned close enough to him so she could whisper without the nearby patrons hearing the conversation. "So let me see if I have the details right from the newspaper reports of Jarod's trial. Rodolfo knew Vinegar Hill from their Brooklyn days. That's how he happened to be hired for the famous photo shoot at the Bluff Point studio and became obsessed with Glenn. Then he was on the lam for an unrelated burglary he committed in Brooklyn and hid in Waco. While there he did gun sales as well as trafficking for his cousin in the Mexican drug cartel. That's where he bought the murder weapon."

"Right. He had set up a drug delivery route for him into upstate, through his friendship with Tom Russo. That connection enabled him to keep tabs on Glenn after the band went their separate ways. Then Tom got busted and chilled out in prison a few years. Meanwhile Glenn kept on the move. After a while his trail went cold. Rodolfo gave up. He moved briefly to Beverly Hills, using the pseudonym Catriona Glass to buy property for his cousin and since then had been making drone videos for weddings and special events.

"Tom reconnected with him a couple of years ago. He mentioned in an email earlier this year that he was going to try and buy back the mansion with Jeremiah. Rodolfo was still obsessed and opened shop here just in case there was a chance Glenn would come back there to record."

"Uprooting your life because you're hoping to reconnect with someone by chance? Wow, that's obsessive."

"Seriously. Now a lot happened in Brooklyn. First of all, the landlord for the studio in Vinegar Hill where Tom was the sound engineer was Ignazio Fracasetti. He met the band there and was hired as their manager briefly. During that summer, Glenn met Iggy's daughter Luna. According to Iggy, there was an immediate attraction between them, though she was fifteen and he was at least twenty years older. Daddy put the kibosh on that, but the two stayed in touch over the years. Eventually they lived together for a time in New York City years later. Then her career took off and she was too busy to focus on their relationship. She didn't want a family and he definitely did. He met a gypsy Irish storyteller in Europe, had a fling and they have a son together."

"Wait, Glenn's married?"

Tara and Maureen turned their attention immediately toward the other two.

"What have we missed? Are you sharing details about the murder? Speak up, Ty."

Kane leaned toward the center of the table and continued. "He never married, but Glenn supports the kid they had. The son lives with his mother in Doolin, County Clare. Glenn and Iggy remained close despite the breakup with Luna."

"Looney and Glenn were an item years ago? That chick gets around." Tara shook her head. "I don't get it. What's the attraction?"

"Shhh," Maureen interrupted. "Keep going, Ty. This is fascinating."

"After getting a tip from a fellow real estate developer, Iggy began investing in Finger Lakes property about five years ago and he mentions to Glenn there's a big farmhouse on the market with acres of vineyards. Glenn's interest in winemaking developed during a vacation in Italy with the Fracasettis—Iggy, his wife, Luna and her new boyfriend."

"Oh, this is getting so convoluted." Kelly's eyes widened.

"But wait, there's more." Ty laughed. "Glenn rents the farm property as well as that lakeside property from Iggy. In the meantime, Luna accompanies her father to view some property on Canandaigua Lake where she meets Gianni. There's some sort of attraction."

"Some sort of attraction? Knowing my ex, the attraction was Iggy's bank sum." Tara rolled her eyes.

"Luna falls in love with the area and moves to the Finger Lakes. You and Gianni break up, Tara. Luna makes her move."

Tara gaped at him.

"How do you know that? Did she tell you that or did Gianni?"

"Iggy told me."

"Looney lassoed Gianni. Well, now."

"Yes. They were living in Canandaigua and from time to time she checks out properties for her father. She becomes intrigued by the house being built on the East Side of Keuka. The owners run out of cash. Her father purchases it, finishes construction and he puts it under his new realty company, Casa Bella. Then he advertises it in several big city papers, including the *LA Times*. The Redferns were in on Tom's plan for regaining the mansion and were actively seeking a place at Keuka. Once they read about the lakeside house, they contact the realty to buy it immediately. At Luna's recommendation, Gianni handles the contract for the sale to the Redferns."

"I don't get why they'd move from bustling LA to here," Maureen said.

"Well, I guess Jeremiah knew his touring days were ending and he wanted to switch to record producing. Angie said he wasn't fond of the California scene and he found the humidity in Nashville unbearable. His best memories of recording music, outside of Brooklyn, were right here. So they moved to Keuka with full hope of getting back the mansion and turning it into a world class studio again."

"So the cast of characters is assembled. How did Jarod get drawn into the mix?"

"Tom Russo was desperate to raise some cash to pay for his part of the mansion purchase. As I said, Rodolfo moved here hoping Glenn might eventually return. Little did he know Glenn was already in residence. Rodolfo opens a video business on the West Side, specializing in drone photography. He's still running drugs for his cousin, though. Turns out, he's also using the drones as a drug delivery system... to Tom."

"Wait, he was dropping drugs in the lake again?" Maureen asked.

"Yep."

"Whoa... wait a minute!"

"What's the matter, Kelly?"

"I'm pretty sure I heard a drone flying up the lake the night of Jeremiah's death. There was also a splash, but the whirring noise kept going up the lake."

"The splash was in front of your cottage?" Kane pushed back his chair.

"My guess was it was over by Thompson's Cove, because after the splash the noise got louder and then quickly softened. So, judging by the Doppler effect, it hadn't passed in front of our house yet when it dropped the drugs into the lake."

"Hmm." Kane scratched his chin. "You said the noise moved up from the south, from below the cove?" She nodded. "You just connected the final dot, Kelly. That wasn't a drug drop. You heard the sound of the gun that shot Jeremiah falling into the lake. Divers found it in a plastic bag when they were searching for Sarah's body. The ballistics test proved it was the murder weapon. If Sarah hadn't drowned, we might not have solved this critical clue in the case. After Jarod confessed, we were able to match his fingerprints to those found on the inside of the gun's magazine. We couldn't figure out how the weapon got into the lake."

"Wow! This is fascinating."

The waitress interrupted them with their orders.

"OK, so who had the biscuits with sausage gravy and a side of bacon?"

Tara raised her hand. Kane gave her a thumbs up.

"Niiiiice."

"Spinach omelet and multigrain bread?"

"Let me guess, Maureen?" He pointed at her and the waitress placed the plate in front of Maureen.

"There's a reason why you're an ace detective." Maureen smiled at him.

"Here's your Belgian waffle with fresh raspberry sauce, ma'am."

"Hmm." Kane raised an eyebrow at the plate. "Always classy, Kelly."

Tara had enough of the chit chat.

"Back to the trial. How did Jarod know Rodolfo?"

"The kid had a taste for drugs. When he ran into money problems after losing his job at the hardware store, he worked odd jobs for Rodolfo. As we know, Rodolfo also enjoys cross dressing and performs at that nightclub, Haute Mama's. Turns out, Jeremiah was a fan of their drag shows, and he used to show up on the nights they had performances knowing that in a small place like this he'd be assured anonymity from the audience.

Jeremiah drank heavily, and when he'd go there with Angie, sometimes they'd get into screaming matches in the middle of a show. It was during one of those episodes when he went into the men's room and muttered aloud that he had no regrets about making millions off Glenn's lyrics. Rodolfo overheard him from his dressing room next door. He was furious and knew he had to do something to avenge the theft of Glenn's work.

"In the meantime, Alejandro Montez contacts Rodolfo's Graceful Creative Studios to see if they can do a drone video of the wedding and fireworks display at the reception. During their conversation, Alejandro lets slip there will be a surprise for his daughter—Jeremiah Redfern will walk out and sing Ryan and Esperanza's song. They sign a contract, but Rodolfo comes up with an additional plan after Alejandro leaves... a murder in the vineyard."

"OK, I'm following you so far. How did Jeremiah get into the vineyard?"

"First Rodolfo dangles the promise of twenty-five grand to Jarod if he will do something difficult for him. Jarod wants to win back Sarah, and he needs money for a down payment on a home he wants to buy for them. Once Rodolfo reveals his target, Jarod agrees. He suspected Jeremiah was hitting on Sarah and told us he deserved to pay for it.

"They try to figure out the logistics of the crime. Jarod's friend Mitch works for the company that Ryan O'Hare hired to run the fireworks display. In the meantime, Jarod was able to get Jeremiah's phone number after he'd called The Eggleston Inn one night looking for a pair of glasses he'd misplaced. Jarod could see the glasses, but thinking quickly, he said they hadn't been found and he asked Jeremiah for his phone number in case they were located.

"Also, a few nights before the murder, Jarod was hired as a bartender for a special wine tasting dinner in Naples. A couple there wanted a selfie taken, but they didn't have a camera. The woman running the dinner borrowed someone's cellphone, took the photos and asked for their email address. She sent the woman the photos using the guy's email app, and set the cellphone down. The man who owned the cellphone forgot about it, but Jarod saw it and slipped it in his own pocket. That was the phone used by Mitch to call Jeremiah.

"And guess who that phone belonged to… Glenn McCann."

"Are you kidding me? *Aha!* So that's why you thought he was tied to the murder?"

"Yes, Kelly. Turns out the day Jarod shot out your store window Mitch was driving the car, stolen from a tourist from Michigan. Jarod returned to the scene later and slipped the cellphone back into Glenn's car. And it continues to get more complicated. The hostess of the wine dinner was Luna Grande. The wines being served were Glenn's. Gianni appeared to be clueless to the fact they were once an item."

Maureen folded her arms and nodded.

"We already figured out the wine dinner connections, thanks to a tip from a client at the spa."

"Speaking of your spa, it was through Monique we learned Luna knew Rodolfo. Guess Graceful Creative also had a sideline of drone surveillance video."

"Holy crap, was that his drone spying on us?" Tara nearly dropped her fork.

"Most likely. He hinted Luna was jealous of you, Tara, and feared you were seeing Gianni on the sly."

Maureen patted Tara's shoulder. "Why wouldn't she be jealous of you." Tara was feeling pretty good about all of this.

Kelly tapped her finger on her lips as she thought about everything Kane disclosed.

"Now if Rodolfo was so obsessed with Glenn, was he the one who put that vinegar bottle on our porch?"

"Yes. Fingerprints on the bottle matched his. It's slightly less fearful than a horse head in a bed, but you got his message."

"Yeah, wished he'd done that earlier."

Kane laughed heartily, knowing what a cad Glenn had been to Kelly.

"So tell me the answer to something else that's been truly bugging me." Tara leaned toward Kane. "Who was responsible for the fireworks screw-up? Mitch?"

Kane continued to explain what went down at the murder scene. How Rodolfo confessed that the plan was Mitch would meet Jeremiah on West Lake Road and take him by ATV into the back of the Riesling vineyard. How Mitch was able to remotely set off the display early by tampering with the firing board. How Jeremiah walked down the vineyard to where Jarod was waiting. How he killed him with one shot. How he was so shocked by what he'd done he dropped the murder weapon in a panic, and how Rodolfo returned to the scene after his performance at Haute Mama's to retrieve the gun.

"There was a sparkly pink feather found near Jeremiah's body... When I found it, and we got deep into the investigation, I was sure that meant Rodolfo was the killer."

Maureen signaled to the waitress for a refill of her coffee, then leaned toward Kane. "What a tangled mess. So what happened to the mansion? Tom won't be involved from prison and Angie moved back to LA after she sold the lake house."

"Ooh, I can answer that," Tara interrupted. "I just heard a rumor at work that Alejandro Montez bought out the partners. Guess who the first artist he plans to record there is—Colin Washington, Sarah's brother."

"So at least someone gets a happy ending from this story."

Kane smiled softly at Kelly. "Well... I'm sure happy I got to meet all of you."

Their discussion continued through the sisters' breakfast. As they walked to the door after paying their tab, the group ran into Gianni outside talking with someone they didn't recognize. He tipped his head and smiled sheepishly at his ex-wife.

"How's it going, Tara?"

"Things couldn't be better, Gianni. How about with you?"

Gianni stuck his hands in his pockets and squinted.

"I suppose you heard Luna left me. Moved in with that rock star to make sweet whines together."

Tara loved that he still had a sense of humor after everything that happened. She took a deep breath and reached out to touch his arm, looking deeply into those eyes she once trusted with all her heart.

"Sorry, Gianni. You deserve better treatment than that."

Her candor caught him off guard. He sighed.

"You always were the classy one in our relationship." The man standing next to him sneezed. "Oh, by the way. I was just telling my new friend here about your interior design talents.

Tara, this is John Ozette. He bought the old sanitarium across the lake from the bluff and may need your expertise."

Maureen stepped forward.

"Oh, we were curious about the lights we saw on there last summer. What are your plans for the site?"

"And these are my sisters-in-law Maureen and Kelly." Gianni looked at Kane, not sure how to introduce him.

"Welcome to Keuka Lake, Mr. Ozette. I'm Ty Kane, a friend of the family."

Gianni raised an eyebrow at Tara, but she was still mulling the fact he didn't use "ex" in front of "sisters-in-law."

Ozette shook Kane's hand and turned toward Maureen.

"To answer your question, I intend to restore the building to its intended purpose—a water cure spa using the onsite mineral springs. We'll have a soft opening sometime this summer. Gianni and I negotiated a deal with the former owners in May of last year. My team has been renovating the building since."

"Best wishes for much success then."

"Oh, no need for those. It *will* succeed. I was told so in a dream by a Coho salmon I caught in Neah Bay." His dark walnut brown eyes locked with Tara's as he pushed shoulder-length, shiny black hair behind his ears with both hands. She couldn't help but notice his muscular arms. Ozette's lips parted slightly as he smiled at her.

Kane raised his index finger to his chin while he was lost in thought for a few seconds.

"Are you by any chance a member of the Makah tribe?"

Ozette turned toward him and nodded.

"Yes, I am. Surprised you know about us."

"I'm very interested in Native American history, particularly the Senecas."

Ozette's demeanor darkened instantly. He glared back, unnerving Kane. *Whoa, did I just offend him somehow?* Everyone went silent; Kelly tried very hard not to laugh. Tara cut through the awkward moment.

"Well, we have to get going now. Very nice to meet you, John. Bye, Gianni."

Tara didn't speak again until they neared their cars.

"Is it just me, or is that man spookier than Looney."

Maureen nodded.

"Did you notice his threatening look toward you, Ty?"

"*That* was intense," Kane said. "Can't imagine why there would be any feud between those tribes."

"Wish I could get a peek inside that old building. They say it could house more than a hundred guests back in its heyday. I can only imagine the stories those rooms could tell... or will tell with that mysterious guy running the place." Maureen cringed.

"Maybe you can get a job there doing séances, Kelly." Tara laughed as she looked over her shoulder. Gianni was still chatting with Mr. Ozette, who turned and stared back at her.

Kelly squinted at the cloudy sky.

"Wonder if it will clear for tonight's full Strawberry Moon. Ah well, nothing like a new day and a new chapter of a story."

Kane looked deep into Kelly's eyes and smiled at her.

"You can say that again."

THE END

Made in the USA
Middletown, DE
04 August 2016